2nd Michigai

l

Blood for I

by

Cody C. Engdahl

Contents

Preface

Thank you so much for your interest in this novel. This is the third book of the *2nd Michigan Cavalry Chronicles* series. Please note: YOU DON'T HAVE TO READ THE FIRST TWO BOOKS TO ENJOY THIS ONE, but I hope you do. I wrote this to stand on its own even if you haven't read the others. This book certainly continues the overall narrative of the series, but everything you need to know to understand and enjoy the adventure we're about to embark upon together is included in this book.

On Language

I try to be as tasteful yet realistic as possible. Initially, I thought I would keep my books clean of foul language altogether, but that came off as inauthentic, especially during battle scenes when my characters are under duress. There was plenty of cussing during the mid-nineteenth century and even though they rarely wrote the swear words down, there're plenty of references to cussing in the firsthand memoirs of the American Civil War. With this in mind, I've restricted the bad words to the dialog and typically only when the characters are in the heat of battle. I'm sure I'd be blurting out expletives too.

That brings us to racial slurs. It is nearly impossible to write about the American Civil War without getting into the racial issues that dominated the war. The war literally decided the fate of slavery and the status of black people in the United States. As a mostly white person, I am loathe to use any racial slurs in my writing. I'm sensitive to how hurtful they can be and I certainly don't want my work to be flagged as offensive by the reviewers at Amazon.

Because of this, I have avoided using the "n-word" in the previous two novels of this series even though that word was widely used by both sides during that time and would have certainly been used in some of the scenes I've depicted. Instead, I've used the word "negro" and "colored" in the dialog and thoughts of my characters, which actually would have been considered polite or acceptable by most people of that time regardless if that particular character would have most likely used the n-word.

Because this book deals a lot with black soldiers and pays homage to their struggles that were not only typical of the war but in the inherent racism in both armies, I felt it would be an injustice not to fully relate their experiences, including the racial slurs they had to endure. I do not take this language lightly so I set up some ground rules. First, these words are only used in dialog and the thoughts of characters and never in a favorable light. In my own narration, I typically use the term "black" to describe people of sub-Saharan African descent as I use "white" to describe people of European descent. At the time of writing this, these words are typically acceptable and not considered offensive.

In dialog and in thought, my characters use the term "negro" or "colored" when they aren't necessarily intending to be offensive. These terms were considered polite or at least neutral during the time of the war. I reserved the "n-word" for only when characters are being insensitive or intentionally offensive. Finally, some of my black characters use the word "nigga," much as some blacks use it today. Although there is much debate over its appropriateness and who's allowed to use it, my characters use it in a way that they refer to themselves or their fellow blacks with a bit of irony or even affection.

Once again, I do not give myself license to use these words in my own speech or narration since I don't know if I have any black heritage. However, I do think it's important in this work, not only for historical accuracy but also to attempt some appreciation of what these American people had to endure as they fought and continue to fight to make us all live up to the declaration that, "We hold these truths to be self-evident, that all men are created equal, that they are endowed by their Creator with certain unalienable Rights, that among these are Life, Liberty and the pursuit of Happiness."

One more note to clear up any confusion: the Federals like to name their armies after rivers while the Confederates like to name theirs after states or regions. Because of this, the Army of *the* Tennessee is a Federal army named after the Tennessee River. The Army of Tennessee is Confederate named after the state. Both armies drew regiments from Tennessee so there is a 7th Tennessee Cavalry (US) and a 7th Tennessee Cavalry (CSA). To make it even more confusing, those two regiments will square off later in this book. I took great care to be very clear on who's who. I think knowing this going in will make it easier to understand as you read.

Have fun! I'll catch up with you at the end with the Historical Note section. There I'll explain a lot of the real history in this book. If you want to jump ahead to it as you're reading I've laid it out in chronological order following the narrative of this book.

Once again, thank you so much for reading my book. I hope you love it as much as I loved researching and writing it. If you do, Please join the Engdahl House email list for updates on new releases, discounts, appearances, and more at https://subscribepage.io/EngdahlHouse.

Cody C. Engdahl, Nashville, Tennessee, 2021

Acknowledgments

I could never do justice to all the people who have been so kind and helpful to me in this journey. Please forgive me if I missed you in this brief section.

First of all, thank you, the reader. You are who I ultimately work for. I appreciate you taking a chance on me. I hope I continue to earn your trust.

Next is my editing team which is comprised of my girlfriend Laura Reinert and my mother Nancy Thompson. Thanks for catching all my mistakes both written and in general. Thank you to Bryan Cummings as well who has also volunteered to help with editing.

I'd like to thank the Lotz House Museum, Parnassus Bookstore, the Robertson County History Museum, Fort Negley, the Salted Caramel Cafe, and of course Amazon for carrying my books.

I'd like to thank the Joseph E. Johnston, Camp 28, Sons of Confederate Veterans; the Sons of Union Veterans of the Civil War Fort Donelson Camp 62; and the Nashville Civil War Roundtable for hosting me for book talks and signings. Thank you, Richard McCardle, at ucvrelics.com. for letting me play fiddle and sell books at your stand. Thanks to Jerry Wooten of Tennessee State Parks for helping me with questions. Thank you, everyone at

for answering my questions and doing a lot of the research for me. Thank you to all the people I've interacted with on the various Civil War pages and groups on Facebook, even if we've argued. I still love you.

I'd like to thank Paul Michael Jason of the Untold Civil War Podcast for having me as a guest. I highly recommend his show as well as the Civil War Breakfast Club, Civil War Podcast, and the Age of Victoria Podcast. All are great resources and highly entertaining shows.

Thank you to my platoon sergeant Rich Werner and the boys from 3/187 Rakkasans. Thanks to all my friends, family, and followers who have supported and believed in me all these years. Thank you to my Aunt Joni Engdahl-Gray who found out that we have an ancestor who fought in the American Civil War. My great great great grandfather Gustaf Wilhelm Anders'son came from Sweden and joined the 43rd Illinois Infantry Regiment. He most likely took part in the Vicksburg Campaign. He returned to Sweden after the war to fetch his wife and son, then settled in Nebraska. He changed our last name to Engdahl when he returned. We never understood why. No one has been able to spell or pronounce our name correctly since.

I'd like to thank my bandmates, Don Masters, Paul Hart, David Johnson, and Rick Fretter of the Inglewood Old Time String Band for playing music with me while I promote my books. We lost Don Masters, our guitar player a few months ago. This book in Memorandum of Donnie H. Masters, 1932-2021. Thanks, Don, for all you've done for me and for your service to our country as an airman during the height of the Cold War in Berlin during the 1950's.

Finally, I'd like to thank my dad and stepmom, Larry and Mary Engdahl, for their love and support. They raised me to love reading and now they read every book that love has produced from me.

Glossary of Terms

Abatis: an obstacle, like a felled tree and sharpened sticks used as a field fortification.

Artillery: the branch of arms dealing with cannons, mortars, and other large projectiles.

Bastion: an extended corner of fort designed to allow defenders to fire at troops climbing the wall.

Battery: a unit of artillery typically made up of four to six guns.

Bayonet: a long knife or spike-like weapon that can be attached to the end of a rifle, turning it into a spear.

Brevet: a rank like "brevet captain" for example, is a promotion for outstanding performance without the raise in pay that would normally come with that rank until it is confirmed and made official.

Breech: the rear of a gun barrel.

Brogans: military-issued leather shoes.

Caisson: a two-wheeled wagon used to carry ammunition boxes as well as a spare wagon wheel and limber pole for a cannon.

Canister: a cannon shell filled with smaller balls meant to disperse upon firing.

Cartridge: a prepackaged bullet and gunpowder unit wrapped in paper or metal casing, as opposed to loose powder and projectiles used in earlier muskets.

Contraband: an ex-slave behind Union lines, often working for the army.

Carbine: a shorter version of a rifle designed to be fired from horseback.*Cavalry:* the branch of arms made up of horse-mounted troops.

Earthwork: a tall mound of dirt piled up as a defensive wall.

Embrasure: an opening in a defensive structure from where cannons can fire.

Enfilading Fire: shooting into the flank of a line of men where the maximum potential targets are exposed.

Feint: a false attack meant to distract the enemy from the real attack.

Flying artillery: light cannons designed to be quickly moved by horses during battle.

Grapeshot: like canister but with larger projectiles often resembling grapes.

Hardtack: a hard cracker-like bread issued as rations.

Howitzer: a low-velocity cannon that uses elevation to lob shells. They can also fire directly at near targets.

Infantry: the branch of arms made up of foot soldiers.

Lanyard: a cord used to fire a cannon.

Laudanum: an opioid in liquid form.

Limber: a horse-drawn two-wheeled cart used to tow cannons, caissons, traveling forges, or battery wagons. It also carries an ammunition chest.

Limber pole: a long pole used to attach a limber to a team of horses.

Minié ball: a conical-shaped bullet as opposed to its spherical-shaped predecessor.

Mortar: a large, cauldron-shaped artillery piece that lobs its shells instead of shooting directly.

Musket: a muzzleloading black powder long gun.

Muzzle: the open end of a gun barrel.

Orderly: an aide assigned to do menial tasks for officers.

Reveille: a bugle call meant to wake troops in the morning.

Redoubt: a small fort.

Picket: a small group of men set out from the main group as a lookout or a guard.

Rifle: a long gun with grooves in the barrel that causes the bullet to spin. Rifles can still be muzzle-loading muskets. Rifles eventually replaced smooth-bore muskets. Cannons can also have rifled barrels.

Saber: a single-bladed, curved sword designed for slashing from horseback.

Sharpshooter: a sniper, marksman, or soldier trained to shoot targets from a distance as opposed to a regular rifleman who provides volley fire.

Sutler: a merchant who follows an army to sell goods.

12-pounder: a cannon that shoots a 12-pound ball. Cannons are often called by the weight of their shot.

12-pound Napoleon: a popular smoothbore field cannon used by both armies. Named after Napoleon III.

USCHA: United States Colored Heavy Artillery.

USCT: United States Colored Troops.

Vedette: like a picket but on horseback.

Volley: multiple muskets or cannons firing in line at the same time.

Works: short for defensive works such as trenches and fortifications.

Worm: an artillery tool consisting of an iron corkscrew mounted on a staff used to clean debris out of a cannon barrel.

<u>Civil War Ranks for both Armies (simplified)</u>
-Enlisted
Private
Corporal
Sergeant
Major Sergeant
-Officers
Lieutenant
Captain
Major
Lieutenant Colonel
Colonel
Brigadier General
Major General
Lieutenant General
General

Both colonels and lieutenant colonels are typically referred to as "colonel." All officers with the rank of brigadier general or higher are typically referred to simply as "general."

<u>Typical Civil War Military Units:</u>
Company or a troop: about a hundred men, but varies greatly. Typically commanded by a captain.
Battalion: an unofficial subdivision of a regiment made up of several companies. In modern times the battalion has replaced the regiment in the US military.
Regiment: made up of several companies, typically ten, commanded by a colonel.

Brigade: made up of several regiments, typically three, commanded by a brigadier general.

Division: made up of more than one brigade, commanded by a brigadier or major general.

Corps: made up of more than one division, commanded by a brigadier, major, or lieutenant general

Army: the largest field command made up of more than one corps, commanded by a major general or higher.

Dedication

This book is dedicated to the soldier who threw off his chains and truly fought for freedom.

Epithet

"Generals gathered in their masses, just like witches at black masses…"
Black Sabbath, "War Pigs"

Act I: The Massacre

Chapter One: Here They Come

April 12, 1864: Fort Pillow, Tennessee

They came through the woods in the pre-dawn darkness like ghosts passing through the ravines and slipping between the trees. Unaware of this impending danger, men of the US 13th Tennessee Cavalry fought their own heavy eyelids as they sat in the rifle pits of the forward picket positions of Fort Pillow.

"Judgement Day, you traitorous son of a bitch!" a Rebel soldier hissed as he leaped into a pit and drove his knife into a nearly slumbering Federal soldier. He covered the dying man's mouth with his other hand and glared into his eyes until the man slumped to the muddy floor.

"You picked the wrong side," he spat at the corpse.

The Rebel cavalryman popped his head up from the rifle pit. All around he could hear the rustle of similar scenes: a whimper from a dying Federal solider, the sound of a knife plunging into flesh. Satisfaction spread across his dirty, blood-spattered face. These home-grown Yankees and their damn negro runaways dressed as soldiers had no idea what was about to happen to them. He waved his hat over his head, signaling the rest to come forward.

More men from the Confederate 2nd Missouri Cavalry, the "Missouri Mongols," emerged from the shadows. They crept forward, clutching their carbines, pistols, and knives. Alarmed by the sudden surge of the butternut-clad cavalrymen, two of the surviving

Federal pickets sprinted from their hiding place towards the fort.

"Shoot 'em!" Captain Smith called out. A blast of gunpowder and the flash of muzzle fire split the darkness. One of the runners cried out as he tumbled to the ground. His companion stopped briefly to look back at the man rolling on the ground in agony before turning back to his all-out dash for safety.

"The Rebels are coming!" he screamed in terror only to be met by another volley of hot lead from behind.

Dr. Charles Fitch's eyes popped open at the sound of gunshots. He lay there for a moment in the darkness of his tiny cabin, wondering if he were dreaming. A second volley caused him to bolt upright. It seemed frighteningly close. Dogs began to bark.

"Good God, they're here…" he gasped, clutching his blanket to his chest. A woman screamed somewhere outside.

"Dear God…" he said, scrambling into his clothes. Manic yelping from the woods caused goosebumps to ripple across his skin.

"Ow!" he hissed, as he banged his head on the low ceiling of his hut. The morning air was cool but fear warmed him as he ran down the bluff towards the river to where the provost marshal's cabin lay. Without bothering to knock, he burst in and started shaking the man sleeping inside.

"Captain Young! Captain Young! You must get up! The Rebels are attacking."

"Jesus!" Young let out as he reached for his pistol next to his bed. He blinked at Fitch for a moment, gathering his thoughts, then focused his eyes. "Start alerting the contraband camp. We need to get the women and children to the landing. Hopefully, we can get the *New Era* to evacuate them. I need to alert Major Booth if he isn't already. This could get ugly fast," he said, turning to put his feet on the floor while he shimmied up his trousers.

Panic was beginning to stir as people popped their heads out from their tents and cabins in the little contraband town that had sprung up outside of the fort's earthen walls. "What's happening, Doctor?" a woman asked as Fitch passed her hovel.

"It's alright, Rosa." He tried to sound calm. "It's just some skirmishers. Major Booth has everything under control. Get your children to the launch so we can get you to safety."

A woman screamed. Droves of people brushed against him as they dashed down the slope towards the river. "Stay calm, everyone!" Dr. Fitch called out. "Get yourself and your families to the launch. We have a coal barge there to whisk you away. There's plenty of room." The sound of crackling wood began to blend in with the tramping of feet. He could smell wood burning. Smoke wisped through the crowd. Dr. Fitch looked up to see the glow coming from the far end of the camp as black smoke rose into the air like a flag climbing a pole.

"Good heavens, they're firing the camp..." he gasped, then to a couple of boys who weren't quite teens yet, "You two! Help me get the sick out of the hospital tent!"

"Are we gonna die?" one of them asked. The whites of his eyes contrasted with the early morning twilight.

"No, not if we stay calm and use our heads, Seddy," Fitch smiled at the boy, patting his soft curly black hair.

A crackle of musketry brought a screech from the women trying to find places for themselves and their children on the largest of the three coal barges docked at the river. Dr. Fitch waved his arms frantically at the *New Era*. The timberclad gunboat sat impassively in the mist on the river. Fitch sighed in frustration. She showed no signs of movement.

"Stay here and stay calm, everyone. I have to go to the fort to signal the boat to come get you. We'll have you away soon!" With that, he ran back up the slope to the little earthen fort that commanded the heights over the Mississippi River. Behind him, the *New Era* finally woke with an eruption of fire and smoke, eliciting more screams from the civilians huddled on the barge. The shells whistled overhead and crashed in the woods on the other side of the fort with a deafening percussive roar.

Dr. Fitch was winded and sweating when he got to the fort. He was relieved to see Major Booth already dressed and giving orders with the confidence of experience.

"Major Bradford!" he called to his second in command. "Get your men to their forward gun pits and hold your position! If we let them get too close they'll get under our cannons and we won't be able to tilt down enough to shoot them!"

"Of course," Bradford replied, Booth's command snapping him out of his wide-eyed paralysis.

"Don't worry, Bill," Booth put his hand on Bradford's shoulder. "With your boys holding those positions, these raiders will be nothing more than target practice for my artillery boys. I trained them myself." Then turning to the newly arrived surgeon, "Dr. Fitch, are the civilians loaded aboard the barge?" Booth called to him.

"Umm…yes, sir. I tried to signal the *New Era* to come get them," Fitch stammered.

"No worries, we'll do it now." Booth said, and then turned to one of his officers, "Lieutenant McClure, signal Captain Marshall to retrieve the civilians! Once they're away he can continue to fire on Ravine No. 1, just as we planned. There's no place those Rebels can hide that we can't hit. Let's give them a warm welcome!"

"Yes, sir!" the young man replied and ran off to the signal station. Soon coded flags shot up the poles causing the *New Era* to stop firing and start steaming towards the landing.

For the first time since he woke, Fitch was beginning to feel relieved. Major Booth was a man who had started his career as a private and rose to the rank of Sergeant Major before accepting a commission to lead the newly formed 6th US Colored Heavy Artillery Regiment as well as two companies of the 2nd Colored Light Artillery. Now at the rank of

Major, he had assumed command of the fort from the well-meaning, but inexperienced Major Bradford. Just weeks before, Bradford had commanded the fort alone with his 13th Tennessee Cavalry. They were a white regiment full of Tennesseans loyal to the Union, although many of them were Confederate deserters who still resented serving alongside the black men they had once known as slaves.

Those white troops were now trotting out to their positions, leaving Booth with his staff and artillerymen in the fort. A crowd of wide-eyed black troops formed around him. "It's alright, boys. Just a little live-fire exercise for us this morning. Get to your guns. Listen to your sergeants. Remember the drill." Then to his officers, "Lieutenant Hill, McClure! Get your men to their guns! I want every man not directly involved in a crew to man the wall with a rifle. Make sure they're ready to replace any crew member shot down!"

Booth then turned to the lithe and well-groomed freeman who had come from Detroit with his oversized friend and enlisted a little over a year ago. These were two he had learned to depend on. "Francis, Elijah, take the rest of these men and go bring those two Parrot rifles back into the fort. Our gunners will be too exposed out there among the rifle pits."

"Yes, sir!" Francis snapped. "Come on, fellas," he turned to the group of men around him. Together they dashed out from the earthen walls to where the newly arrived 10-pound rifled cannons had been placed. They had planned on building earthen works around them to protect the crews, but it was too late now that the enemy was upon them.

"We finally get to try out the new ones!" Elijah huffed with excitement as they ran.

"That's if you don't get shot fetchin'em first, you big dummy," Jerry quipped. "They won't risk a horse to get they guns, but they'll sure spend the life of a nigga on them."

"Come on, Jerry," Francis gasped as they slowed their run just in time to avoid slamming themselves into the cannons. "By the time we fetched horses and rigged them, we'd all be shot to pieces and you know it." A bullet pinged off the barrel of one of the guns causing the men to cringe.

"I guess you right, Frenchie," Jerry looked up from his crouch behind the gun. "Let's get out, quick!"

The two 6-pound James rifles and the two 12-pound mountain howitzers in the fort began firing, scattering the Rebels who were just beginning to take positions in the wooded ravines out beyond the earthen walls, wood cabins, rifle pits, and abatis of felled trees. The white troops of the 13th US Tennessee Cavalry began to fill those rifle pits and answer the potshots that came from Rebels.

Major Booth beamed with pride as his artillerymen wheeled the two iron guns back into the fort with stoic determination just as the intensity of fire from the Rebels began to increase. The 10-pound Parrot rifles had tapered barrels that were a little over 6-feet long. They were made from cast iron with a ring of wrought iron wrapped around the breach to keep them from bursting upon firing. Using less powder than their smoothbore counterparts, the Parrot rifles fired a conical shell nearly two thousand yards with far more precision. That came from the spiral grooves, or "rifling," cut into the inner wall of the barrel that caused the shell to spin.

"Good job, boys! Wheel them into the embrasures here on the south end and commence firing!" Booth commanded.

The men went to work ramming powder charges and shells into the muzzles with well-rehearsed precision. Soon the guns were alive and kicking, bucking backward with jets of fire and smoke. Francis ran to one of the smoking barrels with his worm pole, which was an iron corkscrew-shaped tool attached to a pole. With it, he pulled out the leftover debris from the barrel. Jerry followed by plunging a wet sponge inside. It sizzled and steamed as it cleaned the barrel. Francis then did so with a dry sponge before they reloaded and wheeled the gun back into firing position. Sergeant Weaver squatted to sight it and set the elevation once more.

"By the numbers, boys, just like we drilled!" Major Booth yelled over the thundering cannons. Then to his nearby subordinate, "Lieutenant Hill, take a volunteer and set fire to those cabins outside our walls! They're giving the enemy too much cover!"

"Yes, sir!" Hill answered.

Dr. Fitch watched as the young officer and a civilian volunteer ran down to the cabins with torches in their hands. He flinched as bullets kicked up dirt around them. Soon the first row of cabins was burning. Fitch let out a breath of relief but then suddenly sucked in his next breath with a hiss, cringing as he watched Lieutenant Hill and his companion tumble to the ground and then lay lifeless.

"Do you think you can hold them, Major?" Dr. Fitch asked nervously.

"Certainly, as long as everyone keeps their heads together," Booth assured him. Fitch suddenly dropped to the ground clutching his thigh.

"Good God, Doctor, are you alright?" Booth squatted next to him.

Fitch patted his bleeding leg before looking up, "I think it's just a scrape. I have no idea where the bullet came from."

"Well, we need to get you out of the line of fire," Booth said helping him up. "Isaac, Billy!" he shouted towards the troops manning the wall. "Help Dr. Fitch to the rear. Doc, set up a hospital and prepare to receive the wounded."

A young man about to drive his wet sponge into a barrel suddenly collapsed. His lifeless eyes stared at the sky as blood began to surge from the hole in his head. The gun crew halted for a moment, regarding the corpse.

"Drag that man away! Johnny, take his place!" Booth called to others on the wall. "Keep firing, men don't stop!" The crew restarted their work swabbing, loading, and firing. More of them were dropping. More and more, men were dragging the bodies away and taking their places with stoic determination.

"Well, you wanted to see some action, Frenchie. Here it is," Jerry quipped as they labored.

"Shut up and keep moving," Francis shot back. Both of them cringed as a bullet pinged off the barrel.

"They must have sharpshooters up high somewhere firing down on us!"

"Never mind that, men. We'll spot 'em and drop some shells on 'em, keep firing!" Booth exhorted, stepping over the tail of their gun. "We can't let them get any closer. We can't let them take the colors…!" he shouted, then collapsed. Blood began to pool around his body. For a moment, the sounds of battle seemed far away as the men looked down at their leader bleeding out his lifeblood at their feet.

"…Oh, shit," Jerry mumbled, resting on his rammer.

"Don't just stand there gawking like a bunch of hens, God damn it!" Sergeant Weaver snapped them out of their trance, "Keep firing!" Then to Francis, "Frenchie!"

"Yes, Sergeant!" Francis shouted back.

"Put them dancing legs to work and run down to Major Bradford. Tell him he's in command!" Weaver shouted. "Bobby! Off the wall and take his place!"

Francis crouched low against the inside of the fort's wall, calculating his timing. The crack of a sharpshooter's rifle from one of the high knolls was his cue. With a burst of motion, he was over the wall, out of the ditch, and sprinting towards the log cabins. He slammed himself against a cabin wall just in time to hear the rattle of musket balls pepper the other side. He drew long breaths trying to calm himself. He scanned the rifle pits, looking for Major Bradford. There he was! Once again, Francis waited for a volley before dashing off to Bradford's position. Just as the Rebels had sighted and tracked him he dropped to his hip and slid into the trench feet first, bullets kicking up the dirt around him.

"Jesus Christ, Private! You damn near scared the ghost out of me!" Bradford gasped.

"Sir, Major Booth is dead. You're in command. What are your orders?" Francis blurted over the swelling noise of combat.

Bradford stared at him, blinking, the blood rushing from his face. "We've got to get out of here…" he mumbled.

"Sir…?" Francis prodded.

"Captain!" Bradford called to his subordinate, "Order the men back to the fort! Pass the message along the line. Everyman, back to the fort! We need to consolidate our forces!"

"Sir, shouldn't we leave a line of rifles forward of the fort? The Rebels will get under the tilt of our guns if we don't hold them here."

"Are you questioning my judgment, Private!" Bradford grabbed him by the arm.

"Of course not, sir!"

"Then get back to the fort and tell whoever is in command to cover our retreat!" Bradford shoved him back.

The guns of Fort Pillow opened up in a coordinated volley, cueing the men in the forward pits to make the dash back to the fort. The Rebels made sport of the fleeing men, dropping several of them in their tracks. Soon the men of the US 13th Tennessee Cavalry were finding places along the walls with their counterparts from the 6th US Colored Heavy Artillery and the 2nd US Colored Light Artillery.

"Never thought I'd be fightin' alongside a nigger," one of them protested.

"This nigga may be the one to save your life," the man next to him answered.

The white cavalryman regarded his black comrade for a moment before returning eyes to the sights of his gun, "May God save us all, then…" he mumbled.

Francis panicked when he didn't see his friend working the new Parrot rifle where he had left him. He scanned the bodies lying nearby for the big man. He was only slightly relieved not to see him among them.

"Jerry, where's Elijah?!" He called.

"Th' fool ran off to man the howie!" Jerry called back. Francis rushed off to the north end of the fort. Relief washed over him when he saw his big friend turning one of the mountain howitzers around and pointing it away from the embrasure.

"What on earth are you doing? Why aren't you on the big gun?" Francis hollered, looking at the dead bodies lying around him.

"Sharpshooter on that highpoint," Elijah's bass voice cut through the gunfire. "See!?" he said, pointing excitedly at a puff of smoke that revealed a shooter hidden in the foliage on a hilltop. "I bet I can drop one right on him."

"Alright, big man. Let's see watcha' got." Francis smirked at his friend's fascination for the gun that most of the regiment regarded as an antiquated toy now that they got their new rifled cannons. Elijah set the elevation on the stubby brass tube with studious concentration. "Isn't that a little high?" Francis asked.

"We ain't shootin' directly, watch!" Elijah grinned with boyish excitement. With that, he pulled the lanyard. The brass tube coughed up a puff of smoke. Francis watched the shell arc slow enough into the sky for his eye to catch before it plunged downward and exploded right where they had seen the puff of smoke.

"Woohoo!" Francis leaped with joy. "I do believe you hit him! You are one talented man!" Elijah looked sheepishly at the ground before looking up and returning the smile. "You just have to get the arc right," he said humbly.

Several of the other artillerymen were cheering as well. They began to come over and fill in the places of the previous dead crewmen. "Come on, men," Francis called. "Let's find another target."

The battle raged on as the Rebels inched their way closer to the walls. They began to occupy the abandoned rifle pits and the cabins that had not been burned. The Federal gun crews struggled to tilt their barrels low enough to shoot at them. Then the order came to cease firing. Francis rubbed his ears trying to stop the ringing. Soon he and many others popped their heads over the walls to see what was happening now that they were temporarily safe from the punishing aim of the sharpshooters.

"I think they're demanding a surrender…" Francis said softly as they watched a small party of Confederate officers approach the fort under a flag of truce. They were met by their Federal counterparts.

"I'll die first before I be a slave again," Jerry said quietly.

Cold fear rippled through Francis. The Confederate government had declared that captured black soldiers would be returned to slavery or even summarily executed for insurrection. White officers that led them could be hanged. "I'm…not a slave…I never was…" he mumbled watching the gray and butternut soldiers begin to move in closer.

"Hey!" Elijah shouted, "You ain't supposed to be moving during a truce!" Several of the men shouldered their rifles and aimed them at the creeping soldiers.

A blond-bearded man threw his hands up and smiled, "Take it easy there, Sambo! We just want to get a better look at ya!"

"Yeah, we shoppin' for niggers!" another shouted.

"Take a better look at this," one of the Federals shouted, dropping his trousers and baring his behind to the enemy below. A round of laughter broke out followed by an exchange of insults and taunts between the two forces.

"Quiet! Shut yer damned mouths!" Sergeants shouted on both sides, trying to maintain control.

"We're not helping matters, angering them like this," Francis said softly to his companions.

"They ain't gonna be friendly once they get over these walls either way," Jerry replied.

Elijah frowned as he squinted to get a better view of the exchange between the officers, "I wonder what they talkin' 'bout."

"The Rebs are bluffing like they did at Union City, pretendin' they numbers are big and they got Forrest with 'em," Jerry said. The name of General Nathan

Bedford Forrest brought a worried quiet to the small group of friends. They watched intently as messengers ran back and forth from the meeting of officers to their respective camps.

Finally, a man on horseback appeared in plain view of the fort. He was tall, lean, and sat upright on his horse with an unearthly confidence for a man facing hundreds of enemy rifles. He grinned under his black and gray mustache and chin beard. His blue eyes burned fiercely as he regarded the black and white faces along the wall watching him in awe. He doffed his hat revealing his wild gray-streaked hair and took an ironic theatrical bow.

"Yup," one of the men said, "that's Forrest alright. I spent some time in his slave stockade in Memphis." The men along walls found their voices again and started hurling insults at the Confederate Commander. Forrest smiled, waving his hat in the air to his detractors before riding back to his command post in the woods.

"It don't matter, no how," Jerry spat on the ground. "Ol' Forrest tried to bluff a surrender at Paducah and they sent him packin'."

Francis hardly felt assured. Suddenly, this soldiering fantasy was real. On the other side of the earthen wall was the reality of death or enslavement.

Finally, the two parties of officers retreated to their camps. Not long after, Major Bradford addressed the men in the fort. "You have done well, my boys. Hold out a little longer for there's a boat coming with reinforcements, and if we can hold this place a little longer, we'll have plenty of help. There's a thousand soldiers on board. I'm opening up the whiskey rations for you to share among yourselves for courage, but keep your heads. The lives of you and your brothers depend on it!"

"Well, so much for surrendering," Jerry said with a shrug.

Francis looked up at his big friend with tears brimming in his eyes, "This is my fault, Elijah. I should never've dragged you into this."

Elijah smiled warmly at his friend, "You ain't made me do nothin' I didn't want to do, Francis."

Francis smiled back, wiping away his tear. "You're a good man, Elijah. I'll stand by you and defend you to the end." A bugle called from beyond the wall pulling the two friends from their moment. Then came the chilling sounds of thousands of men yipping loudly in a high-pitched shrill.

"Here they come!" Jerry shouted.

"Everyman to the walls!" Sergeant Weaver shouted, "Shoot the fuckin' bastards!"

With the cannons rendered useless now that the Confederates had crept up under their ability to tilt, the men took to their rifles and found positions on the wall. Many were quickly shot down by the sharpshooters who commanded the heights around the fort.

"Fall back, fall back! Off the wall! Form a line here!" the officers and sergeants shouted. The men backed away from the murderous fire raining on anyone who stuck his head over the wall. Instead, they formed a line twenty paces behind and waited for the enemy to emerge from the battlements. Francis swallowed hard as he clutched his Springfield rifle.

"Hold your fire until enough of them are over! Wait for the command!" the shouts came from sergeants and blended with the high-shrill yell from the ever-nearing Rebels.

Francis began to see the heads of the gray and butternut men appear along the wall like fiends crawling out of hell. They hoisted themselves up and then helped others over.

"Hold!" the sergeants shouted.

The Rebels seemed to multiply as they scampered over the walls in numbers.

"Hold!"

Suddenly, Francis began to think about his friend's warning over a year ago in the comfort of a warm ballroom in Detroit. Francis had been so outraged that Carl, who had ridden off to war and come home a hero, told him to stay out of it.

"Ready!" the sergeants shouted.

Francis pulled his rifle to his shoulder, shook his head, and scoffed as the mass of Rebel soldiers began to surge forward from inside the wall. "Damn it, Carl…I hate it when you're right…" he said softly as the enraged mass of Confederates descended upon them.

"Fire!"

Chapter Two: The Call to Duty

December 1862: Detroit, Michigan

"Francis, do what you feel like you need to do," Carl had said during his wedding reception back in the winter of 1862, "but please be careful. If something were to happen...I would never forgive myself for not stopping you when I could." Francis knew Carl was right to worry, but it still didn't stop him from being annoyed.

Everything seemed to come so easily to Carl. The tall, handsome, olive-skinned young man seemed to tumble carelessly through life while girls swooned and boys either admired him or smoldered with jealously. Carl was now marrying into one of the richest families in Detroit. That is, of course, after he had caused their eldest son to lose his left hand in a duel. Carl had been arrested for that and forced to join the Army. He was sent south to fight the Rebels, a fate from which many never returned, and those who did often came home with broken bodies and broken souls.

But not Carl! A bayonet to the hip, followed by severe fever sent him home a hero. Now, here he was marrying the beautiful and buxom Anna Schmidt. The Schmidts came from Prussia with money. They bought into the iron business and ended up making a lot more. Now even her angry brother, Klaus, was in attendance of this opulent reception for the newlyweds, minus a hand, of course, and now, the bottom half of his right leg. A cannonball had swept it away while he was saving Carl at the Battle of Perryville. Carl seemed to come out of every disaster a winner! But Francis could hardly stay annoyed at his warm and good-natured friend. Still, Francis couldn't help but be a bit jealous. He knew that his desire to take up the cause and win some hero's glory for himself might have been foolish, but it burned greatly in his heart.

Things didn't come so easily for Francis as they did Carl. Yes, he came from a wealthy family too. The Beauchamps' built their wealth over generations of fur trade since the time of the French. But that industry had waned as Detroit passed into the hands of the British and then the Americans. The Beauchamp family had also dwindled down to just Francis and the bitter old widower he called father with affection but got little in return.

Being wealthy and black offered very few peers as Detroit filled with more and more poor and uneducated refugees from the slave plantations of the South. Soon, Francis found himself to be an anomaly. People suddenly seemed to be surprised to see an affluent and educated black man. Even Francis's white friends seemed to treat him more and more like a mascot than a peer.

Now those white friends were going off to fight a war to free the people that only had skin color in common with Francis. They did this while he stayed home, attending balls and making small talk with girls he'd never be allowed to marry, even if he wanted to. The eminent signing of the Emancipation Proclamation was now making this truly a fight for freedom. And with the formation of colored regiments, Francis burned to throw off his dancing shoes and put on marching boots.

"Then, the Arkansans rushed forward and all I had to defend myself was my saber!" Carl lifted his cane to reenact the battle that had left him wounded and sent him home from the war.

The room full of well-dressed men and women gasped with suspense. It was another event to raise money for the troops. Carl, as always, was the keynote speaker and Francis, once again, was his faithful friend sitting in the audience. He sighed and looked out the window at the icicles hanging from the eaves. He had heard this story so many times now that he sometimes caught himself mumbling along, word for word.

The crowds loved it though, and Carl was a rising star. Even the scar on his face seemed to make him more handsome. It was a semi-circle that started from the left corner of his lips and arced down to his jaw creating the appearance of a frown when he wasn't beaming his mischievous grin. For weeks now, Francis had been accompanying him to these speaking engagements where they raised money for wounded veterans and care packages for the troops, sold war bonds, or even recruited new soldiers. Carl's fame rose with each one, but he wasn't the only star.

"How long I was under that pile of bodies," Carl continued as women clutched their expensive crosses to their bosoms, "I don't know, but suddenly a light appeared, and then came the hands of my guardian angel. Folks, I would have died there if it hadn't been for this man right here who found me and brought me home. Ladies and gentlemen, my guardian angel, Elijah Bethune," Carl said, pointing to the large black man sitting among the dignitaries. Francis clapped lazily along with the audience. Elijah: big, sweet, and bashful, dropped his head in embarrassment like he did every time Carl got to this part of the story.

"Elijah, stand up, please," Carl smiled warmly at his friend. The crowd gasped, once again, like they always did, at his size when he stood. "This is why we fight, folks. This fine-looking, well-dressed man was once a slave, considered to be no better than cattle! This is a man among men. This potential is why we fight!" The applause swelled. The host came forward to speak again.

"Ladies and gentlemen, Carl Smith and his comrade, Elijah Bethune!" Cheers added to the swelling applause. "They'll be around to talk and even sign autographs. Don't forget: when you buy war bonds, it keeps fine men like this out there fighting for freedom and for our beloved Union!"

A small brass band started playing *The Battle Hymn of the Republic* as people stood from their chairs and accepted glasses of sparkling white wine. The oak-paneled room was warm with people and a fire that crackled and popped with the music. The oil-burning sconces gave the room an amber glow that contrasted with the late winter gloom that seeped through the windows. Francis stood. He straightened his trousers and adjusted his lapels as a woman approached him.

"Oh, you poor child! Life as a slave must have been awful for you!" She brought her hand to her chest as if to soothe her own aching heart.

"Mrs. Gareth, I'm Francis Beauchamp. My family has been in Detroit for generations. Do you not know me, madam?" he asked.

"Oh, ha! Please forgive me," she put her hand on his shoulder, "sometimes I can't tell you apart."

Francis snapped his head over to where Elijah was speaking to a group of men and then back to her. "Madam, he's twice my size…"

She laughed again, patting him, "Oh, well, I'm sure they'll find something useful for you to do. I do believe they're forming a colored regiment very soon!" With that she moved off to speak with the other guests, leaving Francis agape with frustration.

Francis had inquired about joining the 1st Michigan Colored Volunteer Infantry Regiment, but they would not accept him as a lieutenant or even a sergeant. "All negroes start as privates, boy. Do well and you might be a corporal someday," the recruiting sergeant told him.

"I'll have to think about it," was the closest he came to telling the man to stuff it. If he had to join a regiment full of runaways and paupers as a private, he certainly wasn't going to do it where people knew him. Plus, the colored regiments mustering in the North were rumored to do nothing more than garrison the northern forts and prison camps, far from the front. No, if Francis was going to get in the fight, he was going to go where it was, and his new friend Elijah was his ticket there.

Elijah had been staying with Francis ever since he brought Carl home the previous fall. There was certainly plenty of room at the Beauchamp house. Francis lived there alone with his father, who rarely came out of his office. But Elijah yearned to go back to Tennessee. His sister and one of Francis's dear friends from school, Kyle, were now living together in Memphis with their newborn baby. Elijah and his sister had once been owned by Kyle's family. But the war had changed everything. Now, Elijah just couldn't wait to see his nephew. "I have a family now!" he said with an infectious joy that Francis couldn't help but feel as well. He decided to go with him. Perhaps there he could join a regiment that would see his worth and give him a chance to fight.

"What is it?" Francis's father asked from the other side of his office door.

"I came to say goodbye, Father. May I come in?" Francis replied.

"Come in," Mr. Beauchamp said after a pause. Francis found him sitting at his desk with stacks of papers and piles of fur all around him.

"We'll be leaving for Memphis soon. I don't know when I'll return, Father," Francis told him.

"Hmph, that's a shame. That boy's quite useful," his father mused, looking up from his reading glasses.

"Yes, Elijah's quite a capable man…many talents…" Francis said and then paused for a moment. "Father…"

"Yes..?" Mr. Beauchamp said, closing the ledger in front of him now that there seemed to be more to the conversation.

"They're mustering colored regiments down there…um…I feel it may be my duty to join…to do my part, as it were…"

Mr. Beauchamp looked at him with slight amusement. "Alright, then," he said, reopening his book.

Francis straightened himself, drawing a long breath through his nose, "Have you nothing more to say to me, sir?"

"Don't get shot in the back."

"I feel we've done this before," Carl said with humor. He had one of Francis's bags in one hand and his cane in the other. He lightly tapped it on the ground as they walked.

"Yes, I suppose we must all take our turn at the train station," Francis replied. "Except perhaps this time without murderous Germans demanding duels from us."

"Well, thankfully," Carl said. "Klaus went back to murdering Rebels instead of us for the moment. I guess he could only tolerate seeing me married to his sister and living in his family's home for so long."

"I suppose I'd prefer murdering Rebels too over watching you paw at my sibling," Francis mused.

"I'm gonna miss Ms. Anna and Detroit too, but not this durn cold," Elijah piped in with a shudder.

"Well, if you'd stay long enough, Elijah, we do have a summer here," Carl answered, "and it's a lot more tolerable than Tennessee!"

"Maybe I'll find out someday," Elijah said as they set their bags down on the platform and turned to each other for the inevitable goodbye that they were all trying to pretend wasn't happening.

Francis let out a sigh. "Well, I guess this is it," he said, trying not to sound emotional.

"Francis, I know what you're thinking of doing," Carl said, turning serious. "And I know you don't want me to talk you out of it, so I won't, but please remember, it's alright to change your mind. You can come home. I won't say a word. Everything can be as it was."

Francis let out a soft laugh, looking at the ground, and then to his friend. "I appreciate that, Carl, and I love you for it. But this war is not just some kind of grand adventure, it's for the very soul of this country and the liberty of a people that I have a kinship with. What kind of a man would I be if I didn't heed the call and do my part?"

"A living man. You don't have to fight to be a man, Francis," Carl said softly. "There are other things you can do."

"Like giving dance lessons to widows?" Francis scoffed with bitter humor. "You know, you could come too. I see you're barely using that cane. I know there's plenty of fight left in you."

"I mostly use it to fight off recruiters," Carl said waving his cane at invisible attackers. "Besides, we're trying to have a child and that takes most of my energies if you gentlemen know what I mean."

"Alright, I'm going to pretend I didn't hear you make such a crude reference to my sweet Ms. Anna and hug you goodbye, Señor Carlos de La Vega," Francis laughed, putting his arms around him.

"I told you not to call me that in public. I'm still Carl Smith, regardless of who my father was" Carl said, hugging him back.

"Well, now that you know, I think you should embrace your Mexican heritage. I think it makes you rather exotic and interesting," Francis said pulling away and picking up his bags.

"Not in these times," Carl said looking around, worried that someone might have overheard. "It wasn't so long ago that we were at war with them too." He then turned to Elijah with open arms, "Goodbye, big guy. I must admit, I feel a bit vulnerable without you."

"Aw, you be alright, Carl," Elijah said, hugging him. "I be seeing you again real soon."

"I'm gonna hold you to that, Elijah. Don't let Francis lead you off into any tomfoolery. Be safe."

"I will," Elijah said breaking the embrace and taking his bags.

"Somehow, I don't believe you," Carl said softly, taking in one last look at his friends.

The train whistle broke the awkward melancholy that had settled on the three young men.

"Well," Francis smiled, trying to get back to their previous jovial mood, "I suppose we should get on board then."

"Let me help with your bags," Carl replied.

To Francis, it seemed like the train was driving into spring itself as they traveled south. They changed trains in Chicago. From there they rode to Cairo, Illinois, where they caught a riverboat to Memphis. Francis was miffed that even though his wealth could afford them a cabin on the upper deck, they still had to bunk down below with the other blacks. "You gonna have to get used to it if you gonna spend any time down here. No need causing a fuss," Elijah tried to soothe him.

"Well, hopefully, this war will change all that," Francis mumbled as they carried their bags aboard. Still, the trip wasn't entirely unpleasant. The poor blacks they traveled with seemed fascinated with their two well-dressed travel companions.

"He sounds just like a white man, but different!" they'd exclaim when Francis spoke. Soon people offered them roasted ears of corn and sips of whiskey just to hear them tell tales of the North and read the paper.

"Go ahead, Elijah," Francis smiled at the circle of wide-eyed listeners that sat around them. "Let's hear you read some," he handed him the newspaper.

"I don't know, I ain't ever read in front no one but you and Ms. Anna," Elijah hesitated in taking it.

"Oh, stop," Francis admonished him. "You're an excellent reader! Show our friends here how a man can learn and better himself!"

Elijah looked at the circle of eyes blinking at him in the early twilight. The gaslights illuminated the whites of their eyes in contrast with the evening gloom that seeped in around them. They blinked at him with anticipation. Elijah rolled his eyes and let out a sigh, "Alright then…" He cleared his throat and read slowly and methodically, "CSA President Jefferson Davis had much to say about the North raising colored regiments. In a speech, he said, 'All negro slaves captured in arms will be at once delivered over to the executive authorities of the respective states to which they belong to be dealt with according to the laws of said states.'" He paused and furrowed his brow. "What does that mean?" he mumbled.

"It means if they catch you in them Yankee blues, they goin' send you back to yo master or hang you for insurrection," one of the men sitting before them spoke up. A quiet settled among the small group leaving only the churning of water and the rumble of the steam engine to fill the gap.

"Ahem," Francis spoke up, "Why don't you skip to the next article?"

Chapter Three: New Beginnings and an End

Liza nearly bowled Elijah over as he came down the gangplank, "Oh, my baby brother, look at you all fancy and stuff!"

"Hi Liza..." Elijah mumbled, embarrassed by the attention.

"...And you must be, Mr. Beauchamp! Why, I ain't ever seen a black man look so fancy, no how!" she said.

"Please, madam, call me Francis. How do you do?" Francis doffed his hat and gave a bow.

"My goodness, you sound just like them Yankees, only fancier! Wait till Ms. Kathryn get a load of you!" she squealed with delight.

"Where is she, and Kyle too?" Elijah asked as he recovered his bags and began to walk.

"Ah, they don't show they faces much anymore. Kyle's wanted by both armies. Either one would hang him if they found him, and Ms. Kathryn, well...we'll get to that. They both hidin' out in the colored part of town," she answered.

"Doesn't the family have a house in town? Certainly they'd be sheltering there?" Francis piped in.

"Ooh, Lord, I sure do like hearing this boy talk!" she flashed a smile at him making Francis smile too with a blush as he dropped his eyes. "The Yankees' done took it over. It's full of officers! And they a bit too sweet on Ms. Kathryn. But we got plenty of time to talk about that. Tell me about the North. What's Detroit like?"

"Cold," Elijah said.

The damp cool air of Memphis seemed fresh and full of promise to Francis. He marveled at the sights and sounds of the Southern economic hub while Liza and Elijah chatted happily about how their lives had been since they last saw each other almost a year ago. Above the busy riverboat landing, the city shimmered with activity. They made their way through streets filled with carts, wagons, and men on horses. Soldiers in blue were everywhere. Francis was encouraged to see that some of the soldiers were even black. He marveled at the size and opulence of the Gayoso Hotel and its Greek columns that towered over them. Smaller hotels, shops, saloons, and bordellos lined the streets. Women in satin dresses leered at him from doorways, some even revealing an ankle before Francis could look away.

"Ah," he said as they passed *Young & Brothers Bookstore*. "Now that might be worth a visit…" he said to himself, trying to ignore the woman who called to him.

"Hey there, fancy boy!"

The traffic got lighter and the buildings less impressive as they moved away from the city center to the outer areas. Liza seemed distracted as she scanned the street behind them from over her shoulder.

"What is it?" Francis asked.

"I'm just makin' sure we ain't been followed," she said in a low voice before turning back to her conversation with her brother. Soon the big opulent buildings of downtown were replaced by ramshackle huts, lean-tos, and even army tents. Gone were the soldiers and whites altogether. Small black children in simple cotton shifts ran past them giggling. Francis jumped out of the way to keep his suit from being splattered with mud. A woman yelled after them, then stopped mid-sentence at the sight of Francis. She quickly ducked her head back into her shack. Soon, men and women were poking their heads out to see the two well-dressed men walking through their neighborhood.

At first, Francis barely noticed. He was enthralled with the heavy aroma of cooking and the exotic music. *Is that some kind of guitar?* He was wondering when the music suddenly stopped. Everyone was looking at him.

"Go on, now!" Liza admonished the gawkers after a pause. "Go on about yo business!" she shooed them with her hand. "Ain't you ever seen a man in a suit before? People, please!"

Francis was relieved when the strange guitar-like instrument started plunking away again at some dark and vibrant melody, accompanying itself with rolling arpeggiating harmonics. "What is that thing…?" he mumbled as the crowd began to return to their noisy activities.

Liza knocked on the door to one of the small houses.

"Who is it?" a familiar voice came from inside.

"It's me, baby. My brother and his friend are here, too," she said.

The door opened. "Come in, quick!" the voice said.

"Francis! My God, I thought I'd never see the likes of you again!" the voice exclaimed. Francis's eyes had little time to adjust to the dim light before the figure inside handed off a baby to Liza and threw his arms around him. The baby cooed happily at being in his mother's arms. Francis could feel the rough beard against his face just before they broke off their embrace.

"My God, Kyle, I barely recognize you!" Francis said, still clutching Kyle's upper arms. Only Kyle's bright blue eyes in the dim light were familiar. A heavy blond beard, a mop of hair, a plain shirt, and trousers covered the once well-dressed and well-groomed Southern classmate that Francis had walked to the train station in Detroit almost a year and a half ago.

"Good, then it's working!" Kyle said. "I happened to be a wanted man in both countries."

"Carl's told me about your adventures together. I'm amazed you're still alive!" Francis said.

"Me too, frankly," Kyle agreed. Then pointing to the table and benches, "Come put your bags down, sit. I'll heat up some coffee."

Liza handed the baby to her brother as Kyle lit a match and started the small iron stove.

"Elijah, this is your nephew, James Roger Bethune, but we already call him 'Lil' Jimi B.,'" she told him.

Elijah accepted the child, beaming with happiness. Liza regarded her brother warmly. The child looked so tiny in the big man's arms, yet he held him with gentle confidence. "We named him after our father, James."

"I never knew…" Elijah said shaking his head with awe.

"They didn't want us to know, Baby Boy," She said shaking her head, then looked far off as if she were scanning the seas from inside their dark little shack. "He may still be out there somewhere…"

"A sailor by trade, we think," Kyle added. "If we ever see my parents again, I will press them for answers."

"Where are they now?" Elijah asked with sincere concern for his ex-masters.

"They fled to England," Kyle told him. "We think they have partners there and are now trying to grow cotton in India, Egypt, or somewhere since we're too busy killing each other here to grow anything."

"What about you? Surely you can't hide here forever," Francis asked.

"Well, once we get our money worked out, we're planning on going west. There's land to be had and nobody will know who we are or care," Kyle told them.

"Nobody will know who you are when you're part of someone's scalp collection either," Francis quipped getting a round of chuckles in the room.

Kyle got up to attend the rattling kettle. "Enough about us," he said pouring them coffee, "how's life in Detroit, how's school?"

"Not the same without you," Francis started as the back door opened. "Oh, but you should have seen Carl's wedding! Anna finally reigned him in and now they're trying to have a child!" Francis's voice tapered off as he read the panic flashing across Kyle's face. Kyle shook his head softly, mouthing the word, "No" as two figures entered through the back door.

"Go on," a woman's voice cut through the awkwardness. "I would love to hear about it," she said moving into the dim light that broke through the shuttered window. Francis was taken by the wild red hair and wide green eyes that reflected the narrow sunlight seeping into the room. She was beautiful in her simple frock dress that hung loosely over her bulging belly, which she supported with one hand and a basket with the other.

The old black man that had come in behind her broke the silence, setting down his shotgun in the corner. "I be outside then," he said and slipped back out the back door.

"Ms. Kathryn!" Elijah stood up, handing Lil' Jimi B. back to Liza, "I ain't thought I'd see you again!" he said with an awe-infused joy.

"Oh come here you big oaf and kiss me!" she set her basket down and threw her arms around him, kissing him on the cheek. Elijah smiled bashfully as he leaned over her protruding belly and gently embraced her with light pats. He had never seen the princess-like young lady of the big house look so natural and be so familiar.

"Madam, if I may," Francis sprung to his feet, "I am…"

"…Francis Beauchamp, my brother raves about you," She beamed at him, offering her hand which he kissed with effortless grace.

"My stars, an educated Northerner with class!" she gasped with humor.

"Madam, you do me too kind," Francis bowed.

"Now, please, do tell me about this wedding. I do love hearing about them!" Kathryn said with ill-hidden irony in her voice.

"Ummm, certainly, madam," Francis stammered, trying not to look at her protruding stomach or to make any assumptions.

"Maybe another time," Kyle broke in. Kathryn smirked with slight annoyance at being out-maneuvered by her brother, "Let us first tell you about the wedding Liza and I are going to have, now that you are here!"

Elijah excused himself once the other four started getting into the details of the ceremony to come. He stepped out of the back door into the alley. He was relieved to see he didn't have to look far. Old Man Enon was sitting on a stool next to the house, watching the kids play. From the looks of it, this had become a regular spot for him. Elijah sat on the stoop next to the stool. The old man regarded him with a slight nod before returning his eyes to the children. They were giggling madly, chasing a chicken around the alley

Elijah sat and watched as well until he just couldn't take it any longer. "Liza says you're our granddaddy," he said, not taking his eye off the children.

Enon turned to look at him and then back at the children, "That's right."

Elijah smiled widely and shook his head before dropping it and looking at the ground with a scoff. He looked back up at the kids. "You know, all them years of you looking over us on the plantation…well…I guess I always knew," he said, shaking his head and smiling, tears welling in his eyes.

Enon looked at him and gave up a rare smile before looking back at the children. He patted Elijah on the leg, "You were always a smart boy...big, like your papa too," he said. Elijah just beamed. He knew he wouldn't get much more out of the old man, so he sat there quietly watching the children, happier than he had ever been.

Francis found the wedding to be simple and beautiful. Enon walked Liza down the aisle in the little wood chapel that had recently been built. The smell of fresh-cut wood still lingered and mixed with the smell of the rain that just started to tap lightly on the roof. Once again, Francis found himself in the role of best man. He smiled and nodded to Kathryn who stood as Liza's maid of honor. He then turned to watch Liza's last steps to where they stood with the preacher. Elijah sat among the guests on one of the roughly hewn benches. Elijah had the most important role of all that day. That was keeping Lil' Jimi B. quiet and happy. He did so by bouncing him in his arms and eliciting giggles with funny faces. Lil' Jimi B. coed with delight at the big man.

Francis was stunned by the ceremony. It seemed so raw and wild compared to the Catholic masses he had attended in Detroit, or even Carl and Anna's Lutheran wedding. He had never seen a black preacher before. The tall, thin, kindly man he met prior to the ceremony transformed into a seemingly raving lunatic, but no one else seemed surprised. Instead, the guests played along with him in some kind of call and response routine that seemed so wild and exotic yet well-practiced.

"Every time I turn around, I'm standing on hallowed ground!" the preacher shouted as he spun himself around.

"I know that's right!" someone shouted from the crowd.

"…And I see the bush a-burning with heaven's fire!" he shouted, drawing deep drafts of air through his nostrils. Thunder rumbled softly outside.

"Uh-huh!" a woman let out. Francis shifted uncomfortably, feeling the tension compounding in the room.

"And the bush said onto me, 'Moses! Moses! You must go down, Moses! You must go down!'"

"Yeah!" someone shouted.

"Down!" the preacher shouted again.

"That's right!" another man called out.

"And set my people free!" he shouted. The room was about to explode in ecstasy.

Francis felt he was about to faint when seemingly on cue, a woman started singing, "Go down… Moses…way down in Egypt land… and tell that ole Pharaoh…"

Then everyone joined in, "…Let my people go!"

Now, the whole room was involved, taking turns singing, humming, and clapping hands. The music was dark, wild, and moving. Francis found himself swaying to the beat. He stopped, embarrassed to be caught dancing in church, but then he realized everyone was swaying, dancing, and throwing their hands into the air in an orgy of music, devotion, and fellowship. An elation washed over him, unlike anything he had felt before. Now he was dancing, clapping, and shouting

"Let my people go!" every time the chorus came back around.

The music finally ended and people took their seats. Many of the women were fanning themselves from the exertion of the hymn. The reverend mopped his forehead with a soft laugh, now resuming his previous mild manner. "Now, let's get down to business," he said, "do you, sir, take this woman to be yo wife?"

"Absolutely," Kyle said looking at Liza, shaking his head as if to say, "how could I not?"

"And do you, Miss, take this man to be yo husband?"

"Of course," Liza said, quickly drawing in a sob. She smiled, putting her hand to her mouth as tears glistened in his eyes. Francis felt his own tears trickle down his face.

"Then why don't you go kiss this girl and let's get this party started?! You man and wife now!" the reverend said. A cheer went up. Kyle leaned in and kissed the girl that he had been in love with all his life. Somewhere in the back, a fiddle started sawing off a rhythm. The strange guitar-like thing joined in, and from then on, there was music and dancing all night long.

Francis stared at the strange instrument as people danced and visited with each other in what had become a block party lit by lanterns and sheltered by tarps strung up to keep the intermittent rain off the revelers. There was plenty of smokey roasted pork, ears of corn, butter beans, collard greens, and corn cakes cooked on the flats of garden hoes over the many fires that sprung up along the street. Most of the food and spirits had been "procured" from the US Army although Francis pitched in with the Bethunes for some of the wine. He, however, found the whiskey from one of the unmarked bottles to be exquisite. He sipped it with a little splash of water from a tin mug. Elijah found him and tapped his mug to Francis's, "You enjoying yo'self?"

"Quite, much more than I expected," Francis said taking a sip and hoping he didn't sound too tipsy. "This is marvelous stuff. Where's it from?"

"All over," Elijah smiled, "folks make whiskey all over Tennessee."

"Well, it's the best I've ever had. It's so…earthy but sweet," Francis mused.

"Life's sweet, Francis," Elijah patted him.

"It sure is, Big Fellow, it sure is," Francis mused watching the musician churn out the tunes that set the hips of the revelers in motion. "Say, what is that thing he's playing. It's delightful. Is that some kind of crude guitar?" Francis pointed at the instrument that had bemused him since their arrival. It looked like a drum made from a gourd with an animal skin stretched over it. It had strings and a neck that protruded from it like a guitar, but no frets. Instead, the player's fingers seemed to just find the right place as he plunked along with the fiddler in a mesmerizing tune that was more rhythm than melody.

"Oh, that's a banjo. Seems like someone's always got one when we havin' a party," Elijah said.

"A banjo!" Francis said with new recognition. "I've seen sketches of them in the paper, but they didn't look like that!"

"Yeah, that's one of the old-timey ones like they used to make in Africa. I think the first thing a black man did when he got off the boat was to make himself a banjo and start playing. Masters must've liked it enough to let 'em keep at it. Now the white folk play 'em too!"

"Africa…" Francis said with wonder, watching the man play the ancient instrument from a land far away.

"I thought I'd find you boys together eventually," a woman's voice broke his trance.

"Hello, Ms. Kathryn," Elijah greeted her, "haven't seen you all night."

"Well, I lay low these days because of my condition. There's an ornery Yankee officer living among the squatters at our townhouse. He keeps asking Liza about me ever since I dropped out. We worry he might follow her home someday and find me."

"I see," Francis said carefully, not wanting to pry about her "condition."

"It's alright, Francis," Kathryn said, reading his discomfort. "I'm expecting a child and wanted to get you two alone so we can talk frankly about it."

Francis's eyes widened as he found a place to set his mug. "I am all ears, madam."

She laughed for a moment at his formality, "Francis, I just can't get over the way you speak! You are a darling of a man!"

Francis smiled and looked at the ground for a moment, "Well, thank you, madam. You, if I may say, are a rare beauty."

"Thanks, Francis, although it probably gets me in more trouble than good," She said patting her belly. "I must tell you something and then ask a solemn vow from you as gentlemen."

"I'm entirely at your service, madam," Francis said straightening himself, trying to hide the effects of the whiskey.

"The child is Carl's," she said flatly. Francis's and Elijah's eyes both widened as they stared at her in silence. Kathryn laughed, "Come on, you can't be that shocked!"

"My apologies, madam," Francis gathered himself quickly, "for my reaction and the actions of my friend, but I assure you, Carl is a good man. He'll be happy. He will make it right. My God, does he know?!"

"No, and that's the oath I ask you now," Kathryn said, a bit more sadly. Francis stilled himself and listened intently. "First, I hold no contempt for Carl. He did nothing wrong, or, if he did, I share in the blame. I know he's a good man, trust me, I've seen it for myself. That's why I ask of you this most solemn and sacred oath." Francis and Elijah just stared in stunned disbelief. "He must never know…" she said.

"But, madam!" Francis protested.

She stopped him with a hand on his shoulder, "Please, I beg you. It would cause me much more heartache and trouble if he did. We are going west, away from this war and all its pain and destruction to start again. Let us go in peace. Let Carl have peace with his new bride. She deserves happiness, too. This would most certainly not make her happy."

"Madam, Anna is a kind soul. She would be most accepting…" Francis began. Kathryn cut him short.

"Please, I really don't want to know just what a great person this blonde-headed immigrant living in the North is right now!" she said with a hint of bitter humor.

"I understand," Francis said, dropping his eyes.

"And now, I demand your oath, sir," She said flatly.

"You have it, madam. I shall take it to my grave," Francis said looking up at her.

"And now you, Elijah," she turned to her one-time slave, "I must have your word."

Elijah looked up at her. Tears welled in his eyes, "I promise, Ms. Kathryn, I ain't say nothin', but I wish I didn't know."

Kathryn softened, touching the big man's arm, "I wish I didn't have to tell you, sweet Elijah, but you're too smart to let go on wondering."

Old Man Enon had just about enough revelry for one night. The music, the crowds, the well-wishers had all become just too much and he was tired. He didn't want to talk to anyone anymore or answer any more questions. Too tired to take off his church clothes and lay down, he slipped through the little house that they had made their home and found his stool in the back alley where he liked to sit. There he could still hear the music and the party going on along the street on the other side but now from a comfortable distance. He closed his eyes and leaned his head against the back of the house and smiled as he listened. *Liza sure looked pretty in that dress*, he thought, a*nd Kyle's a good boy, too*.

"There you are, you old fool!" Her voice drifted in through the music and the noise from the party.

"Ester, is that you?" he said opening his eyes. She stood there before him like she hadn't changed a bit. "You been dead for some forty years. Whatcha' doin' here now?"

"I come to take you home," she said extending her hand to him. "C'mon."

"But what about our grandkids? I gotta watch over them," he said.

She smiled and touched his face. The skin on her hand was smooth and youthful like the day of their wedding. "You did yo job. You got Liza to the altar. Now it's up to her man to look after her, and she be lookin' after him, too, and Lil' Jimi B."

"Well, suppose so," he said looking at her, the old love pouring back into him.

"And that Elijah has turned into a fine young man!" she said.

"He always was a good boy," Enon said thinking about the little boy that had turned into such a large and kind man.

"That's because he had you all along to guide him," Ester said. She leaned in and kissed his cheek. "C'mon, now. You done yo work," she bade him to follow her down the dark muddy alley.

"Where we goin,' Ester?" he asked, feeling lighter than he had in years.

"We goin' home, Sweet Pea."

Elijah was pretty torn up over losing his grandfather. "I never got to know him as my grandpa," he said with blurry tear-filled eyes. "There was so much I wanted to ask him…"

They had found him sitting on his stool, as he liked to do ever since they had settled in Memphis. "He liked to watch over those kids back there like they were his own," Liza said, sniffing back a sob. The funeral was at the same small chapel where he had walked her down the aisle just days before. Everyone agreed that at least he got to go peacefully in his sleep.

"…And as a free man," Elijah added.

"So should we all," Francis said, placing a hand on Elijah's shoulder.

"I know that's right," one of the other men said.

The rains finally stopped after a good week-long soaking. "Come on, Big Guy," Francis nudged his melancholy friend. "Let's walk downtown. There's a bookstore I'd like to visit. I'd like to buy you a book. We need to get you back to your reading lessons."

"Alright, then," Elijah tossed the stick he was poking the mud with and lifted himself from his grandfather's stool. After freshening up at the washbasin, the two young men put on their town clothes and started the walk towards Front Street. The sun seemed to come out as if just to light up their way. People were beginning to come out of their homes as well and sweep their front porches after being shut in by the rain for so long. The fresh smells of early spring filled their noses as they walked. Francis noticed the long-absent smile return to Elijah's face as the big man marveled at the large stone buildings along the way.

The shopkeeper at *Young & Brothers Books* eyed the two black men with suspicion as they entered the shop, but then looked at their nice clothes and shrugged his shoulders before returning to his newspaper. Money was money.

"Ah, they have a copy!" Francis said with excitement. "Here you go, big fella. Here's what a man can be. This book was written by the grandson of a slave!"

Elijah furrowed his brow and read the title carefully, "Th' Three Mu-ska-te-ers by Al-ex-an-dre Dumbass."

"It's pronounced 'Ah-leck-ZAN-drah Doo-MAH!'" Francis giggled, "But we'll work on your French some other day. This is what a black man can do! His father was a great general, too! Served under Napoleon himself!"

Elijah thumbed through the book, looking for pictures as they walked along the river toward Fort Pickering. There, the Federals were amassing supplies and men for their ongoing siege at Vicksburg some 200 miles downriver. Francis wanted to get a better look at the big ironclad gunboats that escorted the transports and supply ships.

"Say, there are two fine-looking gentlemen if I've seen one," a friendly voice broke them from their musings. Walking toward them was a handsome young man in a blue officer's uniform with red trimming. A brass emblem of crossed cannons adorned his kepi hat that sat atop a toss of light brown hair. "Lieutenant

Lionel Booth of 1st Alabama Siege Artillery," the man introduced himself offering his hand. The friends both shook it and gave their names in turn.

"Say, would you men like to see the fort? I could give you a tour," Booth told them.

"Well, sure," Francis said, a little unsettled by the pace of this new conversation.

"Excellent!" Booth's blue eyes sparkled with enthusiasm. "You know, we're raising a regiment of colored artillerymen. It takes an intelligent man to operate the cannons, much more than it does being one of those bullet-catchers in the infantry," he told them. "I can tell you now, that I think you two would make fine artillerymen!"

Francis chuckled at the obvious flattery. He looked at Elijah who merely smirked and shrugged his shoulders. "Well, tell us more," Francis said.

"Gladly," Booth replied, beckoning them toward the fort, "follow me."

Chapter Four: Thompson Station

March 5, 1863: Franklin, Tennessee

Two battalions of the 2nd Michigan Cavalry rode down from the heights of Fort Granger overlooking the Harpeth River and through the town of Franklin, Tennessee. They were the vanguard of expedition heading south along the Franklin-Columbia Pike. Behind them were four regiments of infantry and a battery of artillery. The 9th Pennsylvania Cavalry made up the rearguard. They had been skirmishing almost daily with General Nathan Bedford Forrest's cavalry since returning to Middle Tennessee late that winter. Forrest's men seemed to come out of nowhere, seize supplies and prisoners, then disappear before the Federals could react in force.

Now, this force of nearly three thousand men was to link up with General Philip Sheridan at Spring Hill. Combined, the Federals would continue south to probe the Confederate stronghold at Columbia.

"I heard that ol' Forrest can't be kilt," Private Charles Scott said with wonderment to Private Max Bates riding next to him. "They keep shootin' horses out from underneath him and he just gets on another and keeps on killin' without even gettin' a scratch. He's the devil himself!"

"He's a man and can die like the rest of us, Chucky," Captain Newman spoke up from the front of H Company's column. "Now shut your damn mouth before I shut for you." Bates let out a chuckle at

Chucky's big blue eyes bulging in panic at having drawn his company commander's ire. "You too, Bates, goddamnit," Newman added. "Eyes open, boys, mouths shut. Those cousin-fuckers could come out of anywhere." Then turning to Sergeant Barnes, "Ride along the line, George, and make sure they're in good order. Feel free to whack any of them that aren't paying attention."

"Aye, Captain," Barnes said with a chuckle.

Newman slapped the older man on the shoulder as Barnes turned his horse around and rode back along the column to dress the line. Newman's heavy brown mustache hid his smirk but the twinkle in his eyes betrayed the smile. They were all a bunch of dumb kids, but they were his dumb kids and he had no problem being tough with them if it meant bringing them home alive. It was the most he could hope to achieve, he thought absently. It seemed many of the other captains had risen quickly in rank, but not him. Newman chalked it up to not being much of a bootlicker. He had the misfortune of having a wit quicker than his judgment. His mouth caused him more trouble than good.

A crackle of musketry broke his thoughts. He instinctively put up his hand, halting the column. Horses nickered as the sounds of clomping hooves and jangling spurs came to a stop. He squinted at the road ahead, making sure that the men riding hard towards them were indeed wearing blue.

"Easy boys, they're ours," he said, still putting his hand on his Allen & Wheelock revolver. The forward scouts rode in hard past him and up to Major

Leonidas Scranton who halted them with the palm of his hand. Scranton had been a captain as well, until recently. He had been promoted after the Battle of Perryville. Newman seemed to have missed out on the round of promotions that followed, he thought bitterly. Now, Scranton was in command of the two battalions of the 2nd Michigan Cavalry attached to this expedition. Newman wanted to hate the guy, but couldn't help but to like the humble and thoughtful man who now regarded the panting scouts on foam-covered horses.

They saluted, then one spoke breathlessly as Scranton returned the hand gesture. "Rebels in force, sir. They're spread out across the road on the other side of that ridge, possible dismounted cavalry." He pointed to the rise in the road that obscured what lay beyond it.

"How many?" Scranton asked, stroking his beard pensively.

"Thousands, it seems, two…perhaps three brigades, sir," the second scout spoke up.

"Artillery?" Scranton asked.

"None that we sa…"

BOOM!

The sound of cannon fire interrupted him.

"I mean, yes…I guess…" the first scout said nervously, intimidated by Scranton's momentary silence.

"Ride back and inform Colonel Coburn of what you've seen. Tell him we'll put out a skirmish line to hold them here and await his orders."

"Yes, sir!" the scout saluted and began to turn his horse to ride farther down the column. Scranton stopped him short.

"...and, Corporal..."

"Y-yes, sir," the young man replied.

"Make sure you tell him that they have artillery."

Scranton ordered the men to dismount leaving every fourth man behind to tend to the horses. They linked the reins of the three riderless mounts in a chain to the lead horse which the rider used to move them off-road to make room for the artillery and infantry to come forward. The rest of the men pulled their Colt revolving carbine rifles from their saddle holsters and formed into a battle line. Coming over the ridge in a crouch, they could see the Rebel skirmish lines several hundred yards ahead creeping toward them. Both lines halted and began trading shots.

"Get down!" Newman shouted. The men needed little urging to find cover. "Jesus, they are in force," he said, mostly to himself.

The repeating Colt rifles were able to keep the superior Confederate numbers at a draw. But the Rebels brought their cannons forward and began firing shells that screamed through the air and plowed into the earth, kicking up mounds of dirt. Soon, the Federal guns joined in as well as two of the regiments of infantry. Combined, the Federal forces began to drive the Rebels back as the big guns traded shots in what was becoming a running artillery battle. After falling back a mile, the Rebels withdrew altogether. With night coming, the Federals let them go and settled in for the evening.

They continued their march at daybreak. It wasn't long before the 2nd Michigan had to dismount again to engage Rebel skirmishers as the rest of the Union troops marched in column behind them. They pushed forward for miles along the road and rolling wooded hills, drawing closer and closer to the little blip on the map called Thompson Station.

"Pace yourselves, boys, it's going to be a long day!" Newman called out to his men in the skirmish line. "Don't use up all your ammunition!" They were staggered in two rows. The first row fired from kneeling or prone positions after finding whatever cover they could. The back row then moved forward and did the same. The two lines continued to leapfrog each other as they advanced. Officers and sergeants walked behind them, dressing the lines and urging the men forward. The Rebels were doing the same but in reverse: firing and falling back in turns, just enough to keep the Federal skirmishers away and to slow their advance.

Newman didn't like it. It was too clean. The Rebels fired and fell back like clockwork, taking little time to aim. It was as if they were merely practicing a drill… and where were their cannons?

"They're drawing us in…" he said softly to himself. "They're drawing us in!" he said louder as the last line of Rebels dipped behind the next ridge. "Halt!" he called, putting his hand up. Sergeants and officers repeated the order along the line. Newman jogged back to where Major Scranton and his retinue of staff officers followed on horseback. Behind them were the men in reserve who guided the unmounted horse forward.

"What is it, Chester?" Scranton asked, furrowing his brow after returning the salute.

"It's too easy, Leon. It's like they are inviting us in," Newman said.

Scranton caressed his beard with a gloved hand for a moment, looking forward to the ridge before returning his eyes to Newman. "I think you're right. It's a trap." Then to his staff officers, "Ride up and tell the other captains to hold the line here. I'll ride back to Colonel Coburn myself. We're going to need more than skirmishers."

"Poppycock!" Colonel Coburn replied. "You cavalrymen are like hens jumping at your own shadows."

"Still," Scranton pressed on, ignoring the insult, "we haven't seen their cannons all day. I would assume they have found a position of strength with their backs against Thompson Station."

"Nonsense, Major. If you don't think your cavalrymen are up to the task, allow me to show you what real soldiers can do." Then to an orderly, "Bring up the lead three regiments of infantry. Leave the last to guard our wagon train and artillery. Have the 9th Pennsylvania set up a rearguard."

"Sir," Scranton interjected, "would it not be prudent to bring our artillery forward as well to match their guns?"

"Prudence would be not lecturing your superior on tactics, Major. The Rebels are running, not unlimbering their guns. We'll drive them all the way into the Duck River."

The 2nd Michigan moved off the road to make way for Colonel Coburn and his three infantry regiments. They watched as his forward skirmish line and then the rest of the column moved up and over the ridge. Soon the crackle of musketry indicated that a fight had begun. Shortly after, the first cannonade boomed and echoed over the hill. Newman shook his head and scoffed, "...The fool," he said to himself softly.

A lieutenant raced back towards where Major Scranton was conferring with his captains. "Sir!" he saluted, "Colonel Coburn wants you to mount up and charge the enemy's cannons!" he continued breathlessly.

"Is he mad?" Scranton said with sincere astonishment, "We'll be blown to pieces..."

A crackle of nearby musketry caused him to flinch and then turn to the woods on the left. He could see a mix of gray and butternut uniforms along with men in civilian clothing coming through the trees. "They're flanking us!" he shouted. "Captains, get your men along that fence! We must hold them off!"

The 2nd Michigan took positions along the fence that lined the woods on the left side of the road.

There, the rate of fire from their revolving rifles held off the Rebel flanking attack. "Find your targets, men. Make your bullets count!" Newman called to his men. Some were already reloading their cylinders, using the built-in lever on their Colt carbines to pack the powder and balls into each one.

"Notice that?" Sergeant Barnes asked his captain.

"Notice what?" Newman said, not taking his eyes off the woods beyond the fence. He held his pistol aloft, looking for a Rebel to peek out from his cover.

"It's awfully quiet down yonder. The cannons have stopped. I think we're the only ones fighting right now," Barnes replied. Just then a cheer erupted from over the ridge. The two men looked at each other.

"I don't think those're our guys cheering," Newman said.

Barnes's eyes widened, "This is not good, sir."

The thunder of hooves along with the yips and yells from their riders came suddenly from their left. Rebel cavalry was now attacking the column's rear.

"It's about to get a lot worse, George," Newman said. "We're spread too thin!"

"Fall back!" Major Scranton called from his horse as if he had heard Captain Newman's assessment. "Protect our guns!"

The six cannons that made up their battery were hemmed in on the road by the wagon train of supplies in front of them and the 9th Pennsylvania Cavalry guarding their rear. The steep banks along the road prevented any lateral movement. They were stuck.

The men of the 2nd Michigan abandoned the cover of the fence and took positions in and around the gun crews as the artillerymen worked frantically to unlimber and turn their guns toward the enemy that had seemed to have appeared out of nowhere behind them. The 9th Pennsylvanians unleashed a punishing volley, dropping men and horses as they rode in hard like waves crashing on the rocks. The Rebels rode up to just yards of the Federal line, fired their pistols into the mass of blue-clad men, then turned their mounts and dashed back into the woods, each time wounding and killing many.

Abandoning the forward supply wagons, the remaining infantrymen fell back and joined the desperate fight around the cannons. They dragged the screaming wounded men to the center of the defensive square of men, then took their places in the line, fixing their bayonets to discourage charging horses from plowing into their ranks.

The cannons, now turned toward the waves of charging Rebels, erupted in fire, spewing hot canister that dropped men and horses into screaming piles of flesh.

"Jesus fucking wept!" Newman gasped at the grisly sight. The Rebels disappeared into the woods again.

"Hold your fire!" Colonel Jordan of the 9th Pennsylvania shouted as the Rebels broke off the attack. In the absence of Colonel Coburn, he was now the ranking officer of their desperate huddle of men.

Newman squinted his eyes, trying to hear better after the deafening sounds of muskets and cannons subsided. Now only the cries of wounded men could be heard. He wanted to hush them as he listened for the next wave of attacks. Smoke drifted through the square of men. It smelled like rotten eggs and stung his eyes.

"On our front!" a man called.

"Hold your fire!" Colonel Jordan was quick to stop the frazzled men from wasting their shots.

Newman walked towards the forward-facing side of the square. Ahead in the road, the Rebels began to swarm in around the supply wagons. No longer interested in fighting, the Confederates whooped and hollered in delight at the bounty of food and supplies they had captured. Chucky raised his rifle to his cheek and took aim.

"Don't fire, son," Newman squeezed his shoulder. "It won't take them long to figure out that the rest of our ammo is on those carts."

After a brief celebration, the Rebels began to organize their captured carts and animals. Soon, they began to drive them forward.

"What about Colonel Coburn and the rest of the infantry? Ain't they up ahead, sir?" Chucky asked.

"If Forrest's men are between us and them, then they're already lost," Newman said softly, watching the victorious Rebels ride off with their newly won trophies. One of the horsemen turned and rode back toward the Federal square. The blue-clad men rustled their rifles to their shoulders at the approaching threat.

"Easy now, fellas, it's just one man," Newman told them.

Two other riders turned to follow the man, but cautiously held themselves back, watching their tall and slender captain as he defiantly rode closer to the crouching Yankee line. Captain Newman stood upright, crossing his arms, no longer wanting to crouch in front of this man. The clean-shaven face officer with cold, green eyes suddenly looked familiar to him as the two men regarded each other for a moment. The Rebel officer doffed his hat and took a slight bow, "I'd like to thank you, Billy Yank, for delivering our supplies to us."

"Enjoy it while you can, Johnny Reb," Newman said flatly. "The bill's coming soon,"

The man grinned, replacing his hat. "I'll be waiting," he said smiling, then turned back to join the newly acquired caravan of supplies with his two followers in tow.

Confederate Captain Lathan Woods was pretty sure he recognized the heavily mustached officer who stood tall among the otherwise cowering mass of Yankees. "Seven Mile Creek," he said to himself.

"What's that?" Sergeant Tom Billington asked him as he rode up alongside. Sergeant Bill Garret rode up on his other side.

"That was the man who stopped me from killing ol' Cousin Carl back at Corinth," Lathan answered. "Pity, I didn't see that mongrel dog with him."

Lathan thought of the mixed-bred man that had made a fool of him back at New Madrid about a year before. He hoped he'd have another chance at killing him. Perhaps someone had already beaten him to it. But there was still the traitor Kyle Bethune, his sister, Kathryn, and their two slaves whose names were no more important to him than that of his newly acquired horse, courtesy of the Yankees. His last one had been shot out from beneath him in the fight. He didn't know that animal's name either.

What he did know was that he was finally riding with a winner. Unlike the West Point grads he had served under who lost at New Madrid, Corinth, Chattanooga, and Perryville; Nathan Bedford Forrest had the will and audacity to win. This crushing victory over the Yankees was the proof, he thought as he rode along the captured wagons and Yankee prisoners. With Forrest, Lathan was sure they'd drive the Yankee mongrels out of Tennessee and put the runaway negroes pretending to be soldiers back in their place.

Chapter Five: Teamwork

Francis never thought he'd be so proud to wear such cheaply made clothes. He felt absolutely dashing in his red blouse and blue jacket with shiny brass buttons. Each one had a tiny eagle and shield embossed on it. He was particularly fond of the red trim on the sleeves and collar of his jacket as well as the brass crossed cannons on his short-brimmed hat, all of which marked him an artilleryman, a *thinking* soldier, they told him. Most of all, he was proud of the shiny brass belt buckle that had the letters "US" embossed on it. It was his country, a country that believed in him and thought him worthy as a soldier.

Soldiering seemed pretty mundane so far. Most of the training had been how to march with a little musket drilling. "When we goin' get t'shoot th' big guns?" was the common question among the newly enlisted men.

"In all due time, boys," the white sergeants would answer. "Ya gotta learn to be a soldier first, then an infantryman. If you can prove yourself that far, then we'll make artillerymen out of you."

Francis and Elijah stayed in the mostly empty colored barracks as recruits trickled in. Most of them were escaped slaves. Francis was stunned to see the scars on their backs that the others seemed to regard lightly. He wondered if he could take such a beating and then wear the scars as if it were nothing. These were hard men, used to a hard life. They came from farms in Tennessee, Arkansas, Mississippi, and even

Alabama, which was the namesake of their regiment, the 1st Regiment Alabama Siege Artillery of African Descent. Although, that seemed to be about to change. Rumor had it they were about to become the 6th United States Colored Heavy Artillery. That filled the men with delight. No longer were they possessions of a farm, but men of a nation that promised freedom for everyone.

Francis found his fellow soldiers fascinating. They were uneducated, even hard to understand at times, but there was an earnestness to them. They spoke in simple truths that seemed to carry ancient wisdom passed down from the ghosts of their ancestors.

They were industrious, too. Accustomed to labor, they were quick to a task, inventive with problems, and well-suited to the regimented discipline of military life. Francis felt embarrassed and tried to hide the softness he had gained from a leisurely life from these rugged people. They didn't seem to notice or care. Instead, they reciprocated his fascination in abundance.

"I ain't ever heard no color man talk like you. You sound smarter den m'master!" was what they'd tell him followed by a hoot and a laugh among the men.

Hiding his deficiencies at the manly tasks such as building battlements and barracks of the ever-expanding fort, Francis made himself useful to his fellow soldiers by reading newspapers and even Dumas's *Three Musketeers* to them in the evenings. The men were eager listeners. Soon he was reading and writing letters for them, too, a task he encouraged Elijah to help him with. Before long, the two were tutoring other men in the art of letters. Between learning to be a soldier to teaching his fellow men to read and write, Francis felt he was living the purpose his life had so far denied him.

In time, the new recruits crowded the designated colored barracks and spilled into some of the newly constructed ones. Excitement weaved through the men as a large number of recruits marched into the camp one evening. These men had been recruited at Corinth and their addition to the regiment brought them to full strength. Surely, training on the big guns was eminent.

The men gathered on the grounds overlooking the Mississippi River. There, two short stubby bronze cannons had been set up with their ammunition chests set on two-wheeled carts several yards behind them. The guns pointed toward the river. "They don't look that big," one man quipped.

"Yeah, ain't we s'pose to be heavy artillery?" another asked.

"Maybe we just learn on these first, then learn the big ones," Elijah offered, staring at the short stubby barrels with awe.

"Well, I'll be God damn!" an oddly familiar voice snapped Elijah from his trance. "They done put a uniform on the ugliest bear they could find!"

"Jerry…?" Elijah gasped, as he looked up just in time to recognize his one-time companion before the man threw his arms around him.

"Come here y'big ugly bear!" Jerry chuckled, "I thought they done caught and kilt'ya back at New Madrid!"

"Nah, I got away with the help of my friends. What about you? How'dya get away?" Elijah asked.

"Well, they sent me to work on they big dirt walls at Corinth once they figured that ol'Island No. 10 wasn't worth saving. But then they run from there, too! Them fools tried to take me with 'em to Tupelo, but I gives them the slip! Ain't gonna sell ol' Jerry down the river. No, sir!" he told him.

Elijah couldn't believe he was seeing his old friend again. They had met while both of them were on the run, freshly escaped from their plantations. They had been caught and forced into the labor gangs at New Madrid. Now the two men were wearing the Union blue and preparing to fight their one-time masters.

"Jerry, this is my friend, Francis. He's a freeman from Detroit." Elijah motioned to the small, wiry man next to him.

"How do you do, sir? Francis Beauchamp, at your service," Francis said, leaning into the French pronunciation of his name as he offered his hand.

Jerry didn't take it. Instead, he leaned back into friends, covering the side of his mouth with his hand in irony. "Oooh, we got ourselves a fancy nigga here, don't we…?!" he said to them. The men around him gave a low and cynical chuckle.

Francis cocked his head in irritation, lowering his hand as he spoke. "You would do well, sir, not to call me that," he said flatly.

The crowd of men got suddenly quiet. Elijah looked back and forth between the two with a surge of apprehension. Jerry's eyes bulged with feigned comedic surprise. He looked back at his friends before returning them to Francis, "Oh, you ain't a nigga like me? So whatcha gonna do about it, nigga?"

"If you insist on insulting me, I will be forced to demand satisfaction," Francis stiffened himself.

"Oh, you want satisfaction?" Jerry said, extending his open left palm up towards Francis as he stepped forward. "I got yo satisfaction right here…nigga."

Francis made the mistake of looking at Jerry's left hand. He knew it almost immediately as he did. Jerry's right hand flashed across his peripheral toward his face. Francis moved with the open-hand strike, lessening the blow as it grazed his cheek. Without thinking, he brought his left leg up high and then back down hard using the motion to bound himself into the air while lifting his right leg. He spun it around, bringing the back of his heel crashing into the right side of Jerry's face. Jerry tumbled to the ground. Francis landed on his feet and crouched into a fighting stance.

"Aw, damn!" one of the men let out.

"What in tarnation is going on here!" a voice bellowed. The men snapped to attention. Francis rose from his fighting stance and turned to face Sergeant Weaver. Weaver stormed into the circle of men using his hickory stick to separate them. Jerry propped himself up on his arms and shook his head, trying to regain his senses. "Just because you ain't slaves no more don't mean I won't whup the tar out you boys! You wanna fight! I'll give you a beating you'll never forget!"

"Ain't no need for that, Sergeant," Jerry smiled, "Ol' Frenchie here was just showing me some dance moves. Must've lost m'balance." Francis wanted to correct him on his name but thought better of it.

"Boy, don't you get smart with me," Weaver growled propping Jerry's chin up with the end of his stick.

"It's alright, Henry," the newly promoted Captain Booth said, putting a hand on the sergeant's shoulder. "If these boys got enough energy for dance lessons, I think we can make some use out of them with kitchen duty tonight." Jerry let out a breath, slumping his shoulders at the thought of peeling potatoes all evening. "In the meantime, we've got some learning to do. Sergeant if you would."

"Regiment, fall in!" Weaver barked. Jerry got to his feet quickly and joined the rest of the men as they scrambled into position. Weaver used his hickory stick to dress the rows. Once satisfied he turned to Booth. "Sir!" he said with a salute.

Booth returned the salute and smiled at the rows of men in their new uniforms standing at attention. Behind him stood a team of seven men made up of the sergeants and lieutenants of the regiment. "Alright, boys, at ease, in fact, have a seat. Our two dance partners here are exactly why I make this point. If you can't work together as a team…you will die." The dark faces looked up at him in quiet contemplation.

"A full cannon crew has seven men working together in concert to pour fire and death upon the enemies of our Union…and when those enemies come screaming towards you with their guns and bayonets ready to exact revenge for the field of bodies you've left laying before your gun…it'll only be your ability to perform your part and your trust in your brother performing his that will keep you alive."

The men nodded, some even let out an, "mm-hmm," as if they were in church. That got a quick shushing and a menacing look from Sergeant Weaver. Booth smiled, seeing that the sermon was sinking in.

"So today, you must put away all of your petty differences," he said to the group of nodding men. A few more "mm-hmm's" leaked out.

"Silence!" Weaver barked. One of the offenders dropped his head at the glare he got from the sergeant.

Booth smiled at the eagerness of the men to agree. He continued, "Because if you have a problem with any of the other men here, then you have a problem with the whole regiment and that means you have a problem with me. Am I clear?" The men looked up at him blinking silently.

"Oh, for Christ's sake, this is when you're supposed to speak up, you nitwits!" Weaver shouted.

"Yes, sir!" the men shouted.

"Good, let's get on with the demonstration then," Booth told them. "Every one of you will learn to do all seven jobs because when the bullets start flying and men start dropping, there's no telling where you'll have to fill in to keep our guns firing." He then referred to the team of men standing behind him. "These fine gentlemen have served in various artillery units and are all combat veterans. They will be your teachers over the next several weeks as you drill. Our regiment has procured these two 12-pound mountain howitzers from the war department. I'm working on getting us more and bigger guns, but don't be fooled, master these ones here and there won't be anything else you can't handle." Then turning to the team of men behind him, "To your posts!" he shouted.

The seven men took up positions around the gun. Two stood in the front on either side of the muzzle. Two stood in the rear on either side of the breech. A man stood between the gun and the cart set behind it. The last two stationed themselves at the rear of the cart where the ammunition chest sat.

"Sergeant Weaver will be acting as the gunner." Captain Booth told them. "He's directly in charge of the gun and crew. He'll take his orders from the section leader, who typically commands two guns. I'll play that role for our demonstration today. Three sections make up a battery of six guns, which we soon hope to have to bring our regiment up to full force." He paused to look at the faces of the men watching with fixed concentration. Satisfied that they were following, he continued.

"The men in the crew are numbered. Number one and two are in the front," he pointed to each man, "three and four to the rear. Five is next to the gunner between the gun and the cart to the rear which we call a limber. Finally, numbers six and seven are at the ammunition chest on the limber. Don't you worry, we will teach you exactly what each of these men does and drill you until you can do all seven jobs in your sleep. For the time being, I want you to see what it looks like in action."

He then turned to Weaver. "Sergeant, you may commence firing. Solid shot, straight trajectory, just like we discussed. I want them to see the difference."

"Yes, Captain!" Weaver said, then barked, "Gun number one, load!" Then to the number five man, "Solid shot."

The man ran to the limber and repeated "solid shot," opening his leather ammunition bag. The two men there placed a 12-pound lead ball in it. It was a little over four and a half inches in diameter, with a small sack of gunpowder strapped to it. Meanwhile, man number one ran a wet sponge mounted on the end of a long wooden staff into the barrel twice while the number three man in the rear placed his leather-covered thumb over the small vent hole. This was to avoid any accidental discharge while cleaning and loading. The number five man with the ammo bag showed the round to the gunner, Sergeant Weaver. Weaver, upon confirming it was the correct load, gave him a brisk nod. The man then carried it to the front of the gun, opened the bag, and presented the round to the number two man.

The number two man took it and stuffed it into the barrel, bag end first. The number one man rammed it down to the base of the barrel with his rammer mounted on a staff. The two men turned and stepped away from the barrel indicating they were done.

Satisfied with this, Weaver shouted, "Ready!"

The number three man at the rear of the gun removed his thumb and then shoved a priming wire into the vent to puncture the powder bag. Once he removed the priming wire, the number four man shoved a slender copper tube down the hole and into the punctured bag. He then attached a lanyard to it and stepped away, taking out the slack as he did so. Once he and the number three man were outside of the wheels facing back towards the sergeant, Weaver made one more check to make sure all of the men were clear before shouting, "Fire!"

The number four man turned his body away from the gun in a hard jerking motion, yanking the lanyard as he did. This caused a wire inside the copper tube to scrape across the inner walls and spark, igniting the small amount of gunpowder inside the tube which then ignited the bag full of powder attached to the round.

BOOM!

The men sitting on the ground flinched. Some clutched their chests as the gun kicked backward, spitting out flames and smoke. The ball skipped across the water, throwing splashes high into the air before plunging into the depths below.

"Damn!" one of the men let out. Weaver chuckled quietly to himself, deciding to let that one go.

Man three and four rolled the gun back into position. The number two man shoved a worm into the barrel which was an iron corkscrew attached to the end of a pole. He used it to fish out any remnants of the powder bag. The number one man immediately followed with the wet sponge which hissed and steamed as he plunged it into the barrel.

"Cease fire!" Captain Booth called, unable to hide the grin from looking at the stunned faces of the men.

"Cease fire!" Sergeant Weaver repeated. The gun crew snapped to attention, standing at their posts.

One of the sitting soldiers finally let out his breath. Booth chuckled at the awestruck exhilaration that rose like steam off the men. "Quite a show, but we didn't do much but put one in the drink," Booth told them. "The 12-pound mountain howitzer is designed to be light for mobility, but not so much for range and power. The thin bronze walls can't take a full charge of powder like the 12-pound Napoleon. But here's the little trick with howitzers that makes them magical. Sergeant Weaver!"

"Yes, sir!" Weaver shouted back

"Put one on the Arkansas side of the river, fire at will."

"Yes, sir!" Weaver then turned to his team. "Load!"

The seven-man crew performed the same choreographed dance, but this time, Sergeant Weaver set a brass sight on the rear of the gun. Sliding the peephole to the proper range on the ruler-like device, he then turned a crank below the barrel causing the rear end to lower as the muzzle inched its way upward. To the men watching, it appeared to be pointing too high to shoot anything. Still, Weaver seemed satisfied after having the three and four man help him turn the gun slightly to the left. Once the crew was clear, he gave the order.

"Fire!"

The cannon erupted in flames and smoke again as it bucked backward several feet. In a flash, some of the men caught the ball arc into the sky and then come crashing down to earth, smashing into a tree on the other side of the river. They let out a cheer.

"Settle down, boys," Captain Booth told them. "You see, with the right arc you can drop a round on someone who thinks they're hiding safely in a trench or behind a wall. Trust me, once you master the howitzer, nobody will be safe from you." The men let out a chuckle. "But before we teach you how to fire one, you have to learn how to clean it." Then to Weaver, "Sergeant, show them how it's done."

The excitement of the cannon demonstration lasted Francis all through the rigors of cleaning them and then through supper as the men talked enthusiastically about other types of big guns the regiment might get. That excitement died when he and the man he had tussled with were summoned after the meal.

"Boys," Sergeant Weaver smiled at them, "tonight you're going to learn the value of teamwork." Francis gulped nervously as he stood at attention next to Jerry. "You see all them dishes piled up?" He paused for a moment to let the two men acknowledge them.

"Yes, Sergeant," they replied hesitantly.

"You're gonna wash every one of them. Then when you're done, you're gonna wash and peel all these potatoes," he said, pointing his stick to the hundreds of potatoes stacked in bushels. "You better learn how to work together because neither of you is leaving until all the work is done. If you hustle, you might be able to squeeze in an hour of sleep before morning exercise. And if the morning crew tells me you did shoddy work, there's gonna be hell to pay. Am I clear?"

"Yes, Sergeant," the two mumbled.

"Am I clear!" he shouted causing Francis to flinch.

"Yes, Sergeant!" the two bellowed.

The two worked quietly for hours after Weaver left. It was Jerry who broke the awkward silence as they peeled potatoes with their knives. "So what was that shit you pulled on me, anyway, Frenchie?"

Francis thought to correct him on his name, and then decide it wasn't worth the effort.

"It's *savate* or French boxing. 'The foot is stronger than the fist.'"

"Damn, you are one fancy nigga, ain't ya," Jerry shook his head and laughed.

"Good heavens, man! Are we going to have to go through this again?" Francis dropped his hands in exasperation.

"You think just because you born under better circumstances you better than me?" Jerry stopped peeling, eyeing Francis intently.

"You think you're somehow better than me because you weren't?" Francis shot back.

Jerry stared at him for a moment. Both men held each other's gaze. Each with a knife in one hand and a potato in the other. Francis wondered if he was about to get into a bloody knife fight. Jerry finally broke off the contest, returning his eyes to his potato as he continued his work.

"Well, I guess not, Frenchie," he said.

Francis thought about it for a moment before turning to his potato. In that moment he decided he could live with "Frenchie."

Chapter Six: The River of Death

September 18, 1863: Northern Georgia

"What is the meaning of this, sir?!" Major General William Rosecrans fumed, drawing and exhaling long drafts of air through his nose which sat flat and broad on his face. He stared down at the bewildered Brigadier General Thomas Wood from the heights of his horse. The small wiry General blinked up at him in confusion. His staff officers stood around him in stunned silence at the sudden appearance of their enraged army commander.

"I'm sorry, sir," Wood stammered "what do you mean?"

"You have disobeyed my specific orders," Rosecrans replied. "By your damnable negligence you are endangering the safety of the entire army, and, by God, I will not tolerate it! Move your division at once, as I have instructed, or the consequences will not be pleasant for you!"

Wood's face flushed with embarrassment, "Sir, we are in the process of moving now. Clearly, you can see my brigades are forming up to move forward as we speak."

"Why haven't you done so earlier?" Rosecrans demanded.

"I have only just received your orders, sir, mere moments before. I moved immediately upon receipt. My staff here can vouch as much, sir!" Wood replied, completely aghast.

"Do not hide behind your staff, sir. I've had enough of you questioning my orders. I have not forgotten that just last week you demurred when I ordered you to reconnoiter Lookout Mountain. I will not have your damnable hesitancy put my army at risk once again!"

"Sir, on that day I was only concerned about exposing my flanks…"

"Enough!" Rosecrans cut him off. "Hurry up and relieve General Negley on the line, make sure there's no gap between you and General Brannan's division on your left, and from now on, if I give you an order, General, I expect you to obey it immediately!" With that he spurred his horse and rode off, leaving General Wood stunned and embarrassed in his wake. Rosecrans's staff fell in behind him silently. They had just witnessed him dress down two division commanders in the last ten minutes. No one wanted to invite that same rage upon themselves.

"These damn generals think they know better than me just because they fought in Mexico," he said to a nearby aide who was wise enough not to reply. "I won't have their arrogance ruin everything I've achieved."

William Rosecrans had been in the Army during the Mexican War, but unlike some of the veterans he commanded now, he had spent the war teaching at West Point. His return to service at the outset of the current war had been a steady climb in stature and esteem for him. Now he was a Major General in command of the Army of the Cumberland. He had gained the post after Don Carlos Buell had been fired for his failure to pursue Braxton Bragg's Army of Tennessee after the Battle of Perryville.

Bragg's Army of Tennessee had tested him dearly by the year's end. They fought at Stones River, just outside of Murfreesboro, Tennessee. For three days they beat back attack after attack until the Rebels finally withdrew.

Desperate for good news, Washington hailed it as a victory. Even President Lincoln congratulated him with a letter that read, "You gave us a hard-earned victory, which had there been a defeat instead, the nation could scarcely have lived…"

But it was a costly victory, leaving thousands of men dead on the field. Rosecrans spent months rebuilding his army while Washington pestered him for results. Knowing they were running out of patience, he finally moved forward, sweeping the Rebels from Middle Tennessee and taking Tullahoma easily with few losses.

"Hmph!" Rosecrans grunted to himself as they rode into his headquarters camp. The victory at Tullahoma would have been the toast of the nation had it not been overshadowed by the Federal victories at Gettysburg and Vicksburg. Bragg's army had managed to slip away from him at Tullahoma. Rosecrans then drove him out of Chattanooga, as well, but that wouldn't be enough for Washington. They had supplanted General Meade for letting Lee's army escape after Gettysburg. Rosecrans knew if he wanted to keep his job, he'd have to drive old Braxton Bragg into the ground.

Bragg decided to stand his ground just south of the Chattanooga along a creek the Cherokees called *Chickamauga.*

"*The River of Death…*" he mumbled as leaped from his horse and tossed the reins to an orderly.

"Excuse me, sir?" the young man stammered.

"Ah…nothing, as you were, soldier," he said, leaving the man to attend to his horse. The rough translation of the Cherokee name gave him a chill. Everything had been going well up until now. He had spread his forces out widely enough to keep the Rebels guessing where his main attack would come, but now they were exploiting those large gaps in his line as they turned around and began to fight like a cornered dog. Now, he and his staff were scrambling to move divisions around to patch up those gaps quickly before the Rebels could break through. He would not and could not tolerate any of his own generals hesitating or questioning orders.

"Good heavens!" he gasped as he entered his tent. He tossed his sweat-stained hat onto his bed. The table set up in his tent was covered in dispatches. "How'm I supposed to read all of these?!" His staff stood behind him, having followed him in. All of them were too scared to reply. Their heads suddenly turned toward the tent flaps at the arriving sounds of thundering hooves.

A dust-covered rider came bursting in with yet more dispatches in his hand, "General Rosecrans," the man said breathlessly, "I'm so happy I finally found you!"

"Captain Kellogg, what news have you from our left?" Rosecrans asked him.

"Sir, General Thomas's XIV Corps is heavily engaged and needs immediate reinforcements. He requested Brannan's division. I couldn't find you so I went to General Brannan first and asked him to move immediately."

"Damn it!" Rosecrans let out, "If Thomas wanted command of this army he should have taken it when they offered it to him! That leaves a hole in my center."

"Sir," Kellogg was still catching his breath, "there was very little activity on General Brannan's front when I left him. I spoke to General Reynolds, whose division is on the immediate left. He requests that General Wood now closes up on his right to replace General Brannan."

"Fine, you may return to General Thomas. Tell him he may have Brannan's division although I assume they're already moving," he told Captain Kellogg, dismissing him with a salute. He then turned to his staff, "Major Bond!"

"Yes, sir!" Major Frank Bond stepped forward. "Write up an order for General Wood. Tell him he is to now close up with General Reynolds's Division on his left. He is to do it as fast as possible and support him. Have Colonel Starling deliver it immediately when you're done."

"Yes, sir!" Bond said sitting down at the table. He pulled a pen from the ink well and started scratching the order onto paper.

"Now, gentlemen," Rosecrans said, sweeping aside the unread dispatches on his desk to view the map beneath them, "we must see to shifting our right to make up for any gaps in the line. Who do we have on Wood's right?"

General Thomas Wood was quick to move after the humiliating scolding he received in front of his fellow officers. His orders had been to move his division out from a position of reserve in the rear and into the frontline. This was to fill a gap in the Federal center created by all the chaotic shuffling of troops that morning. First, he sent his skirmishers out to provide protective cover while the rest of the division formed up and moved into position.

Colonel Bartleson rode out past the breastworks of felled trees into the clearing before them with his men from the 100th Illinois Infantry. He was placing them where they could best hold off their Rebel counterparts. "Captain, place your men here!" he shouted to one of his officers, motioning with his saber to a little cabin that could provide some cover.

CRACK!

A Rebel ball punched him clean off his horse. He hit the ground with a thump, laying on his back, gasping for air.

"Take cover!" the captain shouted. His men fell in around the cabin and began to fire into the dark tree line on the other side of the clearing. "You two!" he shouted to a couple of privates. "Carry the colonel back and let them know were engaged with Rebel skirmishers."

General Wood needed little notification that a skirmish was developing in his front. The crackle of musketry quickly told the tale. Soon, he had his three brigades of infantry as well as his three batteries of cannons in place along the breastwork. Now with the firepower of his whole division, the Rebel skirmishers had no choice but to slip back into the dark woods from where they came.

"They could have been the vanguard of a much larger attack to come," General McCook put forth.

The other officers paused for a moment to listen. They were conferring in the woods behind the defensive works that Wood's division now occupied. McCook had come by to make sure his corps was properly linked up with Wood's division on his left. It was clear now that the clattering of musketry they had experienced to their front was a small affair compared to the raging sounds of battle coming from far from their left.

"Certainly, General Thomas's corps is getting the worst of it on our northern flank," Wood mused.

"No doubt, sir," his aide, Colonel Bestow, added. "General Rosecrans has been pulling troops all morning from our right to bolster Thomas's defense."

"That could very well leave us vulnerable on our end if we're not careful," McCook added.

A rider came galloping in, disrupting their conference. "General Wood!" the man huffed as he pulled his horse to a halt and saluted.

"Colonel Starling," Wood returned the salute.

"I have direct orders from General Rosecrans," he handed him a folded piece of paper.

"Why are my commands not coming through General Crittenden, my corps commander?"

"There's no time. General Rosecrans says you must move at once!" the lieutenant colonel replied. With that, he saluted and rode off.

Wood watched him go, shrugged, and opened the letter. It read:

Headquarters

Department of the Cumberland

September 20th-1045 A.M.
Brigadier-General Wood,
Commanding Division:

The general commanding directs that you close up on Reynolds as fast as possible and support him.

Respectfully, etc.

Frank S. Bond,
Major and Aide-de-Camp

He frowned, furrowing his brow. "That's odd… What do you make of this?" he said, handing the order to McCook. "Rosecrans wants me to close up on Reynolds's division to the north, but I can clearly see Brannan's division still holding the line between us."

"Perhaps you should ask for clarification?" Colonel Bestow offered.

"After the way he spoke to me this morning, I'm quite sure he would have my head if I delayed for such clarification," Wood said ruefully. "The order says to 'support' him, which I can only infer that he wants me to form up behind Reynolds. Still, that leaves quite a hole in our center if I move now, but he did say, 'as fast as possible.' I can only guess that he has a clearer picture of the whole front than I do"

McCook handed the order back to him, "That's how I read it. I'll shift my corps to the left to plug that hole once I get back to my men."

"Then it's decided, gentlemen," Wood said. He then turned to his aides, "Inform the brigade commanders they are to withdraw from the line immediately and march north. I'll ride ahead to find exactly where we should place them behind Reynolds. Let's move gentlemen, we can ill afford to tarry."

Rosecrans's head throbbed with the constant pulse of artillery north of him. He had hardly slept or even eaten since they crossed the Tennessee River more than two weeks before. Now he was trying to stay focused as he and his staff poured through his dispatches and sent orders. It was hard to keep up as riders came and went carrying communications to and from the front.

"General Rosecrans," the latest rider with urgent news approached his desk with a salute.

"What is it?" Rosecrans sighed.

"General Brannan sends his regards," the man said.

"Of course he does. Get on with it, man. How goes his move to aid General Thomas?"

The man blinked at him for a moment, his mouth open, trying to find words, "He…hasn't moved…yet… uh…sir…"

"What?!" Rosecrans blurted.

"He was going to, sir, but since the order came from General Thomas and not you, he thought he should have you confirm it before he left and created a gap in the line," the man said, confused by Rosecrans's reaction.

"What's with these generals trying to outthink me?! I sent General Wood's division to replace him! Does nobody in this army trust their commanders anymore?!"

The man stared at the furious commander for a moment, not sure how to say what was next, "Sir, I saw General Wood's division on my way here. They were passing behind Brannan's division marching north. I think they were moving to set up behind Reynolds's division in support."

"What?!" Rosecrans sprung from his chair. The courier never answered. Instead, both of them turned their heads to the tent flaps as the sounds of battle from the Federal right and center began to compete with sounds of battle raging to the north of them. Then, above the crackle of musketry and cannon fire came the high-pitch shrill of thousands of men yipping and yelling.

"My God, what is happening…" he mumbled, getting up and walking out of his tent. A flood of men in blue uniforms surged upon them. Thousands of men were running with wild fear in their eyes. Some didn't even have weapons in their hands. Rosecrans reached out, grabbing a soldier by the collar as he tried to run by.

"What is the meaning of this?!" he shouted at the trembling youth who barely filled out his uniform.

The young man looked up at him confused, his wild eyes were filled with panic, "Sir, the Rebels have broken through! It's a blood bath!"

Rosecrans let go of the man's collar, allowing him to scurry away. He stood there watching the confluence of men streaming past him in shock. Then, from across the field, coming out of the woods that blocked his view of the frontline, they came like a river of men in gray and butternut uniforms bringing death and destruction in their wake.

"My God, I am undone…" he mumbled. He then turned to his chief of staff General James Garfield, "Ride to General Thomas immediately. Tell him he's to hold at all cost and cover our retreat to Chattanooga." Then to the rest of his staff, "Gentlemen, If you care to live any longer, get away from here! We must see to the defenses at Chattanooga! Save yourselves!" With that he took to his horse and rode off, outpacing the foot soldiers running alongside him.

Chapter Seven: "At the Peril of Your Life"

In over two and a half years of killing Yankees, Captain Lathan Woods had never seen them do anything so stunningly stupid.

After months of disgraceful running and hiding from Rosecrans's army, General Bragg finally got the gumption to turn around and fight. This newfound courage came with the arrival of General Longstreet and his two divisions on loan from General Lee and the Army of Northern Virginia. The fight on the northern end of the front had gotten them nowhere. Whoever commanded the Yankees at that end of the line was like a rock in which Bragg's troop continually broke themselves upon, wave after wave.

So while that part of the battle raged on, Longstreet formed his corps into a long column and aimed them at the soft center of the Federal line. It was magnificent to see the tight formation of men in grey and butternut preparing to punch a hole in their defenses. Lathan found himself holding his breath as he watched them move forward. Certainly it was going to be a bloody endeavor, marching straight into a heavily fortified line.

But then the Yankees did something completely unexpected.

"What in the world are they doing…?" Forrest mumbled to himself.

Forrest sat on his horse a few ranks in front of Lathan, watching the action unfold. Just as the Longstreet's column broke through the tree line and into the field in front of the Federal fortifications, what seemed to be an entire division of Yankees simply backed away from their breastworks and marched off northward, cannons and all. Lathan and the men around him watched in stunned silence. It was as if a huge door had just opened up right in front of the Confederate advance.

What happened next was an absolute slaughter. Longstreet's corps poured into the Yankee line like water through a broken damn bringing a flood of death with them. Lathan watched in awe as thousands of men in blue started running for their lives. Longstreet's men followed close behind, shooting and bayoneting them in the back. The men in Forrest's personal escort started whooping and hollering. It was a rout. It was tempting to ride into the fray and join the fun, but Forrest and his men had their own work to do.

"Come on, we better get back to our position and be ready," Forrest said to his men. He spurred his horse northward. His escort of roughly two hundred armed men followed him.

The majority of Forrest's command was set up near the junction of Reed's Bridge and LaFayette Road. He had dismounted most of his two divisions and put them in a line along with his artillery. They were guarding the extreme northern flank of the Confederate line. The remainder of his men stayed on horseback, hidden in the woods, waiting for the right moment to burst forward. They were watching the LaFayette Road, ready to fire upon any Federal reinforcements that could come from Rossville or

Chattanooga. Now, they were in the perfect position to wreak havoc on the approaching herd of Yankees using the road to escape back to the city.

Forrest rode up hard on his artillery commanders, reigning in his horse as he gave his commands. "Tell your boys to get ready. In a few minutes, your whole field of fire is going to be filled with runaway bluebellies. Once you fire your first volley, load double canister. It'll be like shooting fish in a barrel, boys. After that, cease fire and we'll make a mounted charge. Pass it along the line."

"Yes, sir!" One of the artillerymen answered and then started relaying orders to the crews. Forrest led his entourage into the woods behind the line of cannons and dismounted troopers. There he found his remaining regiments of mounted men standing at the ready.

"Boys, once they fire their second volley, we go in and start killin'. You ready!" he shouted.

"Huah!" the men shouted back. Forrest turned his horse and narrowed his eyes. He scanned the clearing ahead for the wave of Yankees to emerge from the woods and into the killing field before them.

Lathan's eyes widened with gleeful anticipation. He edged his horse closer to Forrest. Lathan's two men followed behind. Tom gulped hard.

"You ain't gettin' cold feet now, are you Tommy-Boy?" Bill chided him.

"Of course not, but I could use some water," Tom answered.

"Quiet back there, damn it," Forrest hissed, not taking his eyes off the ground before them.

Lathan turned to give his men an incredulous look and an eye roll before returning his eyes to the killing field. Rabbits and deer first emerged from the woods into the field. It was clear they were running from something. Then shadows began to shift in the dark tree line across the way. The sounds of snapping sticks and tramping feet began to increase. Then the first of them came stumbling out of the woods, disheveled, frightened, and confused. Many weren't even carrying rifles. Tom sucked in his breath as hundreds of men in blue began to fill the field before their guns, seemingly unaware of the imminent danger they had run headlong into.

"Fire!"

The order came and the three batteries of cannons opened fire, sending shot and shell into the mass of men. The dismounted horsemen fired their muskets as well. Smoke filled the field, but it was easy to see that hundreds were now laying mere feet away from the Rebel guns twitching and dying. Still, more came from the woods, pushed on by the mobs of men behind them. Many of them stumbled over the bodies of the men that had come before them.

"Load double canister!" the order was shouted and repeated along the line. Tom hissed at the thought of it, knowing the devastating effect double canister would have on the mass of soft flesh at such close range of the guns.

The cannon crews went to work. This time, instead of shells or solid shot, the guns were loaded with two tin cans full of metal balls that would rip apart upon firing and fill the air with deadly projectiles like giant shotguns. Lathan grinned wildly in anticipation at the carnage to come.

"Fire!"

The line of cannons opened up again. A mist of blood shot up like a cloud as the Yankees were torn apart from the savage volley.

"Come on, boys, this is where the fun begins!" Forrest spurred his horse with a "Hyah!" and with that, his horsemen came exploding out of the woods like gods of death and thunder into the mass of broken and fleeing Yankees.

Lathan could feel the hooves of his horse smashing into the soft bodies lying on the ground. He emptied all nine cylinders of his LeMat revolver into the crowd of men, watching them tumble to the ground as he rode by. He reigned in his horse as men ran past him. With a flick of his thumb, he the switched striker on the hammer to engage a secondary barrel that ran along the bottom of his pistol. This under-barrel acted as a short 20-gauge shotgun. He lifted the gun, took aim, and fired. The buckshot split the back of fleeing the man's head, shoving him face-first into the ground with a thump.

Lathan grinned with satisfaction at the versatile little hand cannon as he spun it in his hand and then put it back in its holster. He pulled out his saber and looked for another victim. They were everywhere. He didn't even have to pick as one came to him.

"Sir, I surrender!" a Yankee sergeant ran up to him with his hands in the air. This caused Lathan's horse to rear onto its hind legs. Lathan used the downward momentum to bring his sword crashing into the man's skull as the horse once again planted its front hooves on the ground. The man slumped to his knees, yanking Lathan's arm downward, the saber wedged firmly in the man's head.

"Hey!" Lathan heard General Forrest's voice over the din of combat, "That man was surrendering, God damn it!"

Lathan looked up at his commander's furious blue eyes and offered a slow smile, "My apologies, sir. He came upon me so quickly, I couldn't read his intention."

Forrest eyed him for a moment, then turned his mount and trotted off as he called out, "Start collecting prisoners and their weapons, boys! We need to move them to the rear!"

Lathan looked down at the dying man still stuck to his saber. The man was blinking mindlessly and shuddering as if there was some cold draft only affecting him. Lathan put his boot on the man's head and shoved him to the ground, yanking his saber free. Bill and Tom pulled up next to him.

Bill chuckled, watching the dying man shake on the ground, "I guess we won't need to take this one to the rear."

Tom just stared blankly, all the color had left his face.

"What's a matter, Tom?" Bill prodded him, "No stomach for killin' anymore?"

"…Ah, no, I'm just sick from the bad food, I guess," Tom looked up from the dying man, offering a weak smile.

"Well, it looks like we're having some fine Yankee grub tonight, boys!" Bill whooped.

"There's plenty of work to do before we get to that," Lathan said. "You heard the General, grab some men and start collecting prisoners and their gear. We still have to prove to our commander we're worth having in his escort."

A holler went out at dusk as the shooting died down, then another. Soon the sounds of celebration could be heard all along the line. The last of the Federals had slipped back toward Chattanooga under the cover of darkness. The day was over and the Confederates stood victorious on the field.

General Forrest's men rested in a field near a church that the Federals had been using as a hospital. The Confederates captured it during the day and now were using the medical supplies left behind to treat their own wounded. Lathan could hear the screams of men inside as severed limbs piled up outside the shell-damaged walls. Lathan found his commander sitting alone, leaning against his saddle, cleaning his pistol by firelight.

"Quite a victory today, sir," Lathan said as he squatted on the other side of the fire.

Forrest looked up from his weapon to see Lathan's green eyes sparkle in the firelight. He scoffed and returned his eyes to his revolver, "Hardly, Captain. We let them get away. Our *Commander* isn't interested in victories, he merely fears defeat."

"I'm sure if you commanded this army, our victory would be complete," Lathan purred.

Forrest stopped the work on his gun to look up at Lathan once more, "I'm not one for flattery, Captain, is there something you want from me?"

"I'm merely here to offer my apology once again for my actions today, sir. My men and I are grateful to be riding in your escort. I don't want to disappoint you."

Forrest looked at him for a moment, before returning to his work, "Well, as I always say, war means fighting, and fighting means killing, Captain."

"I couldn't agree with you more, sir," Lathan followed.

Forrest paused, scrutinizing the possible motives of the clean-shaven man grinning at him, "But the reason I *don't* have an independent command right now is because those in power think of me as an uncouth, uneducated barbarian. They love that I can raise and equip thousands of men on my own dime, but then demand that I hand them off to some God damn kid, nearly half my age, just because he went to West Point."

"General Wheeler, sir," Lathan offered, mentioning Forrest's counterpart who commanded the Confederate cavalry corps on the other end of the line.

"The same," Forrest stated flatly. "So when it gets back to them that my men are hacking down unarmed, surrendering men, it only reinforces their prejudice against me. Do I make myself clear, Captain?"

"Crystal, sir. I only want to serve your best interests," Lathan replied.

"Good, it would serve me then to be left alone with my thoughts, Captain."

"Of course," Lathan smiled. "Good evening, sir." And with that, he withdrew from the firelight into the gloom of the evening.

Lathan knew well to keep a distance from his commander over the weeks that followed. He wanted only to show his worth and not cause him any more problems. Lathan had been given command of a company of cavalry before the Battle of Perryville. Many of them died in that battle and during the retreat that followed. More eroded away in skirmishes, sickness, and desertions. Now it was down to him and his hometown buddies Bill Garret and Tom Billington once again. He had gotten them sergeant stripes for their loyalty.

In the constant reshuffling of the Confederate forces in the West, he found them a new place in Brigadier General Nathan Bedford Forrest's personal escort. The escort followed and protected the general everywhere he went. For Lathan, it was an honor to finally serve a commander he could respect, a commander who was just like him.

Lathan wanted Forrest to see that they were the same. But Forrest was too distracted with his own outrage and frustration to take notice. "We could crush them today if Bragg would only move," Forrest said ruefully to himself as he watched the Federals work on the defenses around Chattanooga. The surrounding heights gave him and his men a perfect view of the quickly evaporating opportunity to finish the work they had begun at Chickamauga. But General Bragg seemed too busy fighting with his own officers than going after the real enemy who sat snugly in the safety of the city below. Forrest tried to stay out of the infighting of Bragg's disorganized Army of Tennessee, but Bragg was making that more and more impossible.

For weeks they scouted, raided, and skirmished with the Yankees near Chattanooga and almost as far north as Knoxville. They killed and captured as many as they could, but none of this was appreciated by the high command.

Bragg was distracted with reorganizing his army as he prepared to lay siege to the city. With reorganization came more bad news.

"What?!" Forrest demanded, leaping to his feet at the messenger. The man's horse shuffled back nervously at the sudden movement. The other men sitting around the early evening fire slowly started getting to their feet as well.

The rider cleared his throat, suddenly aware of the glaring eyes around him. But none were more frightening than Forrest's icy blues which made him want to do nothing more than turn his horse and run away as quickly as possible. Instead, he tried not to let his voice quiver as he repeated the message, "General Bragg has re-organized all cavalry units into one corps. You…" He took a moment to swallow, feeling the heat of Forrest's eyes boring into him. "…Um…sir, are to turn over your command and report to General Wheeler for orders, sir."

The man on the horse winced at the silence that followed. Lathan spat on the ground and took a step forward to stand at Forrest's side.

"Ah…" the messenger tried to continue under the hard gaze of the angry men surrounding him, "I have your orders here." He pulled an envelope from his jacket. Forrest snatched it from his quivering hand and tossed it into the fire.

"Here's what I think of your God damn orders. Now you better ride off and tell that old hag of man that I'm coming and he better be prepared to defend himself."

The man's eyes bulged at the threat as his horse instinctively backed away. "Of course, sir. Uh…my apologies." With that, he turned his horse and trotted off into the gloom.

"Get to your horses," Forrest growled in a low voice. Lathan motioned to Bill and Tom with his head to follow. They put out the fire and got to their horses quickly. Lathan moved up through the small entourage, placing himself just to the right and rear of General Forrest. If there was going to be action, he was going to fight alongside his leader. Bill and Tom fell in behind him. Soon they overtook the hapless messenger who kept his eyes forward as he trotted along, terrified to acknowledge the band of men that he was sure were on the way to do something terrible to General Brag.

It was fully dark when they arrived at Bragg's tent. A lantern inside made the canvas structure give off an amber glow. Forrest brushed right through the poor attempt the two sentries made to stop him. Lathan came up quickly behind him, grabbing one of them by the shoulder, and spinning him around to prevent him from following Forrest into the tent. The man blinked at Lathan in shock. Lathan stared the man down, slowly shaking his head and mouthing the word, "No."

"General Forrest!" Bragg sputtered, standing up from his desk, offering his hand. "What a surprise! I'm glad you're here so I can explain…"

Forrest ignored the offered handshake. Instead, he stuck his finger just inches from Bragg's face. "Now you listen here, you son of a bitch, I'm the one going to do the God damn explaining here." Bragg's eyes widened as the blood rushed from his face. He collapsed back into his chair as Forrest towered over him.

"This is the second God damn time you have robbed me of my command and gave it to one of your favorites! Men that I armed and equipped to fight the enemies of our country without any thanks from you or this government! My men have won a reputation for fighting and winning second to none in this army! And now you mean to humiliate again me by stripping them away!" Forrest took a moment to draw in a snarling breath through his nose.

Bragg shrunk deeper into his chair, clutching his chest. "I…I…" he attempted.

Forrest cut him off, "I have stood your meanness as long as I intend to." He drove his finger closer to Bragg's face. "You have played the part of a damned scoundrel and a coward, and if you were any part of a man, I would slap your jaw and force you to resent it!" he paused to glare at him for a moment.

"Please, let me explain…" Bragg offered weakly.

"You may as well not issue any more orders to me for I will not obey them, and I will hold you responsible for any further indignities you endeavor to inflict on me. You're gonna arrest me for not obeying orders?! I dare you, you son of a bitch, and if you *ever* interfere with me or cross my path again…it will be at the peril of your life!" With that, he spat on the ground and stormed out, leaving General Braxton Bragg stunned and shaking in his chair.

"Nice speech, sir," Lathan said as he emerged. Forrest stopped and looked at him for a moment, then down at Lathan's gun which was out and held at waist level, pointing at two terrified sentries. Forrest looked back up at him, "Come on. We're going."

Lathan looked back at the sentries before following, "If we have any trouble leaving, I'm personally coming back and killing both of you. Do you understand?"

The two men looked at each other and then back at him. "Um…yes, sir," they nodded.

Lathan smiled, "Good!" He gave his pistol a spin, uncocking it before shoving it into his holster.

The cool night's air was invigorating as they rode. Lathan felt as if he was drawing power from it. He smiled grandly, tipping his hat at the terrified messenger who was just only now arriving into Bragg's camp.

"Well, that went well," Bill offered as they trotted along.

"Better than you think," Lathan cooed.

"Where are we going now?" Tom asked.

"Back west, I suppose," Lathan said.

Chapter 8: "Fighting Means Killing"

February 1864: Oxford, Mississippi

"Pleeeeease!" the freckled-faced, buck-toothed youth sobbed as he shuddered in the wet and cold February air. He was covered in dirt, weakly clutching his shovel. Snot hung from his nose and intertwined with slobber that clung to his trembling lower lip. "I want to go home to my momma!"

Another one of the condemned men dropped his shovel and stormed over to the crying youth. Lathan's men raised their rifles at the sign of trouble. The man slapped the boy who couldn't have been more than sixteen by Lathan's reckoning. The young man dropped his shovel from the shock of the blow. The man grabbed him by the collar and shook him. "Shut up and die like a man!" he shouted, then shoved him back towards the hole in the ground the boy had been working on. "Now keep digging!"

"Alright…" the boy sniffled as he bent over and picked up his shovel. He wiped the blood, snot, and slobber with his dirty sleeve and started digging again, trying his best to stifle his sobs.

The man who struck him looked back at Lathan and the firing squad then spat on the ground before picking up his shovel and resuming the work on his own grave, as did the seventeen other men who had paused their own morbid work to watch the commotion.

Lathan smiled slowly as he motioned with his hand for his men to lower their rifles. He was happy that the condemned man had done the work of quieting the boy for him.

"Ha!" Sergeant Bill Garret let out. "Don't worry, boys, we'll be shootin' 'em soon enough!" This brought out another fit of sobs and shudders from the boy as he dug. Tears ran clean trails down his otherwise dirty face. Sergeant Tom Billington slowly lowered his rifle, spat on the ground, and looked away. He had killed plenty of Yankees since joining up with Bill and Lathan at the start of the war, but he never thought he would be killing his own.

Lathan, on the other hand, was perfectly fine with shooting these men. They were cowards, deserters, and if they weren't made examples of, other men would think they too could run from the duty that Confederate law demanded of every Southern-born son of fighting age, that is, every man who didn't own twenty slaves. Those wealthy enough to own such a luxury were exempt from conscription. Lathan would be such a man once the war was won. He was sure of it. However, he still wouldn't have hidden behind his wealth if he had been so lucky at the start of the war. He would have joined anyway, just like his commander, Nathan Bedford Forrest.

Forrest had been a self-made millionaire before the war. He had made his fortune buying and selling negroes. Rumor had it he joined as a private, but was quickly made an officer and began to rise in rank ever since. Lathan was sure that as long as he stuck by the fiery cavalry leader, he was on the same path.

Lathan had been a skilled tracker before the war, slowly building his own wealth by catching and returning runaway slaves to their masters. He wondered if Forrest remembered their brief encounter before the war. Forrest had seemed warm and inviting back then. Lathan had brought three runaways to his stockade on Adams Street in Memphis. He wanted to ask him if he remembered, but Forrest was not so warm and inviting now. The man seemed to be impervious to small talk and charm. Lathan knew well not to push his luck. Forrest seemed to be repelled by his attempts at friendship, quickly dismissing him each time, yet he still kept him in his personal escort. Lathan was sure Forrest must have seen his worth, it was only a matter of time before they'd be friends, maybe even partners someday. He grinned widely at the prospect.

He had made sure that he, Bill, and Tom were part of the small collection of men Forrest took west with him. Many of them thought General Bragg was going to have him arrested after Forrest shoved a finger in his face, called him a coward, and threatened his life. Instead, Bragg agreed to Forrest's written request to return west where he could build a new cavalry force and punish the Yankee invaders along the Mississippi River. Not only that but Forrest was promoted to Major General giving him the rank to command such an army.

Forrest had reckoned there were thousands of idle men in western Tennessee, men who had absconded from duty, or had yet to answer the call demanded of them by law. The trip west was a smashing success.

Thousands of men came from states all around just for the honor of riding with the famous Nathan Bedford Forrest. Still, some men ran and hid from duty, like the nineteen men now digging their graves in front of Lathan's firing squad. Their freshly built coffins lay next to the graves as they worked.

Lathan was playing a little game as he watched. He was trying to guess if each man was shivering from the cold or fear when the sound of approaching hooves broke his thoughts. He turned and smiled at the sight of Forrest and his staff approaching. Near him was the ever aloof and aristocratic General Chalmers, who carried a look of mild disdain everywhere he went. Why Forrest tolerated the pompous fop, Lathan could not fathom other than he came from a powerful and wealthy family and Forrest had no choice.

Lathan's eyes then met the other man's eyes next to Forrest. It was Lieutenant Colonel Jeffrey Forrest, General Forrest's little brother. Jeffrey glared at Lathan with unmasked scorn. Lathan dropped his smile and turned back to the scene in front of him, angry at himself for allowing his mask to slip in front of his new rival.

Jeff Forrest was a problem. He was supposed to be dead, killed in action while fighting in northern Alabama. Forrest, at least, had thought so back in Chattanooga. But it turned out that his brother had merely been wounded and captured by the Yankees. It was a rare scene when Forrest learned that his little brother was still alive. Few men could ever claim they saw Nathan Bedford Forrest cry, but the ferocious leader wept tears of joy upon hearing the news. Jeff had returned in a prisoner exchange, and even though he was still recovering from being shot through both hips, Forrest insisted on keeping him close and giving him command of a brigade.

This was all bad news for Lathan. The trust and affection he had hoped to win from Forrest were now being given to his baby brother. Worse yet, Jeff Forrest seemed to see right through Lathan's attempts at building rapport with his brother and blocked him in every way. Lathan could hardly bear the looks of open distrust and contempt Jeff gave him. Now, here he was about to spoil Lathan's big show of devotion.

"Jesus Christ, Bedford!" Lathan could hear Jeff hiss under his breath, "You can't let this happen!"

"If men don't fear me, I'm nothing, Jeffy," Forrest replied in a low voice.

Lathan smiled again. He was winning this argument. It was time to get this done before Jeff Forrest intervened. "That's good enough," he called out. "Bill, Tom, stand them in front of their coffins." That command brought another fit of sobs from the boy.

"Good God, Bedford, that's a child!" Jeff admonished his brother in a low but forceful voice.

"You heard him!" Bill called out to the men. "Stand in front of your coffins!"

The boy fell to his knees and began wailing uncontrollably, "Pleeeeeeease!"

"Damn it!" Tom hissed as he handed his rifle to the man next to him. He squatted next to the boy. "Come on," he said to him softly. "It'll all be over soon. Come, stand up. Make a good accounting of yourself." The boy sucked in a sob and slowly stood. He trembled uncontrollably in front of his coffin as Tom found his place back in the firing line.

Lathan smiled with satisfaction at the efficiency of his plan. He stood the condemned men in front of their coffins so they would fall into them once the firing commenced. Then the coffins could be dragged easily into the holes that the prisoners had dug themselves. Hopefully, Forrest would appreciate his cleverness. Lathan's saber made a metallic zing as he pulled it from the scabbard and held it high.

"Ready!" he shouted. The muskets clattered as the men lifted them from the ground.

"Bedford, do not let this war turn you into a monster," Jeff pleaded.

"Aim!" The rifles clattered again as the men pulled them to their shoulders and pulled the hammers back.

"In the name of your love for me as a brother, Bedford, do not do th…"

"Hold up there, Captain!" Forrest shouted as he nudged his horse forward.

Lathan grimaced. Jeff had beat him again. "At ease, men!" he called. The guns clattered once more as the men eased the hammers down and lowered their weapons. The crying boy went ashen white and collapsed into a pile of unconsciousness in front of his casket. A nervous chuckle rippled through the men. Chalmers let out a sigh and rolled his eyes.

Forrest let a light chuckle and grin escape him. "Help that boy up," he said to the prisoners. The dirt-covered men blinked up at him in wide-eyed awe then quickly obeyed. They fanned him with their hands.

The boy blinked and looked around, trying to understand the scene he had just woken up to.

"Right now, two Yankee columns are marching through our homeland, rampaging and burning everything in their path. The one coming from Memphis is over seven thousand strong. The one marching from Vicksburg is twenty-thousand," Forrest glared down at the condemned men. "We must stop them before they meet and combine into an unstoppable force. These animals are raping our mothers, sisters, and daughters. They are stealing the food from our children. They are turning our slaves against us." The men gulped as they stared up silently at the man on horseback who addressed them. "They are inciting a slave insurrection that will see your parents murdered in their beds by the very hands that once served them. We are staring white armageddon in the face at this very moment! Thousands of good southern men have sacrificed to save this country! They've laid down their lives, which were worth far more than your sorry miserable existences, I'll tell you that!"

Forrest took a moment to glare at the condemned men until each one dropped his gaze to the ground in shame. "Right now," he continued, "they are arming the negroes that flock to their banner. It's a crime against humanity, but I'll tell you what!" He paused to scan the dropped heads, "Those negroes show more fight and bravery than you sorry sons of bitches! Is that what it is, then?! Are you something less than a negro?!"

"No, sir…" one of the men mumbled.

"What?!" he shouted.

"No, sir!" more of the men shouted with conviction.

"I'll tell you what," he continued. "Right now, your lives are forfeit as deserters. You're already dead. Now it can be here on this muddy field for your cowardice or on the battlefield for your country and your honor. What's it gonna be, boys?!"

The men stood in sullen silence, staring at their feet. At last, the man who had slapped the boy earlier stood forward. "With your permission, sir, I'd like to die for my country." After a pause, another stood forward as well.

"Me too, sir," he said.

A third stepped up, "Um…I'd like to kill at least one or two Yankees before I die, but, yeah, I'm in."

A chuckle broke out among the men, clearing the tension that had clung to them so tightly. The rest of the condemned men stepped forward, giving their vows too. Forrest smiled grandly at the flicker of pride beginning to take hold on the dirt-covered men. "Captain," he turned to Lathan. "Issue these men new uniforms. They are reborn. I want the clothes they're wearing to be burned. Those clothes have been worn by cowards."

"Of course, sir," Lathan said with a bow.

Forrest looked at his brother Jeff as he trotted by, "I don't know what you're grinning at, you fool! They're your men now!"

Jeff Forrest smiled. "I can live with that. I can live with that," he repeated as he nudged his horse to follow.

"Pity," Chalmers sighed, "I was rather looking forward to the spectacle of a firing squad…"

"Jeff," Forrest admonished, once they were in the privacy of his brother's newly commandeered tent that evening, "I can't have you questioning my judgment in front of the men like that. It don't look good!"

"Neither does shooting a child," Jeff returned.

Forrest scoffed with humor, shaking his head, "Jeffy, I didn't bring you here to be my conscience, for crying out loud."

"I know, but apparently, that's what you needed," Jeff smiled at his big brother. "Now please don't be mine, I know how you abhor drink, but the pain is tremendous," Jeff said. He pulled a clear bottle of amber liquid from under his cot and poured some in a cup. He then pulled out a smaller bottle and carefully poured a small amount of its brown liquid into the cup as well. Forrest looked away, unable to watch his brother self-medicate.

"I raised you the best I could after Pa died, Jeffy. I tried to do you better than he did me. It ain't my place now to tell you what you can and can't do with yourself."

Jeff drank the contents of his mug, closing his eyes and savoring the warmth of opium-laden whiskey running down his throat. He let out a satisfied sigh and opened his eyes, "And for that, I am grateful, brother. You made a gentleman out of me. I'm the first college-educated of our line. Allow me to return the favor the best I can. You don't even realize the power of your name, Bedford. You're a hero to people all over the

Confederacy. Shoot, even the Yankees revere you. They treated me like a prince as soon as they found out I was your brother in the prison camp. Don't squander that esteem over your rage."

"Them bluebellies were just afraid I'd come up there and murder their entire families if they mistreated you. Respect comes from fear, Jeffy," Forrest told him.

Jeff let out a laugh, "Well, admittedly, I suppose there was a bit of that, too."

Forrest laughed, too, clutching his brother's shoulder and giving him a gentle shake, "Alright, college boy, enough philosophizing for tonight. Soon as you sleep off that laudanum, I want you to take your brigade towards Okolona first thing in the morning. I'm sending out messengers to the other commanders to bring their brigades there, too. We'll trap the Yankee column marching from Memphis and destroy them there, but you'll have to be the vanguard. You'll be the first to get there."

"Of course," Jeff said, feeling the opium beginning to take effect. "Bedford, I think we should give this tent back to General Chalmers. I appreciate it but I really do think we shouldn't aggravate him so. He is your second in command after all."

Forrest scoffed as he rose, "*Little 'Un* needs to know his place if he's going to command one of my divisions. I don't care who his daddy is."

Jeff let out a sigh as he laid back on his cot, the opium carrying him away to an island of sleepy contentment. "You really should stop calling him that as well, but who am I to tell you what to do?"

"You're my conscience, Jeffy," Forrest said, blowing out the lantern, "and I love you for it."

"Alright, now you're just being creepy," Jeff said sleepily. "Get the fuck out of my tent."

Forrest let out a chuckle and left his brother to his drug-laden dreams.

Lieutenant Colonel Jeffrey Forrest's brigade made contact with the larger Yankee column just north of West Point, Mississippi. He attacked the larger force and then began to retreat, exactly as planned.

Major General Nathan Bedford Forrest waited impatiently. Most of his brigades were still spread out but on their way to converge upon the Yankee advance from Memphis. Forrest placed the twenty-five hundred men he had on hand on the other side of Sakatonchee Creek. From there he watched the single bridge, waiting for his brother to cross, drawing the Yankees with him into the trap. They never came. The sound of distant musketry grew in intensity but never got any closer.

"Damn it!" he hissed. "Come on!" he shouted over his shoulder and spurred his horse toward the bridge. Lathan looked around, wondering if he had meant him. He was the only one nearby at the moment, so with a shrug, he spurred his horse and followed. They found Brigadier General Chalmers, looking bored and sitting alone on his horse along the way. Chalmers's newly formed division consisted of Jeffrey and McCulloch's brigades. McCulloch was still on the march, but from the sound of it, Jeffrey's men were heavily engaged somewhere up ahead. Chalmers looked slightly surprised as Forrest and Lathan pulled up in a cloud of dust.

"What the hell is going on up there?" Forrest demanded.

Chalmers pursed his lips in a thoughtful frown as he raised his eyebrows with a shrug. "Nothing more than a skirmish, according to Colonel Forrest's last report, sir. Nothing too severe, I suspect," he said with indifference.

"Jesus! Is that all you know?!" Forrest scowled at him as his horse pranced in place with agitation. "I'll find out myself!" He spurred off towards the fight. Lathan followed close behind. Chalmers rolled his eyes, shrugged, then decided it best to follow as well.

Stray bullets began to ping the ground around them as they drew nearer to the fight. Chalmers flinched as one kicked up a whiff of dust under his horse's feet. Looking up from it, an odd sight caught his eye. A single hatless soldier was running towards them and away from the fight. The youth appeared to be in a new uniform but must have left his gun behind. His freckled face was full of fear as he panted for breath through his wide-open mouth that revealed a large set of bucked teeth.

"God damn it!" Forrest hissed, stopping his horse and tossing the reins to Lathan as he got down. The young man didn't seem to even notice his commanding officer until Forrest intercepted him, snatching him by the collar as he tried to sprint by.

"Come here, you!" Forrest growled. The boy looked up at him in terror as recognition set in. Forrest dragged him to the side of the road, grabbed a stick, and started whipping the boy's behind with frightening ferocity. The boy screeched and howled in pain as Forrest laid it on hard. Chalmers watched with mild amusement. Lathan's eyes bulged with bewildered delight. The stick finally broke under the brutal use. Forrest turned the boy around and with a boot to his bleeding behind, gave him a hard shove back towards the fight.

"Now, God damn you, go back and fight! You might as well get killed there than here. If I ever catch you running away again, I'll kill you myself!" Forrest yelled after the boy who was now running back towards the front with one hand holding onto his swollen rear end. Forrest leaped onto his horse once again and spurred it towards the fight.

Chalmers looked over to Lathan with a slight smile. "I suppose we should follow or we're next," he said as spurred his horse on. Lathan shook his head and laughed as he followed.

Forrest found his brother overseeing the firefight as his men traded shots with an enemy that seemed to be diminishing. Jeffrey turned and smiled at his brother's approach.

"Damn it, Colonel!" Forrest said, ignoring the gleam in his brother's eyes, "I told you to retreat as soon as you engaged them! We've been waiting for you!"

Jeffrey's smile only grew as he shook his head. "We tried, Bedford!" he laughed. "As soon as we pulled back, they pulled back! We keep having to move up to engage them!"

"That's impossible!" Forrest said pulling his field glasses to his eyes. Already he could hear the rate of return fire tapering off. "They outnumber us by far…"

"It's you!" Jeffrey laughed. "You're name is worth twenty thousand of them. They're terrified!"

Forrest paused for a moment, watching the Federals fall back with each volley. "Well, let's keep pressing them until they come to their senses or find some courage."

Colonel Forrest's dismounted brigade continued to press the Federals' rear as his older brother drove one mounted brigade after another into their flanks time and time again in a running battle that pushed the Federals back toward Okolona. Only nightfall stopped the Confederate advance after a friendly fire incident accidentally killed one of Forrest's escorts in the confusion of the darkness.

"Ha! Looks like we're the only ones up for a fight, had to fight ourselves," Bill quipped. No one else cared to laugh.

Forrest's cavalry corps renewed the attack at dawn. They pushed the Federals through Okolona, where at last, the Yankees' calm and organized retreat broke into an all-out run for their lives. The Confederates rolled forward, killing, and capturing those who could not get away fast enough. The Federals finally put up a defense on a farm that sat on a hill north of town. They used the house and farm buildings for cover and threw up crude breastworks with fence rails, dirt, and whatever else they could find. There they hoped to hold off the Confederate onslaught long enough for the rest of the column to reorganize and escape.

Jeffrey Forrest's brigade was in the woods on the side of the road. In front of them lay an open field that climbed to the hilltop where farm buildings lay. Jeffrey organized his men in a column, four men wide, in preparation for the assault. Colonel McCulloch was doing the same with his brigade in the woods on the other side of the road. Forrest rode up to his brother's position with his escort of about sixty men. Jeffrey turned and beamed as his big brother arrived, "My God, at this rate we'll win the war in a week!"

"Don't get too confident, Jeffy, a cornered dog is the most likely to bite," Forrest told him.

"Shoot, this dog's yet to show any teeth," Jeffery laughed.

"Well, just be careful. Bell's brigade should be coming up soon, I'll throw them in as soon as they get here," Forrest told him.

A bugle sounded off somewhere. Jeffery unsheathed his saber with a ringing zing. He smiled at his brother. "It's a glorious day, Bedford," he said with a wink. Forrest nodded and watched as his little brother gave the order, then spurred his horse, leading his men with his sword held forward. The two columns emerged from the shadows of the woods into the light of the open ground that lay before the Yankee defensives. The sun glinted off of Jeffrey's saber and sparkled in Forrest's eyes. He watched with pride as the two columns spread out into a battle line and rolled forward towards the enemy hiding behind their works.

The Yankees seemed awfully quiet. Perhaps they really did lack the gumption to fight. Then came an explosive volley as the Federal guns opened up, obscuring themselves behind a cloud of smoke. Several of Forrest's escorts flinched as cannonballs came crashing into the woods. Dozens of advancing Confederates tumbled to the ground, but Forrest focused on just one. He watched as his brother's head snapped back with a mist of blood that shot out from his neck. Jeffrey let go of his saber, clutched his throat, then fell from his horse, landing in a lifeless clump on the earth below.

"No!" Forrest gasped. He spurred his horse forward. Within moments his entourage was riding behind him. He leaped from his horse, falling to his knees where he cradled his brother's head on his lap.

"Jeffrey! Jeffrey! Jeffrey…!" Forrest threw his head back and sobbed, rocking back and forth while he held his little brother in his arms. Lathan shifted uncomfortably in his saddle as he watched this fearless killer of men cry uncontrollably. Forrest dropped his head, touching his forehead to his brother's, "…Oh, Jeffrey, no…" The men in his staff and escort began to look away. Soon they were removing their hats and bowing their heads in mournful respect.

Forrest's softly kissed his brother's face and then covered it with his hat. After a moment, he raised his head and looked at the men around him causing some of them to flinch at the raw hatred blazing in his tear-ravaged eyes. Forrest didn't bother to wipe the tears away. "Major Strange," he spoke to his aide-de-camp, "see that my brother's remains are conveyed to the rear."

"Of course, sir, with the utmost care," Strange assured him.

"Colonel Duckworth," he turned to another officer, "you are now in command of my brother's brigade. You will shift them to the left and try to get on their flank." Forrest laid his brother's head down and stood. He looked toward the Federal line, then jumped back into his saddle, "They're already pulling back from their forward position. We're not going to give 'em a chance to settle. We're not going to let 'em get away." He pulled out his sword and then turned to his bugler. "Sound the charge," he said flatly, then spurred off before the bugler could even play the first note. Lathan pulled out his pistol and followed. Soon the sixty-some escort was in full gallop behind their leader as he sliced, shot, and trampled his way through the panicked mass of blue-clad men.

Chapter Nine: Bluffs and Calls

March 24, 1864: Union City, Tennessee

"My God, they're here," Colonel Isaac Roberts Hawkins of the US 7th Tennessee Cavalry mumbled to himself in the darkness. He hadn't been sleeping when the gunshots broke the early morning peace. Instead, he had been lying there in a fitful worry, running over every possible variable of the impending attack he knew was coming. Now it was here.

All reports indicated that Nathan Bedford Forrest was on the move, bursting out of northern Mississippi with seven thousand men to take back western Tennessee. Hawkins was sure he was coming to their little undermanned, but well-supplied outpost at Union City. It wouldn't be the first time the Wizard of the Saddle had taken the small town in northwestern Tennessee, and now with Hawkins commanding less than five hundred men guarding a stockpile of Federal supplies, it was likely Forrest would take it again.

Hawkins slipped on his trousers and stepped into his boots while pulling his suspenders over his shoulders. He could hear men running and shouting outside. He grinned bitterly, stroking his dark, short chin beard as he shook his head. The first thing he needed to do was calm the panic.

"Alright, boys," he called out as he stepped into the early morning air, still fastening the belt that carried his pistol and saber around his waist, "get all the supplies you can carry into the fort. We can hold there for days." *That is if they don't have cannons*, he scoffed, thinking to himself. The fort was twenty-five by twenty-five feet. It had small openings every few feet from where riflemen could pick off any attacking force that tried to navigate the abatis of sharpened sticks that surrounded it. The ten-foot earthen walls would protect the men from bullets, but those walls could not sustain a cannonade for very long.

"Captain Gray!" he called to an officer.

"Sir!" Gray replied.

"I want all the surrounding buildings put to the torch. I don't want to afford them any cover. It'll give our boys some light to find their targets as well. Set a ring of skirmishers around the fort. We need to buy ourselves as much time as possible."

"Sir!" Gray replied briskly then quickly set his men to the task. Soon the fort was surrounded by a ring of fire. The glow of burning buildings flickered on the men's faces as they watched from behind the walls for the first sign of the enemy to emerge.

Help was coming. Two thousand men from Cairo, Illinois would be there within twenty-four hours. At least that was the last message he had received before the telegraph line went dead. It had been surely cut by the Rebels. He was alone with his tiny force facing the man every Federal soldier in the West had come to fear, Nathan Bedford Forrest.

Shots rang out as the men behind the walls began to find targets. The skirmishers set outside were soon retreating to the safety of the fort. They were surrounded.

"Here they come!" a man shouted.

Hawkins ran to the south-facing wall after hearing the thunder of hooves and the yips and hollers from the Rebels. They came in hard, firing their pistols as they rode. One of his men fell from the wall screaming as he clutched his face. Blood spurted from between his fingers.

"Keep your fire up!" Hawkins yelled to his men as they frantically fired and reloaded. Several of the Rebels were punched clean off their horses. Some of the mounts tumbled to the ground, squealing in anguish. The charge broke within twenty feet of the wall. The riders broke off into either direction as the defenders cheered.

"Shut up and reload, you fools!" a sergeant shouted over the cheers. The Rebels were far from done. The next assault came by foot. Dismounted Rebels surged forward with their carbines in successive waves. The men behind the walls sent each one back with sustained volleys, littering the grounds with the dead and dying. By sunrise, the Rebels were content to stay behind whatever cover they could find, trading occasional shots with the Federals. Eventually, the firing tapered off as sergeants told the men to conserve the ammunition. There was no telling how long they would need it to last.

Hawkins watched as more and more mounted Rebels paraded past the Fort in the morning light. The hard-looking men in mixed and mismatched uniforms took their time, fearless in the face of their fellow Tennesseans dressed in blue hiding behind the walls. The Federal uniforms didn't scare them. They knew these boys in blue were neighbors, even cousins, who, to them, had picked the wrong side and were now left hanging and exposed in an undermanned outpost of an overextended occupying force of Federal overreach. Hawkins watched the hard eyes examining his walls, seeing all their weaknesses with the smugness of men accustomed to victory.

A distant bugle, followed by cheers from afar broke his thoughts. Captain Gray was quick to put it into words, "That's an artillery call, sir."

Hawkins searched the barricaded Rebel line with his field glasses and let out a sigh. In the distance, he could see them. Black laborers driving carts with large black cylinders loaded on them. "They've brought their guns…" he said to no one in particular. He checked his watch. It was 9:30. How long could they hope to endure once those guns were unlimbered and unleashed?

The Rebels put up flags of truce. Soon a delegation of Rebel officers rode toward the fort with a written message. Hawkins shared that message with his officers as they pondered what to do next. It read:

I have your garrison completely surrounded and demand an unconditional surrender of your forces. If you comply with the demand you are promised the treatment due to prisoners of war according to the usage of civilized warfare. If you persist in a defense, you must take the consequences.

By order of

N. B. Forrest, Major General

"Bullshit!" Captain Beattie blurted. "We just turned back everything they've thrown at us this morning. I tell you we can hold until help arrives from Cairo!"

Hawkins scoffed and shook his head, "They haven't thrown everything yet. Their artillery is arriving as we speak. Once in place, they'll take down our walls in no time. Without our telegraph, we can have no assurance that help is coming. Now, I've had the misfortune of surrendering to General Forrest before back in '62. He's not completely unreasonable. I'll request a conference with him, perhaps I can get better terms, parole for us and our men, but at least it'll buy us more time. I'd rather spend time than bullets right now, I don't know which we are lacking more."

Hawkins and his officers rode out to meet the Rebel delegation and to deliver his request to speak to Forrest in person. They waited as the courier ran the message back to the Rebel line. Moments later, a colonel rode forward. He was a thin man with a chin beard that extended down to the row of buttons on his uniform. He handed a note to one of his officers who then handed it to Colonel Hawkins. Hawkins's hooded eyes dropped as he read it:

I am not in the habit of meeting with officers inferior to myself in rank, but I will send Col. Duckworth, who is your equal in rank and is authorized to arrange terms and conditions with you.

N. B. Forrest, Major General

"…Major General…well," Hawkins said, looking up from the message, "it seems his career has done much better than mine since we last met." His eyes crinkled in a bitter smile.

"I am Colonel William Lafayette Duckworth, sir," the long-bearded colonel said, "commander of the Confederate 7th Tennessee Cavalry. I am here to accept your unconditional surrender."

"Ironic," Hawkins scoffed and shook his head with dark humor, "I command the US 7th Tennessee Cavalry."

"The irony is not lost on us, sir," Duckworth came back with, "however, God favors the righteous."

Hawkins let out a small chuckle, "I see. I'd like some time to confer with my officers."

"You have fifteen minutes, sir. My gunners are itching to blow your fort to Kingdom Come, not even leaving a grease spot where you once stood. It's all I can do to hold them at bay."

"Well, then," Hawkins raised his eyebrows at the threat, "I shall not tarry."

The Federals marched out of the fort and stacked their rifles at 11 o'clock that morning. Some of the Tennesseans in blue wept in shame at giving up so easily after successfully fighting off wave after wave of attacks earlier that morning. Several broke their firearms in defiance before turning them over. They watched in sullen silence as the Rebels helped themselves to the supplies and the many still functioning weapons. The Rebels found their horses too. The ones that weren't immediately commandeered by new riders were laden with the freshly won supplies.

Soon, the prisoners were marched off with armed Rebel soldiers surrounding them on horseback. It was then that Colonel Hawkins began to notice that there weren't many of them, not nearly as many as there were Federal prisoners.

"Where are the rest of your men," he asked one of the Rebels riding alongside the column of walking prisoners.

"Oh, most of them are with General Forrest at Paducah up in Kentucky," the young man said joyfully.

"Paducah!" Hawkins exclaimed. "That's sixty miles away!"

"Well, I guess he can't be everywhere at once," the young man laughed.

Colonel Hawkins blinked in astonishment at the revelation. He then turned to see the black laborers unloading the black painted logs they had mounted onto carts. Some of them laughed and made funny faces at the stunned Federal prisoners.

"Toot, toot!" one of the laborers called out, "I've got your artillery right here, boss!" which got a round of laughs from his fellow workmen.

"Good God," Hawkins said to himself. "I've been had…"

Forrest wasn't sure if he was going to shoot or hug Colonel Duckworth the next time he saw him. He pondered this as he rode to Paducah in the early morning drizzle with a force of three thousand men. They were on their way to take the fort there and capture the large store of supplies, men, and horses.

Duckworth had pulled off a brilliant ruse at Union City. He had forged Forrest's name to fool an enemy who was superior in number to come out of their well-fortified position and surrender to Duckworth's small detachment of a few hundred men with fake cannons. The bluff had won much-needed supplies for Forrest's ever-growing cavalry: three hundred horses, five hundred pistols and sabers, and sixty-thousand dollars in cash. It also took nearly five hundred Yankees out of the fight, five hundred Yankees they didn't even have to waste precious Southern soil to bury.

But the ruse was potentially costly too. Forrest had worked hard to build his reputation. The Yankees typically lost all will to fight once they knew they were facing him. Forrest didn't need to waste his men's lives on taking an enemy position much anymore. He just had to offer them a simple deal: surrender now or die. But that only worked if the enemy truly believed that death was the only other option.

It certainly worked at Union City, perhaps too well. Colonel Duckworth, a Methodist preacher before the war, was certainly a performer worthy of any stage. But like most performers, he was too proud and too attracted to fame. In other words, he had a big mouth. Word of the ruse had run quickly through his ranks before Forrest got an official report. There was talk of the story even appearing on the front pages of the Northern newspapers.

The sounds of cheering pulled him from his thoughts. He looked up from under his hat to acknowledge the Southern-loyal Kentuckians who stood in the rain to welcome him and his men on the outskirts of town.

"Great job nabbin' Union City, boys! You'll have an easier time scaring these Yanks! Most of 'em are niggers!" a man called out.

"Damn it!" Forrest hissed to himself, hiding his anger under his hat as he sheltered his face from the rain. If the townspeople knew about the ploy at Union City, then so did the Yankees in Fort Anderson, regardless if they were negroes. Would they be so quick to surrender if they thought Forrest's threat nothing but a bluff?

And then there were the negro soldiers. The Confederate government had done him no favors by declaring that black combatants were not to be considered prisoners of war, a status afforded to white men by the rules of modern civilized warfare. Instead, they were to be turned over to state governments to have their fates decided. The Yankee press had run wild with that, claiming it meant all negroes would be immediately sold into slavery, or worse, they could be executed on the spot for servile insurrection. Their white officers and sergeants could be hanged, too. With all that noise, it was going to be hard to get any of them to surrender without a fight. That meant more of his men would possibly have to die trying to take their walls.

A distant crackle of gunfire made him look up once more. His eyes narrowed as he listened to the early sounds of battle ahead. "Colonel Thompson has made contact," he spoke to his staff. "Tell the commanders to spread out into battle lines and push forward. I want to capture as many of them as we can before they get behind their walls."

Captain Lathan Woods had ridden at the head of Forrest's column with Colonel Thompson's brigade. It was a homecoming for the Kentucky Colonel who eagerly wanted to rid Paducah of its Yankee occupiers. They pushed the forward Federal pickets through town until they came within range of the big guns of Fort Anderson and the two Federal gunboats that commanded the river. Once under those guns, Thompson's Kentuckians dismounted and took cover among the town's building as the cannons and sharpshooters on the wall opened fire.

The fort sat on the Ohio River. Its high earthen walls were four hundred by a hundred and sixty feet long. The center of each wall extended out at an obtuse angle. A spearhead-shaped bastion sat on each corner creating sharp angles that allowed the defenders to shoot any man trying to scale the walls from multiple directions inside the fort. A fifty-foot water-filled moat surrounded the walls. Around the moat stood an abatis of sharpened logs fastened together in an intricate crisscross pattern.

"Well, they certainly don't want us coming in," Sergeant Bill Garret quipped as they pressed their backs against the brick wall of a town building.

BOOM!

The percussion of one of the big 32-pound cannons nearly knocked the wind out of them. The building next door began to crumble from the blow, sending fellow Confederates scrambling to find new cover. Bill peaked around the corner to get another look at the fort.

"Good Lord, they got niggers on those guns!" he exclaimed, ducking quickly back behind the wall as a splatter of bullets struck it.

"Well, if they can train them to operate a sawmill or drive a steam engine, I suppose they can do most anything…" Sergeant Tom Billington mused.

"It just ain't right," Bill spat on the ground.

"The result's the same no matter who's loading those guns," Lathan said flatly, taking a peek at the Federal defenses. "Those gun crews are exposed, if we can find enough cover to take aim." Movement outside of the fort's walls caught his eye. "Well, look what we've got here…" he said with new interest.

A party of women, children, and old men emerged from the fort and made a dash for the shore. A transport was steaming its way to intercept them. Nearby the two ironclad gunboats kept watch with sharpshooters on their decks looking for targets to present themselves.

"Alright, boys, this is our chance," Lathan said to the men near him. "Stay low and follow me!"

Lathan and a small group of men dashed out from their cover, crouching low as they ran. A spattering of musketry followed them. A man screamed in agony behind him. He knew not to slow down to see who. They had to get to safety quickly before he lost any more men.

The women shrieked and clutched their children as the group of gray and butternut soldiers surged in quickly among them.

"No need to fret, ladies," Lathan smiled, "We're here to protect you."

Tom slung his rifle and offered his hand to a woman who had stumbled to the ground, "Here, ma'am. Let me help you up."

Lathan had other business. "Boys, clear those sharpshooters on the decks, and don't forget the gunners on the fort!" he called out. "It's safe to take aim now." A laugh broke out from the men interspersed among the women, children, and elderly. They shouldered their muskets and fired, sending the sharpshooters on the decks of the gunboats diving for cover, and some to their deaths.

Bill turned toward the fort and spied one of the back artillerists setting down his ramrod and picking up a rifle. Bill shouldered his own weapon and aimed. The artillerist lowered his gun with a grimace. There was no clean shot for him as long as the Rebels were mixed in closely among women and children. Bill smiled and pulled the trigger.

CRACK!

Through the puff of smoke, he saw the man tumble to the ground. "Woo wee! Got the son of a bitch!" Bill shouted in glory. The man was quickly dragged away. A new soldier picked up his ramrod and took his place among the black artillerists, their sergeant yelling at them to continue loading the huge 32-pound cannon.

Colonel Stephan G. Hicks shook his head in disbelief and a little bit of self-shame as he watched the men of the 8th United States Colored Heavy Artillery load and fire their guns. Admittedly, he didn't think the ex-slaves would fight once the bullets started flying, but here they were, stoically working their guns in the face of a ferocious enemy who saw them as nothing more than livestock to be recaptured and tamed.

His artillerists, along with their white comrades of the 122nd Illinois Infantry and the 16th Kentucky Cavalry fought off wave after wave of Rebel attacks until the ground before the fort was littered with their dead and dying. A gray-clad soldier moaned in the eerie silence that followed the last assault. His dying body was hung limply from the sharpened sticks of the abatis. The men peered out into smokey ground before them, waiting for the Confederates' next move.

From the shrouds of dissipating smoke came the clopping of hooves of a single horse. A rattle of clicks spread along the wall as men cocked their rifles, waiting for the target to appear.

"Easy, boys," Hick spoke to them, "Let's see what they have to offer…"

A single rider came forward under a flag a truce.

"Ride out to him and see what he has to say," Hicks commanded one of his lieutenants. The man returned moments later with an envelope. Hicks opened it, furrowing his brow as he read. He let out a scoff and then looked up at the black and white faces that watched him with wide-eyed anticipation. He let out a brief chuckle and then addressed them, "I suppose I shouldn't keep you in the dark, gentlemen. This is from the big bad Nathan Bedford Forrest, whose men lay dead and dying before our walls. He says: 'Having a force amply sufficient to carry your works and reduce the place, and in order to avoid the unnecessary effusion of blood, I demand the surrender of the fort and troops, with all public property. If you surrender, you shall be treated as a prisoner of war; but if I have to storm your works, you may expect no quarter.'"

Hicks looked up to read the faces of the men around him. He saw what he was looking for. "You've been tussling with him all morning. Does he have the *ample force* to take our walls…?"

He scanned the silent faces for a moment, then one of the black soldiers stepped forward, "Hell no, sir."

Hicks smiled grimly, "I didn't think so, sergeant." Then to his lieutenant, "Stand by, I'll have a reply for you to carry shortly."

Forrest sat on his horse, watching his courier ride back with the reply. He had already lost too many men from Colonel Thompson's foolish and overzealous attempts to take the fort on his own. The crossfire from the gunboats and the fort had been punishing. Already, he could see the confidence of his men slipping away. Worse yet, they had been repelled by negroes manning those guns on the wall. A nightmare scenario that he knew was inevitable. They had not faced black soldiers before. The quicker he could get that fort to surrender and bring those negroes back to their proper place the better. The last thing he needed was the press to tell the world that the Wizard of the Saddle had been beaten by a bunch of negroes in blue.

"Sir!" the rider shouted as he handed him the envelope.

"Well, let's see what these Yankee invaders have to say for themselves," he winked and smiled at the rider. His smile fell as he read:

Sir:

I have this moment received yours of this instant, in which you demand the unconditional surrender of the forces under my command. I can answer that I have been placed here by the Government to defend this post, and in this, as well as all other orders from my superiors, I feel it to be my duty as an honorable officer to obey. I must, therefore, respectfully decline surrendering as you may require.

S.G. Hicks
Colonel, Commanding Post

"God damn it…" he hissed quietly to himself.

The renewed attacks brought no better results. The grapeshot and canister from the combined guns of the fort and the boats shredded his men with each attempt to take the walls. The Confederates then tried occupying the town's buildings, using the cover and elevation to fire down at the exposed black artillerists with some success, but the Federal guns started leveling the buildings with solid shot and shells sending his men running for new cover. The only consolation Forrest had was that a cannonball took Colonel Thompson's head clean off his shoulders as the fool tried to visit his own law office in town. This saved Forrest from the temptation of shooting the man himself for starting the assault too soon in the first place.

By dusk, it was clear there was more to lose than to gain by spending any more time in Paducah. "Tell the men to take what they can and destroy the rest," Forrest told his staff. He could hear the cheers from the fort as his column started moving away. Forrest sat silently on his horse. His hat hid most of his face as he listened to the distinctly black voices taunting his men as they withdrew.

Chapter Ten: Friends and Family

"Salut!" Private Francis Beauchamp called out to the line of soldiers standing at attention before him. The men brought their right fists to their hearts then snapped them down and out from their bodies.

"En garde!"

The men stepped forward with their left foot and brought their fists up into a fighting position.

"Le fouetté!...Un!...Deux!...Trois!

With each number, the men brought their rear legs up as high as they could and then snapped them forward at the knee like whips before bringing them down in front of them and returning to a fighting stance.

The newly promoted Major Booth found Sergeant Weaver watching this strange spectacle on the parade grounds of Fort Pickering in Memphis. "What in the devil is this?" he asked.

"It's some sort of French sissy-boxing from what I can tell, sir. Do you want me to stop it?" Weaver said after giving his commander a salute.

"No, let'em play," Booth said returning the salute. "At least they're training to fight." The two men watched as the line of soldiers practiced kicks, blocks, and punches on Francis's command. Elijah nearly bowled over the man next to him as he lost balance.

"Is it effective?" Booth asked.

"Well, Frenchie here dropped Jerry pretty well with some kind of spinning acrobatic kick in the air. They tried to tell me they were just dancing, ha!" Weaver said with a scoff.

"Isn't that Jerry training with them now?" Booth narrowed his eyes as he watched some of the men clumsily make their way through the maneuvers. Francis stopped from time to time to correct their form.

"Yeah, I suppose he figured he ought to join him if he couldn't beat him," Weaver replied.

"We should look to put corporal stripes on that boy if the War Department will allow it. He's already a leader among the men," Booth mused.

"I couldn't agree more with you, sir. Even if he does talk like a sissy," Weaver said, watching the activity with crossed arms.

"Good heavens, do I see white soldiers among them?!" Booth shielded his eyes from the sun.

"These are strange times, Major, strange times."

Elijah finally lost his balance and fell into the man next to him, causing several of the men to go down along the line in a mess of cussing and laughter.

"Alright, Sergeant, time to break it up. We got some real training to do," Booth told him.

"Yes, sir!" Sergeant Weaver snapped stiffly and then stepped forward. "Regiment, fall in!" he shouted. A bugle sounded and the rest of the men of the 6th USCHA ran onto the parade ground. Using their extended arms to space themselves, they formed into neat rows and columns, then stood at attention. Major Booth walked in front of them, beaming at the work he had done. He had taken a gaggle of scared and confused fugitives from the plantations and created a fighting force of confident men.

"At ease, fellas," he said. The men widened their stances and rested their hands on the smalls of their backs in a uniform motion.

"I've got several bits of news for you," Booth said, scanning the black faces before him. "First off, we're getting more guns!" The men gave out a cheer. Booth gave Weaver a nod indicating he was fine with the outburst. Weaver waited for it to die down a bit before putting his hands out to shush them. Booth continued, "The War Department has seen your worth and has decided to invest in you. Today we have taken in a shipment of two 6-pound James rifles. We'll start training on them immediately." Another round of cheers broke out among the men.

"Quiet!" Weaver barked.

Booth smiled at their enthusiasm. "There's more. We will also be getting two 10-pound Parrot rifles..." A murmur of excitement rippled through the men. It was quickly tamped down by their sergeants. "We'll be getting those once we arrive at our new post," Booth paused to look at the wide eyes watching him with anticipation. "Boys, train hard and learn everything you can. In a few days, we'll be deploying to Fort Pillow and manning the guns there." Booth gave the men a moment to murmur among themselves before continuing. "There you will be working alongside the 13th Tennessee Cavalry, a white regiment. Men, there are still many in this army who don't believe a colored man can make a good soldier. I watched enough of your performance to know that is simply untrue. I ask you now to help me prove that to the world. It ain't fair, but you have to be even better than the white soldier to gain respect. I believe you will do that and more. Gentlemen, you fight not only for your freedom but the freedom of your brethren and the betterment of your race. Can I count on you?"

"We won't let you down, sir!" a voice shouted out from among the men followed by around of affirmations.

Booth let out a chuckle, "That's what I want to hear. Sergeant Weaver!"

"Sir!"

"You may commence training."

"Sir!" Weaver snapped, then executing a smart about-face he barked, "Regiment, attention!" The hundreds of men that made up the 6th United States Colored Heavy Artillery snapped to attention in one unified motion.

The men certainly thought the James rifles were a step up from the two small mountain howitzers they had been training with. Instead of lobbing spherical shots and shells, the rifles fired a conical shell that could be aimed directly. The much longer bronze barrels had been rifled, meaning spiral grooves had been bored along the inside. These grooves caused the shell to spin as it exited the gun. This gave the rifle far more range and accuracy.

The men stood in lines behind the two new guns. They took turns at each job of a gun crew before returning to the end of the line to wait again. Francis panted with exhilaration as he jogged to the back of the line. Performing the well-choreographed dance with his teammates to fire the big guns filled him with excitement. The boom of the cannon, seeing the shells hit their targets, moving the gun back into place, even swabbing out the sooty barrel felt like he was really doing something worthwhile. It felt like he was part of something special, something that he'd treasure for the rest of his life.

His smile dropped as he looked around. "Where's Elijah?" he asked.

"Ah, Baby Boy's over there still playin' with the lil' toy gun," Jerry quipped, indicating to the other part of the field. "Guess he ain't ready for the big guns yet."

Francis spotted his friend afar. Elijah was pensively regarding his target and then adjusting the elevation on one of the stubby little mountain howitzers all by himself. The mountain howitzers were mostly forgotten by the men now that they had the new guns. Next to the big man, the mountain howitzer did seem rather toy-like, especially after firing the new James rifles.

"You boys still need to keep up your training with them *howies*," Sergeant Weaver said with a shrug, piping into the conversation. "Those *toys* can still drop a shell in a place where the enemy thinks he's safe."

Francis turned to him, "Sergeant, with your permission."

"Of course," he smiled, gesturing towards the smaller guns with his hand. "Any of you other fellows can go too."

"C'mon, Jerry," Francis tried.

"Nah, I'm alright, Frenchie. Imma stick with the big boy guns for now."

"Suit yourself," Francis smiled and jogged off.

"Try not to break a nail, Frenchie!" Jerry called after him, getting a chuckle from the men nearby. Francis shook his head and laughed as he ran. He had learned to tolerate Jerry's constant teasing. Over the months together he realized that was how the man showed affection to his friends.

Elijah fired his short stubby cannon and watched with a frown as the ball shot into the air and then splashed into the river just short of the trees that lined the Arkansas shore.

"*Qu'est-ce que tu fais, mon ami?*" Francis asked as he slowed his run to trot upon arrival.

Elijah looked up, scratched his head, and searched for words, "I'm…I mean…*Je…pratique…*Dang it, Francis! Why you always gotta be testin' me?"

"Because your masters hid that beautiful mind of yours from even you…a mind far more powerful than your earthly muscles. Now you've got a lot of catching up to do with your education."

"Well, I'm tryin' to catch up with them trees over there. I think I just need to lower the elevation a bit and I'll put one right on top of 'em," he said as he bent over the gun and adjusted the elevation screw. Now that Francis was closer, the weapon looked even more ridiculously small next to Elijah's frame.

"Why aren't you practicing with big guns? Clearly, you could hit your mark with a direct shot. They're very powerful," Francis stated.

"Cause force isn't always the best answer, Francis. Sometimes it's finesse," Elijah said as he pulled the lanyard. The small brass tube coughed up a cloud of smoke as it kicked backward. In a flash, Francis could almost catch sight of the ball as it arced upward and then crashed down on the trees on the other side of the river.

"Bravo, my friend!" Francis gave a little bound into the air while clapping his hands. "You are a cannon-whisperer as much as you are with the horses!"

"The howie will put one where you want it if you treat it right," Elijah said with satisfaction, looking at the broken limbs across the river.

A light rain had settled in as the men boarded the steamboat *Gladiator* which was set to take them forty miles upriver to Fort Pillow. A small crowd had gathered on the shore to watch them as they walked single file across the gangplank.

"Wow, look at all them white folks cheering us on!" one of the men let out.

"Oh, they just happy to get rid of a boat full of niggas, Billy," Jerry quipped causing a ripple of chuckles among the men.

"Why must you always talk like that?" Francis laughed despite himself.

"Oh, they especially happy to get rid of you, Mr. Fancy Pants," Jerry came back, gaining even more laughs. Francis just shook his head and chuckled softly.

Elijah took a hard right turn once he boarded and found a spot along the guardrail. He frowned as he scanned the crowd. Francis came up alongside and looked up at him. "I'm sure they would be here if they could've, big fella."

"I know. I'm glad they not. No tellin' what would happen if Kyle was found or if that officer got his hands on Ms. Kathryn and the babies," Elijah shook his head. He worried about them greatly. Still, he couldn't help but be disappointed at not seeing his friends and family one last time.

Kyle was a wanted man and could easily be hanged as a traitor by the Federals or the Rebels if they found him. And then there was Captain Logan. He was one of the Union officers living at the Bethune townhouse. Logan had taken a powerful liking to Ms. Kathryn. She and Liza had been working at the house, tending to the officers' needs to make whatever money they could, But Ms. Kathryn had to hide once she started showing she was with child. That just made Captain Logan want her all the more. Liza told him Ms. Kathryn had gone to live with other family, but that ol' Captian Logan was not one to be deterred. Liza said she had to shake him off several times as he tried to follow her back to the colored part of town where Kyle and Kathryn were hiding with the babies.

Elijah really missed seeing the children. He had grown quite fond of Lil' Jimi B. and Kathryn's baby, Roger Daniel, or "Roggie," as they were calling him. Roggie was almost a year old now and Lil' Jimi B. was a year and a half. They were cousins, but really more like brothers and already inseparable.

Lil' Jimi B. drew quite a bit of attention from people on the street. He was light-skinned with brown freckles and big blue eyes, but those were the only things that would let you know he had a white father. His light brown hair was a spring of curls. His wide nose, high cheekbones, and full lips spoke more of his African mother. People would often stare at him, trying to figure out which side of the racial divide to place him.

He was wild, too. You couldn't take your eyes off him. The fearless toddler was always crawling into things with reckless abandon. The only concern the child seemed to ever have was for Roggie, whom he was ferociously protective of. It was very sweet the way he cared for his baby cousin who was only a few months younger.

Roggie was an altogether different child. He was darker with olive skin that he apparently got from his father's Mexican ancestry. He had Carl's silky black hair but doe-like brown eyes instead of Carl's green, from which he quietly watched Lil' Jimi B.'s escapades with pensive interest.

Both the boys were sweet and Elijah played with them with his own boyish delight during the times he could visit. Now, he was sailing up the river to perhaps finally get his chance to fight. The boys along with their parents would most likely be long gone once he returned if he ever did. They had been waiting for the children to be old and strong enough to make the journey west. They were also waiting to secure enough funds to make the trip and stake a claim out there in the great unknown. He didn't want them to go. He worried he'd never see them again, but he worried even more about the dangers of them staying.

These thoughts poked at him as the *Gladiator* chugged up the river and the cityscape fell away. He was so lost in the what-ifs and what he'd do that he barely noticed the faint hollering coming from the tree-lined shore.

"Elijah, look!" Francis roused him from his thoughts. "There they are!"

"Elijah, we love you!" he could hear his sister call. She held little Lil' Jimi B. on her hip as she waved from a bluff overlooking the river. Lil' Jimi B. was waving too, trying to emulate his mom, but not seeming to know why.

"Wave for Uncle E. and Frances, Roggie!" Kathryn prodded her child. Roggie instead buried his face in mom's bosom, too shy to look at whatever he was supposed to be waving at.

"They must have found a spot away from the crowd," Francis mused, then shouted, "Ahoy!" as he took off his kepi hat and waved it at the small party ashore.

"You keep your head down, Francis!" Kyle called out to him, "…And look out for Elijah, he's too big of a target to be fighting!"

"I will, Kyle! I'll take care of ol' Baby Boy!" Francis shouted back. Elijah was quietly waving his hat too. Francis looked up at him and caught the tear rolling down his face, even though the big man was smiling. "It's good to have friends and family, isn't it," he said to him.

"It sure is, Francis. It sure is."

Forrest grimaced as he read the paper in his commandeered office at Jackson, Tennessee. The Northern press was having a good laugh at his expense. Nathan Bedford Forrest and his men had been turned away at Paducah by heroic negroes manning the fort's guns. Their commander casually dismissed Forrest's threat of no quarter if he didn't surrender unconditionally and immediately. And why should he? The threat at Union City had been a laughable farce. Now, why would any Yankee commander surrender to him and his toothless cavalry again? Even a gaggle of runaway slaves was able to hold them off. He knew one thing for sure: he was never going to lose face in front of a bunch of puffed-up negroes again.

The paper also boasted that the horses Forrest's men had captured belonged to the Confederate sympathizers that lived in town. The paper claimed the real prize of some 140 horses that belonged to the Federal cavalry had been wisely hidden at the old foundry just outside of town. Forrest let out a bitter chuckle. Now that he knew where they were, he would send a small force back to take them. *Thank you very much, Chicago Tribune, for the tip!* he thought to himself with some satisfaction.

But what really burned was the accusation of cowardice and ungentlemanly behavior. That he could not tolerate.

"Sir," a staffer stuck his head in the door. Forrest looked up from his paper and indicated to the young man to continue, "Captain Lathan Woods is here."

"Send him in," Forrest said, standing to his full height. He turned his back as he adjusted his uniform.

"You asked to see me, sir?" Lathan's silky voice bristled him. He could already feel his blood begin to rise. He let out a sigh and then cleared his voice before turning to look at the clean-shaven, green-eyed man,

"You were with Colonel Thompson's vanguard, is that right?"

"I had that honor, sir. It's a pity we lost him."

"Hardly…" Forrest scoffed, boring his eyes into the man before him. "This paper here says we used fleeing women and children as human shields in the most cowardly way at the beginning of our assault."

"I wouldn't believe the propaganda of the Yankee press…" Lathan started.

"Do not interrupt me!" Forrest snapped. Lathan flinched at the outburst. "I have it on good account that it was you and your men. That you hid among fleeing women and children. That you fired from behind them knowing damn well the Yankees couldn't fire back for fear of hitting innocent civilians. Our civilians, God damn it!" He glared at him for a moment before continuing.

"This is why Kentucky waivers in her support! This is why more and more good Southern men turn to the Yankee banner. This is why they call us a barbaric drunken mob! This is why Richmond hands my commands over to West Point peacocks half my age!" Forrest paused again drawing and expelling deep droughts of air through his nostrils.

"Sir, if I may, we were merely protecting the women from the Yankee invaders and their negro pets. We escorted them to their transports," Lathan offered.

"Do not play me for a fool, Captain," Forrest snarled. "This is the second time you have soiled my name with your dishonorable actions. Do not stain me a third time. Do I make myself clear?

"Abundantly, sir," Lathan bowed. Forrest's silent glare forced him to keep his eyes to the ground. A light knock broke the agonizing pause.

"What is it, Lieutenant?" Forrest said, not taking his eyes off of Lathan.

"A group of women are here, sir," the orderly answered. "They're pleading for an audience."

"Send them in," Forrest replied, then returned his eyes back to Lathan. "Get out of my sight and pray you don't cross me again."

"Yes, sir," Lathan said in a low voice as he slinked away, passing the women entering the room as he retreated.

Forrest dropped the scorn from his face and offered the half a dozen bonneted women the most pleasant smile he could manage. "And what do I owe the honor of this visit from such lovely ladies as yourselves?" he said with a bow.

"We've come to appeal to your sense of honor and duty as a gentleman to rescue us from our terrible plight," one of the women stepped forward, clutching her hands to her bosom.

"They stole all m'damn pigs!" a frail, gray-haired lady in the group spat.

"Grandmama, please! Let me do the talking," the first woman tried to shush her.

"…And m'damn niggers done took off and joined'em!" the old lady added, refusing to be silenced.

"Who?" Forrest's eyes narrowed.

"The Yankees, sir," the first woman answered. "They've garrisoned Fort Pillow on the river. From there, with much villainy, they raid our farms, steal our food, and speak rudely to us women. They beat any man unmercifully that tries to defend us. It's an outrage, sir! Most of them are homegrown traitors who grew up in the county, even deserters from our own army!" She clutched his arm. Tears began to well in her eyes.

"… And worse yet, they have negroes defending their walls. Most of them are runaways from our farms. They hurl insults and even rotten vegetables at any decent white folks who go there to complain. It's an outright travesty, sir. Our friends and family are suffering so…" she said, breaking into a sob.

"There, there…" Forrest said comforting her in his arms as she shuddered into his chest. Around them, the women sniffled and drew their handkerchiefs to their eyes. Forrest drew a deep breath and then called out, "Lieutenant!"

"Yes, sir!" the young man popped his back into the room.

"Send a rider out to General Chalmers. Tell him there's a change of plans. He's to move his men north. We'll converge on Fort Pillow. Get the word out to the rest of the commanders here, We ride in the morning."

"Yes, sir!" the young man replied, quickly turning to the new task at hand.

Forrest gently broke away from the woman. He held her hands in his, then wiped away a tear that sat high on her cheek. He smiled warmly at her before looking up at the rest of them. "You ladies may go home and rest assured that I will take that fort, even if it costs me my life."

Chapter Eleven: An Uneasy Feeling

The trip upriver had been an eerie one. The excitement of leaving Fort Pickering and the Federal stronghold of Memphis faded with the cheers from the crowd and the sounds of the city they left behind. What replaced them was the drone of the steam engines, the pattering of rain, and a rising sense of dread growing in their stomachs.

Until now, the war had been a fantasy in which they saw themselves beating their erstwhile masters. Now, the reality of facing those who'd see them back in chains, or even more so, dead, suddenly seemed real. They sat under the walkway of the deck above them watching the wooded shoreline pass by, imagining hordes of Rebels teeming with guns and whips ready to drag them back to the plantations to endure a most cruel punishment for thinking they could be soldiers.

Francis thought greatly on this. With all his education and refinement, would this enemy think of him any different from those who had fled their farms? What was it like to be whipped? Many of the men he served with bore the scars of corporal punishment. Some seemed to wear them like a badge of honor that they had been man enough to take a beating and survive. Francis wondered if he could endure a flogging or if it would break him. Would he cry out in agony and lose his manhood? Was he a sissy like some men called him? Did his father think he was a sissy?

He shook his head to clear it of these dark thoughts. He looked at the men around him. Some of their faces reflected the same wide-eyed fear that had crept into his thoughts. Others watched the rain-drenched woods go by with stoic indifference.

These men will fight, he thought, slowly nodding to himself, *and I will fight with them.* The sun broke through the clouds and glinted off the rain for a few fleeting seconds. He smiled at the brief moment of brilliance. *I will fight with them.*

Private Washington, sitting next to him, let out a scoff. Francis turned to see the teenager shaking his head and chuckling at some irony which he seemed to be pondering.

"What is it, Billy?" he asked.

"Man, I ain't ever been on a boat before. Now I'm ridin' one on my way to a fight," he said.

"Hey, man. Look at that!" one of the men rose and pointed up the river.

The men clambered to their feet and crowded the rails to get a glimpse of the gunboat moored below a bluff that towered over the river. It was the first sign that they were almost there.

"I sure hope that's one of ours," Jerry said as the men oohed and awed at the gunboat with thick sloping wooden sides and big 24-pound howitzers.

"That's the *USS New Era*, boys!" Sergeant Weaver joined them on the lower deck. "Those guns can drop shells on anything that tries to come up our hill."

"You mean, like shoot up over our heads, Sergeant?" Elijah marveled at the thought.

"Let's hope so," Weaver replied, reaching up to pat him on the shoulder.

Work started immediately as soon as they pulled up to the landing. They unloaded their gear and supplies from the boat and carried them up the path that wound around the bluff to the innermost walls of the fort that sat at the very top. Teams of horses pulled the cannons up along with them. Major Booth was not happy with the muddy ground behind the embrasures. He ordered the men to cut down trees and make planks so the guns would have level platforms where the wheels could maneuver freely. Francis marveled at how his fellow soldiers were able to render wild trees into usable lumber. He wondered if he would eventually have these manly skills that seemed so natural to these men who had labored all their lives.

Booth wasn't happy about a lot of things at the Fort Pillow. It was too spread out to be properly defended by the small number of men he had. He decided to abandon the lower defenses at the bottom of the hill. Instead, he had the men dig new trenches and rifle pits closer to the earthen walls at the top. They felled trees and sharpened logs to create an abatis in front of the ditch that surrounded the wall. The wall created a half-circle facing the heavily forested land below. The back of this uppermost defense was open to the river, but the bluff dropped away dramatically almost like a cliff above the water, making it nearly impossible for an attacking army to climb without using their hands. They mounted cannons inside the walls facing towards the land approach. The *New Era* sat in the river below to protect them from anything that could come from the water.

The black artillerymen set up their tents inside the walls near the rear of the fort and back from their guns. The white cavalrymen who were already there when they arrived had small log cabins they used as barracks that stood between the walls and the lower defenses.

"We don't bother them and they don't bother us," one of the men from the 2nd US Colored Light Artillery told Francis. There were two companies from the 2nd USCLA already there when Francis's regiment arrived. Francis looked back at the little wooden cabins on the other side of the wall with a frown. It seemed odd to him that men who were supposed to fight together would be segregated and have little interaction with each other.

"Some of 'em used to be our foremen back on the farms," the man from the 2nd USCLA explained. "They still getting used to seeing us in uniform I suppose."

The 13th West Tennessee Cavalry spent most of their time on patrol, which Francis soon found out usually meant raiding nearby farms. It made him uneasy to think they were taking food and supplies from civilians. Agitating them wasn't going to win anyone over to their cause. Many of his fellow soldiers liked to taunt the few civilians that came to the fort to complain or even try to reclaim their runaway slaves.

A small town began to grow near the fort. Sutlers came and set up their shops to sell everything from uniforms to liquor. Even though the men were told they couldn't bring their families, many of the wives and children found their way to this little growing community. The officers pretended not to notice, so long as the men kept to their duties. The women found purpose for being there by cooking food and mending uniforms. Some volunteered in Dr. Fitch's hospital tent where they tended to the sick and wounded.

Then came the new guns as promised: two 10-pound Parrot rifles. They had long cast iron barrels that were reinforced with a ring of wrought iron around the breeches. This was to keep them from bursting apart from the stress of firing. Major Booth ordered them to be placed forward of the walls near the rifle pits that the 13th Tennessee Cavalry was supposed to man if there was an attack on the fort. Francis thought perhaps this was a way to ultimately integrate the black and white troops. Soon they would build redoubts around the forward gun placements to protect the crews who'd man them in a fight.

All excitement over the new guns, along with the hard work, and the closeness of their families helped distract the men from the dread they had felt during the journey and when they first arrived. But now that uneasy feeling came creeping back with the return of the rain and the rumors that were spreading among the men.

It started with the mysterious lady dressed as a man. One of the cavalry patrols brought her in. The men mused at who she was and what she was doing in men's clothes while the officers questioned her in the privacy of Major Booth's cabin. Then a small guard detail escorted her to the landing. They put her aboard the *New Era* to keep her away from the men until a ship heading to Memphis could pick her up and take her away.

"He's comin'!" she shouted to them as they took her down to the landing. "He's comin' fer me! He won't rest 'til he gets me back! I'm tryin' ta warn ya! I'm tryin' ta save ya! He ain't gonna take kindly to you darky soldiers neither!"

"Who's coming?" Elijah mumbled as he watched the dark-hard woman being taken away.

"Forrest," another soldier answered. "I think she's one of his spies."

"Shit, that fool still lickin' his wounds from the whuppin' he got at Paducah, man. He ain't want none of this." Jerry said patting the barrel of one of the James rifles.

Francis swallowed hard and looked back at the woman. She was cackling loudly as they took her away. *Such confidence!* he thought with a shiver. He hoped it was just bravado or madness.

More rumors came over the next few days. First, it was that Rebel forces were amassing at Jackson. Then they heard they were on the move.

"I heard they goin' to take back Memphis," Private Billy said.

"They ain't got enough men to take Memphis, fool!" Jerry chided. "They probably goin' back to Mississippi so they can hide."

"Perhaps they're coming here," Francis said bleakly.

Jerry let out a sigh, "Nah, they ain't got no cause for that." For all his bluster, he didn't sound convinced. "What are we to them?" he asked

"Revenge," Francis said simply.

Francis thought on this as he lay in his tent in the predawn darkness. He had spent most of the night fitfully, snapping awake at every sound he heard, then chiding himself for being so skittish. He tried to go back to sleep. His mind raced. *Surely Forrest has better things to do than to attack our little outpost.* Still, the laughing woman haunted him. He shook his head briskly as if to try to shake these thoughts away. Elijah snored peacefully next to him. *So lucky to be able to sleep like he does,* he thought. He started concentrating on his breathing, counting four beats as drew breath in, and four beats as he exhaled. It was a technique he used to calm his mind. He started thinking of a ballroom full of beautiful people swirling around the dance floor to a waltz played by a small orchestra. The women wore grand dresses that swept the ground as dashing young men twirled them around and around.

CRACK!

"Alright," he said, sitting up. "That was definitely a gunshot."

Chapter Twelve: "Yes or No?"

By the time Forrest arrived midmorning, General Chalmers had already ready pushed in, captured, or killed all of the forward Federal pickets. Now the defenders had fallen back to their last line of defense, the earthen walls that commanded the very top of the bluff. His troops had captured the horses in the corral below and much of the equipment and supplies left behind in the hasty retreat. Now, using the deep ravines as cover, they were tightening their grip on the Federal's last position as they traded shots with the defenders.

Not wanting to rely on reports, Forrest rode around his line, scouting for weakness in the Yankee defense. The men who followed him flinched and ducked as bullets pinged off trees and shells landed in the nearby woods and exploded. Forrest felt the dull thunk of impact as something struck his horse. The animal screeched in agony as it reared onto its back legs.

"God damn it!" he hissed through his teeth. He held on tightly as the horse brought its front feet down then slumped over onto its side, pinning him down with its lifeless weight.

"Fuck!" he grunted.

"General!" a staffer shouted as he leaped off his horse and over to his commander. He helped him shimmy out from underneath the dead animal. "Are you alright?!"

"I'm fine, Captain Anderson," Forrest said, dusting himself off after getting to his feet. "Get me another mount."

"Perhaps you should continue your reconnaissance on foot, sir. You'd be less of a target," Anderson told him.

"I'm just as likely to get hit one way or the other. I can see better on a horse," Forrest replied. "I want sharpshooters on all these high points so they can shoot down into the fort," he motioned with his hand to the surrounding hilltops. "That'll keep their heads down and give us some breathing room." Another shell screamed overhead landing behind them with a deafening boom. Forrest turned back to Anderson, "They must have gunboats on the river. Take some cannons and sharpshooters to that high point there to harass them with plunging fire. Shoot into their gunports with rifles. We can't let them navy boys think they're safe hiding in their boats."

"Yes, sir!" Anderson said before dashing off.

Forrest had a second horse shot out from underneath him while continuing his reconnaissance. By the time he finished with his third horse of the day, his own sharpshooters were beginning to quell the enemy's fire. Now, his men could move into closer positions more safely. They began to fill the ravines and even the freshly dug trenches and rifle pits left behind by the enemy. The Yankees tried to burn the log cabins outside of their walls, but his men shot down the two fools they sent out with torches before any damage could be done. Now, these structures made good cover for his men. The trap was set.

"Here," Forrest said, handing his written demand for surrender to Captain Goodman. "Make sure they understand that if they surrender unconditionally now, they'll be treated as prisoners of war, but if my men are forced to die unnecessarily taking these walls, I cannot be responsible for what happens next."

"Of course, sir," Goodman replied and saluted. Forrest watched as the two delegations of officers met under a flag of truce. Soon, Captain Goodman came trotting back with the reply.

"Sir," Goodman said with a salute as he stopped his horse. "The commander says he needs an hour to confer with his officers and the commander of the gunboat *New Era* before he can give you a reply."

"Bullshit," Forrest said. "They're stalling for time. Look there, downriver. Those are reinforcements." Goodman turned to look. Off in the distance, he could see the three boats steaming upriver. Forrest turned to another aide.

"Tell General McCulloch to send three more companies to Captain Anderson. Then go to Anderson and tell him to fire on any ship that tries to land or interfere. Got that?"

"Yes, sir!" the lieutenant shouted with a salute and rode off. Forrest then turned back to Captain Goodman.

"Tell them I only demand the surrender of the fort and the men inside, not their boats. They've got twenty minutes to make up their damn minds or we're coming over the walls and shooting every goddamn one of them!" Goodman blinked at him for a moment.

"Alright," Forrest sighed taking out his stationery, "I'll write it out all polite for them, then."

Before long, Captain Goodman returned again. "Sir…um…some of the Yankee officers have raised doubts that you're even here. They're citing the bluff at Union City as an example, sir…"

Forrest sighed again. "Of course," he said, then trotted off into the clearing in front of the walls.

"Sir! Perhaps you shouldn't…" Goodman tried to stop him from exposing himself to the enemy guns, but realized it was useless trying to hold him back. Men on both sides watched in opened-mouth astonishment as the Rebel commander trotted out into plain view of the armed men behind the walls. Forrest smiled at the worried faces peeping over the top. He took off his hat and gave them a bow. A moment of silence followed and the men behind the wall start yelling insults at him. Forrest laughed, put his hat back on, and trotted back to Captain Goodman.

"There," he said, "that should do it. Now tell them I'm running out of patience and they're running out of time."

Moments later, Goodman returned with a written message.

Your demand does not produce the desired effect.

"What the hell does that mean?" Forrest blurted out, dropping his hand with the paper to his lap. He thrust it back into Goodman's hands. "This will not do. Send it back. Tell 'em I must have an answer in plain English, yes or no."

Chapter Thirteen: The Effusion of Blood

Lathan watched from the shadow of the woods along the Confederate line. His company of men crouched around him in the ravine. He figured that volunteering to lead men in the possible final assault to come would help get him back into Forrest's good graces. He watched with great interest as Captain Goodman rode back for a fourth, between the delegation of Federal officers and General Forrest's command post.

"It doesn't look good…" Sergeant Bill Garrett said in a hushed voice.

Lathan watched Forrest read the written message that was handed to him. The general then slumped his shoulders. After a moment he let out a sigh and started giving orders to his aides. The aides ran off, most likely to convey those orders to the various commanders. Soon, the call to get ready for the assault was shouted along the line.

Lathan turned to his men. "Remember this, boys, they had ample opportunity to end this without any more bloodshed. Instead, they laugh at us. They're laughing at you right now! You wanna know why? Because now, many of you are going to have to die just to prove to them what the fools should already know: that no nigger army can hold back a force of righteous white Southern men."

Lathan paused for a moment, scanning the dirty faces around him. He could see the anger and outrage growing in them. "Look to your buddy," he continued, "it may be the last time you see him alive. Moments from now, when you crawl over that wall, remember his face. You may very well be avenging his death."

One of the men spat on the ground and grunted in agreement. "Get yourselves ready, boys," Lathan said. He turned back to the walls and pulled out his saber with a metallic zing.

A volley of rifle fire crackled overhead as Confederate sharpshooters shot down from their heights at the defenders on the wall. A bugle called. The men started yipping and shouting the Rebel yell. "Forward!" came the shout repeated by officers and sergeants.

Lathan lurched out of the woods with his saber held forward. His men crowded around him, shouting in high-pitched screams as they ran toward the abatis of felled trees and sharpened sticks. He was aware of men in his periphery being punched down by rifle fire. The fort's big guns roared, spraying canister at the attackers, but the balls flew overhead. They were now too close and too low for cannons to tilt down at them.

He grimaced, bracing himself for a bullet to find him. He was furious that he would die at the hands of a negro hiding behind a wall. But the bullet he was expecting had not come by the time they got to the abatis. They climbed over it and into the ditch below. The sharpshooters were doing their job keeping the defenders off the walls and killing the ones stubborn enough to linger. Lathan shoved his saber back into its sheath and set his back against the earthen wall. He cupped his hands and receive a foot of a man who he hoisted upward. He hoisted several men until their hands reached down and grabbed him. They pulled him up as he made the climb. Blood splattered men screamed and fell alongside him as he rose to the top and jumped down into the fort.

"Fire!" someone across the way shouted.

A line of blue-clad soldiers unleashed a volley of musketry that dropped many of the attackers to the ground in screaming agony. Lathan flinched and then patted himself frantically looking for the wound that wasn't there. He looked up to see a mix of black and white men in blue, frantically trying to reload their weapons. He pulled out his sword. "Kill 'em!" he roared. The men around him burst forward, screeching like banshees as they fired into the mass of men who were still ramrodding their next round into their rifles. Many fell. Others dropped their guns and ran only to be skewered from behind with bayonets. They dropped to their knees screaming in horror as they clutched at slim steel points that suddenly protruded out from their chests.

Lathan hacked his way through the retreating men. "Please, don't kill me!" a man screamed.

"Please, sir! We be good! We promise!"

Lathan looked down to find two of the black soldiers had thrown themselves at his feet. The blood from his saber dripped onto their heads. "It's too late," he said. He pulled out his LeMat pistol and shot them both. He looked up from their slumped bodies to see similar bloody scenes all around him. He smiled. Now the Yankees would know to take them seriously next time they demanded a surrender. The chase was on and the game was just getting started.

"We got to get out of here!" Jerry shouted, grabbing Francis and Elijah's shoulders and yanking them back out of their stunned stupor, "C'mon!"

"Sweet Jesus…" Francis mumbled, stumbling back from his position in the line. They joined the mass of fleeing men running towards the tents at the back of the fort. Already men were throwing themselves off the bluff. They tumbled wildly towards the river, breaking limbs and cracking their heads open on trees and rocks as they fell. Francis could hear the crackle of musketry below cutting down the men who had made it to the river. "My God, they've cut off our retreat…"

Rebel yells and screams of terror intermixed behind them as they made it to the tents. Francis stopped to look back. Horror filled his eyes. It was a slaughter. Men with their hands up were being shot down. Others were being clubbed to death with the back end of muskets. He turned back to run. Elijah tumbled to the ground next to him.

"Elijah! Elijah, are you alright?!" Francis dropped down next to him. Elijah hissed, scrunching up his face in pain. He drew his bloody foot up with his hands as he curled into a ball.

"Aghh! I'm hit! Go on! Go on! Run!" he said.

"Nothing doing, big man," Francis patted his shoulder.

"Go on, Francis," Elijah tried to hide the pain in his voice. "I'm injured. They ain't gonna kill me now."

Francis looked up at the bloody scene behind them. Confederates were indiscriminately bayonetting anyone found lying on the ground.

"Ah, I don't think so…"

"Come on, you damn fool!" Jerry shouted. Francis turned back to look at him. Jerry was now at the edge of the bluff. "Ain't nothing you can do for him! No need of you both dyin'!"

"Go on, Francis," Elijah managed a smile. "I be alright."

"Not on your life, buddy," Francis smiled back, tears welling in his eyes. "Go on, Jerry!" Francis called back to him. "I'm not leaving him."

Jerry shook his head, "Suit yourself, fool!" He looked down the bluff at the scene below. The fight was happening there, too. He looked back at the two friends, "Good luck, Frenchie. Good luck, Baby Boy." He smiled bitterly and then dropped down the backside of the bluff, sliding on his hip.

The Rebels were coming. Francis stood up and set himself between them and Elijah's prone body. He sank into his fighting stance. "Francis…don't…" Elijah tried to speak. Nausea washed over him. The world was getting dimmer, the sounds of the slaughter became more and more muffled. Elijah fought for consciousness. He watched as Francis sprung himself into the air, spun around, and threw the back of his heel into the mouth of the first man to reach him. A tooth flew through the air as the man dropped his gun and grabbed his mouth as he tumbled to the ground.

"Shon-of-a-bistch knocked my toof out!" he yelled in protest.

Francis punched the very next man in the nose, but then they were all on him. Elijah felt the tears roll down his face as he heard Francis scream as the men pummeled him.

"Enough! That one's out of the fight for now," a man said.

"I got a couple of teef back from the shon-of-a-bitsch," the man with a bloody mouth smiled. He held up a handful of teeth like they were trophies.

"Tie him down to the stakes inside that tent there, Bill, Tom. I don't want him coming to and trying to get 'em back with all that sissy fighting he was doing," the man told the other two. Elijah watched him approach. "Well, well, well, who do we got here?" he said as he squatted next to him. Elijah shuddered, suddenly feeling cold. He looked up at the green eyes of the clean-shaven man that now leered over him. A wave of recognition slithered through his foggy mind.

Lathan grinned as he saw the recognition in Elijah's half-conscious eyes. "You know, most negroes look the same to me, but you, my friend, I'd recognize you anywhere." Elijah tried to say something but it just came out as an unrecognizable slur of sounds. "Say, looks like you took one to the foot! Well now, I suppose we can help you with that. Bill!"

"Yesh, shir" the man with the bloody mouth replied eagerly. "Looks like you turned out to be a pretty good dentist. How's your surgery skills?"

Bill let out a laugh, "Jesh fine, shir!"

"Good! Let's make sure this negro never runs again."

Major General Nathan Bedford Forrest beamed with pride as his men stormed the walls and poured into the fort. He told them that out of the Missourians, Mississippians, and Tennesseans in his command, he wanted to see who'd be first over the wall. The men took to it like ants to a dropped piece of pie. He couldn't see from his position outside of the walls, but by the sounds of it, his boys were giving the Yankees a licking they soon would not forget. Never again would they be so arrogant to refuse his demand for surrender or foolish enough to pit armed slaves against Southern white men.

He tapped the flanks of his horse and started moving towards the walls. The sounds of fighting had begun to taper. Still, the occasional gunshot rang out and the screams of the wounded could be heard, but it was time to see the prize they had won and for his men to see their leader. He wanted to tell them that this was just the beginning. They could accomplish great things if they just believed in him and in themselves.

He could see the cannons that had once ripped his men apart were now lying idle in their embrasures. "Let's get some men to go in there and get those cannons. I want to turn them on any gunboats still out there," he nodded towards the river.

"Of course, sir!" an aide replied and quickly set off. Forrest dismounted and walked over to admire the first 10-pound Parrot rifle that the men wheeled out from behind the wall. It was quite a prize. He joined in with them, adding his strength to moving the heavy piece. He reveled in their surprise at seeing a major general put his back into the same work he asked of them. Forrest took pride in this hands-on approach.

He was a man and a fighter to his core. He made damn sure his men knew it.

Down below he could see the one remaining gunboat moored upriver with her gunports closed. "Those cowards saved themselves and left their friends to die," he spat on the ground. "I ought to kill them just for that. Turn the cannon a little more to the right, boys. Those sons-of-bitches aren't safe from me yet."

"Sir! Excuse me, sir!?" he heard a man called out breathlessly to him.

Forrest looked up from the gun sights to see a man scrambling up the path from the river with a pronounced limp. He was hatless and wearing a blood-spattered blue uniform.

"Are you General Forrest, sir?" the man asked him with wide-eyed exasperation.

"Yes, sir. What do you want?" Forrest asked flatly, somewhat surprised to be interrupted by this panic-stricken Yankee.

"I am Dr. Charles Fitch, surgeon of this post. I'm asking for your protection as a prisoner of war, sir."

"You're a surgeon of a damn nigger regiment," Forrest spat, putting his hands on his hips, straightening himself.

"No, sir. I am the surgeon of the 13th West Tennessee Cavalry. A white regiment, sir!"

"Then you're a damn homegrown Tennessee Yankee."

"No, sir," Fitch flinched at the fury in which Forrest glared at him. "I'm originally from Massachusetts, but I recently lived in Iowa. Please, sir. I'm begging you to spare my life." Fitch clinched his hands together at his breast.

Forrest scrutinized him for a moment and he narrowed his eyes. "What the hell are you doing down here then? I have a mind to kill you just for being here. This war would be long over if it weren't for you damn Northwesterners comin' down here gettin' involved."

Fitch trembled under his glare, then swallowed. "Sir, I am a man of medicine, a man of mercy. I'm here to help the wounded, sir, your wounded, too! My only motive is compassion. Is that not what makes us human, sir?"

Forrest stared at him for a moment. "Why is it you're asking me for protection now? The battle's over. We won."

Fitch blinked at him for a moment, confused. "Sir...did you not know...? Your men are still killing people...they're killing the prisoners...the wounded. I just escaped a firing squad. They stood us all together. They shot all the men I was standing with...I ran when I realized I wasn't hit..."

Forrest furrowed his brow, "Where?"

"Everywhere!"

Forrest paused to look at the blood-covered man who was shuddering before. He turned to an aide. "Take this man into my custody. See to it that no harm comes to him."

"Yes, sir!" the aide replied.

"Oh, thank you, sir!" Fitch began to sob as he dropped to his knees.

"Shut up," Forrest grunted as he walked into the fort. His eyes widened as he rounded the corner. In front of him were men clubbing black soldiers with the butts of their rifles until their heads cracked open and spilled out their contents. Another man was hacking a black soldier with his saber until his cries for mercy turned into blood-filled gurgles. Others were shooting and stabbing wounded men who were laying on the ground as they reached out for mercy. A wave of nausea washed over him, and then fury.

"Stop!" he shouted. No one seemed to notice him over the sounds of screams, gunshots, and clubbing.

"God damn it, I said stop!" Forrest shouted as he pulled out his saber and pistol. Some of the men began to take notice, freezing in their various acts of violence to look at their commander with a new sense of fear. Forrest tore into the crowd, tearing men off their bloody work and throwing them to the ground. Soon other officers joined in to break up the mob and stop the killing.

"I said stop, God damn it!" Forrest roared. Still, some of the men were too far gone in their blood lust to be aware of the changing scene.

"Hold his leg here, Tom, I'm almost through the bone!" Bill shouted in blood-splatted glee as he readjusted the saw he had been using to take off Elijah's foot.

"Uh…Bill…stop…" Lathan tried to tell him.

BAM!

The back of Bill's head blew out spraying Lathan and Tom with blood, brains, and bone bits. Lathan blinked then whipped the blood from his eyes as he slowly stood up from his crouched position to face his commander. Forrest glared at him through the wisps of smoke that swirled from the end of his pistol. The recognition in Forrest's eyes sent chills through Lathan. Forrest turned back to the other men, holding his pistol in the air.

"Now, I swear, I will fucking kill the next man who defies my orders, you can count on that!"

Forrest looked at the silent and stunned faces around him. He saw fear and the shame they felt at disappointing him. He let out a sigh as he holstered his pistol and sheathed his sword.

"Look, I asked a lot of you today, and you came through as I knew you would. I'm damn proud of you. I thought my heart would burst with pride watching you go over that wall. Now, we got to look at the bigger picture. We can't go losing our heads. These negroes are the property of the very citizens we swore to protect. Killin' 'em isn't going to help anybody. I want the ones still alive rounded up so we can return them to their masters. The others we'll sell. God knows this army needs money for guns, hell, to put shoes on your feet!"

Forrest scanned the faces, seeing his talk was putting them at ease. "If you'll do what I say, I will lead you to victory. I've taken every place that the Federals have tried to occupy in west Tennessee and north Mississippi except Memphis…"

He paused a moment, allowing a grin to spread across his face, "…And if they don't mind, I'll have that place in, too!" He paused to allow the men to chuckle before continuing. "Alright, boys, I'm heading out to my new headquarters at Brownsville to plan our next move. General Chalmers is in charge. We need to clean up here, bury the dead, take what we can…burn then rest. We'll be moving out soon."

Some of the men mumbled their assent. Lathan took the moment to make his move. "I'll come with you, sir. I have some insight on Memphis that can be of help."

"You'll stay here, Captain," Forrest snapped back, regaining some of his previous anger. "See if General Chalmers has any use for you 'cause I swear…if you come into my presence again I may have the mind to kill you myself."

"Of course, sir," Lathan bowed his head, knowing everyone around him knew he had overplayed his hand.

Forrest turned back to the rest of the men. "Collect up the supplies and prisoners, bury the dead, and be ready to march," he said and walked away.

Lathan quickly took control to hide his embarrassment. He turned to his men, "Burn the tents and start dragging the bodies to the river."

"This one's still alive," a man said, nudging Elijah's head with his foot.

"Not for long," Lathan said. "Bury him with the rest."

"There's a man still in there," Tom said, pointing to the tent where Francis was tied down.

"That's no man. Burn it with the rest of the garbage."

Elijah could barely make out what was happening, but he felt it. "Francis…" he mumbled as they dragged him away by his arms. "Francis, no…" he tried to call out as he heard the crackling flames and felt the heat coming off the burning tents. They dragged him down to the river and left him next to a pile of wrecked bodies. Once they finished tossing the bodies into a pit they rolled him on top and then started covering them with dirt. Elijah could make out the shapes of broken heads and distorted faces as the world went black.

Sergeant Tom Billington finally found a moment to slip away. Everyone had been quick to get to work as General Forrest and his entourage made to leave, but once they were gone, the men became more relaxed, helping themselves to the captured whiskey and looting what they could find. It didn't take long for the killing to start again.

Tom had seen enough and didn't want to be a witness to anymore. He found a quiet place to be alone near the river where the passing water helped muffle the sounds of gunshots and cries for mercy from the fort above. He sat near the freshly covered grave where they had tossed bodies into a tangled mess of arms and legs that landed on top of each other in absurd limp positions. *What a way to spend eternity,* he thought, looking at the river flow past the setting sun.

The passing water seemed to have swept away the blood and the bodies of the men that tried to swim across it. He remembered watching them jump into the river as if the water would protect them. They just became targets as his fellow soldiers took aim from the shore. Tom dropped his face into his hands and began to cry.

Suddenly, movement in his periphery startled him. Something in the loose soil of the mass grave moved. Something was now emerging from the ground. Tom watched in horror as an enormous form dragged itself from the ground. It appeared to be some kind of monster made out of mud crawling out of hell to drag him back down for the sins he had committed that day.

The monster froze. Tom held his breath in terror. The thing had eyes. It was looking at him in the twilight. Tom let his breath out slowly. There was fear in those eyes. That fear turned into sorrow and then pity. It was then that Tom realized he was looking at a man. It was the man Tom had held down as Bill attempted to remove his foot. Yet the man's eyes held something that Tom could not understand. The man was looking at him with pity.

Tom turned away. He could not bear to look at the man any longer. He threw his face back into his hands and began to sob anew as the mud-covered man dragged himself away.

Act II: Memphis

Chapter Fourteen: Old Friends

April 1864: Detroit

"There I stood with nothing but my saber to defend myself from the bloodthirsty Arkansans and their bayonets!" Carl held up his cane as if he were about to fend off an invisible army of attackers. The men in the parlor sat quietly in their chairs, listening politely. He could hear the soft rattle of their coffee cups on the saucers in what was supposed to be a dramatic pause, a pause that used to bring astonished gasps the dozens of times he had told this story before. One man covered his mouth and coughed. Carl could feel the effects of the cocaine slipping away from him just as the interest was slipping away from his audience. Worse yet, he could hear people outside beginning to shout. *Oh, fuck,* he thought, *the protesters have found us.*

One of the men got up from his chair to look out of the window. He frowned at whatever it was he saw in street below. The voices were getting louder. *I'm losing them...*Carl thought, as the wound in his hip began to throb. The host motioned for him to continue with his eyes and a rolling gesture of his hand.

"I fought the best I could, but there were far too many of them! A bayonet found me here in the hip and drove me to the ground..." Nobody was listening. Everyone was crowding to the windows to watch the commotion below.

"No more war! No more war!" the crowd outside began to chant.

"Alright," the host stood up. "Thank you, Private Smith, for your heroic tale and of course your service to our country. Private Smith will be here to answer questions and sign autographs if you like…and please, be sure to buy war bonds. It's what keeps brave men like Private Smith armed and fighting for our Union and Liberty for all!"

Nobody was listening.

Carl cringed at being called "Private Smith." *Couldn't they have promoted me before they sent me home?* he thought bitterly. He slumped in his chair. In front of him were a table, pen, and an inkwell to sign autographs that nobody seemed to want anymore.

"Gee, sir, you sure sound like a hero to me! Can I get your autograph?"

The voice was instantly familiar. "Chucky?!" Carl looked up from his sulking. The sandy-haired freckled-face young man stood before him in a civilian suit. "My God, Chucky, you made it out alive! I'm so happy to see you!" Carl stood up and made his way around the table to give him a hug.

"Well, I ain't out yet, just on furlough," he said returning the hug. "They gave all us vets thirty days for signing back up!"

"Jesus, you signed back up?! Why on earth…?" Carl broke the hug to look at him.

"Well…the job ain't done yet, plus they made me a corporal!" Chucky smiled, sticking out his chest and patting it proudly.

Carl let out a scoff, "Am I the only person never to get promoted?"

"You could sign back up! I'm sure they'd make you a sergeant or something!" Chucky said enthusiastically.

"Oh, no," Carl chuckled, picking up his cane and patting the spot where his hip had been jabbed with a bayonet, "not with my injury. My fighting days are over."

Chucky frowned for a moment, then snapped his head around as a brick came crashing through a window.

"No more of our sons for your nigger-lovin' war!" someone shouted from the street. The men in the parlor began to gasp and fret.

"Please, no need to panic," the host motioned with his open hands pushing down on the invisible tension in the room. "There's a back exit, away from the mob. We can discuss the purchase of war bonds later."

Carl turned to Chucky, "We better get out of here before they start burning the city down again."

They followed the rest of the guests to the service stairs. Carl could feel his energy slipping away. He took the opportunity from the commotion in the stairwell to take a pull from his flask of cocaine-infused wine before exiting out the back door into the alley. A trio of men stepped in front of him and Chucky, separating them from the fleeing guests who quickly trotted off at the sign of new trouble.

"Well, here he is," one of the men said, twisting the waxed end of his mustache, "the war hero himself. It's not enough for you to beg for money for your damn war, is it?! You got to lure this boy off to die too?!"

"I'm no boy, I'm a vet, buster!" Chucky growled stepping forward.

"Chucky, please," Carl hissed, putting his hand on his shoulder.

"Yeah, better listen to your boyfriend, little man, you might get hur…"

Chucky smashed his fist across the man's mouth, knocking him into the arms of his two friends. The man grabbed his mouth and then looked up with astonished fury. His friends pushed him back up, shoving him towards Chucky. Carl stopped his forward motion by ramming the end of his cane into the man's solar plexus then whipping it around to smash him on the back of the head as he doubled over. Without giving them a chance to react, he swung it around and smashed the man on the left across the face, sending him tumbling to the ground. Chucky already had the man on the right by the collar, holding him while he punched him in the face repeatedly.

The sound of the crowd grew as some of them were beginning to find the alley.

"Hey! Those warmongers are beating up our boys!" a man yelled, pointing down the alley.

"We got to get out of here!" Carl gasped. He grabbed Chucky by arm. "Let's go!" Chucky looked at the bloodied man in his grip, shrugged, and let him drop. They sprinted as fast as they could, not daring to look back. Ahead were dozens of men dressed in blue uniforms carrying batons running towards them.

"We're vets! We're vets! We're running from the rioters!" Carl called out with his hands in the air. The policemen ran past as the two stood with their hands up, panting for air. The policemen crashed into the mob and an all-out brawl broke out.

"Come on," Carl dropped his hands, giving Chucky a smile, "let's get out of here before the city breaks into a general riot again."

"Wow," Chucky exclaimed, "you and me adventurin' again, just like old times!"

"Yeah," Carl mused, suddenly remembering to use his cane as they walked. "At least they don't have rifles and bayonets like the Rebs did. Do you have plans tonight?"

"Nah, just going back to my ma's house," Chucky said.

"Come over for supper," Carl said, pulling a calling card from his vest pocket. "My wife would love to meet you and you can catch us up on what's going on at the front."

"Sure!" Chucky took the card, reading the address on it. "I think my ma's already growin' tired of me, anyway."

"So, you were at Chickamauga," Carl prodded before putting a forkful of roasted pork in his mouth.

Chucky was caught mid-sip. He put his wine glass down and wiped his chin. "Yeah, we was anchored at the south end of the line for most of the battle, but towards the end, we came up and held them off with General Thomas's men, the ol' Rock of Chickamauga himself!"

Anna smiled, crinkling her nose at Chucky's boyish enthusiasm. Her blond hair was pulled up in a bun with a few strands falling to her shoulders. Carl couldn't help but drink in her loveliness as she beheld Chucky in her big blue eyes. "Do you see my brother Klaus much? He's terrible at returning my letters."

"Ooh, the Brass Baron!" Chucky's eyes widened with awe. Anna's eyebrows raised in surprise. Carl let out a laugh. Chucky suddenly corrected himself, "My apologies, ma'am. I mean Major Schmidt no disrespect!"

"Major?!" Carl Blurted. "He's a major now?!"

Anna let out the light laugh and looked back at Chucky, ignoring Carl's outburst. She shooed away any pretension of bad feeling with her hand. "Put yourself at ease, dear, I'm sure my brother loves the nickname."

"Well, no one dares to say it to his face," Chucky shook his head in awe, picturing the German officer clomping around with his prosthetic leg and brass claw for a hand.

"I know he can seem very intimidating. He must look more like a machine than a man these days, but Klaus has a kind heart, I assure you."

"A heart like a gunboat steam engine, more like it," Carl added taking a sip of his wine.

Anna narrowed her eyes and pursed her lips as she shot him a comical look of scorn. Carl let out a laugh, then quickly picked up his napkin to mop up the wine that had escaped him. "Excuse me…" he mumbled, chuckling lightly.

"Anyway," Anna returned her eyes to Chucky, "how is the *Brass Baron*?"

"We don't see him much, ma'am. He's long since been promoted out of the regiment. He's a staff officer with the higher-ups, I guess.…Oh, by the way," Chucky interrupted himself. "Captain Newman rode back with me. He's in town. Says he's gonna stop by and see you."

"Good God, whatever for?!" Carl let out.

"I don't know…cause he likes you or something?" Chucky shrugged, not knowing how to answer the unexpected question.

Anna gave Carl another chiding look, "You should be kind to your ex-commander. He saved your life."

"My life would not have needed saving if he hadn't clubbed me over the head and dragged me into the war in the first place," Carl was quick to point out.

The boys retired to the veranda after dinner to enjoy a glass of whiskey. Chucky marveled at Carl's silk smoking jacket and the exotic red cap that had a tassel affixed to the top which hung idly on the side. "Wow, is that one of them *Zouave* hats?" he asked. "I seen some strange uniforms with caps like that out there."

"Yeah, kind of. It's a fez. I like to look the part when I partake in the *Oriental pleasures*." Carl said. He opened a lacquered box he had set on the small table between the chairs. Inside was a long smoking pipe, an oil lamp, matches, and a small block of brown gooey resin. Carl lit the lamp, broke off a chunk of the resin, and stuffed it into the pipe. He offered it to Chucky first.

"Um...no thanks..." Chucky stared in awe.

"Suit yourself," Carl said. He held the pipe over the flame and drew in the smoke, then busted into a smoked-filled coughing laugh at Chucky's expression. "Jesus, you'd think I had just pulled out a dead body in front of you!"

"I'm sorry, I heard of opium. I ain't ever seen it. I've been told to stay away from it."

"Oh, it's no different from the laudanum the doctor gives you. Just doesn't taste so bad. Takes the edge off the pain," Carl said, patting his hip, "and helps me sleep."

"I hear people don't wake up for days with that stuff," Chucky shook his head.

"Oh, that's what the cocaine's for. It's a great system really: cocaine during the day, opium at night, it's all-natural, too!"

"If you say so," Chucky said, taking a sip of his whiskey.

"Hmmph," Carl mumbled as his eyes glazed over.

Chucky sat there in the silence that ensued. Carl leaned forward to burn more of the brown goo over the lamp, then fell back into his chair and stared out into the street.

"Umm," Chucky said after a moment, "I think you ought to consider coming back...to the regiment, I mean...We could really use you."

Carl just mumbled something that Chucky couldn't quite understand. He then leaned forward again to take another pull from his pipe.

"We got a lot of new guys now, greenbacks. We need vets like you to help get them in line…" Chucky added. Carl continued to stare, motionless. "I think that's what Captain Newman is coming to say." A ripple of response crossed over Carl's face and then faded back to the plain stare. After a while, Chucky gave up on trying to continue the conversation. He sat for a while with his friend, then finally set his whiskey glass down. "I guess I'll be seeing you then," he said, looking back at the dark house behind him. Carl didn't move. Chucky wasn't sure if he was sleeping. He blew out the lamp, just to be safe, then walked down the steps. He turned one last time to look at his friend who was now slumped in his chair.

"I guess you really never had the fight in you," he said before walking away.

"Goodbye…" Carl mumbled inaudibly in the dark.

He wasn't aware when, but at some point, Anna tried to rouse him from his chair. She gave up then came back out with a blanket to cover him. Later he could hear the birds begin to sing and felt the dampness in his crotch from sleeping in his clothes. Sometime after that, the thump of the newspaper landing on the porch startled him. He dozed off once more. Anna brought him coffee later after the sun had come out. "I really wish you wouldn't sleep out here," she told him. "The neighbors will think you're a vagrant."

Carl mumbled a thanks as he sipped. Anna put her hands on her hips and regarded him for a moment.

"Why don't you clean yourself up and come to church with me? It's been so long."

Carl let out a long sigh, "I still can't understand anything they say."

"How are you going to learn German if you don't try? Come, I'll help you understand."

Carl leaned forward, putting his forearms on his knees and dropping his head. "I can't bear for your friends and family to see me this way," he said weakly. "I know they don't approve of me."

Anna knelt down and ran her hand through his mop of black hair. "That's not true, and even if it were, I approve of you. I love you, Carl."

Carl couldn't bear to look at her. "I love you, too," he said weakly. She let him be for a while. She returned later, completely dressed for church. She brought him a plate with some eggs and pieces of last night's bread which she toasted. "There's still some warm coffee on the stove," she said putting her hands on her hips, "but you'll have to get up and get it yourself if you want any."

Carl let out a groan, "Oh, you're so cruel!"

"I know," she came back with, "see how cruel I can be if you are still in that chair when I get back, old man!"

"Alright, alright, I'll get up," he chuckled. "I promise."

Her eyes sparkled as she smiled once more, "Maybe we could walk by the river later. It's such a pretty day!"

"Of course, my love," He smiled at her. She gave him a smile and turned to leave. He watched her walk away with her thick legs, wide hips, and impossibly tight waist. He let out a groan. He chided himself for being such a fool. He had spent another cold night in the chair instead of snuggling up to her warm body. He resolved not to make the mistake again but knew that he would inevitably.

A shot of "*coca-wine*" from his flask gave him the jolt he needed to get up, use the bathroom, and get coffee before settling back into his chair once more. He was too afraid to look at how much opium he had smoked the night before. He knew he was spending too much money at the pharmacist and there was only so much he could blame on his wound.

He looked at the paper, trying to take his mind off his problems. The headlines on the front page did not help.

Capture of Fort Pillow by the Rebels
Reported Massacre of White and Black Troops
Dead and Wounded Negroes Burned

"That can't be good…" He mumbled to himself, furrowing his brow as he read. *Isn't that where Francis said they were going?* He immediately felt a pang of guilt. He was terrible at writing. Anna kept up with Francis and Elijah better than he did. He remembered something about them leaving Memphis and going somewhere. *Was it Fort Pillow?* The man approaching shook him from his thoughts.

"Well, now, aren't you going to stand up to greet your captain?" the man said.

Carl peered over his paper to see the tall handsome man in a worn-out captain's uniform walking up the path to his front steps. He could see him smiling broadly under his big brown mustache.

"I think I'll sit, Chester," Carl said flatly, dropping his paper. He could see the smile suddenly drop from Newman's face. "Oh, what's the matter, *Chester*? Am I still too beneath you to use your first name?" Carl continued.

The smile reappeared, "Of course not, Carl. You and I are old war buddies, aren't we? It's good to see you!"

"Chucky already told me what you want," Carl said flatly, "I'm not interested."

Newman let out a light laugh, "Of course, I understand. Chucky already told me as much. Still, I would be remiss if I didn't talk to you myself about what I'm offering." Carl just looked at him blankly. Realizing Carl wasn't going to ask, Newman reached into his jacket and pulled out a cloth patch denoting two golden stripes in the shape of a 'V.'

"Here," he said extending them to Carl, "you earned them, Corporal Smith."

Carl looked at the rank and then back to Captain Newman. "You had to club me over the head and drag me into the war the last time. Do you think dangling some petty rank at me now is going to work? Please, just leave me alone, I'm not interested."

Newman dropped his head for a minute and scoffed, then looked back up, "Son, I understand you're bitter. Trust me, this war has been tough on us all. But we've got them nearly beaten! I'm offering a chance to be part of something big, a part of history!"

"Part of something big, huh?" Carl sat up in his chair. "And what has being *part of something big* done for you, *Chester?* Look at you in your ragged uniform, still a captain after everything you've done while your peers have been promoted past you, and now you're reduced to begging men to go die with you? You can give your damn stripes to some other fool."

"Carl…" Newman shook his head.

"Here," Carl said, cutting him off. He pulled out a coin and threw it at him. Newman stood still as the coin hit his chest and fell to the ground. "This is usually how I get rid of beggars."

They stared at each other in silence for a moment. Newman finally let out a chuckle and shook his head. He stepped over the coin and placed the corporal stripes on the porch. "I know the man you are, Carl, and he's not whatever it is you're pretending to be right now. Someday, whether it's tomorrow or twenty years from now, you'll think about this moment and you'll cringe with regret at the way you spoke to me. When you do, I want you to know…I've already forgiven you."

He turned and walked away. Carl watched him leave, fighting back tears of anger and frustration. "I'm not a coward, Captain Newman!" he shouted. Newman stopped. He turned and smiled while shaking his head.

"You're the only one calling you that, Corporal Smith."

There was so much to do, so much Carl wanted to do, but it was getting harder and harder to get from his chair.

"Have you heard from Francis, I'm so worried about them," Anna prodded him almost daily. The truth was, he was behind in his letter writing, his studies, everything. He knew he was being a bad friend. Francis wrote so much it was hard to keep up with him. But he knew it was really because it was hard for him to read the letters. Francis was so excited about what he and Elijah were doing as soldiers and their cause that it made him cringe. He thought about Francis, Elijah, Chucky, and even Captain Newman fighting for this cause that they suffered so much for while he withered away in his chair. He resolved he would make an inquiry tomorrow. He'd write Francis, he'd check for a casualty report from what the papers were calling the Fort Pillow Massacre…tomorrow.

The pain came early. It was more of a nausea that the cocaine-laced wine wasn't going to fix. He drew from his pipe, letting the vapors tame his thoughts and the helpless feeling of needing to do something, but not knowing what. He stared at nothing as people passed by. They glanced at him and quickly looked away. The drool was collecting on his silk robe. Anna would be upset, but that didn't matter right now. Right now he was able to feel nothing.

The shape came slowly into focus. It hobbled into Carl's field of vision. It was a big man. He walked using a worm as a crutch. It was a tool Carl had seen artillerymen use to clean debris from their barrels. It was a long shaft with an iron corkscrew at the end. In the other hand, the big man held a wooden box.

"I brought him home, Carl," Elijah said, holding up the box. "I brought him home to his father...I... can't face Mr. Beauchamp alone," Elijah began to cry. "Oh, God, please, I can't do it alone!" He fell to his hands and knees, sobbing uncontrollably.

Carl sat in his chair and stared.

Chapter Fifteen: The Worst Possible News

Carl was conscious of the front door opening behind him. He felt Anna brush past. "My God, Elijah, are you hurt?!" she gasped as she ran to him.

"I can't do it alone, Ms. Anna! Oh, God, please, I can't do it alone!" he shuddered on his hands and knees, the box sat in front of him.

"Do what alone, child? C'mon, let's get you inside." She struggled to get the big man to his single foot and helped him hobble into the house. Carl just stared at the scene in front of him.

"Do what alone, Elijah?" she asked again as they walked inside.

"Face his father...I...I....brought him home. I brought him home, Ms. Anna," Carl could hear Elijah say.

"Who? What is this box?" he heard her ask. The conversation got muffled as they got into the house, but Carl knew what was being said. A tear rolled down his cheek in the brief moment of silence and then came the scream. Anna was screaming inside the house. The horror and sorrow in that scream broke his trance. The sick emptiness in his stomach boiled over into rage that shot through his veins like lightning spreading across the sky.

"Eeeeeecaaaaaaaagghhh!" he screamed, pulling at his hair. The surge of energy shot through his arms and legs. He drew back his foot and kicked the table over, knocking his lacquered box off the porch. Its contents tumbled onto the walkway below. He picked up his cane and began beating it against the ground until it broke into splinters as he screamed. He then collapsed face down on the ground and sobbed, "Oh, Francis, why? Why, Francis…?"

Hands were on him as he lay there shuddering. "Come on, my love. Come inside."

They sat at the table. Anna brought out glasses and whiskey. She poured the boys one each and then one for herself. She took a hefty draw as she sat, shuddering a bit at the effect.

"There were too many of them," Elijah said, shaking his head, looking at his drink. "Once they came over the wall, there was no chance to surrender. They blood was up and they were just a killin' everyone they could. We was running. I got hit. I told him to run…" Elijah lifted his hand to his face and started crying again.

"It's alright, child," Anna got up and caressed his shoulder. "You don't have to say anymore."

"No," Elijah stiffened. He took her hand and gently removed it from his shoulder. "I appreciate you being so kind to me, ma'am, but if Francis taught me one thing, it was to be a man. He stood up for me. I gotta be strong and stand up for him."

Anna smiled and patted him on the shoulder, "We have all night to listen." Carl watched silently, his jaw twitching with tension.

"I was on the ground, couldn't move. Francis stood over me. He gave the first two a pretty good lickin'," Elijah said, pausing to nod his head to emphasize the truth of it. "But they were just too many…" he followed, shaking his head and looking at his glass.

It took awhile to tell the rest of the story, pausing at moments to gather himself after an outbreak of tears. Carl and Anna listened intently, closing their eyes at moments as the details become too much to bear. Anna cried softly. Carl ground his teeth in rage.

"They own commander, General Forrest, had to shoot one of them to get them to stop, else I be dead, too, I guess," Elijah said, shaking his head, looking at the floor. "But I'll never forget the face of the man who did this to Francis…" He then looked up at Carl.

"It was him, Carl," he said in a low voice as if he was afraid to be overheard. The blood ran from Carl's face as rage turned into fear. "It was that Lathan fellow, you know, the one we tussled with at New Madrid," Elijah added. Carl's eyes widened with shock.

"Who's Lathan?" Anna asked, wiping the tears from her eyes.

"He's the man in my nightmares," Carl answered.

Carl knocked on the big oak door of the Beauchamp home. Elijah was shuddering next to him. Carl put his hand on his shoulder. "It's gonna be fine," he whispered. He perceived a curtain move from the bay window on his right. The door opened. Mr. Beauchamp looked at the boys for a moment, then down at the box in Elijah's hand. He looked back up at them again and let out a sigh.

"Come in, then," he said.

They sat in the downstairs parlor. Mr. Beauchamp poured them brandies then settled into his chair. "How did he die?" he asked.

"Like the bravest man I ever knew," Elijah said, fighting back his tears. Carl reached over and squeezed his hand. Mr. Beauchamp allowed a brief bitter smile as he looked out the window for a moment.

"I would expect so," he said, then turned his eyes back to Elijah. "Tell me the story, please." Elijah did so, pausing at moments to sip his brandy to regain his composure. When he was done, Mr. Beauchamp thanked him, "…and thank you for bringing my boy home to me."

Carl was surprised, but then again, not surprised, at the turnout for Francis's funeral. "I wish Francis could see this…" he said, looking around at the faces of the people who had come to pay their respects to the young man who had delighted the ballrooms of Detroit and taught so many how to dance.

"He can, my love," Anna said, gripping his arm.

People laughed and cried as several speakers took to the podium and spoke about Francis's life and his passion for the cause for which he ultimately laid it down. Carl felt absolutely inept during his turn at the podium. It was hard to speak about another man's heroism without feeling a tinge of guilt at his own deficiency. He felt his words falling flat. He felt the accusation of cowardice coming from the silent crowd as he spoke about Francis's sacrifice. He shook his head, letting out a nervous scoff. He knew it was all in his mind, yet he could not bear to make eye contact with anyone while he spoke.

Elijah spoke next. He used his worm for support as he hobbled to the podium. His simple and earnest way of speaking about the man whom he loved and admired brought the whole house to tears. "He was everything I always wanted to be: intelligent, kind, and brave. He stood over me like a lion as the others ran. He went down fighting to the very end for what he believed in: that a man should be free, that a man's life matters. Francis..." he said, looking up at the ceiling of the church, "...I promise I won't waste this life you died defending. I'll never forget you, my friend. I love you, my brother." With that, he dropped his face into his hands and cried. All that could be heard throughout the church was soft crying.

The wake was a somewhat lighter affair as people mingled and enjoyed drinks and small plates of food in the ballroom of the Schmidt house. Soft string music mixed with the murmur of conversation and the clinking of plates and glasses. Elijah spent most of the time shaking hands and thanking the well-wishers who were eager to speak to him.

"I'm so afraid I may have insulted him," Mrs. Gareth said, dabbing her tears with a handkerchief. "I told him I couldn't tell you two apart. I said maybe the Army would find something useful for him to do. Oh, dear, I did this! I caused him to go and die!" She began to cry anew.

Elijah smiled, touching her lightly on the shoulder, "I'm sure you didn't, Mrs. Gareth. Francis did what he wanted to do, not because of anything anyone told him. I'm sure he took no offense, ma'am."

"Oh, you're a sweet boy," she said, "I just don't know how to talk to you people."

"Just like you talk to anyone else, ma'am. You're doing fine," he told her.

"Thank you," she said with tear-stained eyes as she squeezed his hand. "You're a kind man, Elijah."

Mr. Beauchamp spoke to him later, once he could get him alone. "We need to get you a proper replacement for the foot you lost. I have a friend who's a doctor. He makes prosthetics. I'll take care of the expenses. We'll get you the finest foot money can buy."

"That's very kind of you, Mr. Beauchamp. You don't have to do that for me," Elijah said.

Mr. Beauchamp looked at him for a moment. A sadness welled deep in his eyes.

"Francis was the end of my family, Elijah. After generations of building a prosperous business, the Beauchamps have been reduced to just me: a solitary man who can't take his fortune to the grave. Allow me to be kind to the man who saw more in my son than I did. Allow me this small atonement."

"Of course, sir," Elijah said, bowing his head with a little embarrassment.

"Now," Mr. Beauchamp's voice hardened, "you say you know the man who did this to my boy."

"I do…"

Carl had the dream again. He was pinned under a pile of bodies. Their dead eyes accusing him. Someone was digging through the bodies to get to him. He was relieved, thinking it was Elijah. Then he saw the green eyes and cruel smile peering through the tangle of limbs and faces. It was Lathan, chasing him through the pile of the dead. Carl turned into the pile, worming his way further into the pit, sensing Lathan behind him. Carl was looking for Francis among the dead. He couldn't find him. He could feel Lathan reaching out to him. Panic tore through him. He turned and screamed. He threw himself at his pursuer, screeching with hate and lust for vengeance.

He woke. Anna was snuggled up next to him, breathing softly. He watched the rise and fall of the bedsheet draped over her. He stared into the darkness of the room. How could he ever leave the comfort of this bed, the warmth of her body, the security of this life he had fallen into? Anna shuddered next to him. She was crying softly.

"Hey…" he said, putting his hand on her.

"You're leaving, aren't you," she said softly. Carl let out a sigh. "You're going after that man, the man that killed Francis."

Carl thought for a moment, then spoke, "I guess I didn't realize I was, but yet…I guess I knew I was. I… just hadn't allowed myself to think it out loud."

"Stay with me," she said, turning to him with tears blurring her eyes. "Stay and build a family with me. There is happiness and sanity here."

Carl's heart ached at seeing her suffer. He drew her nearer. The tears on her cheeks were hot against his chest. He was ashamed at his arousal. She pressed her warm body against him, kissing him hotly. He could feel the firm fulness of her thighs straddling him, the wetness between them brushing lightly against his maddening arousal.

"Anna…" he mumbled, feeling guilty over his pleasure of the sudden turn of events.

"Perhaps God will finally give us the child we've longed for." She whispered in between kisses. "Then you'll find a reason to live, instead of looking for one to die."

Carl fell into a deep, black, dreamless sleep after they finished. The early gray light was seeping through the window when he woke. Anna lay sleeping next to him. He wanted to throw his arms around her, squeeze her with all his might, and tell her how much he loved her, but he couldn't bear to disrupt the beautiful image of her sleeping so sweetly.

He got out of bed and threw on his nightshirt and smoking jacket to guard himself from the chill. Anna mumbled something, reaching out to the spot where he had been lying. He paused for a moment, then let out his breath once he knew she was still sleeping. He slipped downstairs, found his lacquered box, and opened it. His pipe was scratched, but still in good shape after he had kicked it over several nights before. There was a small amount of opium, too. Who would know if he decided to "chase the dragon" this early in the morning? He closed the box and put it away. The nausea and shakes would come soon. He knew he had to endure if he was going to ever break free from this slump and do what he felt he had to do if he ever wanted to call himself a man again.

A small amount of coal still smoldered in the cast iron stove. He opened up the bottom air vent, then added more coal. Soon, heat began to radiate. Anna would wake up to a warm house, he thought, and he'd have some coffee. He toasted some of last night's bread adding butter and jam to enjoy on the front porch. It was chilly in the early morning, but the hot coffee, silk jacket, and smoking cap kept him snug in his chair. The cold air was invigorating. He decided to walk.

He washed up, then put on trousers, a shirt, vest, frock coat, and stovepipe hat. He thought of his cane as he walked out the door. He had broken it. He hadn't replaced it yet. He realized there was no point. Everyone had seen him at the funeral without it. He didn't need to hide behind it anymore.

He walked past his mother's house. He thought about the old, heavy saber hanging over the mantel. This was the sword she said she had taken from a dead soldier during their escape from Mexico City the day his father was lost to them. He was tempted to fetch it and take it to the dueling grounds along the river near Belle Island and practice, but he didn't want to wake his mother or allow her to see through him and read his intentions. He kept walking. He passed the Beauchamp house where Elijah had been staying. Would he tell him his plans? Would he want to go? Would he be a bad friend for allowing Elijah to risk his life and freedom for Carl's need for revenge?

Someone was already there at the dueling grounds. He could see through the trees that helped conceal the spot used for illegal dueling, a man moving briskly with what appeared to be a pole in his hands. As Carl moved through the trees he could see it was Elijah. The big man stood in a crouched fighting stance with his worm in both hands, holding the iron spiral end forward. With his newly attached prosthetic foot, he could stand on both feet now without using the worm for support.

With a grunt, he shuffled forward extending his arms to drive the spiral end into an imaginary opponent, then swung it around over his head to deliver what would be a crushing blow as he stepped forward with his rear leg. The big man moving so quickly with his stiff artificial ankle looked awkward, yet surprisingly frightening.

"You move well with that new foot of yours," Carl said, stepping out from the trees.

'Sweet Jesus!" Elijah gasped, whipping around to face this new intruder.

"Please, don't screw me!" Carl said with irony, looking at the iron spiral end of the pole. "It's just me!"

Elijah dropped his shoulders allowing the worm to hang loosely in his hands, "Good heavens, Carl. You nearly scared the ghost out of me."

"Guard your flanks. It's the first rule of combat," Carl smiled at the big man.

"Well, I guess you got me then, Carl," Elijah said bashfully.

"Trust me, the only way I could get you is by sneaking up on ya," Carl said with humor.

"I was just playing around…you know…getting some exercise or something," Elijah said bashfully.

"Yeah, you look good. I was actually going to do the same. Maybe we could play together, just...um... promise not to hurt me."

Elijah smiled, "I'd like that. Francis and me used to play fight all the time. He taught me a lot, you know, that French boxing stuff. We also practiced with our bayonets or even with these artillery tools," he said, looking at his worm.

"Well, that's unfair. All he ever taught me was how to dance," Carl laughed. "Actually, he was a fine fencer. More of an épée man than a saber. C'mon," Carl picked up a stick holding it up like a sword, "let's see what you got." Elijah stepped forward with his worm looking suddenly extremely menacing. "Nice and easy, of course!" Carl threw up his free hand, "Don't hurt me!"

Elijah's terrifying face broke into the warm smile Carl was more used to. "Of course!"

Elijah broke the first three sticks Carl tried to use as practice blades. It didn't matter. For the first time in months, Carl felt happy and free. It was like being 12-years old again, playing out battles he had imagined as a child with his friend. They practiced, shared tips, and worked up an appetite. They went to a cafe for coffee and eggs with bacon and toast. Carl barely touched his food. The nausea and need for relief from the withdrawal were beginning to mount. He had mostly suggested they take breakfast at the cafe because Carl wanted to talk to him without Anna or Mr. Beauchamp hearing.

They both started talking at once, laughed, then bid the other to start. "Please," Carl said, "you go."

Elijah let out a sigh. "What happened to Francis wasn't war. It was murder," he said, looking off afar. "Lathan once made his living hunting black folk like me. Now, I'm going for him."

Carl let out a light laugh, shaking his head. "I had the same notion. I thought I was going to refuse you once you said you wanted to come with me…I was going to say it was too dangerous for you." Carl paused for a moment. He stifled a sudden urge to sob. "But I realized that you're not some sidekick for me to decide what's right or too dangerous. I realize that this is your fight as much as it's mine, maybe even more." He dropped his head and wiped his tears with his napkin. "I also realize that I'm not strong enough on my own. So I want to ask you now…" He looked up with tears glistening in his eyes, "can I go with you?"

Elijah blinked at him for a moment and let out his breath, "What about Anna?" Carl scoffed as he dropped and shook his head. "You got a life to build with her, a family."

Carl looked back up at him, his resolve now returning. "I have no life as long as that animal is still alive. I am no man until I win this war," he said, forcingly emphasizing each word with his finger jabbing the top of the table, causing the dishes to rattle. "Not the one between the states…my war."

The grim look on Carl's face set Elijah back into his chair for a moment. Then he let out a sigh, "Well, I was going to refuse you too, but honestly, I don't know how I'd do it without you."

Carl vomited.

"My goodness!" Elijah shuttled back in his chair to avoid being splattered. He then leaned forward and put his hand on Carl's back. "Are you alright? What can I do to help you?"

Carl looked up at him with red eyes, pale skin, and slobber hanging from his mouth. "I need you to lock me in a room somewhere and not let me out for a week no matter how much I beg."

Chapter Sixteen: "I Know Who You Are"

Liza scrubbed the floors of the Bethune townhouse in Memphis. She kept the place immaculate most of the time despite it becoming a flophouse for idle Yankee officers. She cared nothing for them. They weren't even really that demanding either. But the constant cleaning kept her in their presence and mostly invisible to them, especially when she made herself small, working the floor on her hands and knees, listening carefully to everything they said.

Most of the conversation was idle boasting, complaining, or what they were going to do when they got home. Every once in a while she'd pick up talk about the war. Usually, it was about that wily Forrest and his band of cavalry bandits constantly raiding Federal supply lines then disappearing before a large enough force could be mustered to catch him.

"Give me enough men and the rank to command them and I'll catch that son of a bitch," she heard Captain Logan say to a room full of fellow officers who had grown weary of his bravado.

"The only thing you'd manage to catch out there is typhoid, you fool," Captain Higginson quipped. A ripple of laughter broke out in the parlor. Liza did her best to suppress her own giggles at the boisterous Yankee officer's expense.

She heard a lot of this talk among them. They were young men from the North eager for action as newspaper stories poured in about battles raging seemingly everywhere but Memphis. They had been left behind as part of an occupying force that held the important supply hub for the war effort in the West.

But the war was heading east. President Lincoln put General Grant in charge of all Federal Armies. Grant promoted Sherman to replace him as commander of the Western Theater. Sherman began to draw his forces together for an all-out drive on Atlanta, the industrial heart of the Confederacy. This left precious few to protect his supply lines that ran through Tennessee. Now, Confederate Major General Nathan Bedford Forrest was running amok, raiding these lines and humiliating the few Federal troops left behind to guard them.

The men spoke boldly about confronting "that devil Forrest," but Liza could hear the fear hiding under their proud voices. And why wouldn't they be afraid? The news of the massacre at Fort Pillow had been shocking. No longer was this war some kind of gentlemen's duel over a disagreement. It was a vicious, ugly, knockdown fight in which each side was continuously upping the ante in brutality.

Liza was sick with worry. She had gotten no letters from her brother or his friend since shortly after they arrived at Fort Pillow. Even with a congressional investigation of the attack underway, there was still no information about who was dead, in a hospital, or taken prisoner. The best she could do was stay close to these Yankee occupiers and listen for gossip.

Liza hung up her apron after finishing her chores for the evening. As always, she was quiet and discreet as she slipped out, hoping to not catch Captain

Logan's attention. Hopefully, he was in his chair, nursing an after-dinner whiskey instead of lurking about. She stepped out the back door, closing it ever so softly to not make a sound.

She turned and let out a yelp as she ran right into a man's chest standing behind her.

Captain Logan caught her by the arms, "Whoa, there missy! No cause for alarm!"

"I'm sorry, Captain Logan. You surprised me," she said, quickly looking down from his smiling eyes to the brass buttons on his blue vest.

"Surprise is the key to victory, my dear," he chuckled. "But you and I are not enemies, are we?"

"Of course not, sir," she said softly.

"Why you're pretty enough to make a man go native…if you know what I mean," he said. He paused for a moment watching for her reaction. Disappointed, he filled the silence that followed, "But I suppose Ma and Pa would not be happy if I brought home a darkie as a souvenir."

Liza put her hand on his wrist to remove his grip from her arm. "I must go now, sir," she mumbled.

Logan tightened his grip. "Where is she? Kathryn?"

"I told you, she's staying with family."

"Where?" he hissed. "I'd like to write her."

Liza's mind raced for a suitable lie, "I'll get you an address, sir, they don't tell me nothin'."

The smile returned to his face. "That's a good girl," he patted her on the shoulder. "That wasn't so hard, was it?"

"No, sir," Liza pulled her shaw up to cover her shoulder. She stepped away as he released his grip. She looked up at him. He smiled and gave her a nod and a wink. She turned and started walking. She looked back. He was still standing there, smiling at her. She turned forward and walked briskly down the alley.

She felt those smiling eyes on her the whole way home. She stopped often to see if she was being followed. There were so many men in blue uniforms moving in and out of the pools of gaslight on the street, it was hard to tell. She took one more look around before tapping on the door to the small house where they had been staying in the colored part of town.

"Who is it?" Kathryn asked cautiously.

"It's me, hurry!" Liza said quietly.

The door opened. She quickly slipped inside, closing the door by leaning her back into it. She closed her eyes and let out a sigh. Kathryn was quick to return the latch.

"What is it?" Kathryn asked, fearfully. She was holding Roggie who had his head buried between her chin and her shoulder. Lil' Jimi B. was sitting on the floor, playing with his wooden horse on wheels which he pulled by a string.

"A ma!" he let out, leaping to his feet and running to throw his arms around Liza's legs.

"Oh, that man, Logan," she sighed, picking up the freckled toddler at her feet. His puff of light brown hair pressed against her cheek. "I was afraid he might follow me. He's adamant about finding you. He say he want an address to write yo…" She interrupted herself with a shriek as the door kicked open behind her.

"That won't be necessary, darlin'," Captain Logan said, bursting into the room.

The girls let out a scream. Roggie began to cry.

"So this is where 'away with family' is!" he growled.

"What in the world do you think you're doing?!" Kathryn shouted, clutching Roggie closer to her chest.

"No longer playing the fool, you whore! Whose baby is that?" he demanded.

"None of your damn business, now get out!" she yelled.

"I want to see his face. I want to know who he looks like," Logan said as he strode toward her. Liza put Lil' Jimi B. down and stood in his way with her hands out to stop him. "Stay out of this, Liza," he growled

He stopped. Something was hitting his leg. He looked down. The child Liza had set down was hitting him in the shin with a wooden horse. Logan let out a laugh. "A tough one we've got here," he said, looking back up at the girls. They weren't laughing. Their stern faces glared at him with fear and anger, then suddenly, their eyes widened with surprise. Logan blinked at them for a moment, wondering why.

A hand gripped the back of his collar and yanked him backward, causing him to tumble out the door onto his back into the muddy street outside.

"Damn!" an onlooker shouted.

Logan barely had time to prop himself up onto his elbows before a heavily bearded man burst out of the doorway and stomped him squarely in the crotch. Logan doubled over, bellowing in agony. The bearded man clutched him by the collar. Logan caught a glimpse of his ferocious blue eyes before the man started pummeling him in the face with his fist.

"Fight!" someone shouted.

Liza ran out and grabbed the man's arm before he could land another blow. "Kyle, stop! Please, you'll kill him!"

Kyle paused, then got back to his feet. Logan coughed and spit out blood. He slowly lifted himself off the ground, trying to brush the mud from his uniform with his dirty hands. He looked past Kyle towards the door, looking for Kathryn. Only the little boy stood there. In his hand was a broken toy horse he was holding like a club. Logan let out a bitter laugh. "Is this the animal you spawned that bastard child with?!" he shouted gesturing toward Kyle. "You threw away your life, Kathryn! I would have made an honest woman out of ya!"

"You better go now, Captain," Kyle said, staring the man down. Logan looked back at the grisly man with bright blue eyes. Liza had her arms wrapped around him.

"Wait a minute…" Logan mumbled. He looked back at the child in the doorway. He had blue eyes, too. But besides his light skin and freckles, he had African features and a puff of light brown curly hair. He looked back at Kyle, "I know who you are…" he stared, backing away. Kyle clenched his fist and made to move forward. Liza squeezed him and held him still.

"I know who you are!" Captain Logan shouted as he turned and hobbled awkwardly down the street.

Kyle watched him disappear into the darkness, "Fuck…"

"Come, get inside, quick!" Kathryn peered outside. She was still holding Roggie in her arms.

Liza looked at the crowd that had gathered around, "Go on, now! Show's over!"

"We can't stay here any longer," Kathryn said as she joined Liza and Kyle at the table. She had just put the children to bed. "It'll only be a matter of time before he returns with a force to arrest you," she said, looking at Kyle

"I'm so sorry," Liza began to cry. "This is my fault! I should have known he was following me."

"It's nobody's fault, honey," Kyle drew her near him. "It was only a matter of time."

"Still, beating the tar out of him probably didn't help matters much," Kathryn quipped.

"Yeah, I probably should have let Lil' Jimi B. finish him," Kyle said. The three broke into a light chuckle.

"That child sometimes…" Liza said, shaking her head.

"By the way," Kathryn interjected, "you got a letter today from Detroit. It's Elijah!"

"Oh, thank God!" Liza drew her hands to her breast. "He's alive."

"Do you want to read it?" Kathryn made to get up.

"I will," Liza caught her hand, stopping her from getting up, "We need to figure this out first. I'm just glad to know they made it."

"It simple, we take what we have and go right now," Kyle said.

Kathryn let out a sigh, "I just put them to bed."

"We might not get another chance, Kathryn," Kyle said flatly. They looked at each other for a moment. In the pause, they began to hear commotion in the street. Liza jumped up to peek out of the shuttered window.

"Oh, God, they're coming!" she gasped.

Kathryn turned back to her brother. "Quick, out the back door. We'll stall them."

"Shit!" Kyle hissed, "I can't leave you behind!"

"You're no help to us swinging from a rope, go!" Kathryn shoved him from his chair. Kyle stumbled towards the back door. He opened it to find several men in dark blue uniforms pointing bayonets at him. He turned. Kathryn was screaming as more of them came in from the front door. He put his hands up. He could feel the points of the bayonets poking at the small of his back. Captain Logan hobbled into the room, still smarting from his fall. His left eye was already swollen shut from the beating. He stopped to look at Kathryn.

"You didn't have to make this so hard," he said softly.

"Hmph!" Kathryn let out with contempt, looking away.

"One day you'll learn your place, woman," he said bitterly. He walked over to Kyle and punched him in the face. Kyle lost his balance and fell to one knee. The soldiers immediately shuffled forward with their bayonets, pinning him to the spot in case he tried to fight back. "That's for the unsportsmanlike attack on me earlier."

"I hardly call attacking women and children part of gentlemanly combat," Kyle grunted, rubbing his aching jaw.

"Take him away," Logan said flatly. Two of the soldiers lifted him to his feet and led him out the door. "Escort the two women back to my quarters for questioning."

"What about the children?" Kathryn gasped. "We can't leave them here alone!"

Logan let out a sigh, "Fine, leave the negress here to tend to them for now, but you, missy, have some answering to do!"

Chapter Seventeen: Preparing for War

Carl spent a miserable week chained to his bed. Short sweat-soaked dreams of delirium were broken up by fits of nausea, shaking, and vomiting. Elijah sat in a chair outside the door, shaking his head as he listened to the pleas.

"Please…" the voice inside croaked, "I'm begging you…"

Anna looked at Elijah with sympathy, knowing he was struggling with hearing his friend suffer. She squeezed his hands and kissed his forehead. They waited until Carl fell silent again to enter the room. The smell of sweat and vomit hit them as soon as they opened the door.

"*Mein Gott!*" Anna let out, setting down her bucket of warm water. She walked sharply to the window and opened it. "Pick him up," she said. Elijah unlocked the chain around his foot and scooped him out of bed. Carl hung loosely in his arms, his head drawn back and his arm dangling.

"He barely weighs a thing," Elijah said softly.

"Francis…" Carl called softly.

Anna quickly pulled the sheets from the bed and replaced them with new ones. Elijah sat down with him in the chair while Anna removed his clothes and washed him with a rag and warm water.

"I'm so sorry…" Carl mumbled.

"Hush, my darling," she cooed as they dressed him in fresh drawers and a nightshirt. Elijah laid him back in bed.

"Are you sure you don't need me to stay?" he asked.

"No, darling, you have done enough. I will see you tomorrow," she smiled.

"Alright, Ms Anna, if you need me, I'm just over at the Beauchamp house."

"Thank you," she said. Once Elijah was gone, she warmed up some broth on the coal stove and fed it to Carl, dabbing his chin with a napkin after each spoonful. When he'd take no more, she put the bowl away, took off her clothes, and snuggled up next to him.

Carl could feel the warmth of her thick and firm body pressed against him and the softness of her breath on his skin. "I love you…" he said softly.

"I know. I love you, too," she whispered.

Carl woke to bird songs and sunlight spilling through the window. It felt like he had crawled out of a black hole. The smell of bacon came drifting into the room. He threw off his sheets and checked. The chain was gone. He found Anna in the kitchen, frying bacon in her corset and bloomers. Her hair was up in a bun but several stands had broken free and were lying softly on her bare shoulders. Carl stood there for a moment watching her. She turned to him.

"Oh, he lives!" she smiled.

"Yeah and he's starving!" Carl said with enthusiasm.

"Good! We need to fatten you up, little piggy. There's coffee in the kettle. I'll make you some eggs."

Carl walked over to her. He threw his arms around her and kissed her neck. "You're the best thing that ever happened to me," he said softly in her ear.

"I know," she said, removing his hands and returning to the bacon.

Carl did his best to rebuild his strength in the days that followed. Long walks turned into runs. Soon he was practicing his fencing drills once again, advancing, retreating, parrying, and lunging along the shoreline of the Detroit River across from Belle Isle. Elijah began to join him, using a practice saber at first but then returning to his worm pole. "I don't think a black man can go walking around with one of them on they hip just yet," Elijah said, "but I got me a walkin' stick!"

"Maybe it's a bit stranger for you to walk around with an artillery tool, but suit yourself, my friend," Carl said as he panted. He found that even though Elijah was a little clumsy in learning proper saber technique, he was bruisingly effective with his improvised polearm.

After a few testing probes with the weapon, Elijah advanced, thrusting the iron screw tip forward. Carl was quick to block it with his practice saber as he shuffled back. But before he could return his front foot to the ground, Elijah sprung forward again swinging the other end of the pole around and sweeping Carl's foot out from underneath him. Carl landed on his side with an "Oof!" and then groaned in pain at the hard fall. He opened his eyes to see the pointy tip of the iron screw, inches from his face. Elijah spun the pole around and tucked it under his arm. He leaned forward and extended a hand to Carl.

"Alright," Carl said, getting up to his feet. "I'm convinced."

They returned to the Beauchamp house for coffee, biscuits, and ham. It was a place they could talk and plan, without upsetting Anna.

"First we have to figure out where he is," Carl said.

"If Lathan is still alive…" Elijah started, then finished what he was chewing, "…he's with Forrest, and they somewhere in northern Mississippi. At least that's what the paper say. I say we go to Memphis. It's not too far from the border. The Yankees, sorry, Carl, the Federals…"

"It's alright, I don't mind being called a Yankee, Elijah," Carl was quick to assure him.

"Alright then, them blue-bellied bastards are crawling all over Memphis, so you be safe there." The boys let out a laugh that had been absent for so long.

"Well, thanks for looking out for me," Carl chuckled.

"It's what I do," Elijah said, shaking his head. "Anyway, Memphis is where we can get information on they movement and make our plans. My sister can help us, too." Elijah looked away from Carl, suddenly worried he had opened up a topic that he shouldn't have.

Carl furrowed his brow, pursed his lips, and nodded his head, "Yeah, I suppose she can…" Carl said, trying not to seem too interested in being reacquainted with Liza, Kyle, and therefore, Kathryn.

"I sent her a letter, explaining what happened to Francis and all..." The two went quiet for a moment, looking away from each other, "Um..." he continued, "she hasn't written back yet."

"There's no telling the fate of letters with the war going," Carl shrugged.

"Boys," Mr. Beauchamp walked into the kitchen. Carl and Elijah immediately stood up. "Come into my office, I have some things for you."

Carl was astounded by the piles of furs and stacks of ledgers that filled the office he had only seen in his imagination up to this moment. "You can't go bumbling into the Confederacy with sabers and worm rods in your hands. I'm afraid you're going to have to be a bit more subtle." The two boys looked at each other then returned their gaze to Mr. Beauchamp. "I think these will serve you well," he continued, opening a wooden box. The boys leaned over to look. Inside were two pistols lying on red velvet lining. Alongside them were powder flasks, cartridge boxes, and boxes of percussion caps.

"They're beautiful!" Carl gasped. The pistols had blued octagonal barrels and cylinders with brass frames and walnut handles. Under the barrels were levers used to pack balls and powder into the cylinders. The back end of the cylinders had nipples where the percussion caps would be placed.

"Go ahead and pick them up," Mr. Beauchamp said. Carl was the first to snatch one from the box. He hefted it, feeling the weight, then pulled the hammer back and sighted down the barrel.

"It's a lot lighter than my old Wheelock and Allen," Carl said admiringly. He eased the hammer back with his thumb as he released the trigger.

"The 1851 Colt Navy is one of the best-balanced pistols ever made," Mr. Beauchamp assured him. "It's only a .36 caliber, but you can depend on it. It'll be a little easier to hide in your jacket than the new .44 Army model. They were given to me as a gift, years ago. I've never had use for them." Mr. Beauchamp then turned to Elijah, "Go ahead, son. It won't bite you."

Elijah carefully picked up the other revolver. It looked suddenly small in his hand. "I don't think I know how to work one. I've only shot a rifle before."

"I'll show you," Carl said. "It's just like your old rifle, but you have to load it six times instead of once."

"I have something else that might suit a man of your size," Mr. Beauchamp added. He went behind his desk and came back with a somewhat larger weapon in his hands. Elijah's eyes widened at the first glimpse of it. It had two large barrels side-by-side, each with its own hammer. The barrels had been shortened to be only 18-inches long. The wooden stock had been sawed off and sanded down to create a pistol grip.

"Twelve-gauge double-barrel shotgun, or as I've heard them called a 'street howitzer.' Fill these barrels full of buckshot and you'll clear a room with it. The kick would break most men's wrists, but I think a big boy like you can handle it."

"Wow…" Elijah mumbled as he held the weapon in his hands.

"Not very accurate at a distance, but deadly up close." Mr. Beauchamp added. "You'll be able to hide this in your bags or even under your coat. The truth is, you'll have to get close to do your work. I have one more thing to give you." He brought out another wooden box and opened it. Lying on blue velvet inside were two knives. They had wooden handles with brass crossguards and pommels. The six-inch blades were broad and mostly one-sided but had a shorter edge on the topside that curved downward dramatically to the tip creating a very fine and sharp point. "You might be in a situation where you can't use your firearms," Mr. Beauchamp explained. "The Bowie knife is the finest weapon for thrusting and slashing in tight quarters."

Carl picked up one of the knives, once again, testing it for weight and balance. "They're like pocket-sized sabers. Thank you, Mr. Beauchamp."

"Don't thank me," he said gravely. "I'm also going to bankroll your expedition." He put his hand up to stop Carl from speaking. "I do this for my own selfish reasons. I most likely am sending you boys off to die. I'm not a young man anymore and I was never much of a fighter when I was…" He paused for a moment, looking down. He looked back up at the boys, "I want you to avenge my son. I want to atone for my own failings as a father." He trembled for a moment, then found control. Elijah put his hand on his shoulder.

"You ain't asking us nothing we ain't want to do ourselves, sir," Elijah said.

The older man looked up at him and offered a rare smile, "If you survive, I would hope that you'd come back. There's a place for you here."

The boys couldn't wait to try out their new guns. They rode out the next day to find a place outside of the city.

"Alright," Carl demonstrated with one of the pistols, "pull the hammer back to the half-cocked position. That should allow you to turn the cylinder. Pour the powder from the flask into each cylinder from the front end. Stuff in a piece of wadding, then the ball. Now, pull the lever to ram balls tightly into each cylinder. Put a little gob of grease on each end to hold it all in. The grease should keep moisture from getting to your powder as well. Now, put a percussion cap on each nipple on the back end of the cylinder, and you're ready to shoot!"

They set up tin cans on a wooden fence and began shooting them, first taking careful aim, then practicing quickdraws from their waistbands and firing.

"Alright," Elijah said at last, "let's see what this 'street howitzer' do." He pulled the shotgun out of his bag and unrolled it from the blanket it was wrapped in. He poured powder into each barrel, then a large ball and four smaller balls followed by some wadding to hold the shot in place. He then pulled the two hammers back and placed firing caps on the nipples. "Alright, then," he said. Since the gun had no stock, he held it out with his right hand alone, straightening his back as he took aim.

BOOM!

The recoil swung his arm back violently. The gun flung through the air behind him.

BOOM!

It went off again as it landed. Both of them cringed with their eyes tightly shut.

"Jesus!" Carl exclaimed.

"Uh…" Elijah uttered as he opened his eyes, coming out of his crouch, "Maybe I ought to use two hands…"

"Yeah…" Carl looked back at him, "do that, then."

This time he only loaded one barrel to be safe. He held the pistol grip close to his side and the forestock firmly with his other hand.

BOOM!

The buck and ball tore the can to shreds as it flipped into the air and cluttered to the ground.

"Whew! Now that's a hand cannon!" Carl exclaimed.

They practiced with their new guns and knives as they planned for their expedition to Memphis over the days to come. Still, no response came from Liza, Kyle, or Kathryn. "Maybe they finally went west," Elijah said with a tinge of sadness in his voice.

"I suppose…" Carl replied, looking off distantly. The thought of not seeing his friends again left an empty feeling in his gut. He was ashamed to admit to himself that he was particularly put out by the prospect of never seeing Kathryn again. Even if he was happily married, he couldn't help but to want to at least see her once more.

"I've got to go home," he said, getting up from the table covered with maps and timetables for boats and trains. "Anna will be waiting for me and this is our last night and all…" the emptiness worsened as the words came out of his mouth. For a moment, he felt the urge to call the whole thing off, to run home and throw himself into Anna's arms and swear he'd never leave again. He shook his head and looked down at the floor. The sorrow began to spread through him as he grimaced. "I'll see you tomorrow," he said.

Anna greeted him at the door. She was in a simple white dress and a blue apron. Her hair was tied up but golden stands hung loosely on her bare shoulders. Her large blue eyes beheld him with sad sympathy. "I want to be perfectly honest, Carl," she told him. "I am upset with you. I think you're making a mistake and I don't want you to go." Carl dropped his head and let out a breath. She put her hand on his shoulder, "I know I can never understand this need to reply to violence with violence, or that it's so important to you that you'd be willing to sacrifice our happiness and even your life to repay it in kind, so I won't try. I love you. I don't want to ruin this night by being angry or begging you to stay. So let us enjoy our time together, fleeting that it is. Happiness is so easy to attain, yet we constantly insist on making it unreachable."

Carl looked up at her, tears blurring his eyes, "I love you…" He choked back a sob.

"I know, my love," she held him for a moment, then broke the embrace. "Come, let us eat, enjoy some wine, talk, and do the things that lovers do."

"You are just like your father," his mother chided him with the French accent she still carried after decades of living in the Americas. "Beautiful but foolish in your never-ending quests for honor and glory." They stood on the platform as passengers boarded the train bound for Chicago. Claudette was still a stunning beauty with her gray-streaked black hair, black dress, and the black veil that could barely hide her aristocratic features from the men that passed by and gawked. She clutched his shoulders with her hands and kissed him on each cheek. "Do not turn your beautiful wife into a wretched old widow like your mother, *mon enfant.*"

"I won't, mom," Carl said with a little shame. "Watch over her for me."

"Of course!" She smirked. "Someone has to be a man around here!"

Carl turned to Anna. He looked down for a moment and then back up at her. Her blue eyes were almost too much to bear. "I'll write along the way. I don't know if I'll be anywhere long enough for you to write back."

"I know," she said. "Carl, I know there's someone down there. Someone who still haunts your dreams."

"I…Anna…I…I love you…" He started.

"I know that, too," she said. "But you are whimsical, following your wild passions without thought sometimes." Carl dropped his head and let out a breath. Anna lifted his chin, forcing him to look at her, "I don't ask for me. I ask for the sake of your own tender heart. Don't hurt yourself over this woman. I may forgive you, but your shame will haunt you for all your life."

Carl hardened himself, trying to show as much strength as he could, "Anna, I love you. You're the best thing that ever happened to me. I would not do anything to sully that."

She smiled, "I know. Live, Carl. Do what you must do to carve this darkness out of your heart, but live, and when you're done, come find me. We can then build the happiness we deserve."

He kissed her. The train whistle blew as bellows of steam wisped around them. Elijah picked up his bags after receiving his kisses from Claudette. "Alright, then," he said, looking back at Carl. Carl broke his embrace with Anna. They looked at each other for a moment. Anna's face broke into a smile that nearly made Carl's knees crumble beneath him. He turned, picked up his bags, and followed Elijah onto the train.

"I thought you weren't going to bring that thing," Carl said, noticing the worm pole Elijah was using to help him walk on his prosthetic foot.

"I still need to walk," Elijah said. Carl shrugged his shoulders, then felt suddenly naked for not packing a saber. He patted the small of his back to feel the knife tucked into his pants there, then patted his side to feel the concealed pistol under his jacket.

Chapter Eighteen: The City of Spies

Kathryn stood on the veranda of the big house and watched the river of men in blue march by. It seemed endless. "They look like they in for a fight," Liza said flatly.

"They might find one they're not ready for," Kathryn smirked. She looked down at Roggie and Lil' Jimi B. The toddlers had gone completely silent as they watched the procession go by. It started with a flourish of drums as they poured out of Fort Pickering. Brass bands marched with them playing *The Battle Hymn of the Republic* and then *The Girl I Left Behind*. "That's me…" she mumbled in frustration to herself.

First came hundreds of men on horseback with their saber sheaths glinting in the morning sun. Then came the infantrymen carrying rifles on their shoulders, their bayonet sheaths bouncing against their legs as they marched. The white faces suddenly changed to hundreds of black men marching with a pride she had never seen amongst the slaves or even the freemen she had known. Their uniforms were buttoned up sharply, their faces held high with determination and defiance. Their sergeants called out a chant to keep them in step which ended with a cue to which the men replied in one voice, "Remember Fort Pillow!" Behind them were teams of horses pulling cannons, caissons, and carts full of supplies. Then came more cavalrymen bringing up the rear.

Kathryn let out a sigh. Among this horde of Yankee invaders was her only hope of saving her brother from the dreadful and infamous Irving Block Prison. Now she'd have to wait and hope that her benefactor survived and returned in time to intercede on her brother's behalf.

Colonel Dearing had certainly been her savior since the night of the arrest. While Kyle was shackled and marched off to prison, she was whisked away to the townhouse that once belonged to her family, but now was a flophouse for idle, low-ranking Yankee officers like the vile Captain Logan.

"Kathryn?!" Captain Higginson had exclaimed as soldiers brought her into the house. He turned to Captain Logan who was following behind. "What is the meaning of this?" he protested.

"Stay out of it, Paul. She's a spy and has been harboring her fugitive brother," Logan replied. Then to the soldiers, "Into my chambers so I can question her."

"This is an outrage!" Higginson exclaimed.

"War is an outrage," Logan shot back with dark humor. "Put her in the chair," he said once inside his room. Kathryn took the opportunity to slap him. "Jesus, woman!" he yelped. "Tie her damn hands down, too," he ordered the men.

"Hmph!" Kathryn scowled at him as the men tied her hands behind the back of the chair. Logan returned her scorn with a shrug and a humorous roll of his eyes. Once the soldiers were done he ordered them out of the room.

"Stand outside the door and don't let anyone in," he told them. "Now," he said, turning to his prisoner, "once you start acting like a lady, I'll start treating you like one. I can be very kind."

"I will claw your eyes out," she growled.

"You know, between you and your brother, I won't have a face left," he said lightly touching his bruised cheek. "Now tell me about all of your espionage activity and perhaps I can save you from the noose."

"I've got nothing to say to you."

"Why were you harboring a dangerous fugitive?"

"He's my brother. Why do think, you imbecile?!"

"Who's the father of your child?"

"A better man than you."

"Hmph, we'll see," he said. The door opened behind him. "I thought I said to not let anyone in!" he yelled turning his head. He immediately stood up. "Sir!"

A man with a gray speckled mustache that ended in twisted pointy waxed ends stepped into the room. His riding spurs clanked on the floor. "Release this woman at once!" he demanded.

"She's a spy and a harborer of a dangerous fugitive, Colonel Dearing," Captain Logan protested as the soldiers untied her bounds. "We captured her brother, Captain Kyle Bethune, the same spy that escaped at the Battle of Perryville. She's been hiding him in her home. God knows what information she's been handing him."

"Colonel, I beg your protection from this beast!" Kathryn pleaded, reading her change of fortune as it unfolded.

"You shall have it, madam," Dearing declared, then turned to Captain Logan. "I want a full report of your activities this evening on my desk first thing in the morning, Captain. I advise you to choose your words carefully. This is exactly the kind of behavior that pushes the locals to that devil Forrest's banner and drives them to murder our men. We cannot win this war without winning the hearts and minds. Now, madam," he turned to Kathryn who was rubbing the feeling back into her wrists, "if you would allow me the honor, I will personally escort you home."

"Why, I'd be delighted, sir," Kathryn purred with as much charm as she could muster. She couldn't help but give Logan a victorious smirk as she left him wallowing in his defeat and humiliation.

"I have to say, young lady," Colonel Dearing proclaimed as he took her arm, "you remind me an awful lot of my daughter Iris back home, who, thankfully, resembles her dear late mother Lilith more than me." He led her away. A small detail of soldiers followed them down the gaslit street.

Kathryn gave a polite chuckle, "Oh, Colonel, you honor me too much."

"Not at all, my dear, not at all."

Colonel Dearing continued to fill her ears with stories of his home in Illinois, his daughter, and his deceased wife. He couldn't help but point out multiple times how much Kathryn resembled them both. Kathryn endured him happily. It meant she didn't have to talk. She spent most of the walk plotting her next move. It was obvious she had this fish on the hook. Now she had to figure out how to reel him in and use him to her best advantage.

Colonel Dearing stumbled over his words a few times as he became distracted by the slow change of scenery. Gone were the gaslights and well-heeled passersby on the cobbled stone streets. Now it was dark and the streets were muddy. Black residents watched them suspiciously as they made their way through the neighborhood of shacks and tents.

"Clearly, this can't be the way," Dearing gasped. The soldiers behind them darted their eyes, nervously scanning the darkness for threats.

"Well, Colonel," Kathryn said, "after our plantation burned down, and then your men requisitioned my family's townhouse, there weren't many options for a Southern girl to lay her head."

They reached the small house where all the drama had occurred earlier. The front door lay broken next to the dark opening to the home. "Good heavens, this won't do at all!" Dearing gasped.

"Kathryn!" Liza called out, then dashed outside to throw her arms around her. "I was so worried! Where's Kyle?"

"I'm working on that," Kathryn said quietly, then to the Colonel, "Colonel Dearing, this is Liza Bethune. She'd been a servant to my family, but she's really like a sister to me."

"How do you do, madam?" Dearing said, taking a slight bow. Liza returned the gesture with a curtsy.

"Ah, mama!" Lil' Jimi B. blurted, running out the open doorway and wrapping his arms around her legs.

"Ugh! I just got these children to sleep!" Liza moaned. Colonel Dearing looked to the doorway where a doleful dark-haired boy peeped out from the darkness.

"The child…?" Dearing began.

"He's mine," Kathryn said, scooping Roggie up in her arms.

"I see…" Dearing said, giving the boy a smile and tussling his hair. Roggie buried his face in her bosom. "Sweet boy…and his father…?"

"Dead for all I know," Kathryn said quickly. "Just another flower cut down and trampled over by this war."

"I see…" Dearing said with reverence. "Madam, if I may…" He cleared his throat. "I've been requisitioned a rather large home for my current abode. Much more than I deserve or need, really. It's a rather dreary place, filled with the ghosts and memories of those who had once lived there. I would so like to fill it with the laughter of children once again. This," he said, motioning to the small rundown house with the broken door, "is a hard place for two young mothers and their children to live, even with the protection of your brother. I'd be much comforted if you would agree to take up residence in my home, with your own private room, of course. Please, allow this poor widower some consolation by allowing him to help a widow in need."

"Colonel Dearing! I don't know what to say!" Kathryn said, clutching her hand to her chest.

"A simple yes would suffice, madam," he said with a slight bow.

The girls settled into a comfortable domestic life that they had not enjoyed since fleeing the Bethune Plantation as it burned to the ground. Colonel Dearing spent most of his time away, and when he was home, he spent most of that time at the dinner table, reading and writing reports, and pouring over inventory lists of supplies and rosters of men. "There's a terrible amount of planning that goes into an expedition," he said as Kathryn brought him a plate of bacon, eggs, and toast.

"Where are you going?" she asked him.

"Wouldn't you like to know, my little spy," he said with humor.

"Well, my superiors in Richmond are expecting a smoke signal from me this very morning. I'd hate to disappoint them."

Dearing let out a chuckle, "Well, I'm sure it's no secret to them that this rogue Forrest is a thorn in our side. General Sherman wants him contained before he makes his foray into Georgia. He can't have Forrest and his band of guerrillas harassing his supply line or attacking his rear."

"I see," Kathryn said softly, wondering just how much information she could get from him and what she could do with it. "I hear General Forrest is invincible."

"Poppycock! Wily, for sure, but with more luck than martial ability, I assure you. He can intimidate small undermanned outposts into surrender all he wants, but I'm afraid the force General Sturgis is putting together will be too much for the 'Wizard of the Saddle.'"

"How many?" she asked.

Dearing peered over his reading glasses at her for a moment, contemplating just how much he had already said, "Enough."

"Of course," she said, bowing her head, then quickly changed the subject. "Have you had any luck with my brother?"

"Well, not for a lack of trying, my dear." His good nature quickly returned. "I'm afraid it's quite a delicate matter. It's been hard enough trying to shelter you and Liza from suspicion."

"He's rotting away in that detestable prison," she pleaded.

"I understand, my dear. I'm doing everything I can. They're very skittish right now with the launch of this expedition. It's a bad time to be asking for suspected spies to be released. Once we have this Forrest dead or in chains, I'm sure their ears will be more susceptible to pleas of mercy."

Kathryn watched as the last of the Federal column passed by the veranda. Behind them came the inevitable chain of sutlers and whores that followed every army into the field. Now that the street was clear, Kathryn took the basket she and Liza had prepared and made her way to the dreaded Irving Block Prison. It had been an office building before the war, four stories high on 2nd Street near the court square. The iron slates on the windows were originally intended to keep burglars out but the Yankees saw it better to keep people in. They converted the building into a dungeon where they tossed anyone who dared to defy their rule.

It was filthy and the men held there were underfed. Kathryn could smell the stench of unclean men and despair as she approached.

"That's far enough, missy," a guard told her, "this is no place for a lady."

"I have a pass from Colonel Dearing. I'm here to see my brother," she told him, allowing her distress to garner as much pity from the man she could. He shrugged.

"Come on, then," he led her inside.

She sat at a table in a small room with just enough light spilling in from the window behind her to see. She was beginning to feel nervous. They locked the door after leaving her to fetch her brother. It had been a while. What if they didn't let her leave? Suddenly, she regretted not using the privy before coming.

The door opened at last, startling her from her thoughts. The guards helped the most wretched creature she had ever seen enter and slump into the chair before her.

"Do you need one of us to stay in here with you, ma'am?" one of the guards asked.

"No, I'm perfectly safe here with my brother, thank you," she said, then turned her eyes to the badly beaten man before her. From behind the mess of blonde hair and grisly beard, Kyle's blue eyes found her. "Oh, Kyle…" she gasped, then found her strength, "I brought you some food," she said, pushing the basket forward. Kyle immediately plunged into it, stuffing himself with biscuits and ham. "Perhaps you should save some for later," she started.

"They'll just take it from me," he said, still chewing.

"The guards, have they been beating you?"

Kyle scoffed. "No, they're the only ones stopping the others from killing me," he said bitterly. "Turns out I'm a traitor to everyone. The other prisoners know who I am. I think some of them even have communications with Forrest."

"Then tell them this," she said in a hushed tone. "A force of about eight thousand men marched out of the city today. Colonel Dearing tells me their intention is to destroy Forrest."

"I think they already know. This city is full of spies."

Kathryn sat back in her chair. She let out a breath of frustration. She leaned forward again. "I'll come back regularly with food, fresh clothes, perhaps even a bucket to wash you if they'll let me. You've got to stay alive, Kyle. Colonel Dearing says he'll attend to your release once he returns from their expedition."

"I think Colonel Dearing is walking into a trap," Kyle replied.

Chapter Nineteen: The Crossroads

The knot in Carl's stomach got tighter and tighter as they got closer to Memphis. Each leg of the trip: the train to Chicago, the train to Cairo, and now the steamboat that carried them down the Mississippi, brought him closer to the enemy he swore he'd kill, and perhaps to the woman he thought he'd never see again, even though he always felt he would. Elijah had grown quiet. He stood at the rail and watched intently as familiar places went by: Island No. 10, New Madrid, and then much later, Fort Pillow. Carl put his hand on the big man's shoulder as they chugged past the steep bluff where their friend stood and fought instead of running, and died for it.

"What keeps us all from just killing one another?" Elijah said softly, staring at the bluff. "What makes someone a master and another a slave?"

"I guess it's all some kind illusion of society… until…of course, it all breaks down and we go to war," Carl said, trying to sound philosophical, but immediately feeling foolish instead.

"Hmm…" Elijah mused. "Maybe sometimes we need to."

Carl looked up at his friend, suddenly aware of the great violence the gentle Elijah could be capable of. He shuddered at the thought, then felt comfort knowing he was a friend.

They scanned the landing on the Memphis shore as their boat weaved its way through the cargo ships and gunboats that were coming and going. There was no sign of their friends waiting for them there. "I don't know if Liza got my letter," Elijah said as they carried their bags down the gangplank. "They probably too busy watching the children."

"Children?" Carl asked. Elijah cringed at the slip, suddenly wondering how they were going to explain Roggie to Carl, his unknowing father. He decided to leave that up to Ms. Kathryn and the others.

"Oh you know, they always be children around…" he said vaguely, feeling a sudden surge of panic run through him. Carl seemed too distracted by all the activity that swirled around them in the river town that had become a major wartime supply hub. Elijah let out a breath of relief. At least he had until they got to his sister's little house to think about what he'd say about the child.

Soon he forgot his worries as he joined in Carl's excitement at being in the busy city. It was Carl's first time and Elijah felt the joy of pointing things out like a well-acquainted veteran of the town. "That's *Young & Brothers Books*," he pointed to a shop along the street. "Francis bought me my first book there. Ooh, and that's the Gayoso Hotel! They say it's one of the finest in the world!"

Carl dropped his bags and let out a breath, "We need horses. How far is it to your sister's?"

The scenery began to change as they made their way through the streets of Memphis, stopping occasionally so Carl could catch his breath. The cobblestone streets eventually turned to mud. The stately homes and buildings turned to shacks and tents.

The white pedestrians had tapered away until Carl was the only one around who wasn't visibly of African descent.

"There it is, there, up the street," Elijah said, motioning with his head. "Won't they be surprised to see you! That is unless my letter got through."

Once again, Elijah felt the dread of Carl seeing Roggie and asking too many questions. Ms. Kathryn had made him swear an oath of secrecy about the child's father.

Carl shared in his friend's apprehension, but for different reasons. He was sure he truly loved his wife, Anna, but he couldn't help but feel a tinge of excitement at seeing Kathryn again, and that gave him a tinge of guilt as well.

"Well, that ain't right…" Elijah mumbled.

At first, Carl worried that the big man had read his thoughts, but then saw the scene that caused the concern. The small shack-like house had a broken door laying next to the entrance.

"This is where they live?!" Carl asked in wonderment. He couldn't imagine Kathryn living in such a hovel.

"Yeah…" Elijah said softly, cautiously approaching the doorway. "Hello!" he called, knocking on the doorframe. No response came. The floorboards creaked as he stepped into the dark house. "Liza?" The place was empty. He picked up an envelope laying on the floor. It was damp from exposure. The writing was blurry from the ink running, but he could still recognize it as his own. "Well," he said, turning to Carl who was now standing in the doorway, "they got my letter, but I don't think anyone read it. It's unopened."

"Where do you think they went?" Carl asked. Elijah was about to say he didn't know when a voice outside interrupted.

"They gone," a woman said. Carl turned to see a woman walking by, holding a basket on her head. "Soldiers done come and took 'em away, white folk and all."

"What?" Elijah asked as he stepped out to hear her better.

"They took that white boy and his sister first. Then came back and got the black girl and the babies too."

"Babies…?" Carl mumbled.

"When?" Elijah asked quickly, avoiding any more talk about the children.

"A coupla weeks, maybe. We already talkin' 'bout who goin' live in this house now," she said.

"Where'd they take them?" Carl asked.

"Don't know, but all them soldier done left," she said.

"Left?!" Carl asked.

"Uh-huh," she said, "nearly the whole lot of 'em, by the thousands, 'bout a week ago. They out huntin' after that Forrest fella."

The boys looked at each other then back to her. "Do you know which way?" Elijah asked.

"I don't know," she said, shrugging and rolling her eyes as she walked off. "Wherever that fool at."

It didn't take long to find out. Memphis was full of gossip and people were more than happy to share their knowledge with the two strangers who were asking for the latest.

"So we head southeast toward Corinth," Elijah said, sopping up his pork stew with a piece of cornbread. "Armies march pretty slow. We'll catch 'em."

They had finally found a tavern that allowed Elijah to eat at the table with Carl. The rain began to fall outside again.

"But they've been on the road for a week, there's no telling which way they've gone since," Carl said, taking a sip of his whiskey.

"Eight thousand men leave quite a trail from what I recall," Elijah said, then shoved the cornbread into his mouth and chewed while looking out at the rain.

"We're going to need horses," Carl said, watching the rain fall off the awning outside.

Captain Lathan Woods swatted the back of his horse's head to keep the beast quiet. They had ridden hard for nineteen miles through the hot and muggy Mississippi terrain to get to the fight. The last thing he needed was the animal giving away their position before they could pounce on the Federal rear.

His brigade commander had gotten an urgent message just hours before. Major General Forrest was holding down the vanguard of a superior Federal force just south of Brice's Crossroads, the place where the road from Memphis to Guntown intersected with the road between Jericho and Baldwin. All units were to converge on the crossroads with great haste before the enemy could reinforce his line of cavalry with his infantry, which at the time of the message, was still a few hours march behind.

A bridge crossed Tishomingo Creek just north of the crossroads in the Federal rear. There they had left over a hundred supply wagons guarded by colored troops. The narrow bridge and the cluster of wagons would stymy any attempt at an orderly retreat.

"Dismount," came the hushed order along the line.

Lathan hopped off his horse and handed the reins to one of the men charged with holding the horses while the rest of them took part in the attack. He checked his LeMat pistol to make sure each cylinder was loaded and had a percussion cap. He looked up at the company of men he commanded. Their dirty faces held him with serious anticipation.

"Stay together, boys, and keep killing until I tell you to stop, even if you have to club them to death with your pistols. You got me?" he said quietly. Men nodded, some smiled grimly and mumbled affirmatives. Lathan turned back and peered through the thick underbrush at the bounty of supplies guarded by the unsuspecting troops in blue. He smiled. He and his men were about to make a grand slaughter. Forrest was somewhere on the battleground. Hopefully, he would see Lathan's performance.

A bugle called out from the front to his left over the occasional crackle of musketry. It was repeated all around the battlefield. A cannonade roared from his left.

"Hold…" he could hear his colonel hiss. The men around him bristled with anticipation. They were excited. He was excited. A wave of men in blue fell back and flooded the area near the carts and the black soldiers guarding them. They clustered around the bridge, pushing and shoving each other out of the way as they tried to cross to safety. The retreat was on.

"Forward! his colonel called. The men started screaming their shrill yell as they lurched out of the underbrush.

"Come on!" Lathan shouted, as he burst forward firing his pistol into the mass of panicked blue men. He watched with great satisfaction as the man he had aimed at went tumbling to the ground. Some of the Yankees threw down their guns and jumped into the water to get away. They were trampled by the men behind them. Chasing them were Rebel artillerymen rolling their cannons forward by hand then firing canister into the masses of fleeing Yankees with devastating effect.

Lathan and his men moved forward, shooting down men as they walked over the dead and dying. Fire began to flicker in the darkening sky. Several of the carts were burning.

"Get those fires out, boys! Those are now our supplies!" someone yelled.

The raging fire was drying the blood splattered on his face. It was like some kind of hellish paradise. He could feel the crusting blood crackle on his face as he grinned. Smoke and glowing embers swirled around him as he fired the small shotgun barrel under his LeMat pistol. The man he pointed it at went sprawling face-first into the creek.

Then came the call, "C'mon, boys, back to your horses! The chase is on!"

"You hear that?" Elijah asked, removing his large-brimmed hat to listen.

"Hear what?" Carl asked with frustration. He was trying to get his boot unstuck from the mud without pulling his foot out of it.

"Listen…!" Elijah hissed. Carl stopped squishing his foot around to hear better. He felt it more than he heard: a low thump that pulsed against his chest.

"Them's cannons," Elijah said with confirmed confidence, replacing his hat on his head

"From where?" Carl asked looking around.

"No tellin' th' way the sound bounce around and all, but I figure, whatever they looking for, they found it."

The boys had been following the army's trail for days now on foot. Horses proved to be impossible to find. What the US Army hadn't already requisitioned, the Confederates captured on raids. Even donkeys, mules, and oxen were snatched up. So, the two packed what they could carry and started walking. Then the rain came again. The roads turned into rivers of mud, especially after thousands of men, horses, and cannons had passed through.

"At least they easy to follow," Elijah said.

"Cold comfort there," Carl answered. But it was hardly cold comfort when the rains tapered off and the early June heat set back in.

At dusk, they found a dry place off the road to put up their shelter halves to keep the rain off. They enjoyed some of the ham and hardtack they had purchased for the trip. They passed the bottle of whiskey between them to wash it down, listening quietly to the occasional sound of battle somewhere far off. They woke several times in the darkness, startled by gunshots, but not sure from where or how far off.

"Why are they shooting in the dark? Are they still fighting?" Carl whispered.

Elijah made a fire at sunrise and soon they had hot coffee to soak their hardtack for breakfast. Carl felt uneasy in the morning quiet as they set off once again. The occasional gunfire startled him from time to time.

"Maybe we close enough. We should stay off the road," Elijah suggested. It seemed like a good idea. Other than patches of thickets and undergrowth, it was easier to travel in the wilderness than on the mud-soaked road.

Once again, Carl pondered what their plan was if there was one at all. They had agreed that if Lathan still lived, he was most likely with Forrest's army, as he had been at Fort Pillow. Since General Sturgis's army was intent on destroying Forrest's forces, it seemed inevitable that the two would find each other. There was a lot of confidence around Memphis that the Federals had finally gotten serious enough to put together a force that could finally track down and kill the wily Rebel leader. Perhaps once that battle took place, the boys could search the dead and the prisoners for the man that had caused them so much grief. If he was still alive, they'd make sure he didn't stay that way for long.

Secretly, Carl hoped he was dead. Once the anger faded, the fear set back in. Lathan was the man who saw right through his ploy at New Madrid. Lathan had beaten him so easily in a fight there even though Carl tried to take him down with a surprise punch. He came face to face with him again outside of Corinth. Carl cringed at the paralyzing fear he felt when they stood before each other. Who knows what would have happened if Captain Newman hadn't intervened? And now more than ever, Lathan still haunted his dreams.

Carl looked up at Elijah who was using his worm pole to make a trail through the brush in front of him. He felt a sense of relief at seeing the big man with him. Then he felt ashamed. Was he hiding behind his friend?

He tried to shake the thought from his mind. He then started thinking how much easier this would have been if they had horses. That's when the horses came trotting by.

"What in the world…?" Elijah gasped as the riderless horses ran past.

Carl looked at the saddles as they went by, "Those are Federal cavalry horses! We should grab them!"

"I think we got a bigger problem," Elijah said. "Listen!"

Carl stopped for a moment to concentrate. Beyond the sound of the riderless horses nearby, he could hear heavy hooves galloping not too far off. Then he could hear men yelling in high-pitched voices.

"Run!" Carl shouted.

Elijah flinched as a pistol shot ricocheted off a tree near him. He started running as fast as his prosthetic foot allowed. The galloping and yelling got louder behind him. He ducked behind a tree as another bullet struck it. He pressed his worm pole to his chest and closed his eyes for a moment to listen. Then, sensing the timing, he swung back around with his pole, catching the rider's clothes with the iron screw attached at the end. He gave the pole a quick twist, snagging up the material of the man's shirt. Then with a mighty heave, he cast the man to the ground as the horse rode by. The man hit the dirt with a heavy thump. Elijah swung the pole around, ripping the man's clothes, then brought the other end crashing down on his head.

He panted as he looked at the blood oozing from the rider's broken skull. He only had a moment to think about it as another rider came bearing down on him. He dropped his worm pole, pulled out the shotgun, and fired as he looked up at the new threat. The rider tumbled to the ground as the horse brushed by. Elijah reached out and snatched the reins with his right hand while holding the forestock of the shotgun in his left. The horse slowed and then circled around to bump him with her muzzle. She let out nicker.

"That's a good girl," Elijah stroked her snout, then looked down at the two men he had just killed. The sound of pistols brought him back to the situation at hand. "...Carl," he murmured. He collected his worm pole and mounted the horse. She did a quick circling dance as she bore his weight then read the light taps of his heels and trotted forward under the command of his touch.

Carl had shot one of his pursers. The other was still out there, circling his hiding space which he had found under a fallen tree in a mess of brush and bramble. He looked down at his pistol as he panted. He wasn't sure how many times he had fired or how many shots he had left.

"Come out of there, God damn it, so I can shoot you!" the man called out in frustration, reigning in his horse as it stomped the ground and nickered with impatience.

"Like hell!" Carl couldn't help but to answer, then bit his lip and cringed at his own stupidity.

"So you *are* in there! I swear if you make me crawl up in there it'll be worse!" the man spat on the ground. Carl was weighing his options when a shotgun blast went off. He saw his pursuer hit the ground with a thump, his dead eyes staring at nothing. Carl stared at him for a moment until a deep voice broke him out of his trance.

"C'mon, man, we got to go!"

Chapter Twenty: On the Run

The news trickled in slowly. Rumors of a disaster spread through Memphis after riders arrived at Fort Pickering carrying dispatches on their nearly dead horses. In the days that followed, weary and broken men began to appear on the streets in tattered and muddy uniforms. The story came more and more into focus as the soldiers arrived. Forrest had crushed General Sturgis and his army in a stunning and devastating rout. Hundreds were dead, captured, or missing. Even more were wounded, clogging up the hospitals as doctors and nurses worked around the clock amputating limbs and comforting men as they died.

Kathryn was worried sick. If Colonel Dearing was lost, so was her chance at saving her brother. She was contemplating her next move when the front door opened with a creak. Leaping to her feet, she ran to see who it was. Colonel Dearing stood in the foyer. He took off his cap and rubbed the bald top of his head wearily. His once immaculate uniform hung on him, worn and muddy.

"My God, Loyd, you're alive!" she said, throwing her arms around him.

"Yes, my dear," Dearing smiled bitterly. He returned the embrace with some embarrassed awkwardness, "Although, I barely feel so."

"Come," she beckoned him into the house, "I'll have Liza draw a bath. Let me get you a whiskey. There's food, too."

"They seemed to come from every direction," Dearing told her as he looked down at his half-eaten plate of food. "Our cavalry had been holding them off just south of the place they call Brice's Crossroads. We had to march at the double-quick for miles to relieve them. The men were exhausted and parched by the time we got there. We barely had a moment to get in position when the Rebels descended upon all our flanks. It was a terrible slaughter. I saw so many a good man shot down…" Dearing's voice broke. He pulled his napkin to his mouth to stifle a sob.

Kathryn looked at him with sympathy. She got up and took his plate. "I'll bring you another whiskey, Loyd."

Colonel Dearing had pulled himself together by morning. The girls had cleaned his uniform and polished his boots as he slept. He gushed with gratitude when he awoke to the surprise. He sat at the table sipping his coffee and read the *Memphis Daily Appeal,* scoffing as he shook his head. "That's a pity…" he mumbled.

"What's that?" Kathryn asked.

"It seems General Sturgis has asked to be relieved of his command, and it's been granted," he told her. "I suppose there'll be another shuffling of command before we try again."

Kathryn paused for a moment, wondering if it were the right time. Then decided to go ahead with her plea, "Loyd, do you think you could tend to the matter of my brother, now that you're back and all?"

Dearing let out a sigh as he dropped the paper on the table. "I'm afraid these are trying times, my dear. There's talk of informants giving away our movements. That perhaps these whisperers are to blame for the thrashing we took from that devil Forrest. They're looking for scapegoats. It'd be a terribly inconvenient moment to ask for the release of a man thought to be a spy."

"Anymore inconvenience and my brother will be dead," she said flatly.

Carl and Elijah rode all day on their captured horses, trying to outpace the Rebel pursuers. It was clear that the Confederates were chasing the remnants of the Federal force, killing and capturing men as they went. The boys pressed eastward, away from the road to Memphis, hoping to stay out of the running battle between the hunters and their prey.

"Those four we encountered must have broken off from the main group to chase the horses," Carl mused. "Hopefully, we'll be able to swing wide enough around the rest of them." Still, every time they thought they were in the clear, the sound of men on horses somewhere behind them pushed them on.

By dusk, it had been several hours since the last sign of pursuers. They decided it was safe enough to stop and camp for the night, although it was still too risky for a fire. The boys munched on hardtack which they soaked in whiskey to soften it. They nibbled on the last of the ham while the horses picked away at the undergrowth growing around the tree where they were tied.

The next day they started swinging their path back north and west, trying to find a way back to Memphis while still avoiding Confederate cavalry. They passed miles of overgrown and abandoned farmland. The land had been stripped of resources by both armies constantly marching through and taking everything that could be eaten as they went until finally, families gave up and fled.

"We better find some food soon or we 'bout to run out," Elijah said.

They searched an abandoned farm, tying off their horses and taking their bags with them which they hoped to fill with anything missed by the last army to come through. They found very little but broken doors and empty cupboards. They checked the barn next.

"Plenty of hay for the horses," Elijah mused.

"Yeah…" Carl said softly, examining the stacks of loose hay on the ground and loft above. His eyes were adjusting to dark inside which contrasted with the thin lines of sunlight that spilled through the cracks between the wooden slats of the walls. "Something doesn't feel right…" he said, scanning the hay slowly until his eyes fell on another set of eyes peering back at him from under the hay, "…like we're being watched!" Carl drew his pistol quickly, aiming it at the eyes in the hay. Elijah whipped out his shotgun, cocking both hammers with two quick clicks of his thumb.

Two hands popped out of the hay, and then a head. "Don't shoot, mister! We…I mean, I mean you no harm!" A man emerged from the mound of hay. Strands clung to his black curly hair and ragged clothes. He looked over at Elijah in confusion as he recognized another black man, but this one was holding a shotgun on him. He looked back at Carl. "Wait, you ain't slave catchers, are you?"

"No," Carl said, as he uncocked his pistol and slid it back in its holster.

"And you ain't Confederate soldiers neither," the man said, lowering his arms.

"No, we're actually running from them ourselves," Carl said looking over at Elijah. Elijah gave him a shrug and uncocked his shotgun before tucking it back under his jacket.

"Hmm…you with the Yankee army? You sure do sound funny."

Carl let out a chuckle, "Well, not really, I guess. We've got our own business to attend to."

"I see…" the man said, then turning back to the mounds of hay. "Alright, I think these fellas are friendly. You can come out."

Carl blinked in amazement as several people suddenly emerged from the hay. He was doubly surprised to see some of them were white.

"We's runaways lookin' for the Yankee army. I hear they got jobs for color folk like me. And once you get to them, you free," the man told them.

"You wanna get to Memphis, then," Elijah told him. "They on the run theyselves. Rebel cavalry be runnin' 'em down all over the place."

Carl was still gawking at the white men hiding among them. "Surely, *you're* not runaway slaves," he said.

One of the men laughed and stepped forward. "Damn well feel like one!" he said. The others murmured in agreement. "Some of us are deserters or avoiding conscription altogether. I ain't got no money to own no negro, so I ain't gonna die so someone else can."

"If they find us," another spoke up, "they either force us to fight or shoot us for desertion. I ain't got no cause to fight. So I'm a runnin.'"

"I see…" Carl said, scanning the group of men, wondering what to do next. In that quiet moment, he heard the far-off rumbling of hooves and the calls of yelping men.

"Damn it! You led them right to us!" one of them shouted. Several of them bolted out the door in panic.

"Wait!" the first man they had spoken to called out, "Don't run! You'll give away our hiding space!" It was too late. The rest of them sprinted out of the barn and into the light.

"Come on," Carl turned to Elijah. They darted for the door. In the blinding sunlight, they could see the ragged group of men dashing for the wood line. Riders began to appear across the field in the other direction.

"We're cut off from our horses!" Carl gasped.

"Come on!" Elijah grabbed him by the shoulder, spinning him around in the direction of the fleeing men. They broke into a run, trying to catch up as the rest of the men were disappearing into the woods. They could hear hooves pounding the ground and the Rebel yell behind them. Once in the woods, they could see their fellow fugitives clustered together, scrambling to get through the thick brush ahead.

"Get down!" Elijah hissed, shoving Carl to the ground. They scrambled under the brush, trying to quiet their heavy breathing as horsemen came thundering past. Carl was sure they'd be trampled if not found outright. Gunshots rang out followed by cries of pain and fear. The two kept as still as possible, too scared to look at the commotion taking place deeper in the woods. After what seemed like an eternity, the horsemen returned, ambling slowly by. Carl sneaked a glimpse of the line of men following them. Their hands were tied behind their backs and their necks were bound together with a rope led by one of the horsemen. He froze, terrified they'd be spotted, and added to this chain of misery.

They didn't move or make a noise until it was completely dark. Carl was the first to break the silence. "God damn, I have to pee," he hissed.

The big man next to him started shaking, alarming Carl at first until Elijah let out a stifled chuckle. "Boy, you tickle me sometimes!" he said, trying to hush his own laughter. They got to their feet, stiff from lying in place for hours. Carl took a few steps away to relieve himself.

"Do you think we caused them to be captured?" he asked.

"I don't know," Elijah said, thoughtfully. "Truth is, they out everywhere looking for runners: slaves, Yankees, they own deserters, ain't nobody safe. Big group like that, they'd be found sooner or later I suppose."

"Yeah, I guess so," Carl said softly, but neither of them was convinced. Carl decided it was better not to bring it up anymore.

They ate the last of their last pieces of hardtack for breakfast before heading out again on foot. The horses were gone, another prize for the Rebel cavalrymen. Carl was just happy they hadn't been captured as well.

They came across more wetlands in the afternoon. "I've had about enough of this," Elijah said. Carl watched in quiet wonderment as the big man took off his boots, rolled up his trousers, and took off his shirt.

"What are you doing?" Carl asked.

"Getting dinner," he replied, as he waded in the water using his worm pole for balance. Carl watched with great curiosity. Elijah waded to a large fallen tree that sat half-submerged. He leaned his pole against the trunk, then bent over, digging around the tree with his hands.

"What in the world…?" Carl murmured as he watched his friend search around the trunk. Elijah's eyes brightened at last.

"Gotcha!" he let out in triumph as he jerked upright.

"Holy cow!" Carl gasped. Elijah stood in the knee-deep water, wrestling with a large fish that had a wide gaping mouth and what appeared to be whiskers. He had one hand deep in the creature's mouth, the other held on to its gill.

"Catfish tonight, brother!" Elijah called out, unable to ride his excitement. He slung the leviathan over his shoulder and waded out of the water.

They climbed up a small outcrop of rock in the woods. There they found a narrow entrance to a small cave which they hoped would hide the smoke and the light from their cooking fire as evening set in. Carl watched with fascination, helping where he could as the big man made a fire and then tore the skin off the fish, starting with his knife, then using his bare hands to rip it off with one swift pull. He then sharpened the end of a stick and drove it through the fish's mouth until it poked back out near the tail fin. He cradled the stick between two others that he had stuck in the ground on either side of the fire. Then rubbed salt, which he kept in a small leather pouch in his haversack, on the meat as he turned it. Soon the small cave was filled with the smell of smoky roasted fish.

"You are a remarkable man," Carl said, accepting the chunk of meat Elijah offered him.

"You learn a lot, growing up on a farm," Elijah said, stuffing a morsel in his mouth. "Can't always depend on the master to feed ya. My grandaddy took me fishin' a lot. Didn't know he was my grandaddy back then, though," Elijah said, looking off distantly.

Carl uncorked the bottle and handed it to him, "I'm glad you got to see him before he died, Elijah."

Elijah smiled and returned his eyes back to Carl. "Yeah, me too," he said, then took a swig before handing it back to Carl. "Here, you finish it."

Carl accepted the bottle, swirling the last of the whiskey around in the bottom. "I don't suppose he taught you how to find a bottle of whiskey under a log as well, did he?"

The two chuckled. "No, but we find some soon!"

Carl could see the early morning sunlight creeping into the cave as he opened his eyes. Wisps of smoke from the embers swirled and found their way out of the entrance. He was thinking it might have been a good idea to put the fire out completely before they fell asleep when he heard the nicker of a horse outside. Elijah's eyes popped open at the sound.

"Alright, come on out of there with your hands up if you don't want to get shot!" a man outside shouted.

The two looked at each other in panic.

"Don't make us climb up there and get ya!" another man shouted.

"Um…Just a minute!" Carl called back. Elijah's eyes widened at Carl's response. Carl whispered quickly, "Stay here. They don't know how many of us there are."

Elijah shook his head and started to speak, "Carl…"

"You know I'm right," Carl cut him off. "It'll be a lot worse for you than me. No point in both of us getting caught. Go to Nashville and wait for me there. The path to Memphis is cut off."

Elijah dropped his head and sighed. Carl smiled and squeezed his shoulder.

The first voice shouted again. "I'm gonna count to ten and then we're coming for you!"

"No need! I'm coming! Just gathering my things! Let me get my pants on!" Carl called back then rolled his eyes as he looked back at Elijah with humor. Elijah dropped his head again and shook it with a light but sad chuckle.

"Boy, you crazy," he said softly.

Carl crawled out of the entrance of the cave and looked down at the horsemen gathered below the outcrop. There were about a dozen of them, all in different variations of uniforms from both armies and civilian clothes as well as carbines, pistols, and large knives.

"Boy, I'm glad to see you!" Carl called down to them in the best Southern drawl he could muster. The men below furrowed their brows at the sound of him. "I was afraid you were Yankees."

One of the men leaned toward their apparent leader, motioning with his head toward Carl. "I think this boy may be feeble-minded. Doesn't sound right."

The leader stroked his heavy beard with a gloved hand. "You have a funny way of talking, friend. Where're you from?"

"Um, Texas. I'm here to join the fight!" Carl called back.

"Hmm..." the man mused for a moment. "You don't sound Texan to me."

"Yeah, I get that a lot, my dad's Mexican," Carl realized that this was the first time he said so openly. He wondered if it was a mistake in the silence that ensued. Finally, the leader spoke again.

"Well, come on down here and hand over your weapons, *amigo*, until we get this sorted out. I gotta tell ya, I'm not quite buying what you're selling here."

"Of course," Carl told him, then climbed down the rocks that made up the little outcrop he had been standing on. He tried his best not to seem nervous. "Here you go!" he pulled his pistol out, making sure to grab it by the cylinder and not the handle to be as nonthreatening as possible. He then reached around his back to pulled out his Bowie knife, holding it by the blade as he presented the weapons to the bearded leader. The man motioned to one of the men near him.

"Take his weapons, and bind his hands," he said, then to Carl, "Just a precaution, friend. Come with us, please."

"Certainly," Carl said, maintaining his smile as he handed the weapon to one man. Another leaped off his horse and tied his hands in front of him. He then remounted, holding the other end of the rope. Their leader gave a signal and the squad of horsemen moved off. Carl stumbled forward as the rope tugged him along. "Wouldn't it be easier to put me on a horse?" he asked, noticing the riderless horses the men were also leading along.

One of the men scoffed, "Sheesh! This feller ain't with us a minute and he's already tellin' us our business!" A round of chuckles passed through the men. Carl realized that it was probably best to keep his mouth shut from this point on.

Chapter Twenty-One: The Liar

Carl walked in silence for hours behind the Rebel squad along with their captured wagons and horses. He spent the time thinking through his options. He realized his current situation might be the part that was missing from his plan. He could very well be walking straight to the man he had set out to kill, Lathan Woods. The trick was to convince these men that he was truly an eager volunteer and not a conscription dodger, deserter, or worse, a Yankee spy. He reaffirmed that it was best to keep his mouth shut as much as possible, lest his hard consonants and short vowels betray his Detroit upbringing.

He also thought this new plan would end quickly if he were truly being brought directly into the presence of his enemy who would recognize him immediately. He hoped that wasn't the case, at least not yet. He was happy he had lapsed in his shaving these last few days, and probably wouldn't have the opportunity anytime soon. He resolved he'd let his facial hair grow, even if it typically came in uneven patches. For the time being, he'd let the grime and dirt from travel cover his face as much as possible.

The march was grueling as the heat began to rise. It didn't take long to feel the lack of food, water, or the need to relieve himself. He was about to ask when the halt came and some of the men dismounted. "Come on," one of them told him, giving his rope a tug. Apparently, several of them also had to relieve themselves. They took turns while others kept a lookout. Carl was allowed to go as well. Once finished, one of the men offered him his canteen.

"Drink up or you won't make it to camp," he said in a gruff voice.

"Thanks," Carl said, accepting the unexpected kindness.

They stopped again at mid-day. The man who had been leading Carl at the other end of the rope tied it to a tree and beckoned him to sit down. "Now, don't get any crazy ideas," he said as he turned to join the rest of the squad around a newly lit cooking fire. Others were sent off in various directions to watch for any approaching dangers.

The men talked in low voices, occasionally let out a chuckle. Soon, the smell of bacon wafted its way to him, teasing his hunger even more. Then the smell of cornmeal frying in the bacon grease poked at his stomach. Carl let out a groan as he saw the men sharing out the meal and carrying portions to the men keeping watch. At last, the leader of the band came and squatted near him. "Here," he said, handing him a tin plate with flat corn cakes and a few chunks of bacon. "Courtesy of the US Army," he said with irony. Carl lifted his bound hands for the plate.

"Thanks!" he said eagerly.

"Hang on a minute," the man put the plate down and untied Carl's hands. "There," he said, then handed him the plate. "Just so you're fairly warned: we'll shoot you if you even look like you're about to run."

"I understand," Carl said with his mouth full of fried cornmeal. The man remained squatting next to him as Carl chewed. Carl slowed his mouth as he moved his eyes nervously back to the heavily bearded man.

"I'm Captain Jedidiah Ranker. M'boys call me Captain Jeb. Who might you be?"

"Um, Carl..." he said then swallowed his food, "Carl Smith, sir."

"I thought you said your daddy was Mexican. Why isn't it Carlos?"

"Well, I guess it is," Carl said. "My mother kept my father's identity from me growing up. I suppose I'm really Carlos De La Vega."

"Why would she do that?" Captain Jeb said, sharpening his eyes as he scrutinized Carl's story.

"Well," Carl said, realizing the more truth there was in his story, the easier it was to tell, "because he fought for the other side in the Mexican War."

"I see," Captain Jeb said, nodding his head. "Why?"

Carl looked off as he thought for a moment, then returned his gaze to Captain Jeb, "I suppose because the US was invading his country."

"Exactly!" Captain Jeb said as his eyes twinkled with satisfaction.

No one bothered to retie Carl's hands after the meal. Better yet, they put him on one of the captured horses. "We'll move quicker this way," one of the men replied to Carl's surprised look. Still, they made sure Carl was kept in the middle of the column. He realized that Captain Jeb was not a man who felt like he needed to say anything twice. Carl understood that the threat remained. If he ran, they'd shoot him.

They didn't speak to him much for the rest of the journey, but they watched him carefully, always keeping him in the center of the group, even as they slept. Carl knew the lookouts would certainly be alerted if he even got up to relieve himself in the middle of the night. But Carl wasn't going anywhere. If he played it right, this might be his best opportunity to find and kill Lathan. He'd worry about escaping later, that is, if they didn't find him out first and put an end to his folly and most likely his life.

At last, they made it to Tupelo. The first thing that struck Carl was the number of blacks in the streets. They drove carts, shod horses, and worked the forges and kitchens. The women moved about carrying baskets on their heads. The streets were also full of soldiers in various forms of mixed uniforms and rags. Some loitered idly, playing poker and rolling dice, others marched smartly with their sergeants calling cadence as they passed. He was careful to keep his head down and not make eye contact with any of them. Still, he couldn't help but scan the faces, looking for Lathan.

The squad came to a halt. Captain Jeb saluted a man in a gray officer's uniform. "We were able to capture these horses and supply carts. We also have a prisoner." Carl frowned at the word "prisoner."

"A Yankee?" the officer returned the salute, then turned his eyes to Carl.

"Sounds like one, but he says he's from Texas. I don't know if I believe him. Says he came to join. He hasn't shown any indication of running yet."

"I see…" the officer mused for a moment. "Well, put him in with the absconders for now. We'll decide whether to give him a gun or a hanging later."

That didn't sound good at all. "Wait…" Carl started.

"Come down from the horse now, *Carlos*," Captain Jeb hushed him with his hand. He passed Carl off to two of his men who took him to the city jail. Carl winced at the musty smell of unwashed men inside. He turned to face his fellow prisoners in the dark overcrowded cell once the guard closed the door and turned the lock with a loud click.

"You!" a voice shouted, causing him to wince again. From the crowd of men came an accusatory finger and then the face of one of the white men he and Elijah had encountered in the barn just days before. "You're the reason I'm in here!"

The man charged, swinging his fist wildly. Carl jumped back, bumping the back of his head on the iron bars. The other prisoners cheered as the man rushed forward, wrapping his hands around Carl's throat. Carl coughed and gagged as he swung his fists wildly against the man's face. A whistle blew. The lock clicked. Guards rushed in, clubbing their way to the brawlers. They pulled the man off him as Carl landed a parting blow.

"Take him out of here!" their captain yelled. "He should never have been put in with them in the first place!" Then to the prisoners, "Next man to start a tussle will get a whippin'! Am I clear?!" The men hung their heads. Some mumbled affirmatives. Carl rubbed his throat in exasperation. He had only been locked up for a few seconds and was already fighting for his life. He wondered how'd he survive the night.

They came in the morning with buckets of water for the men to wash themselves then handed out tin cups of cornmeal gruel for breakfast. Afterward, they lined up the prisoners and marched them out to a field where soldiers stood in an open-ended square formation. A crowd of spectators was gathered around them. They were all facing a single wooden post sticking out of the ground at the open end of the square.

My God! Are they going to shoot us one at a time?! Carl wondered as gut-wrenching dread poured through his body. The sergeant leading them told them to halt and to stand at attention. Carl scanned the soldiers, looking for Lathan. A group of officers approached on horseback. At the head rode a tall slender man with a gray-streaked chin beard and ferocious blue eyes. Carl looked away quickly, terrified that those eyes would find him gawking among the prisoners.

"No! Let me go!"

The shouting snapped his attention away from the terrifying Confederate leader. They were bringing out the man that he had tussled with the day before. The man struggled against the soldiers who were mostly dragging him to the post. With some effort to contain him, they finally had him tied securely to the post.

"Put a gag on him," a captain said. Carl found himself ashamed that he was relieved not to have to hear the man's lamentations anymore.

"Private Robert Carter, you are convicted of desertion two times over, first from the Army of Tennessee and then from Major General Nathan Bedford Forrest's Cavalry Corps. You are sentenced to die." With that, the captain gave a nod. A sergeant called out.

"Firing squad, forward march!"

The riflemen marched into position, halted, then turned sharply toward their target. The captain pulled out his saber and held it aloft. The sergeant barked out the orders.

"Ready...! Aim...!"

Carl watched the man tied to the post try to squirm out of his bounds and try to speak through his gag. *Jesus, where does he think he's gonna go if he gets free?* Carl thought shaking his head. The sickening feeling roiled in his stomach. The captain brought his saber down.

"Fire!"

The crack of the rifles made Carl jump. The smell of rotten eggs from the gun smoke wisped past his face contributing to his revulsion. He regretted not looking away fast enough. Soldiers untied the limp man from the post and dragged him away leaving a trail of blood behind them. Carl turned and watched the captain of the firing squad speak to the frightening blue-eyed general who towered over him from his horse. He shuddered as the general looked up and caught Carl's eyes as he looked at the ranks of prisoners. Carl

277

quickly looked away. He watched the exchange of salutes in his periphery. The general and his staff turned their horses and left. Carl let out his breath of relief at seeing them go. He looked back as the captain walked towards him and the rest of the prisoners.

"Being of fighting age and not already in the service of our country already counts you as absconders, if not outright deserters, as per the conscription laws of the Confederate States of America," he told them. He eyed each man as he scanned the ranks. Carl fought the urge to somehow clarify that he was trying to volunteer. But once again, it seemed wiser to be quiet.

The captain continued, "Being that we're short on bullets…and of men, General Forrest has graciously decided to allow you into his service and give you the opportunity to redeem yourselves as men… instead of shooting you." That got a sinister chuckle from the group of sergeants standing by.

"If any man wishes to refuse this offer, please step forward. I'm sure we can find enough spare rounds to shoot you." Once again, a round of chuckles came from sergeants followed by silence as the prisoners looked down and pawed the ground with their feet.

"Excellent. These sergeants will take your oaths. I recommend you mean what you repeat. We'll assign you to units later," he said, then turned to the collection of noncommissioned officers near him. "Sergeants, swear these men in," he said then strode away.

Carl waited idly, listening to the men make their oaths, wondering what he had gotten himself into and how'd ever get out of it.

"Alright then, son," a sergeant approached him. "Raise your right hand." Carl suddenly felt the verge of panic run through him now that the moment was upon him.

"Um...yeah," he said, raising his hand.

"Repeat after me: I, state your name..." the sergeant said.

"I, Carl Smith..." Carl repeated.

"You're a liar," another voice interrupted. Carl and the sergeant turned to see from whom. "Go on to the next, sergeant. I'll handle this one," Captain Jeb said.

"Of course, sir," the sergeant said and moved off.

Captain Jeb moved uncomfortably close to Carl, reading him with his eyes. Carl could smell the campfire smoke in his beard. Jeb spoke low and pointedly, "You're a liar, *Carlos*. If I weren't a civilized man, I'd whip the truth out of you." Carl swallowed hard, trying not to look away. "I can't rightfully denounce you as a spy until I know for sure. So until I know, I'm keeping you close to me so I can shoot you myself once I do. You understand me?"

"Yes, sir," Carl said feebly.

"...and you can knock off that fake accent. You ain't foolin' no one, and frankly, it's just hard on the ear. Now, raise your right hand, *Carlos De La Vega*, and repeat after me."

Like in a trance, Carl lifted his hand and repeated the oath that Captain Jeb dictated to him. It felt like a dream in which he was both tunnel-visioned and hyper-aware at the same time. It felt so alien to repeat the name he supposed the father he could not remember had meant for him, a name he had never used for himself.

"I, Carlos De La Vega," he repeated, "do solemnly swear and affirm that while I continue in the service, I will bear true faith, and yield obedience to the Confederate States of America, and that I will serve them honestly and faithfully against their enemies, and that I will observe and obey the orders of the President of the Confederate States, and the orders of the officers appointed over me, according to the Rules and Articles of War."

Captain Jeb smiled slowly upon finishing, revealing the chilling facial expression for the first time to Carl, "Welcome to the Confederate Army, Carlos," he said as he handed him back his Colt revolver and Bowie knife.

Chapter Twenty-Two: The Trap

Kathryn would have almost enjoyed the panic that ran through the streets of Memphis if it hadn't been such an inconvenience for her in her effort to save her brother from the hellhole that was the Irving Block Prison. Still, she took great satisfaction at seeing the look of terror on the Yankee soldiers' faces as they prepared for Forrest and his hellions to surge into the city at any moment as they rode down the last remnants of Sturgis's army.

Let them come, she thought smugly, ignoring the hat-tipping and bowing from the pathetic Northern men she passed in the street. She smirked with contempt as she fanned herself. *Forrest would teach these cowards how a real man fights,* she thought. She reaffirmed this belief in the changes she saw in her brother. True, his face still bore the cuts and bruises from fresh violence, but there was a growing confidence in his demeanor. He was beginning to win fights. Still, he was cautious as ever when it came to family.

"I want you to take Liza and the children as far away from here as possible," he told her from the other side of the table in the visiting room.

"And go where?" she laughed. Kyle sighed. He closed his eyes and rubbed the bridge of his nose as he thought.

"Look," she said, "we're perfectly safe with Colonel Dearing. He promises he'll help once things settle down...Or even better, if General Forrest takes the city, he'll certainly release all of our boys from this

God-forsaken place." She saw all the confidence in Kyle wash away. His face went pale at the mere mention of the name.

"The Confederates want to hang me more than the Yankees do," Kyle said, shaking his head. "That's why I'm constantly fighting off the other prisoners. Forrest knows me personally. The first thing he'll do is take me out and shoot me."

Kathryn bit her lip as she thought. Then leaned forward with new energy. "Look, maybe we could show them that you're truly loyal to the cause. That you're useful." Kyle slumped back in his chair and shook his head.

"Give me the names of every important Confederate you know that are held here. Surely, General Forrest won't abide by the cruelty they've endured. Surely, he'll see your shared misery as proof of innocence."

Kathryn's newfound hope quickly slipped away in the days that followed. Forrest dropped his pursuit of Sturgis's stragglers and withdrew to Tupelo. The Yankees' fear of an attack on the city and their general wound-licking gave way to a new confidence as thousands of veteran troops arrived daily by riverboat. The talk in the city went from defending against Forrest and his unstoppable hordes to a new force, fourteen thousand-strong, preparing to hunt him down and put an end to *Wizard of the Saddle* for good.

Preparing for the new expedition also took up much of Colonel Dearing's time, once again, distracting him from being any help in her brother's plight.

"My dear, I assure you," he said, as they stepped onto the platform at the train depot, "once we have Sherman's supply lines secure, there won't be such worry about *spies* lurking in the jails. The authorities will be much more amenable to our efforts to free him."

Kathryn sighed, looking past the colonel. Thousands of men behind him were loading into boxcars. Even more climbed on top of them, crowding the roofs until the rickety structures swayed under the weight, threatening to collapse and crush the men inside. Hundreds of horses were loaded into other cars, their riders also found places to sit on top. Men and mules labored to hoist cannons onto the flatcars. Once secure, the crews found places among them to sit for the ride. This was just one of many trips the train would be taking out to La Grange, the staging ground for the expedition south into Northern Mississippi. Kathryn wondered what General Forrest and the other Confederate leaders could possibly have out there to contest such an enormous force.

"Kathryn," Dearing drew her attention back softly. She returned her eyes to his. His eyes softened as he took her hands, "I would hope that once I return…" he dropped his head for a moment, searching for words and courage. He looked back up at her and cleared his throat. "…I hope that I may court you properly." He smiled softly, relieved that he had finally said it, but then quivered slightly as he braced himself for her answer.

She smiled sweetly at him, reaching out to touch his cheek. "Loyd…" she said. He reached up and pressed her hand to his face. She continued "…in the absence of my father, you will have to ask my brother for permission."

Dearing let out a light bitter chuckle, dropping his eyes to his feet and shaking his head. He knew she had played the moment well. He returned his gaze to her, "Of course, my dear."

"…And to do that, you have to survive," she said. Loyd's smile returned in earnest at the hint of concern for his own well-being from this beautiful lady before him. "Come back to me, Loyd. I'll be waiting."

"Of course, madam," he said, kissing her hand, then strode away, beaming with a boyish delight he hadn't felt in decades.

Kathryn watched her last chance to save her brother board the car which was reserved for officers of his rank. The train belched out a cloud of steam and black smoke. The whistle blew and the train lurched forward with a chug. She watched it slowly pull away, increasing its speed ever so slightly. She suddenly furrowed her brow as she watched a man sitting on top of one of the cars. He stuck his leg out to touch a post as the train passed, lost his balance, and tumbled to the ground with a hard thump. His friends called to him with alarm. They reached out in a useless gesture to help. He lay there on the ground, sprawled and unmoving. At last, he sat up and shook his head to clear it from a daze. The train rolled by him. Realizing he was missing it, he jumped to his feet and began to run, desperately trying to keep up as the train began to outpace him.

She watched the scene play out in the shimmering hot summer air for a moment before turning and walking away. She fanned herself and scoffed. *This was why the Yankees can't accomplish anything,* she thought.

"Here they come again," Lathan told his men. "Hold your fire until I say. Remember, we're just bait. Kill as many as you can, but be ready to pull back in an instant!" He wiped the sweat from his eyes and peered back down from their trench on Pinson's Hill. Men in blue spilled into marshy land below. Lathan and his boys were with Brigadier General Chalmers's Division. They had been sent out to harass the two Federal columns that slowly rolled southward, robbing, raiding, and burning farms as they went. Lathan's boys were furious and hot for revenge. He had to remind them that this was not the fight they were aching to have, it was just the beginning of a trap.

The Yankees had made it Pontotoc, Mississippi, a town nearly twenty miles west of Tupelo. The Rebels built defensive lines on Pinson's Hill, just south of town, cutting off the road to Okolona. There they would try to hold the Yankees off just long enough for Major General Forrest to set his trap, then let them through.

Forrest and his immediate commander, the newly promoted Lieutenant General Stephen D. Lee, were sure the goal of the Yankee expedition was the rail line at Okolona. It fed the Confederates supplies and reinforcements from as far south as Mobile, Alabama, on the Gulf of Mexico. Chalmers was to hold the Yankees off as long as he could to give Forrest time to dig in and fortify. Then Chalmers was to fall back and draw the enemy south to Okolona where Forrest and the rest of his men would be lying in wait to destroy them.

The sun baked down on Lathan and his men's heads as they watched the dismounted Federal cavalrymen creep cautiously across the marshy valley below. He flinched as their own Rebel batteries opened up with a roar. "Too soon…" he mumbled. Rifles and carbines crackled to life along the Confederate trenches. His own men started shouldering their weapons, excited to join in the fight. "Not yet!" he told them, "they're too far away." Then peering back down at the Yankee troops below he let out a hiss, "Damn it! We spooked them!"

The Yankees stopped, flinching at the sudden barrage from above that had not yet found its range. Some of them started shouting and twirling their sabers in the air. Soon, they were slinking back into the woods on the other side of the swampy bottoms, disappearing from sight.

The Confederates waited for them to reappear. They clutched their weapons as they scanned the woods for the next assault. It didn't come. Eventually, the tension eased. Men set their rifles down and relaxed. By nightfall it was apparent, the assault wasn't coming. Now the Rebels were beginning to worry.

Carl took a moment from digging to wipe his brow before shoving his spade back into the ground. He certainly didn't want to be yelled at by one of the sergeants for shirking. He had forgotten how hot and humid it could get in the South. Now he wondered how he'd bear it again.

He worked alongside Rebel soldiers and hundreds of slaves that had been taken from the nearby farms and forced to help build the fortifications at Okolona. They were digging trenches and building dirt walls on the north side of town. He worried at times that he might be mistaken for one of the slaves as much as he was prodded to work. He shook off the thought. Unlike them, he still had his pistol and knife on him, marking him as a soldier. This was required by Forrest's *General Order Number 56* stating that every soldier had to be armed and ready to fight at all times.

His time with the Confederates so far had been a whirlwind of ever-changing circumstances. He had hardly any time to worry about fitting in after taking the oath. News of the advancing Federal columns set them into a flurry of activity. Carl and his new company marched south to Okolona with the rest of Forrest's corps which was a mix of cavalry, infantry, and artillery. Many of the infantrymen were actually dismounted cavalry since serviceable horses had become a precious commodity.

He considered himself lucky to have been claimed by Captain Jeb, even though he found the man to be terrifying and dangerously suspicious. Still, Jeb took care of his boys making sure they stayed mounted, well-equipped, fed, and watered. He also made sure they had a good spot to set up camp every time they stopped for the night.

Carl marveled at how loose, yet fluid, the Rebel army operated. It was hard to tell who was who or what their ranks were as men wore all sorts of combinations of uniforms and civilian clothing. Some even dressed in Federal blues taken from captured supplies. Units were shuffled and reassigned to different commands. It was all quite confusing to him, yet everyone seemed to know where he was supposed to be and what he was supposed to be doing. There seemed to be a deeper commitment and cooperation among these men that didn't require the stiff regulation he was used to in the Federal Army.

The men carried different weapons as well. He recognized plenty of British Enfield muskets, which had been popular among the Rebels from the start of the war. Many of the men carried captured US Springfield rifles as well. The rest carried all sorts of carbines and even sawed-off shotguns from home. More than anything, men carried pistols, and usually more than one. They were easy to draw and fire from the saddle. They could be fired multiple times before needing to reload and the more pistols you had, the more you could fire without reloading. Carl felt particularly under armed with his single pistol. Still, here he was among what had been the enemy from the start of the war and they still allowed him to carry a pistol and a fighting knife.

The job detail might have been another step in gaining trust. That, or they finally decided he was more useful as a slave than a soldier. As watchful as Captain Jeb had been of him, he had no problem volunteering Carl when the call came for men to join the labor parties once they got to Okolona. Carl found himself worrying that this was where he'd be stuck for the rest of the war. Would Captain Jeb even take him back later, or was he a slave now?

The work was hot, dirty, and backbreaking, but at least it kept him away from the prying questions of the other soldiers. So he dug and dug, lost in his thoughts as he listened to the black workers around him sing hymns and labor songs. It seemed cruelly ironic that these people would be forced to work to help those who fought to keep them in slavery.

A bugle call broke him from his thoughts. A rattle of snare drums followed. Carl looked up from his work. The slaves around him kept working, ignoring the call altogether. The soldiers, however, were dropping their shovels, wiping the dirt off their hands, and running off to find their units. They were happy to break away from the work they felt was better suited for slaves. Carl looked at the black workers around him. They returned his gaze with large, doleful eyes.

"Um, sorry…" he said as they blinked at him, "I got to go." He carefully set his spade down and ran off to join the rest, feeling slightly guilty at his happiness at leaving the black men to finish the job.

One of the workers shrugged his shoulders as he watched the last of the white men flee the job, leaving the slaves alone and unsupervised. He set back to work, starting the next hymn.

"When Israel was in Egypt land…" he sang out in a rich baritone voice.

"Let my people go…" the others joined in.

Carl ran along the ragged groups of men collecting into their companies, regiments, and brigades on the ground between town and the newly built defenses on the highland they called "Prairie Mound." He felt a bit of panic, worried that he wouldn't find them in time, that he'd still be bumbling around looking once the corps was called to attention.

"Hey, *Carlos*, over here!"

A wave of relief washed over him at hearing the newly familiar voice, regardless of the chuckles that came from the others at his expense. He found his place among Captain Jeb's men and waited to be called to attention. He waited a while, quietly listening to the other men talk. Chalmers's division was supposed to be drawing the Yankees southward to Okolona where the rest of Forrest's corps would envelop and destroy them. Something must have gone wrong and now the men guessed at what it could be.

"Here he comes now," one of the men said. Carl looked up to see the heavily bearded Captain Jeb approach.

"Alright boys," Jeb told them, "I just spoke to the colonel. We need to break camp and mount. We're riding north to Pinson's Hill at Pontotoc immediately."

"What's going on, Captain?" one of the men asked.

Jeb paused for a moment, then told him what he knew. "The Yanks didn't take the bait. Instead of chasing Chalmers to us, they demurred. Now Stephen Lee and Forrest are afraid the Yankees are going to scurry back to Memphis without a fight. We got to catch them and force 'em into one before they do, even if it's on the ground of their choosing."

"Ha!" one of the men let out. "We ain't even started and we already got 'em licked!"

The column pulled out within the hour. Carl was relieved not to be left behind with the work crews. He considered himself lucky to be on horseback, as well. Several of the cavalry regiments had been dismounted for the lack of horses. They marched in the rear as infantry. He couldn't imagine making the march on foot in this blistering heat.

Captain Jeb's partisans remained mounted. They rode in the column not far from where Lieutenant General Stephen Lee and Major General Forrest led. He knew this luck came from Jeb's desire to keep him close due to his mistrust and not for any merit Carl had shown. Still, Jeb had regarded him with something of a smile when Carl had first returned to the company covered in dirt. "Looks like you've been making yourself useful, Carlos."

"Um, yes, sir," Carl had replied sheepishly.

Now Carl followed him quietly as his horse ambled along the dusty road. He tried to scan as many faces of troops around him without appearing to be doing so. He was looking for Lathan among the thousands, hoping to find him before Lathan found him first.

Lathan slept lightly in the trench of their forward picket position with his men. He was semi-conscious of the changing of the watch through the night. He kept himself at a half-sleep, ready to leap into action as soon as the occasion arose. He popped an eye open at the sound of a distant bugle. He checked his watch by the light of the waxing moon now hanging low in the western sky. It was only two past midnight.

"At it early this morning, they are," Sergeant Billington whispered, detecting that Lathan was awake.

"Run back to the colonel, Tom. Make sure they're aware at headquarters," he said quietly, then peered into the darkness of the valley below that separated them from the enemy. The "ra-ta-ta-tat" of drums followed, then the sound of men moving around came from across the way. The Yankees were up to something.

Tom returned after a few moments. "Colonel says to hold tight and keep listening. Forrest's Corps is still arriving and getting into position as we speak. He says if the Yanks attack, we'll be ready. If they run, we'll ride them down."

Lathan nodded with a grunt then resumed his snoozing. He dipped in and out of consciousness, still listening for clues of what the Feds were doing. They got quieter and quieter as the early hours crept on. At the beginning of the soft gray light, he sent Tom with a small team to creep forward and see what was happening. He watched the men shuffle out in a low crouch, disappearing into the early morning mist that rose up from the wetlands below. Moments later, they came trotting back, fully upright.

"They're gone!" Tom called out breathlessly as he leaped back into the entrenchment.

Chapter Twenty-Three: A Change of Course

Carl felt he had barely closed his eyes before he was roused from the spot on the ground he had found to catch a few moments of sleep. "Saddle up. We're heading out," someone said, nudging Carl with his foot. It seemed they had just arrived at Pinson's Hill moments before after a long hard march, but the early daylight was evidence that he had slept longer than he thought.

"The Yanks have stolen a march on us," Captain Jeb told them, heaving himself onto his horse. "We've got to find their rear and force them to turn and fight us." He gave his mount a light kick on the sides, pulled the reins to the right, and put the beast into motion. The rest of his men fell in behind him.

Forrest's mounted troops fanned out in search of the Yankee column. By the time they realized they had guessed wrong, it was too late. The Federals weren't retreating to Memphis. They had instead marched due east for Tupelo, which the Confederates had left undefended. Now the Yankees were hours ahead of them. No longer could the Rebels hope to entice the Federals to attack them in their fortifications at Okolona or even Pinson's Hill. Now, the best they could hope for was a fight on open ground before the Yankees could take up a strong, fortified position at Tupelo and force the Rebels to wreck themselves attacking their works instead.

Forrest lashed out at the Federal rear with frantic urgency, driving his six regiments of horsemen and two pieces of flying artillery into their column. But the Federals put up a well-organized rearguard. Their cavalry found multiple defendable positions on hills and in groves along the road to Tupelo. There, they would fire on their pursuers before falling back to find another position behind the next line of the defense. They played this methodical leapfrog in reverse as the rest of the column hurried to Tupelo. The Rebels had to dismount to save their horses in order to contest these defensive lines. This slowed their pursuit as the Yankees got away.

Losing patience, Forrest ordered mounted charges to break through the Yankee rearguard. Carl cringed as he watched men race forward on their mounts, screaming the terrifying Rebel yell and firing their pistols only to be punched off their horses by Federal ambushers. He dreaded the moment that Captain Jeb would tell them to mount, that they were next. He walked forward with his line of dismounted men, holding his pistol. Behind them, one out of every five men held the horses ready to be mounted and charged forward in the running fight to Tupelo. Carl wondered what he'd do once he came into range of someone in a blue uniform and had to shoot.

The Federals crossed a creek that cut across a low point in the road. They were cresting the next ridge. Forrest brought forward his two field pieces and started lobbing shells at them in frustration. The Yankees responded by unlimbering their cannons and firing back. They pinned the rebels down while the rest of the blue army put more distance between them.

Carl marveled at seeing black soldiers across the way work the cannons and man the lines of musketry that supported them. He thought about how proud Francis had been in his letters. Francis wrote so much about everything he was learning about artillery. It saddened Carl, then made him furious that he'd never get the chance to hear Francis's passionate voice talk about it in person.

He looked at his pistol and then at the men around him. He could kill six of them before they could stop him. He let out his breath. That would be pointless. Who knew what any of the men near him had to do with his friend's gruesome death? There was only one man he knew for sure who was responsible, Lathan Woods, and Carl was going to make him pay.

"Walk up, Carlos," the man he was beginning to know as Tim said. Tim was the man who led him on the end of a rope when he was first captured, then later offered him water in an unexpected act of kindness. "We're moving," he said.

They shuttled further down the creek before crossing in an attempt to get around the enemy's flanks. They traded shots with the Yankees as they passed through the cornfields far on the northern end of the Federal line. Carl flinched as Minié balls came whistling through the corn stocks. By instinct, he fired his pistol back in their general direction, only thinking to pull the shot high at the last minute. *My God, whose side am I on?!* he thought.

He looked around at the men near him. They were reloading in a crouch or sighting down their barrels, looking for targets. When another volley from the enemy didn't come, it was clear the Federals were withdrawing again. The drive was back on.

Eventually, Forrest's men converged with Chalmers's division at a crossroads where a farm and blacksmith shop sat. Evidence of a battle was everywhere. General Chalmers and his men had attacked the Federal flanks but failed to stop their drive to Tupelo. Carl rode down the road that was littered with overturned burning carts, dead mules, and men. The smell of blood, gun powder, and burning wood made him queasy in the hot July sun. He wondered if Lathan was among Chalmers's men. He felt it best to keep his head down until he knew.

The pursuit continued through the smoldering afternoon. Men stripped down to their sweat-soaked shirtsleeves. They managed to engage the Federals in small skirmishes, but the Yankees refused to turn and give battle. Still, this gave Carl opportunities to fire his pistol uselessly at the fleeing enemy in front of his new comrades. He hoped it looked like he was trying. He was thankful that they hadn't bothered arming him with a rifle or anything that might actually have a chance at hitting someone. His pistol was almost useless from the range they had been able to get within the fleeing enemy so far.

A rumble of distant artillery gave evidence that a battle was raging ahead later that afternoon. It was over by the time Forrest's column caught up. Another flanking attack had failed. The Yankees merely stopped long enough to turn their cannons on the Rebel ambushers that had fired at them from the woods along the road.

By dusk, it was over. The Yankees made it to the heights of Harrisburg which was a hamlet just two miles outside of Tupelo. Deeming it good defensible ground, they turned their guns around and held back the arriving Confederates as they dug in. By the time the full Rebel column arrived, it was too late. The Yankees were firmly set in their defensive works and only a well-organized assault could pry them loose.

The Federals had turned the tables. The Confederate commanders stewed in their frustration over their failure to stop them. Now the Rebels would have to attack a fortified position instead of defending one. The Confederates dug in on the high ground across the way and kept a wary eye on the Federal encampment. There they planned the next day's attack while the men made their camps and rested.

Carl followed the lead of his comrades. They fed and watered their horses then found food for themselves. Carl sat next to Tim. The two quietly spooned salted pork and beans into their mouths as they watched the flickering campfires twinkle on the Federal held heights in the evening gloom. Men around them spoke in low voices about the day that had passed and the day to come.

He was cleaning his revolver after supper when Captain Jeb came to check on them. "Looks like ya got some use out of your pistol today, Carlos. Did ya manage to shoot any of 'em?"

"Well, I hope so. I certainly tried, sir. I'm almost out of ammo," Carl said, looking up at the bearded man towering over him. He hoped the darkness would hide his nervousness.

"We'll make sure you get what you need for tomorrow, son," he said, then to the men around them. "Rest up, boys. Tomorrow we take it to those Yankee invaders." A muted round of affirmations came from the men.

Carl returned to working on his pistol, scrubbing out the fouling that had built up in the barrel and the cylinders from firing it all day. He considered himself lucky. In a day of chasing the Federals, he avoided having to shoot anyone and he also didn't get shot. Tomorrow would be different. Tomorrow they'd be attacking the enemy's works in an uphill assault. If he wasn't cut down by cannons and musketry in the open fields, he would come face to face with the army he had also sworn an oath to, an army that somewhere his friends still fought for. *What have I gotten myself into,* he thought, as he looked at the Federal campfires dotting the landscape from afar like terrestrial stars.

Little sleep came to him. Musket and even cannon fire interrupted the peace through the night. He thought about his bed back in Detroit and how much he'd like to curl up next to Anna's warm body. Was she right? Did he throw away his life for some fool's adventure? He wanted to write her and tell her that he still lived, but how would he send a letter back north from deep in the Confederate Army. They were already suspicious of him. How would she be able to write back?

Then Kathryn crept into his mind before he was able to shoo her away. Where was she? Where was Kyle? He wondered what a child between Kyle and Liza would look like. *Children...Did Elijah say something about children...*

He could hear a solitary bird begin to call out in the darkness. Soon more joined the early morning chorus. Men began to stir. They mumbled softly to each other. The smell of freshly stoked cooking fires drifted around him. He knew he was done sleeping even before the bugle call.

At least there was breakfast. The Rebels took great satisfaction in sharing the spoils of captured Federal supplies. There was even coffee! "Here you go, Carlos! Courtesy of Uncle Sam!" Davy from his company chimed with glee as he handed him a cup.

"Thank you!" Carl brightened at the smell.

"I got something else for you, Carlos," another voice said.

Carl looked up to see Captain Jeb standing over him.

"Here," Jeb said, handing him a short-barreled rifle. Carl took the weapon, examining it with fascination. "Sharps carbine. Here're some cartridges," he said, tossing Carl a couple of cardboard boxes. Carl had to drop the weapon to his lap as he clumsily tried to catch them. "It may not be as fancy as some of these new repeaters, but at least you can load it with loose powder once we run out of cartridges. Have you shot one before?"

"Uh...no, sir," Carl said.

"Have Tim show you how to load it. You'll be doing a lot of that today."

Tim sat alongside him and patiently ran him through the process. "Pull hammer to the half-cock position, then push the lever forward." Carl pushed the lever that also functioned as a trigger guard. The breech block lowered, exposing the rear opening of the barrel. "Place your cartridge in the breech and then shut the lever." Carl pulled out one of the cartridges which was a bullet wrapped in a paper full of black powder. As he closed the lever, the sharp edge of the breech block cut off the back end of the paper cartridge, exposing the powder in the chamber. "Blow away the excess powder or it'll flash in your face when you fire," Tim warned.

"Yeah, I don't want that to happen," Carl said, thinking about the Colt revolving rifle that blew up in his face over two years before. He still had a small scar on his face to remind him of it. It made a semi-circle from the left corner of his mouth to his jaw. It gave him the appearance of a permanent half-frown.

"Then you can put a primer cap on the nipple when you're ready to fire, just like a regular musket," Tim finished.

"Thank you," Carl said, lowering the hammer for the time being.

"Just don't shoot any of us, you damn Yankee spy!" the man Carl was beginning to know as Toby called out. The rest of them laughed. Carl was stunned. He had worried that the men suspected him. Now it was being said in the open. The only thing he knew to do was to laugh with them.

"I keep trying," he called back, "but I'm a terrible shot!" The men laugh even more.

Davy gave him a slap on the back, "Hopefully all them Yankees are bad shots today!"

"Hear, hear!" someone else shouted.

For a moment Carl felt at ease with his Rebel comrades, maybe even liking them. He then wondered if he could shoot any of them if the time came. The laughter died down. In the quiet that followed, he wondered if he'd have to shoot a Federal soldier first.

It would be a while before he'd have to shoot anyone. They had been placed on the right end of the Confederate line under General Forrest's direct command. From there they watched the opening moves. The plan was for the left wing to entice the Yankees to come out of their works and attack them. Once that happened, they would fall back and use the woods as cover. General Forrest's right wing would then jump in and slam into their flank. The Yankees didn't budge, preferring to fight from behind their defenses. Now the right wing was forming up to attack their works directly in hopes of dislodging them by force.

"Why isn't General Forrest commanding the whole assault? Doesn't he command all of these troops?" Davy asked as they watched the left-wing emerge from the woods and start their run across the open field towards the Federal works. Their Rebel yell was barely audible above the Yankee cannons.

"There's something in the plan he doesn't like," Tim answered, not taking his eyes off the scene unfolding before them.

"Why don't he just change it?" Davy asked, flinching as he saw dozens of men mowed down by the relentless cannonade.

"It's not his to change. General Stephen Lee outranks him," Tim said, watching the waves of men tumbling to the ground as they desperately tried to make it to the Federal entrenchments.

"I'm sure he ain't happy about takin' orders from a pup twelve years his junior," Toby piped in.

"I don't suppose he is," Tim said flatly.

"I guess that why he's letting ol' Stephen Lee take the loss," Davy said softly.

No one dared to affirm that statement out loud, although, to Carl, it was apparent there was a silent agreement among them that it was true. Carl looked down at his Sharp's carbine. He thumbed the top of the breech block idly, listening to the battle intensify. He hoped the others didn't notice his inability to watch. The men dying in the hopeless attacks were his enemies he supposed, but they were still men. They were men like the ones that were around him now, men he had been sharing meals and even an occasional laugh with over the last few weeks.

He dared himself to look up again. It was terrible. Hundreds lay dead or wounded in the field. Still, more waves of Rebels dared to make the dash. Carl felt sick at the terrible loss. He feared he, too, would soon be called to make the hopeless run on the Federal entrenchments. *This is where I die*, he thought with burning, ironic bitterness. He took in a deep breath and resolved to pretend to be as brave as the men around him.

He didn't need to.

By noon it was over. Whatever cue General Forrest was waiting for to throw his wing into action never appeared. Some of the men quietly mused that Forrest wasn't going to waste any of them on such a hopeless and meaningless effort.

A somber quiet fell over the Confederate camp that evening. Rising above the now subdued sounds of camp life came the cries of wounded men as doctors did their bloody work to save as many as they could. Gone were the jokes, laughter, and bravado from the night before. The men that had been so eager to finally fight it out now stared at their cooking fires, lost in their thoughts. The specter of defeat haunted them. The myth of invincibility that swirled around General Forrest was dissipating like the last wisps of gun smoke from the battlefield. Carl made sure to match his mood to the men around him. If there was ever a time not to talk, it was now.

The Federals pulled out of their positions the next day and marched north, leaving Tupelo burning in their wake. Once again, Forrest rallied the men still able to fight and gave chase. They harassed the stubborn Federal rearguard with renewed vigor, but the pursuit began to fall apart after Forrest himself had to be carried to the rear. Rumors of his death ran through the ranks, sucking away their resolve. Eventually, the pursuit was called off. The Yankees had done their damage and were now retreating to resupply and prepare for their next punishing foray into the Southern heartland.

Forrest was not dead. He had taken a bullet to his big toe. Frustrated at watching his last chance of victory slipping away, he rode out on his horse once his foot was wrapped, grimacing in pain as he tried to rally his boys one more time. But it was over.

He lay in bed days later with his right foot bandaged and elevated. The saddle-worn boils on his rear end burned dully, adding to his frustration and discomfort.

"Tsk!" he muttered as he threw the Yankee newspaper to the floor. It landed in a way where he could still see the headline as it lay there mocking him:

A *Three Days' fight with Forrest: Rebel's Handsomely Whipped*

He tried to kick it over with his good leg then hissed in pain from agitating his boils and his throbbing big toe.

"Aren't we a bit cranky today?" His wife entered the room with a cup of hot coffee and a handful of letters.

"I'm not in the mood, Mary Ann," he said grimly, then regarded the comic frown on her face. "I'm sorry, dear," he said, accepting the cup. "The Yanks never cease running their mouths and now they're talking about taking another run at us, this time with twenty-thousand men…and here I am…laid up with busted toe and boil-ridden ass. I've got possible five-thousand effectives at best and a bunch of broken-down horses…even if I could ride." He paused to take a drink, mad at himself for showing weakness to his wife.

"There, there, Bedford," she soothed, stroking his gray-streaked hair. He leaned into her for a moment, allowing himself the brief luxury of affection.

"I brought you some mail," she said at last. "Looks like mostly fan letters to cheer you up…and this one…!" She held up an envelope, "Looks like the fancy handwriting of a pretty young maiden. It has no return address, the little sneak!" she said, putting her hands on her hips in feigned outrage.

"Trust me, Mary Ann, ain't no woman gonna put up with me like you," he said taking the envelope with an ornery smile. His smile faded as he read.

June 14, 1864

My Dear Major General N. B. Forrest,

    I hope my letter finds you well. Please forgive my impertinence in writing you and for trying to keep my anonymity. I fear for my life and that of my child. We are living among the most vile of Yankee occupiers. Still, at great peril to myself and child, I am compelled to write you as it is my duty as a true daughter of the South, and sister to a dear brother, who at this moment rots away in the cruel Irving Block Prison here in Memphis.

    The prison is full of true Confederate patriots, like my brother, who suffer greatly under the deprivations of their jailers.

I've sent you a list of their names with this letter, including my brother, whom I won't name here for fear of identifying myself. These are proud and loyal gentlemen who grow sick and starve under the terrible conditions put upon them. Please, sir, I beg you, won't you come and liberate them? Bring the flaming sword of justice to these loathsome tyrants who infest our soil, torment our sons, and violate our daughters.

Your faithful servant,

K.B.

Forrest leaned back in his bed and closed his eyes for a moment to organize his thoughts.

"What is it?" Mary Ann asked.

He handed her the letter and watched her read. Once finished, she slowly raised her eyes to her husband. The fire had returned and was raging in his eyes.

"The Yankees are out in force, looking to hunt me down," he said. "There is one place they'd never expect to find me, and they've left it undefended."

Chapter Twenty-Four: The Casualty

Kathryn walked to the train depot. She held her nose high and avoided the jubilant faces she passed in the streets. She couldn't bear looking at them. The news had been a hardly credible rumor at first, but as more and more confirmation trickled in, people in Memphis became more willing to believe until their cautious optimism finally broke into an all-out celebration. Nathan Bedford Forrest had been defeated at the doorstep of Tupelo. It was even said that he was most likely dead from his wounds. The city was safe. Sherman's supply line was secure. He could now confidently march into Georgia and take Atlanta.

The happy faces looked at her with an expectation of shared joy. All they'd get from her was silent contempt if she even bothered to acknowledge them at all. Her hopes of Forrest liberating the city and freeing her brother were dashed. Now she'd have to go back to feigning interest in the nostalgic, middle-aged Colonel Dearing to save Kyle and to keep their little family alive, fed, and decently housed.

She stood among the crowd fanning herself as the soldiers poured out of the train cars. A damp wave of body odor radiated from the masses in the late July heat. She tried her best to fan it away. Everyone else seemed too excited to notice. They greeted the soldiers with cheers and refreshments as the brass band played *The Girl I Left Behind*. Families were eager to find their man alive and well among the throng of returning soldiers. So many were terrified that their husband, father, or brother was one of the dead.

Word was they would not be back for long. They'd be in town just long enough to resupply and reinforce before heading out again to destroy the remainder of the Rebel forces that lingered in Northern Mississippi.

Kathryn stood on the platform watching the crowd start to dwindle. Finally, she recognized a face among the thousands of blue-clad soldiers. She turned away quickly, hiding her face in her fan. It was too late. A hand clutched her shoulder and turned her around.

"Waiting for me, Sweet Kate?" Captain Logan leered at her. His left arm was bandaged and in a sling. The unwashed smell of campaigning rolled off him. She tugged her arm free, allowing her anger to replace her fear.

"Unhand me, you cretin. I'm waiting for your superior officer. I'm sure he'll not appreciate your brutish behavior."

Logan smiled at her for a moment. Kathryn glared back, her face twitching as the unexpected pause unnerved her. "I suppose he wouldn't…if he lives."

Kathryn's jaw unclenched as her eyes widened, "…What?"

"My apologies, madam," Logan grinned. "But, you might want to find another protector for you and your mixed-breed pups. Perhaps you should start being a bit more cordial with me, my dear." Kathryn didn't say anything in return. She stared off. Her mind was racing. Logan's grin returned as he watched the news sink in, deflating her haughtiness.

A woman began to scream. They both turned to see her screeching, "No, no, oh, God, please, no!" as she fell to her knees. The baby in her arms began to wail. A confused toddler clutched her arm as soldiers tried to comfort the grief-stricken woman and get her to her feet. Logan broke the momentary silence between them.

"Perhaps I could call upon you, once you've thought it through."

Kathryn said nothing, only perceiving that he had withdrawn as she watched the newly widowed woman sob inconsolably.

Hours of asking and searching brought her to the Officers' Hospital on Front Street. It was one of the many mercantile buildings the Federals had commandeered and converted for medical purposes as the war brought more and more wounded into the city. She walked down the bay of beds, scanning the faces of the sick and broken men. The stench of unwashed bodies, urine, feces, festering wounds, and blood mixed with the harsh chemical smell of disinfectants. She tried to fan it away, grateful that the open windows brought in some fresh but hot summer air.

At last, she found him. The well-groomed, proud man now laid disheveled and sunken into his bedsheets. "Oh, Loyd!" she gasped, bolting to his side. Dearing looked up at her weakly and formed a smile.

"If I could've, I would've sent word to you not to come. This is no place for a lady," he said weakly. The comment got him a scoff from one of the passing nurses. "Except, of course, the wonderful angels that work here like you, Beth."

The woman rolled her eyes then smiled at Kathryn. "I'll get you a stool, miss," she told her.

Kathryn placed her palm on Dearing's chest and caressed the bald top of his head as she sat next to him. "Oh, Loyd…" she said again.

He smiled weakly. "I would embrace you, but I'm not all the man I used to be," he said, indicating with his eyes the stump where his right arm used to be.

"Oh, Loyd, you're plenty a man and more!" she protested.

More blue-clad men poured into the city in the days that followed. They clogged the streets along with horses and carts. Kathryn was relieved once they finally loaded onto the trains and headed out once more to engage the Confederates in Northern Mississippi. They left behind only a few to guard the city, run the prison, and perform the administrative duties of occupation. She noted that the men left behind weren't the best and brightest. Most of them were injured or found some other way of avoiding the latest campaign, like the detestable Captain Logan, who always seemed to find a way to bump into her while she was out on her errands.

She split her time over the next few weeks visiting her brother in prison and Loyd in the hospital. As one seemed to grow stronger with the food she brought, the other began to diminish. Kathryn penned letters to Loyd's daughter as he dictated. At times he seemed to confuse Kathryn for her and his long-lost wife. She didn't mind so long as it brought him comfort.

She sat at his bed as he dozed, wondering how she was going to free her brother as her last hope was dying in front of her. Loyd opened his eyes. A lucidity had returned since the last time he feverishly called her "Lilith," the name of his late wife to whom he professed his undying love.

"Kathryn…" he mumbled with a faint smile. She smiled back, gripping his hand.

"I'm here for you, Loyd," she said.

"I'm not long for this world," he said softly.

"Don't say that…!" she started.

"Shhh…" he stopped her. "Listen to me. I have money stashed away in the mattress at home. You must take it and go somewhere safe with the children and Liza. I will rest better knowing you're safe."

"Oh, Loyd," Kathryn said as a tear rolled down her face, "I can't leave while my brother is trapped here in prison." Dearing let out a breath. He looked at the ceiling for a moment. A new determination spread across his face. He returned his eyes to her.

"Run back to the house and fetch my stationery. I will pen an order for his release. I don't know if it'll work."

"Oh, you sweet man! How can I ever repay your kindness?"

"Perhaps you could write my daughter," he smiled and squeezed her hand. "Tell her how I died. Perhaps tell her I was a good man."

"Of course, my dear Loyd," she sniffed back a tear, caressing the top of his head.

"Hurry, I don't have much time," he released her hand and closed his eyes.

Kathryn dashed back to the house where she, Liza, and the children had made a home with the colonel in what almost felt like family. Liza's eyes were wide with anticipation as she read the focused purpose in Kathryn's face.

"What is it?" she asked.

"There's little time to explain, we're leaving soon. Come!" Kathryn grabbed a knife from the kitchen and dashed up the stairs and into Colonel Dearing's room. They tore off the sheets from the bed and frantically examined the mattress.

"Here!" Liza said. Kathryn crouched next to her. She could see the loose stitching along the side that Liza had found. She cut the threads and reached into the opening. Liza watched with anticipation, her eyes reflecting the flash of excitement that crossed Kathryn's face as her hand found the prize. Her fist emerged full of Federal dollars. Liza let out a gasp then covered her mouth.

"Here, take this," Kathryn shoved the money toward her, then drove both hands back into the mattress. She pulled out more stacks of currency in ones, twos, fives, even tens and twenties. "Apparently, he doesn't trust our Southern banks," Kathryn quipped, handing Liza most of the stash, then stuffed a few notes into her bosom. "Take this, buy a wagon and a pair of sturdy mules. There's got to be some somewhere that aren't out on campaign with those damn Yankees. Get provisions, too, for at least a few weeks if not months. We're getting Kyle out tonight and headed west."

Liza blinked at her in astonishment. She turned to see Roggie and Lil' Jimi B. clutching the door frame, watching the women and the pile of money in quiet awe. "What about the children? I can't take them along as I do our business."

Kathryn blew her bangs out of her face and turned to regard the toddlers. "Lil' Jimi B. can watch over Roggie for a few hours until you return."

"He ain't two!" Liza protested.

"We're in a war, Liza. He's got to grow up sometime."

Kathryn rushed through the city with Colonel Dearing's leather satchel that held the stationery he used to write orders. Her mind was racing. It was getting late in the day. She worried that Liza wouldn't be able to find the wagon or the supplies they needed. The Yankees had taken almost everything useful with them. A twenty-thousand-man force required a lot. They had repaired the rail line from Memphis to Holly Springs in Mississippi. There they had set up a base of operations that could be sustained by a constant flow of supplies from the rail. Surely somewhere between the supplies unloaded from the steamboats on the river to where they were   loaded onto the railcars, Liza would be able to procure what they needed. She was clever, charming, and armed with a lot of cash. These corrupt Yankees would be easy for her.

"Well, hey there," a familiar voice made her cringe. She looked up to find him standing in her way. "We have to stop meeting like this or people will begin to talk," Captain Logan grinned at her, his left arm now out of the sling.

"Trust me, people in this town know well enough that I don't associate with people beneath my class. Now, please step aside."

"Judging by the looks of your child, I doubt that. Whatcha got there, missy?" he asked looking at the leather satchel she clutched to her chest.

"It's something for your colonel and none of your business," she huffed.

"He's still alive? I heard not for long."

"What are you still doing here?" she changed the subject. "Aren't you supposed to be leading your company in battle right now? I hear they're already heavily engaged, fighting and dying like men while you're here loitering and harassing women."

A flash of anger flitted across his face, then shifted into a smile. He lifted his arm, "I just got the bandages off. I'll be back in action soon, until then I am here to guard you and your fellow citizens from the savages you call your countrymen."

"Well, perhaps you could make yourself useful in the meantime by pulling a cart or cleaning up the messes left by the horses," she said, brushing him aside.

Evidence of a battle was trickling through the streets. Ambulance carts rolled past her carrying men that had been unloaded from the railcars that were beginning to arrive from Holly Springs. The medical district was once again abuzz as nurses and doctors triaged men into the various hospitals. Kathryn picked up her pace, worrying that visitors would be shooed away now that they were about to get busy. She entered the large bay of the Officers' Hospital. Already, she could hear the sounds of wounded men crying out, as the treatment was often more painful than the wound.

She spotted Loyd's bed. Nurse Beth and another were stripping it of its bedclothes and replacing them with fresh sheets. Then they lifted a groaning half-conscious man from a stretcher and placed him onto the bed.

"Where's Colonel Dearing?!" Kathryn gasped, clutching his leather satchel to her chest. The two nurses looked at each other, unsure who should speak and what should be said. Finally, Beth turned to her and spoke.

"I'm sorry, dear, he…passed peacefully in your absence. We needed the space. He's in the morgue now, would you like to see him…?"

"My God…!" Kathryn gasped. The women looked at her with sympathy.

"We're so sorry…" the other added. Kathryn had already turned and was running toward the door. Now she was running through the streets clutching the bag tightly to her chest. Tears streamed down her face. Everything was going terribly wrong. She'd never get her brother out. She, Liza, and the children would soon be homeless once the Federals decided to move someone else into the house.

She slammed the door behind her, let out a breath and thought for a moment. It was getting dark. She was running out of time. She set the satchel on the dining room table and stared at it. She threw her face into her hands and began to sob, pulling back the strands of hair that had come loose. She felt a small hand on her thigh. She looked down to see a puff of curls and big blue eyes surrounded by freckles regard her with sympathy.

"Don't cry, Aunt Kate," the little boy said.

Kathryn looked at Lil' Jimi B., smiling through tear-blurred eyes. "You're, right child. We've got work to do. Where's Roggie?"

"Sleepin'," he pointed upstairs.

"How's his diaper?"

Lil' Jimi B. giggled mischievously, "Stinky!"

Kathryn let out a laugh, sniffing back the last of her tears. "Well, we'll tend to that promptly," she said, getting up from the table. She picked up the boy and carried him upstairs. Roggie was sleeping soundly. She hated to wake him, but he needed to be cleaned and changed. Lil' Jimi B. watched intently as she did so. She wondered just how much she could teach the toddler to help with Roggie. They needed all the help they could get.

She fed them eggs, toast, and beans. She smiled at how the two giggled and seemed to have a way of communicating with each other that was deeper than spoken words. She went back into Loyd's bedroom after putting the children to bed. The torn open mattress still lay on the floor. She sewed the hole back shut and remade the bed. No sense in leaving behind any evidence of the treasure they found. She looked at Loyd's spare colonel's uniform which he used for dress occasions. *If only Lil' Jimi B.' was twenty years older…*she thought, musing over what use she could get out of it.

She decided to pack it. She took his sword and pistol, too. These were definitely useful things for their trip west.

Then the idea struck her. She dashed downstairs to the dining room table. The satchel sat on there like the obvious solution she had been failing to see all evening. She could hear the approaching rattle of the iron-rimmed wagon wheels outside on the cobblestone street. She let out a sigh of relief. Liza had done her job. Now it was time to do hers.

She opened the bag and pulled out the paper inside. She looked at Loyd's journal and notes, examining his handwriting. Then found blanks of the pre-printed stationery he used to write orders. She could hear Liza opening the door. Kathryn pulled out a pen and ink jar. She dipped the pen and started writing.

Chapter Twenty-Five: The Raid

A heavy fog rolled in overnight. It hid the hundreds of horsemen creeping through the outer suburbs of the city. "It's proof that God is on our side," Captain Jeb told them as they checked their pistols and the sharpness of their blades one last time before riding out to do their bloody work.

Carl tingled with fear and yet no small measure of exhalation. It was a terrifying and insane plan. He felt guilty at how excited he was to be a part of it. Wasn't he on the wrong side? Would he finally be forced to kill a Federal soldier just to maintain his ruse? Would he ever find Lathan among these wild Rebel horsemen? Was he becoming one?

He shook off these thoughts and focused on Francis's happy and laughing face. Francis, his sweet friend who cared so much about the freedom of others that he laid down his own life for the cause. Francis, who only wanted to be treated with the same dignity as others, died a tortured hideous death at the hands of a man who thought him nothing more than an animal. Rage coursed through Carl's veins. No, even the most callous butcher would not subject an animal to the brutal and painful death that Francis had suffered. Carl focused on Lathan's cold and smirking face. Rage and fear swirled in his stomach. He tightened his resolve. He would find this man. He would find his own courage. Francis would be avenged. He would remove that smirk from Lathan's face. He would do whatever he had to today to do so. *This* was his war.

He rode with a column of cavalrymen, barely able to make out the man in front of him in the dark morning fog. The wildly frightening Captain Bill Forrest led them. Tim told him that the only man Nathan Bedford ever feared was his own brother Bill. Carl could see why. The wild hair and icy gray eyes gave Bill an air of raw uncontrollable violence. Bill walked with the confidence of a man who could not imagine himself losing a fight. That was probably why Nathan Bedford chose him to lead this part of the raid. Only a man with an iron nerve like Bill could pull off such an audacious plan.

Bill had only recently returned after recovering from a wound he got at the Battle of Sand Hill in Alabama the year before. A musket ball tore through his thigh and broke the bone. Now he was back in the saddle, ready to bring slaughter to the Yankee fools who thought themselves safe hiding in the occupied city of Memphis.

"Get ready…" Bill gritted through his teeth. They were approaching the first Federal picket guarding the entry into the city.

They had been riding for three days, sweeping wide around the large Federal force that spilled into Holly Springs in Mississippi by railcar. They came to take up the fight once more after their success at Tupelo. General Chalmers's division engaged them at Oxford, fooling the Yankees into thinking that they were the main objective. But Forrest had other plans. He handpicked two thousand men with serviceable mounts and four pieces of artillery to attack Memphis while the Yankees were away. They were to capture three generals there and possibly free the Confederate patriots stuck in the Irving Block Prison. Most importantly, they would teach the Yankees a lesson. There was no place safe for them on Southern soil.

The journey had been tough. They had to build bridges of felled trees lashed together with muscadine vines to cross some of the rain-swollen rivers along their way. Forrest ended up having to leave two of the cannons behind and send five hundred men back after their broken-down horses finally gave out. They got to Hernando, Mississippi, Saturday afternoon, just south of the Tennessee-Mississippi border outside of Memphis. They ate and rested for a few hours then broke into separate teams to make the final twenty-five-mile ride to Memphis.

Bill's team was to capture the forward pickets without firing a shot, then ride to the Gayoso Hotel and take General Hurlbut prisoner. Once the teams had captured their assigned targets they would then use them to leverage the release of the Confederate prisoners held at Irving Block Prison. Nathan Bedford's team along with the two remaining cannons would position themselves along the escape route and cover the retreat. With their high-level prisoners and the proof that they can strike anywhere at any time, Forrest and his men would force the Yankee Army out of Mississippi in order to protect Memphis from further attacks.

Everything depended on this moment. Bill and his men drew closer to the guard post at the foot of the bridge over Cane Creek that led into the city. A soldier in blue walked out holding up a hand to stop them, in the other he held a lantern in.

"Who goes there?" he demanded

Bill put his hand up, indicating to his men to stop. He brought his own horse to a halt. "We're a detachment of the 12th Missouri Cavalry with Rebel prisoners," he said gruffly.

The soldier winced as his lantern reflected off of Bill's icy gray eyes in the darkness. He paused for a moment and rubbed his chin.

"I'm gonna have to ask you to dismount, sir, and come forward alone."

"Alright, then, have it your way."

Bill touched his spurs to his horse's flanks and bolted forward. The soldier flinched, widening his stance and throwing his hand out to stop the rider. Bill's horse reared as he pulled out his army model Colt revolver, clenching his hand around the cylinder in a reverse grip. He brought the butt of it down on the man's head like a hammer, using the momentum of his horse returning its front hooves to the ground to magnify the force. The soldier collapsed like a pile of rags on the ground.

"...boring conversation anyway," he mumbled, then shouted to his men. "C'mon!"

Carl's horse lurched forward with the rest of them as they clattered loudly across the bridge. Catching his balance, he worried about the noise they were making. There were tents just on the other side of the bridge. Bill's men had already surrounded them, pointing their pistols at a few dozen men who were trembling in their underclothes. "Take these prisoners to the rear," Bill said to Captain Jeb. Jeb nodded to two of his men who bade the men in their underwear to march back across the bridge.

"What about our clothes? Surely you'll give us the dignity of our clothes?!" one of them protested.

"If you're gonna invade our country, you should have dressed for it, damn you," Bill growled, then to Jeb, "Shoot the next son of a bitch that opens his mouth."

CRACK!

They all flinched as a Minié ball whizzed through the group like an angry bee. Bill snapped his head towards the direction of the shot. Bewildered Federal soldiers were scampering in their various stages of dress, fumbling with their guns.

"It's on now, boys! Let's go!" he shouted, spurring his horse forward. Carl followed, leaving Captain Jeb and his small detail behind with the prisoners. Rebel horsemen poured into the city from multiple directions, riding hard toward their assigned objectives, whooping and hollering as they rode. *This was not the plan,* Carl thought, as he galloped along with the rest of them through the dark city street. The Gayoso Hotel with its grand white columns loomed ahead. Carl gasped as Bill plunged straight through the front door on his horse. Carl dismounted with the others and followed him in.

"Where's General Hurlbut?" Bill growled, pointing his pistol at the night clerk. His horse pranced nervously in the grand lobby of the hotel. The man trembled as he held up a key. Bill looked to his men. "Go!" he said, indicating to the key with his head. One of them snatched it and off they ran. Carl followed the rest as they dashed down the corridor. The man in the lead was opening the locked door as Carl caught up. They spilled into the dark room with their pistols in hand.

"Wake up, you son of a bitch!" one of them called out. They were rummaging in the darkness. Carl listened for the protests from the Federal general. There were none. Finally, someone struck a match. In the flickering light, they could see the dress uniform of a major general hanging in the closet, a desk littered with papers and dispatches, and a bed only recently unmade by the men searching for the officer.

"He ain't here!" one of them called as they ran back to the lobby. Bill cocked and raised his pistol once more at the terrified clerk.

"Where is he?"

"I swear," the man pleaded, "I don't know! He goes out sometimes and doesn't return until morning." A cannon sounded somewhere outside causing the man to jump. The sounds of fighting were intensifying. Carl flinched as Bill's steely eyes fell on him.

"Go to the jail, see if it's well defended. We're running out of time," Bill ordered him.

Carl fought the instinct to ask, "Me?" Thankfully, others were moving with him. He realized Bill had been speaking to the group and not just him.

Outside, the early hints of dawn were showing. Gunshot, screams, and galloping hooves could be heard all around as they mounted their horses.

"Hello, handsome!" a woman's voice startled him. He looked up to see an open window in the house nearby. A woman in her nightclothes was leaning out, waving her handkerchief. Once again he was about to ask if she were referring to him. Instead, he meekly waved back.

"Um…hi."

He could see all around, people were peering out of their windows, some with fear, others were cheering, even waving Confederate flags.

"Go get 'em, boys!" one of them called out.

"Come on, Romeo!" one of Carl's fellow raiders yelled at him.

Kathryn could hear the commotion outside of the prison. Something was happening and it was more than a drunken street brawl. She looked back at the fool of a guard who was scrutinizing the order for her brother's release. She was running out of time and options. She had waited until just before dawn to try her ruse. The night guards were usually the dumbest. They'd be more concerned about ending their shifts than harassing a lady carrying an officer's order, even if it was forged.

She had been stunned earlier that morning when she climbed onto the front bench of the covered wagon Liza had bought. "What are these?" she said, indicating to the two large horned beasts attached to the yoke.

"You know damn well they oxen, Kat," Liza climbed in next to her.

"I thought I said mules," Kathryn said looking at the tan animals.

"Army's got 'em all, besides these are better for a long haul," she told her. Kathryn gave her an unsure look. Liza rolled her eyes. "These are the matters in which you shouldn't question a black woman," she said, cracking the whip. The wagon started rolling down the cobbled street toward the prison. Kathryn shrugged in acceptance. She looked back in the wagon. The boys were peering back at her huddled among the barrels and sacks of supplies. Roggie was wide-eyed with bewilderment. Little Jimi B. beamed with devilish delight.

"You boys be quiet and stay back there until we're out of the city," she had told them.

Now she wondered if they'd make it out at all as she watched the guard shake his head at the order.

"I'm sorry, ma'am. This is quite irregular. Why would he send you instead of a soldier with this order?" he asked.

"Because they're all out fighting Forrest in Mississippi, I suppose," she offered.

"Hmmm, I'm going to need some clarification on this..." he said, frowning. The sounds of fighting caused him to pause and look toward the high window. Hints of morning light were seeping through. Something was happening. Kathryn considered digging under her skirts and pulling out the colonel's pistol that she had tucked into her drawers. She reached into her bosom instead and pulled out two twenty-dollar bills.

"I think you have bigger problems to worry about currently," she said, indicating to the noise outside with her eyes. "Now, you can make this ordeal hard or very easy on yourself," she said, flashing the money. The guard looked at it and then back at her.

"Give me a minute, ma'am," he said, leaving her in the room. She wondered if she had miss-played her hand as she waited. She feared that she was about to be arrested. The door opened.

"Kathryn…" Kyle said.

"My God, you need a bath!" she replied.

The faint glow was growing in the east once they got outside. Kyle caught a brief glimpse of the wagon before someone overtook him.

"Damn, you stink!" Liza told him as she threw her arms around him.

"Liza, my love…" he gasped as he held her.

"Come on, we've got plenty of time for all of that on the trail," Kathryn chided them. The battle sounds were getting louder.

"Time's up!" a man's voice interrupted. Kyle felt a hand on his shoulder spin him around. A fist crashed into his jaw, knocking him to the ground. Kathryn let out a scream. Kyle caught a brief glimpse of Captain Logan before a boot connected with his face and then continued to stomp on his body.

"Not so tough when you're not sneakin' up on someone!" Logan said, punctuating each word with a stomp. Liza lurched at him, clawing at his face. Logan sent her to the ground with a backhand slap. She clung to Kyle, protecting his battered body with her own.

Kathryn fumbled under her skirts, trying to pull out her gun.

"You animal! I'll shoot you!" she screamed.

"Oh, no, you won't!" Logan said, grabbing her wrist and yanking her back to slap her with his other hand. Kathryn's head snapped to the side from the blow. She looked back at her attacker, then saw the horsemen bearing down on them.

A man with wild black hair and a scraggly beard leaped from his horse and dove headlong into her attacker. Captain Logan hit the ground with an "Oof!" as the wind ejected from his lungs. The man pummeled him mercilessly with his fist as Logan tried to utter, "Stop…" through his bloody teeth.

"Good God, Carlos," one of the other horsemen said as they pulled him off of the bloody Yankee captain, "you'll kill him!" Carl got up, dusting off his trousers. He looked at Kathryn with a mix of pain, astonishment, and ferocity.

"I just knew that was your voice screaming," he said, panting.

"Carl…" she gasped, walking slowly to him. She moved his overgrown bangs to the side and looked into his eyes. "How in the world…?"

A bugle called off in the distance, followed by another. "They're calling the retreat, Carlos. We got to go!" one of Carl's comrades told him.

"Take the prisoner back. I'll catch up in a minute," Carl said with an authority that even surprised him.

"Alright, Romeo, you're just full of surprises!" the man chuckled. "Don't take too long or you'll become a prisoner yourself."

Carl looked back into Kathryn's eyes, wondering what to say that wouldn't ruin the moment. Kathryn finally spoke, shaking her head in disbelief. "You certainly have a way of disrupting my life," she said with a smile.

"Seems just in the nick of time," Carl said, then immediately felt foolish. She gave a small incredulous laugh. Finally, Kyle gave out a moan, breaking the moment.

"Oh, Kyle!" Kathryn gasped, bolting to her brother's side. Liza was helping him up.

"I'm fine," he grunted, getting to his feet. He looked at Carl with open-mouth disbelief. "What in the world is going on, Carl?"

"Well…um…I," Carl stammered. There was so much to explain as the chaos around them swirled. Gunshots, screaming, cannons, and galloping threaded through his attempts to speak.

"We gotta get out of here!" Liza gasped clinging to Kyle as she pleaded.

"Go," Carl said finally. "There'll be time to talk later." A sense of resolve washed through him as Kyle blinked and then smiled.

"Seems like I owe you another one, friend," he said as Liza led him to the wagon.

"I've lost count," Carl said.

"You…" Kathryn once again pulled his attention to her.

"Kathryn, I…" he stopped, realizing he had no idea what he wanted to say.

"I heard you got married," she said with a sly smile.

"I did," he said, looking at the ground and then back at her. "I did…"

"She's a beautiful girl, Carl. You're a lucky man." Carl dropped his eyes to the ground and let out a small embarrassed chuckle. He was surprised when he felt her lips on his cheek. She gave him a small kiss. "You deserve to be happy, my pretty friend." He felt a warm rush of blood fill his cheeks. He looked up as she walked away. "Take care of yourself, whatever this is you're doing," she said as she climbed onto the wagon bench.

"Thanks…you, too," he said meekly. She smiled and turned away. He stood in the middle of the street, watching the wagon begin to move. Its wheels clattered on the cobblestones and mixed with the sounds of fighting and bugles calling the retreat. The sun was burning away the fog and casting his shadow forward as he watched the wagon draw farther away. Exhilaration, frustration, longing, and grief swirled in him as he watched it go, like the dream he'd had so many times before.

Then, suddenly, the dream broke as two small faces pulled him from his thoughts. A blond curly-haired boy peered over the wagon's backboard and waved at him. Stunned, Carl lifted his hand and waved back. A second toddler popped his head up and stared at him with his large brown, doe-like eyes. Carl slowly dropped his hand, staring back at the boy, watching him pull away.

Act III: Nashville

Chapter Twenty-Six: The Crossing

October 29, 1864: Tuscumbia, Alabama, General Hood's Camp, The Confederate Army of Tennessee

The old man finished his evening chores, then walked away. It was really that simple. No one seemed to notice the faithful old slave walking through the evening camp, past the pickets, and into the wilderness along the southern side of the Tennessee River.

Why would they? He had always been a good worker, did his job, and never complained. That's why his master and the white men around him that he commanded trusted him and treated him well. He had seen a man whipped when he was just a boy. The sound of the lash and the screams haunted him. He had watched in horror as a strong and proud man was reduced to a whimpering child. He was terrified he'd suffer the same fate someday.

"Do what the master say, work hard and be honest, and you'll never have anything to worry about," his momma had told him a few years before she died.

"Keep your head down, your mouth shut, and stay out of trouble," his father had told him. Those were the last words he said before leaving. He was sold away, never to be seen again.

The old man may have lost his parents at a young age, but their words carried him through a relatively good life. House slaves lived far better than those working the field. They were almost like a lower tier of family to the master. Sure, some of his own kids had been sold away. "You're a good breeder!" his master had told him. It hurt to see them go, but he supposed raising a family of his own probably would have distracted him from his duties with the master's family.

Once his wife died, he was able to completely throw himself into caring for the master, and then the master's son, and then that master's son's son. For three generations of masters, he made their meals, dressed them, and oversaw the other house slaves. He brought order and cleanliness to the master's home as it passed from one to another.

It was no surprise then, when the war came, that his young master took him along. "The Yankees are coming to take our farms and violate our daughters," his master had said. That seemed true, judging by all the destruction they left in their path. But some of the slaves said the Yankees had come for a different reason, that the Yankees were coming to free the negroes. A fool's dream he had thought. Yet many dreamt it. He had seen many slip away and make the run to freedom. They're were even black men in the Yankee army! Imagine that! Perhaps it was true. Either way, it was looking like the Yankees were going to win.

His master's army changed leaders once again. The masters at the very top were tired of the Army of Tennessee constantly running away and losing. They fired ol' General Joe Johnston and replaced him with a younger man who promised to put up a solid fight against the Northern aggressors, General John B. Hood, though he heard some call him "Sam." This Hood was a surprise. He was tall, handsome, with a long face and deep-set soulful eyes. His full head of hair and long beard gave him an air of dignity, but the man was missing a leg! He had a bum arm, too, that he often kept in a sling.

"Man, things are so bad, they can't even get a commander with a full set of limbs anymore!" some of the slaves joked in private.

But what he lacked in limbs, he sure made up for with a gumption to fight. They fought the Yankees all around Atlanta, but Sherman's army was far too big to stop. Hood was losing men by the thousands in the effort, so they ran, hoping Ol' General Sherman would leave the city and chase them. He did for a bit, but Atlanta was too big of a prize to walk away from. So the Yankees returned to their spoils, and now Hood's army was too far west to do anything about it. So Hood decided to take Tennessee instead.

The white men said it'd be easy. The Yankees were so busy tearing up Georgia and Virginia that they left the West wide open, just plum for the taking. But the old man didn't see it that way. He was surprised they couldn't see it for themselves. Despite all the talk of victory, Hood's army was underfed, under-clothed, and undersupplied. What started out as a call to glory turned into a long, drawn-out refusal to admit defeat. The old man had had enough. If he was going to be free, he might as well be free now.

He waded into the river. It was cold but invigorating, like a bucket of water thrown at him, waking him up from a lifetime of sleep. He went farther, deeper. The water rose around him, soaking his clothes until his feet could no longer touch the bottom. He dipped his head under and rose back up a newborn man, baptized in freedom. He swam with a vigor he thought he had lost long ago. He made it to the first shoal, stumbled across, not looking behind him, just forward toward the northern shore. Once more, he was in over his head, swimming hard against the current that wanted to drag him downriver. He wouldn't let it. He'd decide where he was going from now on. He felt the bottom once more. He was walking, wading to the shore.

He stumbled toward the light of the campfires and glowing tents. He was wet and shivering in the cool night air. It didn't take long for the Yankees to notice him.

"Stop! Who goes there?" a young man called. There were two of them wearing matching blue uniforms which were far cleaner and well-kept than the ragged old mismatched clothes he saw around the Rebel camps. These boys looked official, they looked like establishment. They also looked scared, shaking as they held their rifles to their shoulders. They aimed at the old man. Their bayonets glinted in the darkness. He could see their eyes behind the weapons, watching him with trepidation. The old man smiled as he raised his hands. *Why…they just boys! h*e thought.

"A free man," he answered.

"General Croxton?" a voice called softly through the tent flaps. Brigadier General John Croxton let out a sigh. He wasn't sleeping anyway, but now he was sure he'd have no chance with the constant interruptions.

"What is it?" he asked, trying to sound patient.

"A runaway, sir. Says he's got information for you only."

"Alright, give me a minute," he said, sitting up in his cot. He shimmied into his trousers, pulling the suspenders over his shoulders. Then draped on his jacket before lighting the lantern on his little wooden writing desk. "Alright, bring him in," he said, still buttoning his jacket. He straightened his beard with his hand and slicked back his long brown hair. He looked up at the old man wrapped in a blanket.

"What do you got for me?" he asked.

The old man offered a clumsy salute then quickly caught the blanket as it slid off his shoulder. Croxton smiled softly at the man's attempted military decorum.

"General Hood fixin'ta cross the river tomorrow, sir," the old man said.

Croxton's eyes widened. The smile dropped from his face. His small cavalry brigade was spread out over twenty miles along the north bank of the river. They'd been watching for the Rebel army's next move. Most had thought they'd return to Georgia, once Sherman began his march to Savannah. Now it appeared the Rebels had their own conquest in mind.

"How so?" Croxton asked.

"They got pontoons, sir," the old man said. "They be arriving for days now. Gonna build a bridge, they are. They crossin' at Bainbridge, sir, bringing the whole lot of them. Gonna march all the way up ta Nashville and plant they flag."

Croxton's eyes bulged. He turned to a staff officer, "Who do we got closest to Bainbridge?"

"Colonel Smith, 2nd Michigan, sir"

"Send a message to Smith. Tell him to concentrate his men at Bainbridge. They're to hold them there while we gather the rest of the brigade."

"There's over forty-thousand of them, sir! We got a thousand men at best!" another staffer let out, barely hiding his alarm.

"We've got to buy Nashville time," he told them. "Get on the wire. Tell General Thomas Hood's Army is crossing near Florence. He's marching on Tennessee. Nashville is threatened. We'll try to hold them as long as possible, but we need help." He then turned back to the old man. "Thank you, sir."

"Certainly. I can help, sir. Do any job you like. I can even shoot one of them guns. I just don't think I could shoot m'master, though. He ain't so bad, you know. I very much raised him m'self."

Croxton smiled once again at the old man, "Well, maybe we can find something less violent for you to do, but you'll have to accept pay. You're a free man now."

"No sign of them, sir." Sergeant Barnes rode up to Captain Chester E. Newman's vantage point. They had been combing the banks east of Florence on the northern side of the river all night. Newman grimaced as he peered out into the black water. It was full of shoals and small ever-changing islands from erosion in the current. It was a place where the big Federal gunboats could not go for risk running aground. This had to be it! He looked to the east. Hints of gray light were seeping into the horizon. He turned back to the weary faces around him. They were   waiting for orders. He let out a sharp exhale through his nose, dropped his shoulders, and sunk deeper into his saddle.

"Alright, set out a picket line along the river. The men can sleep in turns, but I want constant eyes on that other shore. They ain't sneaking through on our watch."

Newman woke with a jolt. "Take it easy, sir. It's just coffee," Sergeant Barnes smiled, handing him a steaming tin cup.

"Thanks," he mumbled, taking a sip, feeling his mustache soak into the hot brown liquid. He peered up from the rim back at the sergeant. "How long have I've been sleeping?"

"A few hours, sir. I didn't have the heart to wake you."

"Any sign?"

"No, sir, not of the Rebels or our reinforcements."

"Hmm…get the word out. I want our boys to start patrolling again. If they're crossing here, I don't want to be caught sleeping."

The dreary afternoon brought the threat of sleep once more. Newman fought his eyelids as his horse ambled along with the others. *Just five minutes,* he thought.

CRACK!

The sound of a distant rifle snapped his eyes open. Soon there were more. The sharp and rapid report of the 2nd Michigan's newly issued Spencer repeating carbines was unmistakable.

"It's coming from downriver!" Barnes called out.

"Bugler, sound the assembly!" Newman shouted. He stood up in his stirrups and waved his hat in a circle as the bugler spurted out the jaunty melody. "On me, boys!" he called. The rest of H Company were soon around him. Their horses pawed the ground.

"We're missing the fight, Captain," Chucky said, snapping his head back and forth between the sounds of battle and Captain Newman.

"Don't be in such a rush," Bates mumbled.

"Not for long, boys. In column, follow me!" Newman shouted. They were off, thundering along the shore of the Tennessee. Newman slowed them to a trot as they neared the crackling sounds of a firefight. Already several companies of the 2nd Michigan had dismounted. They had taken up positions along the shore, firing their Spencer repeating carbines.

They fired, then pulled back their hammers to the half-cock position. Pushing the levers under the guns forward, they opened the breeches and shook out the spent copper casings. Pulling the lever back fed another round from the magazine which was hidden in the shoulder stock. Then they pulled the hammers back again to the full-cock position and fired once more. After seven shots, they pulled the tubular springs from the butts of the rifles and inserted seven more rounds before replacing the spring and firing again.

Newman shook his head at the sight as he dismounted. "Leave your horses here and fill in on the firing line," he told them. He was still amazed at the modern weapons, even though they'd had them since March. The metal cartridge firing weapons replaced the old cap and ball revolving rifles that they had carried at the start of the war. No more did they have to pour powder and push balls into the cylinders

He looked over to a heavily wooded island in the river. The Rebels were coming out of the woods, firing back at a much slower rate as they were still ramming powder and balls into the barrels of their muskets for each shot.

"Where did they come from?" he asked one of the captains, motioning to the ever-increasing numbers spilling out of the woods.

"They used the island to shield their crossing overnight," he told him.

"Sneaky bastards," Newman said, returning his eyes to the enemy growing in numbers on the island shore. In time, they were overwhelming, even for their Spencer repeaters. At last, the other regiments arrived from Croxton's brigade. They added their firepower to the 2nd Michigan, but it wasn't enough. Their small cavalry brigade was no match for the forty-thousand-strong Confederate Army of Tennessee. Once the Rebels unlimbered their artillery on the shore and started firing, the Federal horsemen had no choice but to fall back and watch in frustration as Confederate engineers built their bridge out of pontoons and planks. Attempts to pick them off as they worked were quickly answered with cannon volleys that sent Federal riflemen running. Overnight, a team of volunteers took canoes into the waters. They were to cut the pontoons loose and destroy the bridge. Those men never returned. They were most likely dead or captured. The bridge remained. There was nothing they could do to stop the Rebels from crossing.

Lieutenant General John B. Hood hoisted himself up with his one good arm onto his crutches. He used them in concert with his one good leg and the prosthetic leg he wore for riding to move toward his horse. His staff watched quietly. An aide took his crutches and strapped them to the back of his saddle. Two others hoisted him onto his mount. Hugging the horse's flanks with his leg and remaining stump, he felt complete. He sat tall. His 6'2, broad-shouldered frame towered over his subordinates. He gathered his long, tawny beard with his good hand and straightened it between the rows of brass buttons on his gray uniform. A raindrop splattered on his shoulder. He looked up at the cloud-covered skies. His deep-set blue eyes scanned for hints of sunlight. There was none. He nudged his horse forward. His staff fell in behind him. The drums, horns, and fife started a jaunty version of *Dixie* for the men to find rhythm in their step. Thousands of men followed in ranks of four.

More drops fell. The weather had been fine for days as the first troops crossed and occupied the northern shore. They shooed away a small detachment of Federal cavalry and secured the bridgehead for the rest of the army and their leader to cross. It was appropriate now, he thought, that it should rain on his crossing. Like the gray clouds covering the blue skies, his gray army would completely blot out the invaders in blue. Like the countless drops of rain, they would shower the Yankees with cannonades and musketry. The rain started coming steadily as his horse took its first steps onto the bridge and found its footing on the swaying and rocking pontoons that kept it afloat.

Sherman may have taken Atlanta and was reported to be mounting a campaign to bring the rest of Georgia under his heel, but he left Tennessee poorly defended. Hood held his face up high, allowing the cold rain to splatter against it and soak his thick blond hair. The Confederate battle flags flapped in the wind behind him. Caesar was thirty-six years old when he crossed the Rubicon and claimed Rome for himself. John B. Hood was thirty-three, in command of an army, and on his way to take Nashville.

Chapter Twenty-Seven: They're Coming

Elijah ducked under the eaves of the State Capitol. The rain was now coming down hard. The Greek columns towered over him as he huddled against the cold. From here, he could see the network of uncompleted trenches and fortifications that sprawled from the Capitol Hill to the far forward picket lines on the outer edge of the city. He shook his head. Nashville was just not prepared for the storm to come. He let out a sigh and hobbled back out into the rain. A tarp had blown off one of the big guns that were mounted around the building. He could not justify keeping himself dry while the rain splattered against the exposed barrel.

The city had been in a frenzy ever since the news came. General Hood's army had crossed the Tennessee River, just below the Alabama line. They were marching north to Nashville. The Federals did not have the manpower to stop them. General Sherman had taken most of the troops on his rampage through Georgia. What he left behind was just enough to occupy the city and a few more to spread out through the state in a failing attempt to guard the supply lines from partisan guerrillas and Forrest's cavalry. Nashville was woefully undermanned in the face of the Rebel army that was coming.

Desperate calls went out to all available forces in the region, but some would take weeks to arrive. The only significant force that stood between Hood's army and Nashville was General Scofield's two corps from the Army of the Ohio. They were at Pulaski, just fifteen miles north of the Alabama line. But Scofield's smaller force could only hope to slow Hood down without being completely enveloped and destroyed themselves.

Everyone in Nashville was put to work. Press gangs rounded up free black men and forced them into labor teams. They dug trenches and built fortifications. Elijah didn't wait for the press gangs to find him. He jumped in as soon as he heard the news. "If the Rebels capture Nashville, ain't none of us gonna be free no how," he told the others who lamented that their liberators had just become their new masters. He may have been missing a foot, but he still had a gift with horses and experience with cannons. That made him invaluable to the undermanned artillery units. He threw himself into the work, driving the horse teams that moving the big guns into position. The white artillerists were happy to have the help. Some treated him like a mascot or a junior member of their batteries. Elijah endured it. Still, he wondered if he was doing enough. He looked at the soldiers around him who, following his example, came out of their shelters and continued their work of setting up and protecting the big guns around the Capitol. Their blue uniforms set off another wave of guilt through him. Should he be in blue, too?

Rejoining the military was not in the plan, even if they did accept him with a missing foot. He was supposed to wait for Carl. Once together again, they'd continue searching for that awful Lathan Woods and make him pay for the terrible things he did to Francis.

But months had gone by. Carl had surrendered to a Rebel patrol so Elijah could escape. He acted like he was trying to join, but Elijah didn't think they were buying it. For all he knew, they hanged him and Elijah was waiting for nobody. Now it seemed two of the best friends he had ever known were gone, and the city he thought was a safe place of refuge was threatened by an army of those who would make him a slave again.

He had another friend, however, a friend that had been quite a surprise in the early days shortly after he got to Nashville.

"Well, I'll be damned!" the familiar voice had startled him from his thoughts back in late June. With nothing to do and nowhere to go, Elijah found a place in the shade to watch the riverboats come and go on the Cumberland. "They done put white man's clothes on a big ugly bear, but he still ugly!" the voice said.

"Jerry?!" Elijah gasped, turning his eyes to his long-lost friend.

"Corporal Jerry, fool!" Jerry smiled, pointing to the twin stripes on his arm. His unbuttoned uniform jacket hung loosely and open on him, allowing the sweltering summer heat to escape from his body.

"You made it!" Elijah said, bounding to his feet and overwhelming his friend with a hug.

"So did you, Baby Boy," Jerry chuckled, then looked down at Elijah's prosthetic foot. "Well, at least most of you."

"Ah, it ain't nothin' but a thing," Elijah said, looking at his false foot and then back to his friend.

"Where Frenchie at?" Jerry asked, smiling broadly. The smile fell away slowly as he saw the wild change of emotions flash across Elijah's face.

"He...he..." Elijah suddenly covered his mouth, trying to smother an unexpected sob.

Jerry's eyes softened. "Hey, take it easy, big fella," he said, putting his hand on his shoulder. "I got some liberty time. Why don't you buy me a drink? We talk about it."

They found a stand in the shantytown built up in the shady alleys behind the big building streets where the white people walked. It was a shack that served hot plates of chicken and beans with cool cups of lemonade fortified with whiskey. Jerry listened somberly as Elijah told him about the terrible moments that followed after they had parted ways.

"You mean that fellow that caught us way back in the New Madrid days?" Jerry asked.

"The same." Elijah shook his head, then described the beating and burning Francis had suffered by him and his men. Jerry cringed at the details.

"Damn, I see why you got it in for him. I owe him a few lumps, too. They was pretty rough with me, too, as I recall."

"Yeah, he a bad man," Elijah said distantly, sipping his lemonade.

"You right," Jerry said nodding. "But you know what? Frenchie was a good man. I wish I had the chance to tell him that. Toughest sissy I know..." he said shaking his head. Elijah let out a laugh that helped clear some of the sorrow he felt in his stomach.

"Stop it," he chided, giving Jerry a soft elbow.

Jerry let out a soft laugh, "I know, I know. Truth is, he more a man than I'll ever be." A silence fell between the two. Elijah tried to think of something to say. He was grateful when Jerry broke in once more. "Say, you wanna go around killin' white boys, you oughta join up with me. We always lookin' for good men in the 13th, even if they ugly."

Elijah smiled, "I don't think they'd take me without two good feet to march with."

"Sure they would! We got all sorts of busted niggas up in there."

Elijah shook his head and laughed, "Jerry, you ain't changed a bit." In the end, Elijah had to beg off, claiming he had to wait for Carl and stay true to his mission.

For days, he watched over the roadways that led into the city, hoping to catch Carl straggling into town. He made the rounds to all the hotels, taverns, and flophouses, or at least the ones that would allow a colored man to enter. He thought maybe Carl had slipped into town when he was unaware.

Eventually, he found work as the summer weeks rolled on, shoeing and tending to horses. He had plenty of money. He kept it hidden in the hollow of his false limb. Mr. Beachamp had promised to send him more if he needed. But he grew restless and didn't want to be seen as an "idle negro" loitering around town. He did well and, once again, had to beg off offers of a permanent job. He needed to be free and ready for when Carl arrived.

He was beginning to doubt that would happen when autumn arrived. He feared he had been wasting time waiting for someone who was never coming when he should have been moving on his own to fulfill the promise he made Mr. Beachamp to avenge Francis.

"Last chance, Baby Boy," Jerry chided him as the 13th US Colored Infantry prepared to load the train. They were once again called to protect the rail lines that allowed supplies to flow from the rivers, through Nashville, and ultimately to Sherman's Army in Georgia. This time they were heading to Johnsonville where supplies were unloaded from riverboats on the Tennessee and sent east on railcars to Nashville. Elijah couldn't understand how the river could be both due west and straight south of him at the same time.

"That's 'cause the Tennessee run west along the Alabama border then makes a hard right and then runs straight north to the Ohio River on the Ohio-Kentucky border," Jerry explained, drawing a crude map in the dirt with a stick.

"How do you know all this?" Elijah asked. He couldn't imagine how someone could comprehend something bigger than what he could with his own eyes. The world was truly an enormous place outside of the plantation where he grew up.

"Oh, they got maps and stuff tryin' t'esplain why we gotta go die by some ol' river somewhere," Jerry said, shrugging his shoulders.

"Gee, you really make me want to join up when you put it like that," Elijah nudged him with his elbow.

"Alright, Baby Boy, you got me there. If I see that ol' Lathan Woods, I'll shoot'em for you. You just look out for my girl while I'm gone," Jerry said.

"Which one?"

"I don't know, whichever prettier. Just don't go takin' any turns in m'absence, you big ugly bear."

Elijah watched the men board the train as their wives and children waved and cheered. Jerry stopped and turned to give him a wink before disappearing into the boxcar. The train gave off a blast of steam and then slowly started pulling away. The empty feeling churned in Elijah's stomach as he watched it go. Should he have been on that train too? Where exactly did his duty lie?

Duty found him easily like the rain that soaked his coat as he tightened the rope that held the tarp over the big gun outside of the Capitol building. Jerry could very well be fighting Forrest's raiders on the Tennessee River to the west right now. Rumor had it that some sort of disaster happened out there. He worried about him greatly. It seemed all his friends were dying while he hid in the city. He tried to learn more about what happened at Johnsonville, but bigger news came and no one was talking about Johnsonville anymore. Now everyone was in a panic. A large Rebel army had crossed the Tennessee River to the south and were marching to Nashville. The city would need every man to stand up and fight, with or without a blue jacket. Elijah may only have one foot. But his duty was clear, he would stand. He would fight.

Chapter Twenty-Eight: The Burning of Johnsonville

Jerry didn't say a word as they boarded the train. The handful of privates he bossed around knew not to talk when their corporal was in this mood. Wisps of smoke still swirled around them carrying the smell of burnt wood, meat, sugar, and whiskey. It was all that remained of the supply depot at Johnsonville. Behind them were the smoldering ruins of the warehouses, the wharf, and the twenty-eight steamboats and barges that were tied there. Now they were nothing more than burned-out husks in various sunken states spread out for a mile along the eastern shore of the Tennessee River. The millions of dollars' worth of supplies that the 13th US Colored Infantry had been sent to protect were gone. All of it had been nothing more than fuel for a fire that lit up the night for miles around.

What burned Jerry the most, was that they had done it themselves. He barely got a glimpse of the enemy on the other side of the river before the order had come to burn the supplies, anything to keep them and the gunboats out of the hands of the Rebels. The fire got out of control. It spread from boat to boat and then to the buildings until everything was burning. They tried to douse the flames, but the Rebel cannons and sharpshooters fired on everything that moved from across the water. Soon it was clear that it wasn't worth losing any more men over an inferno that could not be contained.

The next morning, they had stacked their rifles and walked down to the waterfront to see what could be salvaged. There was nothing left but smoldering remains. Bits of ash drifted in the air like snow, but the heat still rising from the ruins made it unseasonably warm for early November. Many of the men removed their wool jackets as they searched the remains for anything of worth.

The frustration lay on them thick like the ash that covered the ground. They had lost a battle that they never got the chance to fight. The Rebels had come quietly. They found places hidden in the woods of the opposite shore to set their cannons completely undetected.

It had been another busy day on the wharf loading and unloading ships, and stacking supplies on the docks or in the warehouses. Civilians strolled along the wharf, waiting for their boats to embark once more. There were wild stories of Rebels stealing gunboats and raising hell downriver to the north. But a squadron of Federal ironclads, crewed by experienced Navy men, put a stop to that. They forced the Rebels to abandon and burn their stolen vessels then flee into the woods on the western shore. Hopefully, that was the end to General Forrest and his raiders' threat to the busy river port of Johnsonville.

A sudden eruption of smoke and fire startled everyone from their afternoon tasks. The first shots plunged into two of the gunboats just as they were leaving port, immediately disabling them. More shots followed. Men leaped from the boats and swam to shore as steam and smoke billowed out after them. Others could be heard inside, screaming as they were scalded alive from a direct hit to the boiler.

The Rebels reloaded and fired relentlessly. Complete panic broke out on the wharf. Women and civilians ran up the hill to the protection of forts as their big guns awoke and began firing back, blindly at the other shore. The still functioning boats opened fire, too, trying to find targets in the woods across the river before the Rebels hammered them into silence as well.

Jerry grabbed any man he could find. "Get y'goddamn guns, you fools!" he barked. They dashed to where their rifles were neatly staked in tepee-like structures of four. The weapons rattled as men grabbed them and detached the bayonets for easier loading. They ran back to the waterfront. "Don't wait for orders, just shoot!" Jerry shouted, as he spat out the bit of the paper cartridge he had torn off with his teeth. He poured it into the barrel, flinching at the shells landing around him as he rammed it home. He set a percussion cap on the nipple, brought the rifle to his shoulder, and fired blindly into the smoke that hid the enemy on the other side. A crackle of musketry rippled along the shore. The men of the 13th were giving it back. The cannons on the other side responded with a deafening roar, punching men down with a spray of shell fragments. Jerry felt the hot wind carrying deadly projectiles blow past him. He hissed and cringed. Something had scraped along his side, cutting his jacket. He felt the blood beginning to trickle there.

"Damn!" he let out as he dropped. He patted his side for the wound. He couldn't tell how bad it was, but he was still breathing so he decided to keep fighting. He rolled onto his back and loaded another round. He rolled back onto his stomach and fired again into the general direction of the Rebel guns. The cries of wounded men around him found gaps between the popping of muskets and the booming of the cannons.

"Who the hell told you to get your rifles, damn it?!" White officers had shown up just in time to tell them what they were doing wrong again. "Get the wounded out of here! We need you with buckets, not rifles, you fools!"

They fell back and re-stacked their rifles behind the warehouse. It was already on fire. Soon they were running buckets of water from the river to the raging flames. Jerry burned with indignation each time he saw a man shot down while fighting the fire instead of the enemy. It was a fire the foolish commanders had ordered themselves, hoping to keep the supplies and gunboats out of Rebel hands. Now the fires were out of control and it was up to a black man to put it out.

It was hopeless. And too many men died in the useless effort. The command finally came to fall back to the fort. From there all they could do was watch everything burn along the shore. The fire raged all night. The big guns of the fort blasted blindly through the wall of flames at the opposite shore. Eventually, they too gave up.

Jerry kicked around the ashes and smoldering wood in a half-hearted attempt to look like he was doing something useful. They came out the morning after to clean up the white man's mess, as always. He was careful not to overextend himself. He didn't want the stitches along the side of his ribs to bust loose and start bleeding again. He figured he had been lucky. He watched so many die uselessly. He wondered if any of the rounds he had fired at the other shore even hit anyone.

"Hey, look! They still there!" one of the men shouted. Soon more of them were shouting, yelling insults, and shaking their fists at a collection of Rebels across the river. Having done their work, the Confederates were packing up their cannons and preparing to leave. Still, Jerry had the sense to step away from the crowd. No point in being part of a target, he thought

He watched the men across the water. He had been an artilleryman himself. It was still interesting to watch how the big guns were handled. They were attaching them to limbers and pulling them away with horse teams.

Then he noticed it.

The Rebels unlimbered one of the cannons and were pushing it back to its firing position.

"What are they…?" he mumbled to himself.

Then it became clear.

"Hey!" he shouted at the men who had crowded together to yell insults at the Rebels. "Get out of there, you damn fools! They 'bout to fire!" It was no use. The angry crowd couldn't hear him over their own voices.

BOOM!

The cannon fired, sending birds scampering from the trees. Several men fell to the ground, reeling in agony, others were dead.

"Get out of there, you fools!" he shouted. It was unnecessary. The men were running in all directions now. The Rebels were loading another round. "Get your rifles!" Jerry yelled at them. They should be firing back, he thought, now that they had a chance to actually fight someone. But the men were running wildly to get away from the exploding shells. By the time some of them had fetched their rifles and returned, the Rebels were gone. Everything was gone. There was nothing to fight for, and nobody to fight.

Broken and defeated, the 13th loaded onto the train. With nothing left to defend, they were heading back to Nashville. Jerry found a spot on the wall inside the boxcar. He slumped against it and rested his back. He closed his eyes and let out a breath. A young private turned to look at him.

"Shut up," Jerry said without bothering to open his eyes.

Chapter Twenty-Nine: The Mexican

Carl, or Corporal Carlos de la Vega as his comrades knew him, couldn't help but cringe as the 10-pound Parrot rifle fired into the mass of unarmed men on the other shore.

"Ha! Look at'em darkies run!" one of the cannoneers shouted with glee.

Carl quickly recovered. He was careful not to show any queasiness at seeing Federal soldiers shot down in front of his fellow Confederates, especially now that he had a reputation to keep. The men quickly reloaded and fired again. The mass of jacketless soldiers on the other shore had broken up after the first shot. The second round burst into a cloud of lead fragments, tagging a few of the fleeing soldiers and knocking them to the ground. This sent howls of laughter among the gunners.

"Pickin' cotton don't seem so bad anymore, do it now?!" another gunner called out after them.

"Alright, boys," a young officer rode up after the second shot, "you done had your fun. Pack it up and get on the road. We're already behind. General Forrest don't take too kindly to stragglers."

The last sentence brought an air of seriousness to the gunners. "Of course, Captain," the sergeant of the crew saluted, then turned to his men and gave them a sharp nod. They quickly swabbed the barrel and began to roll it back to its limber. Captain Morton turned to Carl. "Corporal *Carlos*," he said with some irony.

"Uh, yes, sir," Carl replied, startled at being addressed directly by the artillery commander. "Have your boys watch over them as they work. I don't want any of those negroes taking potshots at my men."

"Of course, sir."

"Your team will stay with them until you catch up to the main column. If I lose any gunners, I'm coming to you for the tab."

"Of course, sir."

Captain Morton eyed him for a moment, then rode off to check on his other crews.

"Alright, I guess we should watch that other shore for sharpshooters," Carl told the handful of men assigned to him. "They might come back with rifles." The men looked at him for a moment then turned to their assignments. He felt a little foolish giving obvious orders to men who knew what to do anyway.

They were hard to read. Carl wondered if they liked or resented him. He felt it might have been a mistake to tell Captain Jeb that his dad had been a Mexican. That marked him as a Mexican as well among his new comrades ever since, even though he had never been to Mexico nor could he speak a lick of Spanish. They playfully called him "*Carlos*" and would say things like "*si, señor*" when he tried to give an order. Most of it seemed to be good-natured, but others seemed to take offense to the half-breed, Yankee-sounding stranger who suddenly had corporal stripes and was telling them what to do.

Carl tried not to push them too much. Still, it was exhilarating to have been given rank and recognition at last, even if had come from those he had considered the enemy. He watched Captain Morton ride off. The commander of Forrest's artillery couldn't have been more than a few years older than him. It was proof that a man could be anything in this wild and improvisational army.

Carl thumbed his Sharp's carbine and scanned the burned wreckage on the opposite shore. He had to be careful not to be seduced by this strange acceptance from the other side.

"Alright, *Capitán*," the gun crew's sergeant called to him. "We're moving out, if you and your boys would be so kind as to escort us, *Señor.*"

Carl let out a polite laugh and rolled his eyes. "Of course, Sergeant." He nudged his horse away from the shore and rode behind the limbered gun and its crew. The rest of Carl's team rode in front and on the flanks, guarding the gun and its team from any possible surprise attacks as they traveled.

He liked a lot of the men he was with, even if they teased him. In a way, it felt like acceptance. He had to remind himself from time to time to hold on to his anger. Lathan Woods was his enemy and he was somewhere among them. Carl was going to find and kill him for what he did to Francis and hopefully soon. It was only a matter of time before they saw through his ruse and denounced him for the imposter that he was. They were most certainly going to hang him as a spy if he stayed with them too long. He looked down at the two golden stripes on his still new gray uniform. He scoffed and shook his head at the irony and absurdity of it all. He had thought they were going to hang him, just before they gave him his stripes.

"Carlos!"

Carl had just closed his eyes. The voice startled him out of his drowsiness. He looked up to see Captain Jeb standing over him. "The General wants to see you."

"The who…?" Carl asked, slowly getting to his feet.

"General Forrest, son, and I wouldn't keep him waiting."

"Of course!" Carl said, dusting himself off.

They had just gotten back to Hernando in Mississippi after their early morning raid on Memphis back in August. It had been an exhausting romp. They had ridden all night to get there, attacked at dawn, then had to fight their way out. They spent the rest of the day driving hundreds of captured horses, mules, and prisoners through the steamy summer heat, trying to put as much distance as possible between them and the angry Federal hornets' nest they had kicked.

It wasn't until they crossed Hurricane Creek that they felt safe enough to call a halt and give the men and horses a much-needed rest. Carl had found the shade of a tree to steal a wink or two just before Captain Jeb came to fetch him.

"Am I in trouble?" he asked, as they walked through the streets filled with lounging men and tied-up horses.

"You tell me," Jeb answered. "Is there something you ought to be in trouble for?"

Carl thought it was best to not answer. They reached the town square. General Forrest and his staff were sitting in chairs they had taken from the courthouse. It was cooler to sit in the shade than inside the stuffy old building. Several of the Yankee officers were standing under guard nearby. One stood before the general. Carl recognized him as soon as the man turned to look at him.

"That's the one, General!" the man said, pointing his finger at Carl. His eyes were blackened and nearly swollen shut. His lip was busted and his face was heavily bruised. "That's the soldier who assaulted me, sir, in an unduly and outrageous violation of the civilized conduct of war. I am an officer, and furthermore, I was unarmed. I demand justice!"

Carl unconsciously took a slight step back as Forrest's cold blue eyes moved from the Yankee captain to him.

"Is this true?" Forrest asked flatly.

Carl gulped as he looked around at the faces staring at him. "He, um…was attacking a woman… sir."

"Liar!" the Captain screeched, then snapped his head back to Forrest. "Sir, I am an officer and a gentleman. Would you take the word of this rogue…"

Forrest put up his hand, stopping the man mid-sentence. "Captain Jeb, this is one of your boys. Can you say who's telling the truth here?"

"No, sir, but some of my other boys were with him," Jeb answered. "I'd take their word on it."

"Fetch 'em, if you would, Captain. I'd be most interested in hearing their rendition." Forrest said, stroking the beard on his chin. He propped a riding boot on the small writing desk set in front of him and leaned back into his chair. Jeb gave a nod to his man, Tim, who Carl now understood to be a sergeant. Tim nodded and left. Carl could feel the late August heat soaking into his now road-worn civilian clothes as he stood before this summary court. Sweat trickled down his back. The Yankee captain glared at him as they waited.

Tim returned with Davy and Toby. Carl felt a little better as the boys had taken a liking to him, especially after his fight with the captain. They walked up wide-eyed and apprehensive as they approached their general. Toby caught a glance of the badly beaten captain. He elbowed his friend to take a look.

"Dang…" Davy let out at the sight.

"Stand at attention in front of your general," Jeb told them. The boys straightened themselves, snapping their arms to their sides.

"At ease, boys. We're all friends here," Forrest told them. "Can you tell me how Captain Logan here came to be so abused?"

Logan drew in a breath, puffing himself up as he turned to listen to the Rebel soldiers.

"Well, sir. We was headin' for the jail, lookin' to see who we could bust out when all of sudden we heard a lady scream," Toby started. "It didn't take ol' Carlos here but a second to go a chargin' in, no care at all about what he was ridin' into. We tried to stop him."

"We did," Davy nodded in agreement.

"We got there just in time to see Carlos jump from his horse right on to the Captain here and then just started a'pummelin' him, sir, somethin' terrible. We had to pull him off before he kilt 'em!"

"We did, sir!" Davy once again affirmed.

Captain Logan sucked in a breath through his nose, puffing out his chest as he turned to the general, waiting for his response.

"Was there a lady there?" Forrest asked.

"Why, yes, General," Toby said, "a pretty one too! He had her by the wrist…"

"I was escorting her to safety," Logan interrupted.

Toby stopped and blinked at him before speaking, "Pretty sure I saw you strike her, sir."

"Yeah, looked that way to me," Davy nodded in agreement.

A silence fell among the proceeding. Logan finely turned to Forrest, "She was hysterical, General. Panicking from the attack…"

Forrest put his hand up and stopped him cold. The Federal officer seemed to tremble under his gaze. At last, Forrest spoke. "I'm going to parole you and the rest of the captives, Captain. I haven't the time or resources to watch over you." Logan let out a breath in relief. Forrest continued. "I have the mind to give you a lickin' myself, but it looks like Private…"

"Carlos, sir" Jeb interjected.

"…Private *Carlos* did the job well enough, but let me be clear…" Forrest took his boot off the desk and leaned forward, focusing his eyes on the captain, "…if I ever catch you on Southern soil again assaulting our women, I will personally make you pay for it with your life, and I won't be quite as tender as Private Carlos here. Do I make myself clear, Captain?"

"Yes, sir," Logan mumbled, looking at the ground, unable to meet the general's eyes.

"Get him out of here," Forrest ordered. "The sight of weak men sickens me."

Captain Logan kept quiet as the soldiers led him away with the others. Carl watched them go, feeling like he had barely survived the encounter himself.

"Private Carlos…" Forrest spoke at last, startling Carl from his thoughts.

"…de la Vega," Jeb added.

"…*de…la…Vega,*" Forrest said each syllable in a measured rhythm, "Come forward."

Carl stepped forward, trying to hide his fear.

"That sounds Spanish to me," Forrest said.

"He's a Mexican, sir," Jeb said.

"Half Mexican, sir…" Carl blurted before catching himself. He fought the urge to cringe.

"*Half*…Mexican…" Forrest said again measuredly. He put his boot back on the desk and leaned into his chair. "You know, I had the mind to kill Mexicans once…" Carl just blinked at the general, wondering what was coming next. "…rode halfway 'cross Texas just to do so…but the war was over and I didn't get my chance." Forrest paused to examine Carl with his icy blue eyes. Carl worked hard not to tremble. "Now when I think of it…I'm glad I didn't." Carl felt a wave of relief run through him. "They were just fightin' to protect themselves from an invasion of Federal bluebellies like we are." A ripple of murmured agreement spread among the men.

"No, I think I understand the Mexican now," Forrest said, "…and I like a man who will throw it all in the defense of a lady. I like fighters, Carlos." Forrest paused to stare at him for a moment before continuing.

"I'm making you a corporal effective immediately, Corporal *de la Vega*." He then turned to one of his staff officers. "Take Corporal de la Vega to the quartermaster. I want to see him in a uniform with his stripes."

The weeks that followed were a whirlwind of raids and hard riding. Carl rarely had a moment out of the saddle. Charged with harassing Sherman's supply line into Georgia, Forrest and his men raided depots and tore up train tracks all over Northern Alabama and West Tennessee. With the best of the Yankee fighting forces in Georgia, the small garrisons left behind were no match for Forrest and his men. Spread out in separate commands, Forrest seemed everywhere at once to the Federals. The small Yankee detachments left to guard the backwood supply routes were quick to surrender at the mere mention of the general's name.

Carl's company rode with Forrest's personal command while General Chalmers commanded his other wing. The two arms operated separately. It had been a wild ride including commandeering a couple of Yankee gunboats and rampaging on the Tennessee River before running them aground and burning them once the Yankees showed up with a whole squadron of Navy boats to take them back.

Marooned on the western shore with no way to cross, they decided to take one last parting shot at the Federals at Johnsonville before withdrawing south. Carl took a last glance at the smoldering ruins as they rode away. Even Forrest couldn't have guessed that the attack would be so utterly successful. The Federals were so terrified that he would cross the river and capture the depot that they burned their own supplies, then lost control of the flames until everything was gone.

Now, the once jubilant Rebels marched south in somber silence. The party was over. After months of independent command, Forrest and his cavalry corps were assigned to General Hood's army. It was no secret that Forrest resented being put under the command of younger men. They were constantly promoted past him for their West Point educations and not for the kind of battlefield grit and genius that brought Forrest victory after victory.

Hood was waiting for them in Florence, Alabama, writing impatient dispatches to Forrest almost daily, too afraid to start his invasion of Tennessee without cavalry to scout his front and protect his flanks and rear. Now with Johnsonville destroyed, there was nothing more they could do to stall inevitable. They marched south to link up with Chalmers's men. Once united, Forrest would bring his corps into Hood's Army of Tennessee.

"Where's my Mexican?" Forrest asked with humor as Captain Jeb and his men rode up to relieve the general's security detail.

"I got him right here, General, where I can keep my eye on him," Jeb said indicating with his head to Carl riding behind him.

"Good, Chalmers may have a woman-beater with him that we'll need our Mexican to whup," Forrest said with a chuckle. A round of laughs spread among them. Carl felt his face flush with embarrassment.

They had made it to the rendezvous point early. The men were at ease, mostly because Forrest was showing the first signs of good humor since leaving Johnsonville. Jeb placed his men around the general and his staff to protect them. He put Carl near Forrest, knowing that the general enjoyed the novelty of his exotic cavalryman, and also knowing how much it made Carl uncomfortable. Carl knew his captain would be watching him with great amusement, waiting for him to finally break down and reveal this crazy charade.

Soon Carl began to grow bored. At first, he listened to Forrest and his staff speak about their plans for the coming march but then began to drift into his own thoughts. He wondered if he'd ever get a letter off to Anna without it being caught. He wondered if Elijah had made it to Nashville and was he there now? Then, invariably, his thoughts turned to the redheaded beauty that said goodbye to him at Memphis and the little boys in the back of her wagon.

"He's coming, General."

A scout rode up to them to deliver the news. "General Chalmers and his escort are about five minutes behind me, sir," the man saluted.

"Very well," Forrest returned the salute, then straightened himself in his saddle. Carl tried to shake off his afternoon sleepiness. He straightened his uniform and groomed his mustache and chin beard with his gloved hand. He had allowed the facial hair to grow over the months since he left Detroit. Now he felt it added to his Mexican persona and possibly hid his identity, but then again, who among these men would know him from before?

"James! It took you long enough!" Forrest called out to the group of horsemen entering the other end of the clearing.

"I came as soon as you beckoned, General," their leader said calmly. His sleepy eyes and aristocratic bored expression were such a contrast to Forrest's ferocity. It surprised Carl that a man so different would be his second in command.

"Aw, you know I'm just giving you a hard time, James," Forrest chuckled.

"Of course, sir. Your humor is always appreciated," Chalmers replied.

Once again, Carl began to drift as the two commanders spoke. His thoughts were far away as he scanned the faces in General Chalmers's retinue. They were worn out from the long march to link up with their corps commander. Some wore uniforms of mixed style. Others were in civilian clothes. This army was much more loose and fluid than what he remembered from his time in the 2nd Michigan. These men seemed to contrast each other as much as they did their enemy.

Carl flinched. He felt the blood drain from his face. He quickly looked away, hoping the other pair of eyes among Chalmers's men didn't notice him. He stared at the ground, panicking. Everything inside him screamed to spur his horse and run away. He'd be shot down in a minute, he told himself. He let out a breath, gathered his courage, and looked back up. The man was looking right at him. At first, the green eyes held him with some kind of curiosity, as if he were trying to figure out where he knew him from.

Carl straightened himself. There was nowhere to run. He could shoot him now. He could spur his horse forward and empty his revolver into this man then throw himself on top of him and tear out his eyes before anyone could stop him. Anger and hatred ran through him suddenly like hot lava, pushing away the fear.

Lathan's eyes seemed surprised at the change of emotion, then widened in stunned disbelief. Recognition had finally set in. He tilted his head and mouthed the word, "How?"

Carl mouthed back, "I'm going to kill you."

Lathan nodded, smiling maniacally. His eyes sparkled with irony as he winked.

"Until our next rendezvous in two days, General," Chalmers gave a slight bow to Forrest before turning his horse.

"Until then, James," Forrest said, touching the brim of his hat.

Chalmers trotted off. His men turned to follow. Lathan gave Carl one last nod and a smile before turning and following his commander.

"C'mon," Forrest told the men around him, "the clock is ticking." He spurred his horse forward. Carl fell in behind his captain and the general. He could almost hear the clock ticking.

Chapter Thirty: Captured!

"Hold the line here, boys! If they cross this creek, we're through!" Captain Chester E. Newman told the men of H Company. "Take this moment to reload. They may not give you another," he said grimly.

He looked back across Saw Mill Creek expecting to see Rebel cavalry come howling through the woods at any moment. He pulled out his Allen and Wheelock pistol, pondering whether to take his own advice and reload the cylinders that he had already fired. The men of the 2nd Michigan Cavalry were scrambling along the line of the creek, looking for places with good cover to shoot from. Many were also taking his advice, pulling out the springs from the butts' of their carbines and inserting cartridges into the magazines to bring them back up to a full seven rounds.

It had been a nonstop running fight since the Rebels rolled out of Florence, Alabama, and into Tennessee. The 2nd Michigan had been the rearguard, constantly holding off Rebel cavalry as General Schofield pushed his small army north. The Confederates furiously nipped at their heels, desperate to get in around their flanks, envelop, and crush them before they reached the safety of Nashville and the rest of General Thomas's army. It was an all-out race and the war in the West was the prize.

Time and time again, the Michiganders dismounted, formed a line, and held off the Rebels with the superior firing rate of their Spencer repeating carbines, then fell back just before the Rebels were able to ride around their flanks.

The Rebels had nearly succeeded at catching them at Spring Hill the day before. They attacked from the east as the Federals were evacuating Columbia and got caught with their cannons and supply wagons stretched out along the road to Franklin. The Rebels poured in wave after wave against the under-protected Federal right, but then inexplicably halted at sunset and began to set up their camps. Stunned at this reprieve, the Federals did not waste the opportunity. They scurried to Franklin through the night, keeping a wary eye on the Rebel campfires which were easily within rifle shot of the long line of march.

Once in Franklin, they dug in. The town sat snug in a bend of the Harpeth River. A rail bridge and a burned-out wagon bridge were the only ways across. Once they got on the other side of the Harpeth, the safety of Nashville's fortifications and General Thomas's army would be an easy day's march away. But the engineers needed time to repair the bridges before the wagon trains, artillery, and men could cross.

So the sleepless and footsore soldiers spent the morning repairing the town's trenches and earthworks, digging new ones, and building an abatis to create a half-circle of fortifications that connected each end to the river. These fortifications and the bend in the river created a complete circle of defense for the engineers to do their work and the wagons to begin crossing the river.

The cavalry was guarding the fords in the river along the Lewisburg Pike on the eastern flank. This was to keep the Confederates from crossing south of town and attacking Federals from the other side of the narrow bridges. The 2nd Michigan sat with the river anchored on their left. In front of them ran Saw Mill Creek which fed into the river. They hoped it was a good enough obstacle to slow the unstoppable Confederates down.

"Yeee! Yip! Yip! Yip! Yeeeee!"

A chill shot through Newman as the screeching echoed in the woods. "Damn it…" he mumbled looking down at his pistol. He had missed his chance to reload. "Here they come boys!" he said looking back at the woods across the creek. "Hold fast! Don't fire until you see the fuckers!"

The first of the gray and butternut men came bounding out of the trees. The Spencer carbines crackled to life, dropping some of them near the water's edge and sending the rest tumbling back into the woods for cover.

"Agh! I'm hit! Help me!" one of the fallen Rebels screamed. He twitched and squirmed in agony. Half his body was in the water. A man appeared from the brush, eyeing the Federals harshly. He held up his hands as he slowly crept out of the woods.

"Hold your fire," Newman said, watching the man. They locked eyes on each other.

"Paul, I'm dying," the soldier cried out. "Oh, God, I'm dying!" It was clear now that he was not much more than a boy.

"I got you, Thad," the man said, holding his eyes on Newman. Newman uncocked his pistol and raised the barrel showing the man that he was no longer pointing it at him. The man nodded as he slowly lowered himself and grabbed the boy's arms. Newman nodded back and watched as the man dragged the boy away into the cover of the woods.

"Alright, stay sharp," Newman said, turning to his men. "They'll be coming again soon." They waited quietly, hearing nothing but the water running over the stones. Newman shifted his revolver to his left hand. He reached for his powder flask with his right. He stopped. He heard a rumble, then the Rebel yell once more.

"Damn it…" he gasped, putting his flask away and transferring his pistol back to his right hand. "The lunatics are charging us." He straightened his pistol arm, leveling his aim at the trees. "Hold!"

An avalanche of horsemen burst from the woods. Newman fired at the first man he saw, not knowing if he hit him through all the smoke. The Spencer carbines crackled to life. The men quickly worked the levers and fired again, pouring lead into the charging enemy. Newman fired again. The attack fell apart as men and horses tumbled to the ground. The rest turned around and darted back into the woods.

"Jesus Christ, the fucking madmen…" Newman shook his head. "Get ready! They'll come again," he said, once more reaching for his powder flask. He quickly poured the powder into the empty cylinders then rammed in the lead balls. Satisfied, he looked back at the wood line across the creek and waited.

They did not come again.

Carl followed along with the rest of the escort as Forrest rode to meet with his commanding officer. It was no secret that the two were not fond of each other. Forrest, as always, resented being commanded by a younger man. General Hood still seethed at Forrest's delay in meeting him at Florence and thus holding up his invasion of Tennessee. They had certainly made up for lost time since as they chased the Federals through Colombia, Spring Hill, and now had them pinned against the river at Franklin.

Carl had plenty to worry about along the way. The Yankees with their repeating rifles were as dangerous as a rabid dog in a corner. Every encounter with them seemed likely to be his last. Even worse, every encounter could have forced him to fire on his old friends, although he figured he had been more of a threat to the birds in the trees than any bluejacket with his intentional high firing.

But more than anything, he had his true enemy to worry about. Lathan Woods was somewhere out there with Chalmers's division. Lathan had clearly recognized him. It could only be a matter of time before the game was up. Each day Carl expected to end up hanging from a tree. He spent the few opportunities he was given to sleep clutching his revolver in one hand and his knife in the other, determined to go down fighting when they finally came for him. They hadn't yet. It was maddening. Surely Lathan would denounce him any moment if he hadn't already. Perhaps it was the constant skirmishing and the distance between the two wings of Forrest's command that kept him alive. Lathan was with

General Chalmers's Division on the far left of the Confederate line. Carl was with Forrest and his other two divisions on the right.

Whatever it was that had kept him alive so far, he was sure it would not last. Time was running out on this ruse. He had to find Lathan, kill him, and get across Federal lines before they figured him out and hanged him as a spy. First, he'd have to get through this battle that seemed to be looming before him at Franklin.

The Federals had fortified themselves there with their backs to the river. Forrest and his escort had spent the morning surveying their defenses, looking for weaknesses. They found few. They tried to get around them by crossing the river south of town, but stubborn Yankee cavalry with their repeating rifles held them off at the crossing.

Now Forrest and his small security detail approached a handful of generals collected on Winstead Hill which sat along the Colombia Pike, south of town. From there they could see the rolling fields that climbed gently toward the Federal works. Forrest nodded to General Chalmers, his second in command, as he reined in his horse, then acknowledged the other generals. Chalmers nodded back, then turned his eyes slowly to Carl. He regarded him with aristocratic disinterest. It was immediately unnerving.

Does he know? Is Lathan here too?

Carl scanned Chalmers's escort, looking for the terrifying green-eyed devil. He wasn't there. Carl let out his breath then turned back to Chalmers. He was still eying him. Panic began to rise in his stomach. Chalmers finally moved his eyes back to Forrest and joined the conversation.

I've got to get the fuck out of here, Carl thought.

"Where is he?" Forrest asked.

"He rode forward a bit to get a better look," Chalmers said.

"I'm afraid we're not going to like what he sees, gentleman," General Cheatham added.

"Here he comes now," Chalmers motioned with his head.

Carl turned to see. General Hood was a surprise to him. He was a young and handsome man with deep-set blue eyes, a long face, and a long tawny beard. He sat high in his saddle. His wooden leg bounced clumsily against the side of his horse as he trotted up the hill. He held the reins in his right hand while his left arm hanged limply in a sling.

"We will make the fight," he said boldly as he brought his horse to a halt before his generals. Cheatham let out a short breath through his nose and looked once more at the half-ring of fortifications that locked the town to the river. A moment of silence followed among the generals. Forrest finally spoke.

"General, having been the first of us here, I've had the opportunity to reconnoiter their defenses thoroughly. Their position is exceedingly formidable, and in my opinion, cannot be taken by direct assault without a great and unnecessary loss of life."

"I do not think the Federals will stand strong pressure from the front," Hood replied quickly. "The show of force they are making is a feint in order to hold me back from a more vigorous pursuit."

The two stared at each other for a moment. The other generals watched them quietly. Carl began to feel uncomfortable. At last, Forrest spoke again.

"General Hood, if you will give me one strong division of infantry to go with my cavalry, I will agree to flank the Federals from their works. I will clear them out in two hours' time."

Hood smiled slowly. "I appreciate your offer, General Forrest, but we've run out of time for wide flanking maneuvers. They certainly didn't seem to work for us at Spring Hill," he said, shooting a sideways glance at General Cheatham. Cheatham let out another short breath and looked away, back at the Federal lines.

"The Federals are at the point of breaking, gentlemen," Hood continued. "One good push and we'll destroy them. The plan stands. Cheatham and Stewart's corps will attack their center in full force, Stephan Lee's corps will be in reserve once they arrive. General Forrest, you will keep your cavalry split between the two flanks. Once we break through, you'll ride down and destroy any of them that try to escape to Nashville."

"I don't like the looks of this fight," General Cheatham finally spoke. He had been quiet since taking much of the blame for the failure at Spring Hill. "The Federals have an excellent and well-fortified position."

Hood turned his smile towards him. "I'd rather fight them here where they've only had a few hours to fortify than at Nashville where they've had three years." A silence fell on the generals once more. After a moment, Hood spoke again. "Gentlemen, you have your orders. God is on our side. This council is adjourned." He sat quietly on his horse smiling at his corps commanders as they slowly turned their horses away and rejoined their own staffs.

Carl watched General Cheatham shake his head as he trotted toward his division commanders. A handsome dark-haired general greeted him with a smile and a twinkle in his blue eyes. "Well, General," the man said with a lyrical Irish brogue, "if we are to die, let us die like men."

"C'mon," Forrest said to his own men. Carl fell in behind the general as they trotted away.

The late morning skirmishing had fizzled out to an eerily quiet afternoon. The Federal cavalry fell back a mile closer to town and started to build a barricade across the Lewisburg Pike facing southeast. Once again, they anchored their extreme left on the Harpeth River. There they would hold off any attempt the Rebels might make to squeeze between the road and the river and pour into the Federal defensive works from the flank.

Brigade commander General Croxton rode out to inspect this new forward line. The men, done with their work, were now taking the opportunity to eat and rest, carefully snuggled away in the cover they had created. Lieutenant Colonel Ben Smith, who now commanded the 2nd Michigan, greeted Croxton with a salute.

"Awfully quiet, Colonel," Croxton returned the salute. "Any sign of the enemy?"

"Not a hide nor hair since we moved back, General," Smith replied. "Makes me a little nervous, actually."

BOOM!

A distant flash of cannon fire was followed by a sharp whistling of shell in flight.

BAM!

The shot buried itself in the ground a few feet from the general's horse, showering them with dirt and causing the animal to rear up on its hind legs, whinnying loudly.

"Whoa! Whoa! Easy!" Smith shouted, grabbing the reins and forcing its front feet back to earth. Croxton had already leaped off and was crouching, bracing for another shot. When it didn't immediately come, he stood up and dusted himself off.

"Well, I suppose I should be a bit more careful," he said with some irony. "Be sure to keep your eye on them, Colonel, and keep your line of retreat open."

The men welcomed the quiet that followed. Some snoozed behind the walls of dirt and the abatis made from osage orange limbs. Others wrote letters or puffed pensively on pipes, occasionally looking off to the woods afar, wondering what the enemy was doing in his silence. By mid-afternoon, the wondering became too much, even for the commanders.

"Nothing more than a mounted reconnaissance, Captain Hodges," Colonel Smith told the I Company commander. "Do not bring on an engagement."

"Aye, Captain," Hodges saluted. Smith returned the salute, then patted the horse's rump as he rode off. I Company rode out past the abatis. "Don't shoot us on the way back, Chester," Hodges said as he passed.

"Why not?" Newman grinned. "What have you done for me lately?"

I Company spread out in a battle line as they trotted forward. The men behind the barricades watched quietly as the horsemen moved farther toward the unseen enemy. Suddenly, they broke into a trot and began firing their pistols.

"How is that *not* 'bringing on an engagement'…?" Smith groaned to himself.

Croxton rode up within minutes of the shots. "What's happening, Colonel?" He said, returning the salute.

"I sent a company out to reconnoiter the enemy, sir. I told them not to start an engagement but it seems they've stepped into something."

"Hmmm…" Croxton mused. He pulled out his field glasses and scanned the ground ahead. A lone trooper came galloping back. The man wove his way around the abatis, then reined in his horse in front of the two officers.

"What's your report, Lieutenant?" Smith asked, returning the salute.

"Sir, we pushed back an advanced position of the enemy. It was lightly defended. We're holding it now."

Smith turned to Croxton with raised eyebrows and pursed lips.

Croxton took another look through his field glasses, then brought them to his lap "Well, Colonel," he said, "if you're whipping the Rebels, go in."

The 2nd Michigan mounted their horses and formed into battle lines in front of the abatis. They left one company back to guard the retreat. Newman checked his pistol one last time before the order to advance came. The lines of horsemen, several hundred strong, lurched forward, first at a walk, then slowly picking up speed. The men of I Company were waiting ahead. They sprung to their mounts and joined the formation as the regiment pushed forward toward the dark woods across the field.

Several Rebel pickets sprung up from their hiding spots in the tall grass. They fired wildly then ran for the safety of the woods. The horses were now at a full run. The men were taking shots at the fleeing Rebels as they galloped.

Suddenly, and seemingly from out of nowhere, thousands of Confederates sprung to their feet and fired their rifles at the charging horsemen. The shots were rushed and many flew high, but the effect was immediate. Horses reared and some fell over, throwing their riders as the men reined them in too hard. Newman pulled his reins to the left and fired his pistol into the mass of gray and butternut men as he wheeled around. The Confederates were moving forward now, reloading and firing as they went. Their cavalry came exploding out of the woods, spilling around their lines of infantry.

"Shit! Fall back! Fall back!" Chester shouted, firing his pistol wildly at the river of horsemen thundering towards them.

BOOM!

Cannons on the heights from across the river came to life, pouring enfilading fire into the Rebel ranks.

"To the river! To the river!" men were shouting.

Chester rode with the fleeing Federals, turning back to fire at the masses of Rebel cavalry chasing them. He looked forward again to the river. Men and horses were plunging into the water, clinging to their saddles as the horses swam. He turned back to fire once more before taking the plunge himself.

"Gaaaaaa! Fuck!" he shouted as he tumbled into the mud at the river's edge. His horse plunged into the water and swam away without him. Newman rolled into the water. Something had stung him in the back of his thigh and now his leg was on fire. He couldn't move it. Raw panic coursed through him as he struggled against the rain-swollen current. He gasped for air as he clawed his way back to the bank and crawled out of the water, dragging his useless leg behind him. Panting, he looked across the river. Men were pulling each other out of the water and mounting their horses once more. Then he heard the thumping of hooves around him.

"Surrender or I'll shoot!" a Southern voice commanded. Newman raised his hands slowly. He looked up at the Confederate horsemen towering over him.

"I've lost my pistol in the fall, friend. I'm injured and no threat to you now," he smiled softly.

"Trust me, you never were," the man said, then looked over to his men. "Carlos!"

"Yes, Captain," one of his soldiers replied, edging his horse forward.

"This man is an officer. Take him back to the rear and have our doctors look at him," the heavily bearded officer said, then looked back at Newman. "You, sir, are now a prisoner of the Confederate States of America. Your war is over."

Newman laid his head back on the ground and groaned. He clutched at his leg. He was beginning to feel nauseated and dizzy. The soldier the Rebel captain had been speaking to leaped from his horse and came to his side.

"Take it easy, sir. I have to wrap the wound to stop the bleeding," he said.

That voice, Newman thought. He saw the man through his blurred vision. He was dark-complected with locks of wild black hair spilling from his cap. He had a scraggly beard and mustache that barely hid the youthfulness of his face. The young man suddenly froze, as if startled by something.

"What is it, son?" Newman said weakly, finally finding the man's eyes. They were green and wide with astonishment and recognition.

"Chester…" the young man gasped.

Hearing his name uttered from this stranger was a shock. It brought a moment of lucidity to his eyes. Now he saw it, too, and shared the young man's surprise. He smirked as he laid his head back down and closed his eyes. "If I ever wake up again, I'm going to beat the living shit out of you, Carl."

Chapter Thirty-One: The Confrontation

Captain Newman did not wake up. At least not while Carl and his team carried him back to the grand plantation house that was already transforming into a hospital. Carl felt a pang of guilt for being relieved by that. Certainly, he wanted his old captain to live, but having to explain himself amid the Rebel army would certainly blow his already crumbling ruse.

"Haven't we got enough of our own boys to tend to?" a soldier sitting on the steps asked. His bandaged arm hung in a sling.

"He, uh…fought nobly…" Carl fumbled for an answer.

"Well, you can nobly toss his Yankee carcass into the river," the man said.

Carl stood agape, holding Newman's shoulders while Davy and Toby held his feet. He was trying to find something more to say.

"Oh, nonsense," a woman came out wearing a blood-spattered apron. She swatted the man in the back of his head. "Go make yourself useful and bring me a bucket of water," she said, then turned to Carl and his team. "Bring him in, boys. We're busy, but not at the expense of our humanity."

Broken men in various states of consciousness littered the floor. Puddles of blood oozed around them and soaked into the rugs. They found a place and set him down gently. Davy gagged at the stench of chemicals and body fluids. "Wait outside," Carl told them. "I've got to talk to the nurse and then I'll be out, too."

Toby nodded, tugging on the other's arm, "C'mon." Davy didn't need much convincing. Carl smiled as he watched them navigate the blood and bodies on the floor. A warm breeze blew through the open window, momentarily clearing the room of the heavy stench. He closed his eyes and savored it for a moment. For the first time, he realized that it turned out to be a warm sunny day after weeks of cold rain. It was a surprise for the last day of November. His smile slipped away. He could hear the battle intensifying clearly. He opened his eyes and stared out the open window. The ground shook with the regular thundering of cannon. Rifle fire rattled and overlapped itself like hail on a tin roof.

"What's the matter with him?" the nurse entered the room.

"He's shot in the back of the thigh, I think. I wrapped it the best I could," Carl said, looking up at her.

She paused for a moment, examining Carl's face. "He means something to you," she said flatly.

Carl suddenly sucked in a sob that sprang out of nowhere. "I suppose he does," he said.

"Well, leave him here. We'll do what we can with him, darling."

"Thank you," Carl said, wiping his nose with his sleeve. She smiled at him warmly. Carl nodded then clumsily made his way out, feeling her eyes on him the whole time.

Toby and Davy were waiting for him, wide-eyed and listening. The cannon and rifle fire was becoming more and more constant. "They're going at it something furious!" Davy said, shaking his head.

"I supposed we should be throwin' ourselves back into it then," Toby said, looking up at Carl as he came down the veranda steps. Carl stopped and looked off toward the sound. He could see the golden sunlight casting long shadows through the trees, but not much else from the steps of Carton Plantation house. He looked back at the two young men in his charge. They were no older than he was for sure, mere teenagers mostly likely. He bit his lip and looked toward the sound of raging battle again. There was no way in hell he wanted to *throw* himself back into whatever it was that was going on.

He looked back at the two young men, trying to gauge their enthusiasm relative to their fear. They blinked at him with wide-eyed anticipation. He couldn't betray his reluctance to fight the Yankees or his fear. His leadership over these two was already razor-thin, and so was this ruse he had been living for months now. If he acted like a coward, they'd see right through him. They'd see him for the imposter he was. Everything depended on what he said next and how he said it. He cleared his throat.

"Well, we gotta figure out where our boys are before we go running blindly into a wall of bullets," he told them.

"I'm pretty sure they crossed the river, chasin' them Yankees," Toby said, not blinking as he looked to Carl for a reply.

"That was over ten minutes ago," Carl told him. "You know how quickly things change in a fight. They could be anywhere now."

The two stared at him silently as the cannons raged on. "Let's ride up that hill," Carl pointed, "and see if we can't find where they are."

Toby blinked at him. Davy spoke finally. "Makes sense to me!" he said, nudging the other.

"Yeah," Toby said at last, "me too."

Carl felt a fleeting moment of relief as they mounted and rode for the high grounds sitting before the rolling field that led into town. He knew it couldn't last. At some point, he'd have to do something about these two and the enormous battle that was just beginning. Running away was awfully tempting, but how and when?

They came out of the woods into an open patch on the hillside. The low sun sunlight blasted them from the left as they emerged.

"Good Lord…" Davy let out, shielding his eyes.

The great rolling field spread out below them. From their vantage, they could see about twenty-thousand men in gray and butternut marching, their flags fluttering in the breeze. Their formations spread over a mile on each side of the Columbia Pike. In front of them stood a salient of a few thousand Yankees set out a few hundred yards from the main Federal line.

"My God, they'll be crushed out there…" Toby said softly.

The Yankees left out in the forward position desperately poured rifle fire into the approaching ranks, dropping dozens of the marching Rebels.

Federal cannons on the hilltops further back cut down swaths of men, creating momentary gaps in the Confederate formations that quickly disappeared as men moved in to fill them.

Carl cringed at the sight. The Confederates left behind a trail of hundreds of fallen men as they marched farther into the firestorm. Their enormous mass of humanity was on the verge of swallowing up the forward Federal line. At last, the Yankees there broke. They turned and ran for the main defensive line behind them.

"Follow them in!" the Rebels shouted, breaking their clean formations to run in and among the terrified Federals. The Yankees in the main fortifications had to hold their fire, now that the enemy was mixed in with their fleeing comrades. The Rebels were cutting them down as they ran, stabbing them in the back with their bayonets. The officers rode along with them, hacking down at men with their sabers and shooting them with pistols. The officers sitting high on their horses made easy targets for Yankee sharpshooters behind the line. Carl watched in horror as these officers were snatched off their horses by an invisible force, leaving the animals to run wild and alone toward the abatis in panic. Other horses fell kicking and screaming in agony, throwing their riders to the ground.

One of the officers picked himself up, shouted to his men, then continued forward on foot, pointing at the Federal earthworks with his saber.

*Let us die like men…*Carl thought, recognizing the handsome general from before.

The Irishman's body jerked and convulsed as bullets tore through him. Still, he staggered forward then finally collapsed on the Federal earthworks, his body straddling the top, his sword still extended forward. A desperate fight broke out as men played a morbid version of tug-of-war over the prized General's body.

Hand-to-hand fighting spread along the line. The fleeing Yankees had crashed into their own works and the Rebels slammed into them from behind. Without room to reload or aim, the men hacked with sabers, stabbed with bayonets, and pummeled each other with the butt of their rifles.

From Carl's distance, it appeared to be an enormous caldron of humanity boiling over with violence in the darkening gloom. He looked at his companions. They were staring in open-mouthed horror at the sight of tens of thousands of men in a desperate struggle to either break or hold the Federal line. He looked off to the right, across the river. Wherever Forrest's two divisions were, there'd be no way they'd find them in the darkness tonight. He looked back at his two men. They didn't seem to be in any hurry anymore to *throw* themselves into what now looked like some terrible medieval battle.

Other than sporadic muzzle flashes along the line, it eventually got too dark to witness any more of the fighting, but they could hear it rage on for hours. The boys sat in stunned silence around the campfire they built as the sounds tampered off. None of them cared to talk or eat after witnessing the horrors they had seen.

The dream came again. Carl was once again under a pile of bodies, fighting for breath. Panic surged through him. But then suddenly, he was standing outside of the pile, staring at the corpses. They wore both uniforms, blue and gray. They were all in different stages of mutilation and decay. He wanted to look away, but he couldn't. To his horror, the pile began to move. Blood started running down the sides like some gory fountain. Something was crawling out of the top. It was in the form of a man, covered in blood. It pulled itself out and stood on top of this mountain of death. It pulled out a sword and pointed it at him. Carl could see his cruel face.

"I'm waiting for you, Carl," Lathan said.

"Huh!" Carl woke with a gasp.

He was damp with sweat. It was dark. His two companions were sleeping. A single bird broke the silence with a lonely song. After a moment, another joined in. It was time. He was never going to get a better chance. He got up slowly and quietly untied his horse. A pang of guilt struck him again as he looked at the two dark lumps sleeping on the ground. They were good fellows. Perhaps he could have been friends with them in another life.

"Be safe, boys," he whispered as he mounted, not daring to look back at them as he rode off. Down the hill he went, grateful that his horse could find its way because he was completely blind in the dark woods. They found the road and moved towards town. The horse weaved through the bodies littering the road. Some of the bodies moved as they passed.

"Water…" he heard a voice gasp. He wanted to stop, or rather, he wanted to want to stop. More voices called out, groaning for help. The growing gray light in the east began to reveal the hellish scene. Hundreds, maybe thousands, of dead and dying men and horses lay in all directions. He couldn't save them all, he thought, he couldn't even save one. He drew in a sharp breath and steeled himself to the tragedy.

His horse reared in terror as they approached the abatis. The bodies hanging from the sharpened stakes created some kind of grotesque monument to death.

"It's alright," Carl patted his horse's neck as he got down and led it around the obstacle. The earthworks on the other side were covered in bodies as they passed. On the other side, men were stacked on top of each other like cordwood, Rebel and Yankee alike, passing into eternity in each other's arms.

It seemed he and his horse were the only living creatures left on Earth. He walked along, scanning the faces, knowing he was being foolish. There was no way he'd find or even recognize his enemy among the legions of the dead.

He stopped cold. She seemed to have appeared out of nowhere, like an angel here to collect him. He patted his chest, looking for a wound, wondering if he were dead too? She smiled at him. The little brown-haired girl could not have been a day older than six. She wore a simple white shift that contrasted greatly with the blood, ash, and charred wood around them.

"I drew this," she said, handing him a small scrap of paper. He looked at it.

"What is this? A dog?" he asked.

"No, silly," she giggled. "It's your horse!"

"Oh, I see it now," Carl said. He smiled at the girl, wondering where she came from.

"Matilda, *Komm her!*"

The German voice startled him. *My God, is Klaus here?!* His brother-in-law was somewhere among the Federals as far as he knew. He turned to see a bearded man calling for the girl from across the street.

"*Bleib weg von den Soldaten, Mädchen!*" the man yelled. Carl was relieved to see that it wasn't his one-time enemy, and now family a member by marriage, here to fight him too.

"*Ja, Papa!*" the little girl called back and scurried over to her father. The man gave Carl a suspicious glare as he herded his girl back toward the bullet-ridden house behind him. Carl let out a light chuckle as he looked back at the crudely drawn charcoal horse. He folded the paper and stuffed it in his pocket. He drew in a breath, looking back at the scene around him. The small moment of levity was gone.

The living began to appear. They crawled out of their hiding spaces and were now seeing the result of all the terrible noise they had heard through the night. Some searched the piles of bodies for men still living, others for loot.

Who won...?" he wondered. The Federals were gone. They had left their dead and wounded behind. Soldiers in gray and butternut were now beginning to appear, ambling among the corpses in stunned silence. Soon there would be officers and sergeants giving orders, organizing burial parties, and reforming what was left of their commands.

I've got get out of here… he thought. A sudden resolve broke him out of this strange sleepwalk. He knew what he needed to do. He was going to get on his horse and ride north until he could go no farther, rest, then ride again and again until he could crawl back into his warm bed and snuggle up next to Anna, far away from all this misery and death.

"Well, now…Cousin Carl."

The voice was like a bucket of cold water dumped on his head. His cheeks began to tingle as the blood rushed from his face. There was no leaving now.

"I don't know how or why…but I knew you'd be here," Lathan said.

Carl turned to face him. Lathan sat on his horse. Both his hands were relaxed on the pommel. His sword and pistol hung loosely at his side. Carl felt his hand tingle. He could draw and possibly shoot him before Lathan could react. Lathan smiled, looking down at Carl's twitching hand. He turned his eyes back to Carl's.

"Not a good plan, Carl. Even if you hit me, you wouldn't get far."

"I'm here to kill you," Carl found his voice.

Nathan pursed his lips into a frown and nodded. "Alright, fair enough," he said. "Let's at least give you a fighting chance. Pick up that sword and follow me."

Carl looked around. The soldiers and townspeople sorting through the dead and wounded were completely unaware of the confrontation unfolding between these two men in gray uniforms.

"Come on now," Lathan said, "if you wait too long they'll put us on a burial party."

Carl reached down and pried a saber from a dead man's grip. Then undid his belt and scabbard.

"Do you really need all that?" Lathan sighed.

"Well, I've got to carry it somehow," Carl said with impatience. "It's an open blade!"

"You there!" a voice interrupted them.

Carl turned to see who spoke.

"Put that down immediately!" the officer spoke. "There'll be no looting of our dead, soldier!" Carl froze as the other man approached.

"It's alright, Lieutenant," Lathan intervened. "The...*corporal* is under my command."

The man stopped and frowned at Lathan. "We need every man here to help with the clean-up and burial, Captain," he said.

"That's for you walking bullet-catchers, Lieutenant. Right now the enemy is running to Nashville and we need every able-bodied cavalryman to ride them down. Now do we have a problem here, or do I need to report your interference to General Forrest?"

The man blanched at the name. He stammered for a moment, then opened his mouth to reply.

"Now if you're done wasting our time," Lathan cut him off before the man could say anything, "we've got Yankees to kill." Lathan shot Carl an ironic look with the last bit. The man stood agape in silence. "I thought so. Corporal, follow me."

Carl dared not look at the man's face, knowing his own bewilderment would give him away. None of this was happening the way he had imagined. He sheathed the sword and slung it on his saddle, mounted, and followed Lathan through carnage and wreckage.

I could shoot him in the back right now, he thought. He felt the handle of his revolver, watching his enemy in front of him. *Damn him!* he thought. The man knew him so well. He didn't even bother looking back. Lathan knew he was safe. He knew Carl lacked the nerve. *How can I fight a man so confident?* The urge to run came washing over him. All he had to do was spur his horse and hope that Lathan couldn't catch him. Fear locked him into inaction. He sat passively on his horse as it carried him to his fate, like an unmanned locomotive steaming toward a cliff.

They rode along the interior line of the Federal defenses until it ended at a hairpin bend in the river, northwest of town. Only a few active soldiers remained there. Some nodded and saluted the captain as they passed. Most had their heads down in their work, dragging bodies and taking inventory of captured arms.

They continued along the river, which now flowed impatiently away from town. It was swollen from the recent weeks of rain. Branches and debris raced along with the current. Carl thought he'd feel some peace in the woods by the water, away from the scenes of ruined men. But the sound of rushing water just amplified his sense of urgency. The birds seemed to scream at him from the trees to run.

At last, they came to a clearing. It sat high on the river which hurried by several feet below its banks. Lathan tied off his horse. He took off his jacket, rolled it up, and secured it to his saddle, then drew his saber.

He whipped it through the air as he walked across the clearing, still with his back to Carl. He widened his arms and stretched his chest and shoulders which suddenly seemed alarmingly large for a man so thin. Carl dismounted and tied his horse up as well. The two animals regarded each other with doe-eyed shyness, unaware of the animosity between their riders.

Carl removed his jacket, then pulled out his borrowed saber. He slashed the air as well, testing its weight and balance. It felt heavy and he felt awkward holding it. He was already breathing hard. He drew a deep breath through his nose, trying to calm himself.

Lathan turned and smiled. He stood tall among the high grass, "Tell me, Carl, so why are you killing me?"

"You killed my friend!" Carl blurted.

Lathan let out a light laugh, "Well, we're in a war, Carl, I should hope I killed quite a few of them."

Carl's face tightened in rage and frustration. "Not like this. You killed Francis, you son of a bitch! You tied him down and burned him alive!"

Lathan blinked at him with confusion for a moment. Then he raised his eyebrows with realization. "Ah, yes! The flying negro! Kicked the teeth out of one of my men with that trick. Impressive...like a trained circus animal." Carl flinched at the insult. "Friend of yours, huh?" Lathan continued noticing the effect of his words. "I knew you were a half-breed Northern mongrel, Carl," he said with self-affirming satisfaction.

"I'm half-Mexican, for the record," Carl said with annoyance.

"Ah! Interesting! Well, I'm sure you Yankee mutts are half of everything. But from what I've seen, you're not much more than half men." Lathan smiled, watching the anger ripple across Carl's face.

"You killed a better man than you," Carl growled

"It's war, Carl. People die." Lathan shrugged his shoulders.

"You didn't have to burn him alive!"

"And your people don't have to burn our farms either," Lathan was quick to retort. "None of this would have happened if you people had just stayed home."

Carl glared at him for a moment, trying to find something to say. He finally spoke. "Are you done?"

"Sure," Lathan chuckled. "it was a boring conversation anyway." He raised his saber hand high and overturned, baring the blade forward with the tip pointing down. Carl held his forward and sank into his stance. They eyed each other for a moment. Lathan finally raised his eyebrows, "Well…"

"YAAAAAGH!" Carl howled as he charged, burning with hate and rage. He raised his blade and then brought it slashing down towards Lathan's head. Lathan blocked the blow with the flat of his sword, stepped aside, and kicked out Carl's foot as he passed. Following through with his blade, he scraped Carl's back with the tip as Carl went tumbling into the grass.

Carl hissed in pain as he went down. He quickly rolled and scrambled to his feet bracing for an attack. Lathan let out a chuckle. "That was your plan? You came all this way for that? C'mon Carl! At least make this sporting!"

Carl glared at him, panting, sucking in draughts of air through his nose, trying to calm himself. He stepped forward again. They touched blades. Carl feigned a flicking wrist cut to the head, then redirected his point to Lathan's heart with a lunge. Lathan stepped in, closing the distance, snapped his blade to the left, diverting Carl's attack, then swung his fully extended arm back to the right, bringing the back of his fist and the brass hilt crashing into Carl's cheek. Carl stumbled backward from the blow, fighting for his balance. He stabled himself, then touched his throbbing cheek. It was already beginning to swell.

"I guess they never taught you how to actually fight in any of your fencing lessons, rich boy," Lathan snickered. "At least your nigger friend put up a better fight than this."

That did it. Carl stomped forward with a flurry of short tight slashes and jabs, giving his opponent little time to counter. Lathan shuffled backward, quickly parrying the frantic attacks until finally finding an opening. He drove his tip towards Carl's gut. Carl circled his blade underneath and then swept Lathan's blade aside. Following the momentum, Carl stepped in, picking up his back foot and burying it into Lathan's stomach. Lathan went reeling backward, pinwheeling his arms as he teetered over the bank.

"Fuck!" he cried out he plunged into the fast-moving water. Carl rushed to the edge. Lathan floundered as the water threatened to sweep him away. He caught a branch with his hand. Carl let out a howl of frustration. He pulled his pistol and aimed it at him. Lathan collected himself and stared back at him with tense anticipation. Carl's hand shook as he aimed. He dropped his hand and howled again at the sky in torment.

"Ha!" Lathan called out over the rushing water. "I knew you couldn't do it! You ain't got the nerve!" Carl picked up a rock and chucked it at him. Lathan's eyes went wide with fear and surprise just before the stone struck him in the forehead. He instinctively clutched the bleeding wound with both hands, letting go of the branch. "Ow! Now that was uncalled for! Carl! … Carl, damn you, Carl!" He called out as the river swept him away.

"Fuck!" Carl cried out in frustration. He ran to his horse, untied it, and leaped into the saddle as quickly as he could. He paused, looking at Lathan's horse. He got down and untied it too. He looked to the north. All he had to do was get to Nashville. It was just twenty miles away. He could get there before nightfall and be safe. He got back on his horse and sat, unable to start. "God damn it…" he whispered. He was frustrated at his failure, frustrated at his cowardice. Then decided what he must do. He let out a sigh and laughed. He laughed at his own foolishness, but then again, better a fool than a coward he thought.

He spurred his horse, leading the other with him. They headed south, away from Nashville, back into Franklin and into the very heart of the Rebel army.

Chapter Thirty-Two: "Oh, Captain, My Captain!"

Captain Newman woke up. He propped himself up on his elbows and scanned the lawn around him. There were hundreds of men lying on the ground. Some squirmed and moaned, others were still, sleeping, or staring off into nothing with dead eyes. Many of them were missing arms or legs. Bandaged stumps had taken their places.

He looked down at his throbbing leg. His boots were gone. His left pant leg had been cut away revealing his bandaged thigh, but otherwise bare leg. He let out a sigh of relief. They were expensive boots, but at least those were replaceable.

He sat up, hissing and grimacing in pain. The men around him were mostly in the gray or butternut uniforms of the enemy. Still, there were several in blue intermixed with them. *Who won?* he wondered. Rebel soldiers were coming and going, bringing broken men on stretchers to the big plantation house. Others carried men out to the expansive lawn and found places for them on the ground. It was clear that regardless of whoever had won the battle, the Confederates were running this hospital. *Am I a prisoner...?* he wondered.

He watched as a Rebel soldier rode up to the house in a hurry. The young man had a second horse in tow. He leaped from his horse, tied them off, and scurried up the steps, removing his cap before entering, revealing a bruised and swollen cheek, and a mop of wild black hair.

"That fucking kid…" Newman mumbled, shaking his head.

Carl emerged from the house moments later. A woman came out with him. She pointed toward Newman. Carl clutched her hand in both of his and said something to her. He stumbled down the steps, nearly falling as he shoved his cap back onto his head. Newman watched him as he approached, nearly stepping on the other men along the way. Carl squatted before him, panting, his big green eyes wide and frantic.

"Son," Newman began, "I can't tell you how disappointed I…"

"Shut up and listen to me," Carl cut him off. Newman was stunned into silence. "We are leaving now. There's no time to explain. I'll do that later. Can you walk?"

Newman blinked for a moment. "I suppose with some help."

"Here, put this on. It's going to get cold again," Carl stuffed a gray jacket into his hands. Newman looked at the captain's insignia on the collar.

"Well, at least you got the rank right," he said.

With Newman's arm around his neck, Carl helped him hobble towards the horses. He was sure that every pair of eyes was on them as hoisted his one-time captain into the saddle.

"For crying out loud, son. If you keep acting like we're guilty of something, they're going to start believing you," Newman chided.

"Sorry, sir," Carl mumbled, then was immediately mad at himself for falling back into the old habit of addressing Newman as his superior officer.

"Allow me to lead, Carl," Newman said, almost as if he had been reading his thoughts. "Unless you want to switch jackets," he said with a wink. Carl looked down at the corporal stripes on his own sleeve.

"Of course," he mumbled, stopping himself from adding 'sir,' then felt foolish for being petty.

He soon realized that he was happy to let his old captain lead. Newman sat high in the saddle, smiling broadly under his big mustache and winking at the somber stretcher-bearers and ambulance drivers that passed them on the Lewisburg Pike into town. The man's confidence gave him such a natural aura of command. Carl marveled at how many of the downtrodden soldiers saluted him as they passed. Then came the real test. A major put his hand up to halt them.

"Where is your hat, Captain?" he asked, examining Newman's ragged, barefoot appearance. His own uniform was immaculate, denoting him as an officer in someone's command staff and not a man who led troops in the front.

"Shot off the top of my head in the fight, Major," Newman saluted him. "I see you were able to keep yours on through the worst of it, as well as your uniform clean."

The man glared at him, outraged by the implied accusation. He opened his mouth to protest. Newman cut him off.

"If you don't mind, Major, we have urgent business to attend. The enemy's still out there and we are on the chase. The fight's not over yet for the cavalry, sir, although, I suppose for some…it still hasn't begun." He gave the man a sharp look as he urged his horse on, not giving him a moment to reply. Carl kept his head down, terrified at making eye contact with the outraged senior officer.

"What is your name and regiment, sir!" The man called out.

"Captain Chester E. Newman! I'm with Forrest!" Newman shouted, not bothering to turn back to look. Carl held his breath, tensing his neck and shoulder muscles as he waited for the man to ride up on them and demand more. At last, he relaxed once it was evident that the man had given up on the unruly captain.

"That's a thing, right? Forrest's Regiment…?" Newman asked casually.

"It's a corps," Carl answered, then hissed under his breath, "You are going to get us killed if you keeping talking to them that way."

"Eh, fuck that guy…" Newman said calmly. "He was about to get *himself* killed."

Carl watched Newman's high-headed bravado melt away as they approached the fortifications that wrapped around the outer edge of town.

"Good God…!" Newman gasped.

Thousands of dead and wounded men still littered the ground, abatis, and earthworks despite the hours of work the Confederates had already put into collecting them. Carl wondered if Newman would stop to find a pair of shoes or trousers among the dead but then realized it'd be too risky to tarry. Instead, they rode on in silence, finally finding a ford to cross the river. Carl kept his eyes on Newman's back the whole time, afraid that looking around would give them away.

At last, they had put some distance between them and the remnants of the Rebel army at Franklin. Carl was beginning to breathe easy.

"Ha, I knew it!"

The familiar voice shattered any sense of relief. Captain Jeb emerged from the brush on horseback. He held a double-barreled shotgun in his right hand, cradling it on his left arm which he used to hold the reins. He leveled it at them. "That's far enough, boys."

"Take it easy, partner," Newman said, raising his arms. Carl raised his, too.

"We ain't partners, Captain," Jeb spat on the ground. "and you're a terrible cavalryman. I've been trailing you since the hospital. You never once bothered to notice." He then looked to Carl, "I knew you were a no-good spy, *Carlos*. I've just been waiting for you to make a mistake and prove it."

Carl swallowed hard.

"It just don't make any sense, though," Jeb spoke again. "After everything you've done to gain our confidence, why would you blow it just to save a mere captain?" He looked back to Newman, "No offense, sir."

"None taken, my friend," Newman replied, his hands still up in the air.

"He's my…other captain, sir," Carl said.

"Your *other* captain?" Jeb asked.

"Yes, sir. From when I was in the Federal army," Carl said.

"So you're a spy?" Jeb said, raising his shotgun higher.

"No, Sir. I was discharged…because of an injury. I came back, though, for…personal business."

"*Personal* business?" Jeb said the word slowly, chewing on its possible meaning.

Carl let out a sigh. He decided it was best to come clean. "I came back to kill Captain Lathan Woods of General Chalmers's division. He tortured and murdered my friend at Fort Pillow."

Captain Jeb's eyes burned into him from under his cap and behind his heavy beard. Carl shuddered at the ferocity of his gaze. His arms began to feel heavy from holding them in the air.

Jeb let out a light chuckle, then broke into a full-hearted laugh. Carl sat in stunned silence. He had rarely seen the man smile before, let alone laugh. Then Newman started to laughing too.

"You know," Jeb said, wiping away a tear, "I would've shot almost any other man for lying to me, but somehow I think you're just dumb enough for that story to be true."

"I can confirm that he's pretty stupid," Newman added.

Jeb let out another laugh, then recovered his normal seriousness. "Alright, boys, off them horses. They're property of the Confederacy, that saber, too, and the rifle I gave you, Carlos. You can keep your sidearms. Those are yours." Carl blinked at him in confusion. "Get off my damn horses," Jeb said more firmly. Carl got off his horse, then helped Newman ease himself down. He handed the reins to Jeb.

"Corporal de la Vega, you are to conduct your *other* Captain back to the Federal lines. That's my last order to you, son. And just so you know, I'll be shooting at you next time we meet."

"Of course, sir," Carl said, stunned at this sudden change of fate.

"Thank you, my friend," Newman said.

"We ain't friends, Captain," Jeb said flatly, "and I'll be shooting at you, too, by and by."

"Fair enough," Newman shrugged.

Jeb turned to leave.

"Why?" Carl asked. "Why are you letting us go?"

Jeb let out a sigh. "One more battle like we had last night and this army is through," he said. "This war's comin' to end…and it ain't goin' our way." He paused for a moment to choose his words. "I don't see any point in killing you…or handing you off for someone else to kill you." He stuck his shotgun into its saddle holster. "You stuck your neck out to save this *other* captain of yours. Maybe someday somebody might do that for me."

Carl stood in silence for a moment then spoke, "Stay safe, Captain."

"I'm still going to shoot you next time I see you, *Carlos de la Vega*," Jeb said, then gave his horse a light kick and trotted off with the other two in tow.

Newman turned to Carl, "*Carlos de la Vega?*"

"It's a long story," Carl sighed.

"I can't wait to hear it," Newman replied.

"Son, that has to be the dumbest story I've ever heard," General Wilson said, "not even worthy of a two-bit novel." Carl swallowed hard. He felt naked, standing in the room full of officers at the Saint Cloud Hotel in Nashville. "Captain Newman," the cavalry corps commander turned his attention, "can you attest to any of this wild tale?"

Newman stepped forward on his crutches. "Most of it…no, sir, but I can tell you that Mr. Smith did once serve under me, he did rescue me from behind enemy lines, and from what I've seen, his descriptions of the enemy's dispositions are accurate, sir."

Wilson looked over to his own commanding officer, General Thomas. Thomas gave him a nod to continue. Wilson looked back at Newman, "Does any of this seem credible to you, Captain?"

Newman looked at Carl with a smirk, "Smith is certainly a fool and a troublemaker, sir, but I've never known him to be a liar."

Wilson leaned back into his chair. "I see," then after a pause, "Mr. Smith, please wait outside while we decide what to do with you."

"Uh…yes, sir." Carl started backing away

"And please keep in mind that even though you are not yet under arrest, I'll have you shot if you attempt to flee. Do I make myself clear?"

"Absolutely, sir," Carl said, bumping into the door. He turned and fumbled for the knob, sure that everyone in the room was watching him. He was far too nervous to sit in the hotel lobby. Instead, he stepped outside to take advantage of the pause in the rain. The air had become cooler since the almost summer-like weather during the battle. Still, it was a lot warmer for December than he was used to back home. He thought of Anna and cringed with regret. It had been six months since he left. He hadn't written her since he first arrived in Memphis. For all she knew, he was dead. He resolved to write her at the first opportunity.

Without warning, an enormous man snatched him up into his arms, startling him from his thoughts.

"Woo, boy! I knew it was you!" Elijah said. "They said two of ours boys showed up in Confederate clothes and I just knew it was you. I knew you'd come!"

"Elijah, you made it!" Carl said, feeling happy for the first time since he could remember.

"Yessum," Elijah smiled broadly, "I've been helpin' out the white artillery boys with they horses and all, tryin' to stay busy, you know, but waitin' on you. I haven't forgotten our mission."

"I fought him, Elijah. I fought him and failed," Carl said, looking at the ground.

"Mr. Lathan?"

"Yeah, we dueled after the battle at Franklin. He was too much for me. I got lucky and kicked him into the river then ran away," Carl sniffed in a tear. He buried his face into his hands and began to cry in earnest. "I failed, I failed Francis…"

Elijah put his arm around him and squeezed. "Francis was never about killin' nobody or gettin' revenge…nothin' like that. Francis was about fightin' for his cause, Carl. He laid down his life so a man like me can be free, so we *all* can be free." Carl wiped his tears with his sleeve, looking up at his friend. "Right now those men that would put us back in chains are coming to Nashville. They comin' for us, Carl. Everyman gotta do what he gotta do so that this *can* be the land of the free and the home of the brave just like they sing in that song. This is how we honor Francis, not by killin' one man, but by finishin' the job, fightin' for this cause, fighting for the free America Francis dreamed of."

"You're right, Elijah," Carl sniffed, "but I still want to kill that fucker."

Elijah laughed, patting him on the shoulder, "Boy, you crazy! That's why I love you so much."

"I love you too, Elijah," Carl said sheepishly, looking at the ground.

"Smith!" the sergeant startled him. "You're wanted inside."

"Of course!" Carl turned to him, then back to Elijah, "We'll talk soon."

"Wait, Carl…" Elijah caught his arm. "You kicked him into the river?"

"Yeah," Carl smiled, "and it was fucking glorious."

Once again, Carl entered the drawing-room filled with Federal officers. Cigar smoke wafted through the gloomy daylight that seeped through the rain-splattered windows. A few oil lamps on the wooden desks created a warm glow that flickered off the brass buttons of the uniforms. Carl stood as the men lounging in chairs regarded him silently.

General Wilson spoke at last. "It's my inclination to have you tried for espionage and treason, Mr. Smith, and then have you hanged." Carl felt the blood drain from his swollen face. "Unfortunately, this army can barely spare the time or the lumber to build a scaffold, nor can we really spare the bullets to shoot you, as much as I'd like to." Wilson paused to see the effect his words were having. He smiled at the result. "As it turns out, we're also short on cavalrymen to protect our flanks from that devil Forrest and his unholy hordes of maniacs." Wilson then shifted his gaze to the collection of men sitting behind Carl. "Captain Newman!"

"Yes, sir," Newman hoisted himself onto his crutches, "do you think you can make use of this rogue of questionable loyalties?"

"I suppose I can find some horse shit that needs shoveling, sir," Newman answered.

Wilson turned his eyes back to Carl, "Well, son, what's it going to be? Are you going to make us go through the motions of having a trial just so we can hang you, or will you allow us to move on with more pressing matters by taking the oath?" Carl sighed and dropped his head. "Excellent!" Wilson said. "Captain, you may take your recruit and rejoin your regiment. They're currently encamped on the east side of the river at Edgefield."

Chapter Thirty-Three: Welcome Back

Elijah was still waiting outside when Carl and Newman exited the Saint Cloud Hotel. His eyes were wide with unspoken questions. Carl looked to Newman for permission. Newman nodded. "I'm back in the cavalry, Elijah," Carl turned back to his friend. "I didn't have a choice."

"That's alright, Carl. I think it's what we suppose to do. We ain't fighting *our* war no more, Carl, we fightin' Francis's war. This is the way."

Carl smiled bitterly, "I suppose it is. Come find me when it's done. If we live."

"I will," Elijah replied.

"Jesus, son," Newman called back, as he climbed into an ambulance cart waiting for him. "Stop being so damn gloomy. Say goodbye to your boyfriend and let's go."

Elijah and Carl chuckled for a moment. Carl hugged him, "Goodbye, my friend. Stay safe."

"You do the same, Carl. I be lookin' for you when we done."

Carl walked behind the ambulance that carried Captain Newman across the Cumberland River. He was happy he didn't have to endure the awkwardness of sitting in the cart in silence with his once-again commanding officer. Instead, he took in the sights that the bridge spanning the river afforded. Below, a monstrous ironclad gunboat chugged laboriously towards them. Its lanterns glowed in the early evening gloom. Watching the behemoth approach gave him an exhilarating sense of vertigo. Its smoke and steam billowed up as it passed, shrouding the bridge with a warm steamy fog and the strangely satisfying smell of burning coal.

Carl opened his mouth in astonishment at the red bands painted on the smokestacks and the emblem of an anchor suspended in between. He wondered if it was the *Carondelet* that had made the famous night run at the Battle Island No. 10. He decided it must be. He smiled at the ironic circumstance. Seeing the famous gunboat from his early days in the war again gave him a strange sense of coming home.

He could see the rows of tents on the other side of the river as they passed the mid-point of the bridge. They were neatly aligned in a grid. The campfires dotted among them created an orderly pattern in the gloom that looked like the stars arranged on the old flag. He suddenly worried about how he'd be received by his old comrades, especially now that he was showing up, once again, in an enemy uniform. Newman had the ambulance stop in front of the sentries guarding the entrance into the camp. Its boundaries were protected by an abatis of sharpened stakes bound together in a criss-cross pattern.

"That's far enough, Sergeant," he told the driver. "I'd rather walk from here."

The sentries saluted him as he hobbled past them on his crutches. They eyed Carl suspiciously.

"Captain Newman, back from the dead!" Sergeant Barnes embraced him, nearly knocking him off his crutches. "I've been waiting for you ever since I heard of your return."

"Good to see you, too, George," Newman chuckled. "It's all thanks to our newly reenlisted Private Smith!"

"Private Smith, lost at Perryville!" Sergeant Barnes gasped, "Back from the dead as well. Looks like they be handin' out them Rebel uniforms in hell, then."

Newman looked down at the Confederate jacket he was wearing. "It ain't easy crawling out of there unless you dress like one of those devils."

"Well, sir," Barnes said, after finishing his laugh, "the Colonel will be wanting to see you right away."

"Of course," Newman smiled, patting the man on the shoulder. "Can you see to it that Smith here has a tent mate and blanket for the night?"

"Sure thing, Captain. It's good to see you both."

Carl spent the next hour standing uncomfortably in Lieutenant Colonel Smith's tent as the two officers sat in chairs. Newman debriefed the colonel on all that had occurred since he had been missing in action. Smith occasionally raised an eyebrow and shot a glance at Carl as Newman told the story. At last, the meeting was over. "Come see me in the morning, Captain, and we'll decide what to do with Private Smith," the colonel finished the meeting with. Carl didn't like the sound of that.

"Of course, sir," Newman said, hoisting himself onto his crutches. He gave a salute. Carl did the same, then held the tent flap open for his captain. He was surprised to see a crowd of men had gathered outside.

Some held torches that flickered light against their brass buttons and the gold trim of their cavalry jackets. Their faces appeared grim in the torchlight.

"What is this…?" Newman stopped to look at the hundreds of men standing before them.

One of the captains stepped out from the crowd. "We thought you *Southern Belles* looked so pretty in your Confederate jackets," he said, "that we decided to serenade you, just to make sure you ladies remember what you fighting for." He then nodded to another man in the crowd who stepped forward with a fiddle on his shoulder. He started to play a sweet and simple melody. Carl recognized it immediately. The men began to sing:

> *Oh, we'll rally round the flag, boys, we'll rally once again,*
> *Shouting the Battle Cry of Freedom,*
> *And we'll rally from the hillside, we'll gather from the plain,*
> *Shouting the Battle Cry of Freedom.*
>
> *The Union forever, hurrah! Boys, hurrah!*
> *Down with the traitors, up with the stars;*
> *While we rally round the flag, boys, we rally once again,*
> *Shouting the Battle Cry of Freedom!*

The men raised their fists in the air with each shouted "hurrah!" Two of them brought out an American and a 2nd Cavalry Regimental flag and wrapped them around Carl and Newman's shoulders. Carl felt tears welling in his eyes as he listened to the regiment sing together as one. He was mouthing the words, trying to remember them, when someone handed him a bottle of whiskey. He took a full pull from it and passed it along. The men broke into the *Battle Hymn of the Republic*, then switched the older *John Brown's Body* lyrics. Fifes and brass instruments began to join in.

The evening continued with more music and singing. Men danced around the fires in their vests and shirt sleeves, kicking their feet high with their hands on their hips as fiddlers whipped up rollicking Irish jigs. More whiskey came around. Someone handed Carl a plate of beans, salted pork, and cornbread, which he greedily shoveled into his mouth, licking his fingers as he did so.

"Sergeant Barnes told me to give you this."

Carl looked up to see his old comrade and adversary, the one-time Private Bates now wore corporal stripes on his sleeve. Bates handed him a blanket.

"Thank you, Max," Carl said carefully, remembering the animosity they had shared in the past.

"He says you're to bunk with me…since I've got space in my tent now," Bates said.

"Well, I'm sorry for any intrusion I may have caused, Max," Carl said earnestly.

"Eh, better you than one of these greenhorns, I can't stand those guys," he said plopping down next to him. Carl took that to mean things were fine between the two.

He was awake before reveille. Lying in a two-man tent in a Federal camp was awfully familiar. He lay there staring at the canvas remarking how everything thing since Perryville seemed like a dream, like he never went home, never married Anna, never came back for revenge, and never was impressed into Forrest's cavalry. He shook his head. No, it did all happen, he thought, and he needed to get a letter to his wife as soon as he could.

Camp life in the 2nd Michigan Cavalry wasn't much different from what he remembered, except there were many new faces and only a few he remembered from before. With the constant drilling and being pulled for guard duty, patrols, or work crews, it was hard to find time to write as they prepared for the coming battle.

"Smith," Sergeant Barnes found him as Carl was searching for words to start his letter to his wife, "the captain will be seeing you now."

"Yes, Sergeant." Carl got off the ground and returned his borrowed writing material to his tent.

He found Captain Newman sitting at his small writing desk outside of his tent. He was wearing a new blue jacket and had shaven the stubble that had popped up around his heavy mustache during their adventure. "Ah, Carl," he said, returning the salute. "At ease, son. I've got something for you." He handed him a slightly worn jacket. "Try this on. It might be a little snug." It was clean but had some washed-out bloodstains on it. What really caught Carl's notice were the stripes.

"It's got corporal stripes on it, sir," he said.

"Well, I meant what I said back in Detroit, even though you were rude to me," he smiled.

"I'm sorry, sir…I…" Carl started, looking at the ground.

"Don't worry about it, son. I told you then, I already forgave you. Besides, getting me out of Franklin goes a long way toward an apology. Now it seems your *other* captain thought you worthy of the stripes, so who am I to question his judgment?"

"Thank you, sir," Carl said sheepishly, not wanting to correct him that it was actually Forrest who promoted him, not Captain Jeb.

"Try it on, let's see if it fits," Newman nodded to him.

Carl put on the jacket, "It seems to fit well enough, sir."

"Yeah, it was always a little too big on him," Newman nodded.

"On who, sir?"

"Chucky," Newman said.

"Doesn't he need his jacket?" Carl said, realizing he hadn't seen his friend since he returned.

"Not anymore, Carl," Newman shook his head slowly. "He's dead."

The world seemed to start spinning as the realization settled in. "Take a seat, son, before you fall over," Newman spoke again. Carl felt his way to a stool like a blind man feeling his way in the dark. Waves of sorrow, regret, and nausea washed over him. "Take it easy, kid," Newman handed him a tin cup. Carl drank down the whiskey then shuddered from the effect.

"How…?"

"Fighting for what he believed in, Carl. Took one to the head as we fought our way into Franklin. For all I know, it could have been one of your boys."

The words stung him to the core. "I...I...don't..."

"It's alright, Carl. I know where your heart is, even if you don't. That's why I'm trusting you with this responsibility...Chucky's responsibilities, I know you will do him proud."

Chapter Thirty-Four: The Opening of the Dance

The Rebel army crawled out of Franklin and into the hills on the southeastern edge of Nashville. There they dug in, building their own defensive line that connected the hilltops with rifle pits, trenches, and redoubts. From there they peered back at the Federal line, daring them to come out and attack. The weather attacked instead.

The temperature plummeted. The rain froze as it fell. It rattled against shelters, pelted the men, and clung to their beards. Soon, everything was covered in a sheet of ice including men found frozen to death at their posts. The snow came next. It fell for days, adding a blanket of white to the sheet of ice. Both armies sat frozen in place as men on both sides ignored orders against chopping down trees and stripping homes of wooden floors to feed their fires.

At last, the snow stopped. Wilson's Cavalry Corps broke camp and moved back across the river. The men had to dismount and lead their horses on foot because the bridge was far too icy for riding. The animals slipped and struggled to find footing on the wind-swept bridge as they crossed. They rode out along the Charlotte Pike and set up camp west of the city with the Cumberland River at their back. Here, they waited for orders to begin the assault.

The attack would begin on the Rebel right flank which was anchored on the deeply entrenched Nashville-Chattanooga Railroad on the southeast side of town. Once the Rebels started shifting their troops to defend their right flank, the Federal cavalry would sweep around from the west and clear out any Rebel horsemen protecting the Confederate left. Then, three corps of infantry would swing around in an enormous wheel-like motion to drive the Rebels from their fortifications.

Carl woke up feeling something he hadn't felt in days. He was warm. He threw off his blanket. He had been sleeping in his clothes and now he was damp with sweat.

"Go back to sleep, Carl," Bates mumbled, "they'll be calling for us soon enough."

As if on queue, the trumpet called reveille.

"Damn you, bastard," Bates groaned, "they heard you movin' around!"

Carl let out a laugh. Other than the constant snide comments, Bates had become a surprisingly welcoming tent mate. Carl had soon found out that not only had he inherited Chucky's jacket and rank, he was also assigned his horse and gear, including the shelter half that made up the other part of Bate's tent. It was an ironic exchange of tent mates. Carl and Chucky had once shared a tent. Bates became Chucky's tent mate once Carl left. Now Carl was back and sharing a tent with this sardonic corporal from Pontiac. They had not gotten along in the early days of the war, even coming to blows once. But now, Carl assumed that Bates had found some kind of familiar comfort in him, someone to fill the void left by Chucky, someone to grieve with. Carl was happy about the new friendship.

"Good Lord!" he exclaimed as he undid the tent flaps.

"Is that smoke?" Bates said sitting up and rubbing his eyes as vapors rolled into the tent.

Carl swirled the ghostly fumes around his fingers. "It's fog and lots of it!" he said.

It was still dark outside. The air was warm and clammy. The morning campfires glowed dimly in the thick mist. The smell of coffee and bacon drifted through the heavy air. Carl could hear the nickering of nearby horses but couldn't see where they were.

The ordnance sergeant came through while they ate breakfast and issued rounds to the men. Then they received three days' worth of rations. "I think they're expecting a fight today," Bates said, tucking the hardtack crackers into his haversack. Before Carl could think of anything clever to say, cannons opened up on the river. Hundreds of heads turned toward the sudden interruption of the morning peace.

"Someone's fighting…" Carl said, looking off toward the sound.

Lathan had heard them coming, or more so, felt them coming at first. His company of men was sleeping on the ground near the battery of cannons placed on the heights that overlooked the bend in the Cumberland River, west of the city. He hadn't truly been sleeping. He never really did. He would slip into a semi-state of consciousness but always stayed aware of what was going on around him.

It started as a faint vibration in the ground as he slowly became aware. Then he heard the low rumble of steam engines and the churning of water displaced by paddle wheels.

"Get up, they're coming!" he said, leaping to his feet.

They were at the very left end of the Confederate line, although there wasn't much of a line to their right. Most of Hood's army was concentrated on the southeast side of town. Their fortifications ran about four miles from the Nashville-Chattanooga railroad to Hardin Pike. It was dwarfed by the Federal fortifications that ran about seven miles with each end securely anchored on the river.

Hood had sent Forrest with two cavalry divisions and five infantry brigades to Murfreesboro to attack the Federal garrison there in hopes of drawing the Yankees out of their fortifications at Nashville. This left only Chalmers's cavalry division to protect the four miles of open country between the Confederate fortifications that ended at Harding Pike and the Cumberland River. They had set up a battery of cannons on the heights overlooking a bend in the river. From there they were able to bring shipping between Clarksville and Nashville to halt. Federal gunboats had tried to dislodge them before, but having to fire up at the Rebel guns from the river caused the shells to fly harmlessly over their heads and dropped into the woods behind them. Now it seemed they were back to try again.

The cannon crews shuffled to their feet and began cramming rounds into the barrels. Lathan's men scanned the foggy darkness, looking for the source of the sound in the river below.

"There!" a man yelled.

Lathan could see the faint glow from the smokestack passing through the stew of fog.

"Fire!" the lieutenant colonel in charge of the guns yelled. The six cannons roared to life, spewing jets of flames into the thick fog. Lathan could hear the splashes in the water made by the shells, but there was no sound of them punching through the iron armor of the gunboat.

Spears of flames cut through the fog as the ghostly vessel, now having spotted the Rebel guns, fired back. Lathan stood watching as the men around him ducked and cringed. The shells whistled overhead, then crashed and exploded behind him.

The men worked frantically to reload and turn the guns to follow the path of the vessel hidden in the fog. They fired again. The guns kicked backward with great violence as smoke and the smell of sulfur mixed into the fog that swirled around them. Once again, splashes were all they gained. More shells came screaming overhead, now from upriver.

"There's more of them waiting to pass!" one of the crew members shouted. The boat they were firing upon passed, disappearing into the mist. The gunners held their lanyards, waiting for the order to fire to come again. Some of the crew stood up from their crouches and unplugged their ears. An eerie silence rested on them in the dim morning light. They listened to the hum on the river, trying to imagine what was happening below. The humming to the left began to get grow louder once again.

"It's coming back!" someone shouted.

"Fire!" the order came. Once again, the guns kicked backward as they threw spikes of flames into the fog. Shells came again, screaming overhead.

Lieutenant Commander Leroy Fitch stood on the foredeck of the *USS Moose*, stroking his beard as he strained to see through the fog. The river monitor class *USS Neosho* had returned from her run past the Rebel guns. He was anxious to hear her report.

"There, sir!" a sailor called.

The faint glow of a lantern emerged from the fog. He could hear the splashes of the oars as the outline of the longboat appeared. He smiled with relief.

"Well, I see you managed to survive, Lieutenant!" he called out as the boat pulled alongside the *Neosho*.

"They certainly made a go at it, Commander!" Lieutenant Howard replied joyfully as he climbed aboard the command ship and offered a salute.

Fitch returned the gesture, "Any damage?"

"None that we noticed so far, sir. I'm having my boys do a thorough inspection now, but I don't think they hit us."

"Excellent. How many guns?"

"Six, by my count, sir."

"Hmm…The fog must have delayed the cavalry from clearing them out. We'll hold here until they've done so. In the meantime, I'm ordering a general cease-fire. We don't want to hit our own boys once they show."

Elijah held his breath as the gunners of the 12th Indiana Light Artillery adjusted the elevation and aim of the big siege guns at Fort Negley. The fort sat on a hill in the southeast corner of the Federal line near the Nashville-Chattanooga Railroad. Normally, the fort had a commanding view of the hills south of the city where the Confederates had built their line, but now there was nothing to see except the stew of dense fog that filled the space in-between. Still, the gunners had recorded the locations of their targets and were now dialing the screws that adjusted the elevation and direction of the big 32-pound Parrot rifles.

Elijah could hear cannons were already rumbling from somewhere in the early twilight as he waited. It was most likely coming from the river, the men had guessed. They had been waiting for the attack to commence on the Federal right to start their own bombardment. Now that the battle was commencing, it was time for the big guns of the forts to join the dance.

"Fire!" Captain White yelled. The eleven guns of Fort Negley erupted in flames and smoke, kicking back several feet, hurling their projectiles into the Confederate lines over a mile away. A second round of explosions sounded from afar as the shells exploded on their targets. The guns of the other nearby forts along the line opened up as well. Soon there was no break in the overlapping thunder of cannon fire. The ground shook as the Rebel shells began to slam into the hillside near them and explode.

"Easy!" Elijah steadied his team of horses. He stood by, ready to move cannons, haul rounds, carry gunpowder, or whatever they needed him to do, even work the guns if they'd allow a one-legged black man to do so.

Down below, he could see in the morning sunlight, through the breaks in the dissipating fog, a column of blue soldiers emerge from the earthworks and move south along the Murfreesboro pike, parallel to the railroad that marked the end of the Rebel line. Pride and a bit of regret swirled in him as he watched the black men in blue uniforms march tall into battle with a contingent of white troops behind them. The black man was going to get his chance to fight.

The guns at Fort Negley had been pounding the southeastern flank of the Rebel line all morning. Now these troops were forming into battle lines preparing to drive the Confederates from their works.

"Cease fire!" Captain White called, silencing the guns. Elijah's ears were ringing from the constant firing. Now in the sudden quiet he thought he could hear the distant rattle of snare drums and fife.

The Federal battle lines lurched forward from the Murfreesboro Pike toward the railroad. The colored troops led the assault with white troops marching behind in reserve. The Confederates had some rifle pits and light earthworks on the east side of the railroad. The men there fired at the approaching blue troops, then quickly scurried out of their positions, and dashed back toward the main fortifications on the west side of the tracks. The black troops fired, dropping several of the Rebels as they ran.

Elijah let out his breath, realizing he had been holding it as he watched. Things were going well. The relief was only momentary, however. He furrowed his brow as he tried to make out what he was seeing. There was motion in what looked like a cluster of trees and piled logs that sat on the east side of the tracks, north of where the black troops were nearing the railroad. Elijah was pretty sure he could make out men moving around in there, turning their big black tubes toward the blue troops now reaching the rails.

"It's a trap…" he uttered to no one in particular.

The soldiers came to a halt at the tracks. The rail line was dug deep into the bedrock, twenty feet below them. There seemed to be some confusion as to how to cross and what to do next when the Rebel guns opened up. They were caught in a crossfire between the guns hidden in the cluster of logs east of the tracks and the guns west of the tracks that had now turned from facing the main Federal line to the black troops advancing on their flank.

The effect was devastating. Elijah cringed as he watched dozens of soldiers fall to the ground as canister and musketry poured into them at close range from two directions. Hundreds of them jumped into the deep railroad cut to get out of the hail of lead that was tearing men to shreds. The line of white troops surged forward toward the now revealed Rebel battery on the east side of the tracks. The guns there opened up on them as well, mowing men down by the dozens. Some of them made it to the walls of stacked lumber only to be shot down as they tried to crawl over the top.

The Federal formations broke. Soldiers ran back toward the Murfreesboro Pike in a chaotic panic. The Rebel guns flailed them with canister. Men arched their backs and fell to the ground as hot metal tore through them from behind.

"We got to help them!" Elijah called out to any who'd listen.

One of the gun sergeants looked at him with sympathy, shaking his head sadly, "We'd only be firing on our own men, Elijah."

Bitter, impotent frustration coursed through him as he watched. Hundreds of men were now trapped in the railroad cut. Some were trying to climb the twenty-foot rock walls to get out. Rebel soldiers moved forward, crowding the edge of the narrow chasm. They started firing their rifles into the densely packed cluster of humanity below.

Elijah turned away, no longer able to watch. Light-headed, he sat down as the tears rolled down his face.

Carl was beginning to get bored. The attack was supposed to have started early in the morning, but the fog had delayed them. The fear was that the horses would lose their footing, formations would lose cohesion, and the men would be riding blindly into the enemy's guns. Eventually, they got down from their horses and rested while they waited for the fog to lift.

Carl spent much of that time checking and rechecking the Spencer carbine, the Allen and Wheelock revolver, and the saber he had inherited from Chucky. Then he checked the weapons Mr. Beauchamp had given him, a Colt Navy revolver and the Bowie knife he kept tucked in the back of his pants. Both sets of weapons came with their own set obligations.

Carl smiled at the "C. S." Chucky had carved into the stock of his carbine and the handle of his saber and pistol. It was a practical thing to do. He supposed this was so Chucky could identify his gear from everyone else's, but Chucky was also immensely proud of the weapons he'd been issued and the jacket that Carl now wore. Chucky had always looked at looming battles with boyish excitement. To him, they were opportunities for heroics. To Carl, they were opportunities for being just another one of many shot down by a random bullet meant for anyone and no one in particular. Battles were something he dreaded. He let out a sigh. "Alright, Chucky," Carl chuckled to himself, "I'll be brave for you."

It wasn't just for Chucky that he had to be brave. As a corporal, he had been assigned a handful of privates to watch over. He was still learning their names, Joey, Israel, and Albert. They were new recruits from Macomb County, Michigan. They replaced men who had gone home at the end of their enlistment, had been wounded, or were dead. They looked at him with wide-eyed fear as he inspected their weapons. "Don't worry. Stay close to me. Listen to orders. You'll be fine," he told them, trying to hide his own fear. For all he knew, they'd all be dead by the end of the day.

The fog burned away by mid-morning revealing yet another obstacle. Some of the infantry had moved up into position during the dark foggy hours and were now in front of them instead of behind, where they were supposed to be. They were blocking the path of the cavalry. After much bickering and shuffling, the way was finally clear. Carl put his left foot into the stirrup, grabbed the saddle horn, and swung himself into the saddle. It felt good. He steadied the brown mare he had inherited from Chucky, patting her on the neck as he took up the reins. He checked his pistols and saber once again, made sure his Spencer carbine was in its saddle holster and patted the knife stuck in the back of his trousers before turning to his privates to sure they were ready too. The nods they gave were all he needed. He didn't want to overdo it with them, mostly so they wouldn't see how nervous he was.

A lone bugle called out followed by others. Over twelve thousand men and horses began to move forward. Major General James Wilson's Cavalry Corps was made up of four divisions. Each division had two to three brigades and a battery of horse-drawn artillery. Each brigade had anywhere between three to five regiments. The corps was an enormous mobile army onto itself, and to Carl, it was an awesome sight to behold as he rode amid the massive force.

The four divisions began to spread, reaching out with their flanks from the Cumberland River to Hardin Pike where Major General A. J. Smith's detachment of the Army of the Tennessee was wheeling around to sweep into the enemy's fortified line from the flank. Most of Carl's division was in Kentucky, hunting down Rebel raiders. This left only General Croxton's Brigade to take part in the battle commencing at Nashville. They rode in the rear of the huge formations, ready to go galloping into wherever they were needed.

Much of the corps had dismounted and pushed forward on foot. Their horses were led from behind by the remainder of mounted troops in case they needed to quickly mount and give chase. Several of the regiments spread out far to the front as skirmishers to feel out the enemy's forward positions. Carl could hear the crackle of Spencer repeating rifles ahead. They had certainly found something!

Soon, hundreds of prisoners were shuffled to the rear. He scanned their faces, wondering if he'd recognize any of them. He wondered if Lathan would be among them. It had been only two weeks since he kicked him into the Harpeth River and ran away from the Rebel army. Still, the sight of these, once again, enemy soldiers was shocking. Their faces were thin and despondent, although some looked relieved to be done fighting. Many were barefoot and dressed in rags, making him wonder how they survived the week's worth of frozen weather. He couldn't help but feel sorry for them.

"These are the men you're facing," he told his awe-struck privates as they watched prisoners marched past.

The brigade drew to a halt. Carl moved to check his weapons again, then forced himself to stop. Nothing could possibly have changed since the last time he checked them only five minutes prior.

"Alright, boys," Captain Newman addressed the company at last, "we're moving toward the river to help Johnson's division clear out Rebel artillery. Apparently the ornery fuckers got our Navy pinned down at the bend there. Johnson's already taken losses trying to force them from their works."

The mid-December sun had already set by the time Croxton's brigade linked up with Johnson's division. "They're up there on that ridge," one of Johnson's men explained as he guided the 2nd Michigan to their place in the line. "They're too high up on the river for the gunboats to hit them. The shells just go over their heads." Carl could just make out the glow of campfires on the heights in the darkness. Their flickering light revealed an outline of fence posts and logs the Rebels had placed along the ridge as a barricade.

It was now too dark to attack. The assault would have to wait until morning. Soon, the Federals were starting their own cooking fires. Carl stared into the flames after eating, knowing he should be writing Anna, but unable to make himself move. It had only been a week since he sent his first letter home in months. Did she get it? Has she sent one back? A cheer broke out along the line, breaking him from his thoughts.

"What's going on?" Bates asked.

"The Rebels are licked and Forrest ain't even here!" one of the revelers replied

The news spread through camp quickly. Prisoners taken that day had confirmed that Forrest and most of his cavalry were in Murfreesboro, far from the battlefield at Nashville. At most, they were facing only one division of cavalry. What's more, despite the late start, the day had been a smashing success. Thomas's hastily assembled army had swung around like a sledgehammer into the Rebels' left flank, sending them scurrying from their works. Thousands had been taken prisoner. The Federals had suffered relatively low losses.

"They ain't got any fight left in 'em, boys," Captain Newman assured them. "I'm told they've fallen back to an even smaller, more compact line. Tomorrow it'll just be a matter of finishin' 'em off." Carl looked off to the faint glow of fires on the heights near the river, certain that there was just enough fight left in them to shoot him in the morning.

Chapter Thirty-Five: The Last Dance

They weren't there. After a fitful night of worrying and then a nerve-wracking climb to the Rebel barricades, they found nothing but the smoldering remains of campfires and tracks from horses and gun carriages in the soft ground. Carl looked down at the river as the squadron of gunboats steamed toward them, now that they had been given the all-clear. The last of the early morning fog still clung in pockets on the water. He flinched as cannons opened up again somewhere far off behind him.

"Saddle up, boys," Newman told them. "The party's started, and it looks like our dance partner has run out on us."

Jerry looked up at the Rebel works that lined the top of the hill. "Man, these fools crazy!" he mumbled to himself, shaking his head. This was the far right end of the Confederate line. He could see their regimental flags flapping in the rain from behind the felled trees and the short stone walls that made up their defenses. The men of the 13th USCT stood in formation in the cornfield below waiting for the order to advance. They watched quietly as the big Federal guns hammered away at the Confederates on top of Overton Hill. He was pretty sure that no matter how many shells they lobbed up there, there were still going to be plenty of Rebels left to shoot them down once they began their climb. Suddenly, he wasn't so excited about getting his chance to fight.

Rumor had it that this wasn't even the main assault. Once again, the colored man was going to be used as bait to draw the Rebels to their right, Jerry couldn't help but think, then the main attack would be on their left. He turned and looked around at silent black faces staring at the explosions on the hill. Raindrops struck their upturned faces then ran down like tears. *Ain't we a bunch of suckers,* he thought. He looked to the bayonet attached to his rifle. Raindrops glistened on the steel. *I better get to kill at least one them sons-of-bitches before I die,* he smirked to himself.

"There they go now!" one of the soldiers said, pointing.

Jerry looked back at the hill. He was surprised to see white regiments begin the assault. He was certain they'd sacrifice the colored troops first.

"Damn!" one of the soldiers exclaimed as a burst of canister tore through ranks of men climbing the hill. Dozens of them fell at once. The Rebels began popping up from behind their works and firing muskets into the advancing ranks. More men tumbled to the ground.

"Damn, this crazy!" another soldier mumbled at the ghastly sight.

"Quiet in the ranks!" a sergeant chided them.

"Alright, boys," their captain spoke, "we're next. Just like we trained. Keep in formation. Don't fire until you hear the order. This is our chance to show what we can do."

"That's right," some of the men mumbled.

Jerry sighed. *Yeah, we can die just as good as them white boys,* he thought.

Up ahead the first wave broke. Men tripped over each other and slipped in the mud as they turned away from the withering fire and ran back down the hill.

"Forward…march!" came the command. The 13th USCT moved forward as one. Their brogans sloshed in the muddy ground as they marched. The carnage on the slopes was momentarily obscured as they approached a dense thicket at the base of the hill, but they could hear the battle raging on the other side.

Someone was humming in the ranks above the din. The melody conformed with the rhythm of the snare drums. Soon, voices began to sing the words of the hymn. Jerry found himself mumbling along:

…Mine eyes have seen the glory of the coming of the Lord.

He is trampling out the vintage where the grapes of wrath are stored;

He hath loosed the fateful lightning of His swift and terrible sword…

Jets of fire shot down from the heights as the hill once again came into view. Now he could see hundreds of soldiers, white and black, all the same in their blue uniforms littering the slopes with their broken bodies.

…His truth is marching on.

The 13th USCT continued forward.

Glory, glory, hallelujah!

The men of the 13th turned their bodies sideways at the same time to allow the survivors of the last wave to escape through their ranks, just as they had practiced on the parade ground time and time again, then snapped forward as one once the last survivor was through.

Glory, glory, hallelujah!

Minié balls whizzed around them as the Rebels were now targeting this new threat.

Glory, glory, hallelujah!

"Captain! I'm wounded! What should I do?" Jerry heard one of the soldiers call out.

"Stay down, Josiah," the captain called back, "it's alright, son."

His truth is marching on…

More of the men were dropping all around him. Others quickly filled in the gaps as the regiment climbed the slope. He looked left and right. They were the only ones left still marching forward. A hot wind blew through the ranks. Scorching pieces of metal tore through him. He was suddenly on the ground gasping for air. Men's feet squished in the water as they walked around him. He tried to push himself up only to fall back into the mud. The light was dimming. He tried again, propping himself up on his elbows. Up at the top of the hill, he could see a black soldier standing on the Rebel parapet waving the 13th USCT Regimental flag. The soldier's body convulsed as bullets tore through him. Another soldier picked up the flag.

"...Mine eyes have seen the glory..." he mumbled, then closed his eyes.

The seemingly hopeless assault on the Rebel right flank did what it was supposed to do. Hood shifted troops from his center and left to hold off the relentless Federal attack on his right. This left his already weakened line on the left hopelessly undermanned. What's more, the exhausted and battered Rebels had placed their defenses at the very geographical crest of the hill instead of on the "military crest," which would typically be a bit further down from the top. The result was the silhouette of their defenses made an easy target for the Federal artillery who made them pay dearly for the mistake. Furthermore, defenders at the top of the hill would have to expose themselves in order to shoot down at the attackers climbing the slopes than if they had dug their trenches lower. When the Federals launched their attack, they were therefore protected by the steep slopes instead of exposed.

The Rebels first saw their own forward skirmishers running headlong into the main defenses. Then the Federals surged into view behind them as they crested the hill from several directions. It was more than enough for the men defending the hilltop. After firing a wild volley that mostly flew over the heads of their attackers, hundreds took to their feet and ran. Many dropped their guns along the way. Others threw their hands up and surrendered. They were done with fighting and running.

The Rebels ran through their own line causing an overall panic. Others joined in the flight without even seeing what they were running from. Soon it was a tsunami of fleeing soldiers in gray and butternut rags.

"Stop!" officers tried to rally them. "Turn and fight for your country, for God's sake!"

"You turn and fight for your country, you stupid son of a bitch!" was the answer they got as the river of men flowed past them, unconcerned about orders from officers anymore.

"Here!" Colonel Rucker drew an imaginary line across Granny White Pike with his sword. His horse reared as the endless flow of fleeing soldiers ran past. "We'll hold them off here."

"Who?" Lathan asked, "The Yankees or our own cowards?"

Rucker glared at him. "Dismount and start building a barricade, Captain."

Lathan was furious. Mismanagement had caused the disaster at Franklin and now the Confederate Army of Tennessee was crumbling before his eyes at Nashville. At least the cavalry was still fighting. They had paralyzed the Federal navy for two weeks with just a handful of cannons on the river, but suddenly found themselves isolated and outflanked when the rest of the army retreated. Like thieves, they had to slip away, fearing that the enormous force of Yankee cavalry that had them nearly surrounded would catch them in the dark.

They had spent the day protecting the rear of the new defensive line the infantry had thrown up overnight. Now that that line had broken, they were now guarding the retreat.

"Help me with this wagon, Tom," Lathan told his man. The road was cluttered with discarded gear. Men had dropped their haversacks, bedrolls, even rifles as they ran. Wagons sat idle in the road, their horses and mules having been snatched up by fleeing men. With a grunt, they flipped a wagon onto its side. Others brought more wagons, logs, and whatever else they could find to block the road. More fleeing men flowed by. They ran around the ends of the barricade or climbed over the top in their desperate flight to Franklin.

Lathan rested the barrel of his carbine on the wagon and peered up the road, looking for this monster that had terrified so many men. Rain began to fall again as the afternoon sun faded. He turned to watch the colonel place cavalrymen as they arrived along this new line of defense. Another detachment of horsemen was approaching. The colonel rode up to meet them. His saber, which he was using to direct newcomers, was still in his hand. The leader of this new group rode forward to meet him. Lathan squinted in the rain and fading light, trying to make out the man Colonel Rucker was speaking to.

"Those don't look like our uniforms..." he mumbled to himself.

Rucker must have realized his mistake at the same time. He swung wildly at the man, clipping his forehead with the tip of his saber.

"Shit!" Tom let out. Rifles rattled along the barricade as men pulled them to their shoulders.

"Hold your fire!" Lathan shouted. "You'll hit the Colonel!"

Rucker's horse reared with fear from the sudden violence. He dropped his sword as he fought for balance. His opponent recovered from the scrapping blow and drew his own sword. Rucker grabbed the blade with his gloved hand and the two men grappled and punched at each other from their saddles. The rest of the stranger's horsemen surged forward. Rucker finally broke free taking the man's sword with him.

"Shoot them! Shoot them!" he shouted, wildly motioning to his pursuers as he galloped toward the barricade. The line crackled with carbine and pistol fire. Several of the galloping horsemen and their mounts went down including the colonel who was now lost from sight in the cloud of gun smoke.

The Yankees were upon them before anyone without a repeating rifle could reload and fire again. Lathan dropped his carbine and shot the first man that came over the barricade in the face with the tiny shotgun barrel of his LeMat pistol. The man collapsed on him as more poured over the top, knocking him onto his back. He flinched and squirmed to avoid the boots, brogans, and bare feet stomping in the mud around him. He lifted his pistol and shot into the groin of a man in blue. The man howled in agony and collapsed to the ground. Others in both uniforms fell around him. The sounds of screams, pistols, and sabers clanging mixed in with the rain that splattered on his face making it hard to see. He shimmied out from under the dead body. Feet unknowingly stomped and kicked at him as the melee raged on. He turned onto his stomach and crawled, searching for enough space to stand up in once again.

Wilson's Cavalry Corps surged forward once the Confederate line broke. A bearded man in a ragged butternut uniform ran up to Carl's horse with his hands in the air. "I'm done! I'm done!" he shouted.

"That's good, sir. Just move to the rear to be processed," Carl pointed with his saber.

"Do you have any food?" the man asked.

"Sure," Carl tossed him a piece of hardtack.

"Thank you, friend," the man smiled up at him. Rainwater washed lines into his otherwise dirt-covered face.

There was no resistance as they rode south on Granny White Pike. What was left of the Confederate army had retreated. Left behind were the war-weary stragglers who were happy to be done fighting.

"Alright, look alive, fellas," Newman rode up on H company. "Our boys are engaged with a Rebel skirmish line down the road. They've put up a barricade. We're going to ride around and fall in on their flank. Let's go!"

Lathan finally got to his feet. Men were running past him, trying to get away from the mass of blue jacketed men that had overwhelmed their line. Lathan fired a few shots into them indiscriminately. He turned and began to jog along with the rest of the fleeing troops. He holstered his pistol. The fight was over. It was time to get on his horse and get as far away as possible. There was no way he was going to let the Yankees gloat at him in a prison.

Most of the horses were already gone when he got to the tethering line. He felt a brief wave of panic course through him at the thought of someone having already taken his horse in the all-out rush to escape. To his relief, his mount was still tied to the tether line.

"They're coming in on our flanks!" someone shouted.

Lathan turned to see the dark forms of men on horseback coming out the woods on the other side of the pike. They were surrounding the men fleeing from the barricades and taking them prisoner. He fired a few rounds into the mass of them, turned, and ran for his horse. He untied the reins and stuck his foot in the stirrup. The sound of hooves pounding the wet ground was around him.

"Stop! Hold it right there!" a voice commanded. He put his hands up and turned to face the four horsemen surrounding him. Three held pistols on him. Their leader pointed at him with a saber.

"Alright, hand over that pistol, sir, and everything is going to be fine," the man said. The voice sounded awfully familiar.

Lathan looked up and smiled at the corporal, "Of course, Cousin Carl."

"You!" Carl gasped. They stared at each other for a moment.

"Um, corporal…?" one of his men asked.

"Take his pistol, Joey," Carl said, not taking his eyes off Lathan.

The private put his own pistol away and nudged his horse closer. "Nice and easy, sir," he said, his voice quivering as he extended his hand.

"Of course," Lathan cooed. Keeping his left hand in the air, he undid the flap of his holster and pulled out the gun. Clutching it by the cylinder and barrel, he offered it handle first to the private. Carl let out a sigh of relief as Joey leaned down to take it.

Lathan grabbed his arm with his left hand and yanked him off his horse, pulling him to his body like a shield. He spun the pistol around in his hand and fired. The other two soldiers fired wildly. Muzzle flashes lit up their frightened faces in the rain and gloom. Carl's horse reared in panic, throwing him to the ground. He landed with an "Oof!" He scrambled to his feet. Lathan was already on his horse and gone. "Damn it!" he let out.

Joey was on the ground screaming. "I'm hit! I'm hit!" Israel's horse pawed the ground nervously. Its rider lay in a lifeless clump next to it.

Albert looked at Carl. His wide eyes blinking slowly in bewilderment. "I think I shot him," he said indicating towards Joey with his head.

"There's no telling who shot who, Al," Carl said, thrusting himself back in the saddle. He sheathed his sword and pulled out his revolver. "Take care of him. I'm going to go kill that man." He put his spurs to his horse and plunged into the woods.

Lathan had a good jump on his pursuer, but his horse faltered and then collapsed from a loss of blood. "Damn it," He grunted. He got to his feet. The animal must have caught a bullet from the shootout. He put a boot on its side and pulled his saber from the saddle. A twig broke behind him. He spun around, pulling his pistol with his other hand. A flash of lightning lit up Carl's face. He sat high above him on his horse, his pistol leveled on Lathan. The rain had stopped. A low peal of thunder rumbled through the woods as the two men stared with their pistols pointing at each other.

"Looks like we're in a bit of a standoff, Carl," Lathan said.

"You didn't have to shoot my men," Carl said.

"We're in a war, Carl. Has anyone explained to you what a war is and what you're supposed to do in one?"

"You could have just surrendered, Lathan. I wouldn't have been able to do anything other than take you prisoner."

"Ah," Lathan said with some delight, "but aren't you here to avenge your fellow nigger, my half-breed friend?"

"I'm half-Mexican, you son of a bitch," Carl gritted through his teeth.

"Don't be so hard on yourself," Lathan replied with a chuckle. They fell silent for a moment, pointing their guns at each other. "Well, then," Lathan said at last, "it looks like we're in a bit of a *Mexican* standoff, then."

Carl stared at him down the barrel of his gun, daring himself to pull the trigger and be done with this one way or another.

CLICK!

Carl flinched. The hammer of Lathan's gun had fallen and found nothing but an empty chamber. "I knew it was empty," Lathan laughed as he tossed it to the ground, " but I just wanted to make sure."

This was it. All he had to do was shoot and it would all be over.

"Well…?" Lathan shrugged. Carl let out a sigh and he uncocked his pistol. "I knew it!" Lathan said triumphantly. Carl holstered the weapon, got down from his horse. He tied it to a tree, pulled out his saber, and turned to meet his enemy.

"You know," Lathan said, "I'm beginning to like you, Cousin Carl."

"I will hate you for the rest of my life," Carl said, holding his saber up and setting into his stance.

"Well, that shouldn't be too long, then," Lathan smiled, sinking into his stance. Carl sprung forward, raising his saber and swinging it down at Lathan's head. It was met with a clang of steel. Lathan deflected the blow, whipped his blade around, and swung at Carl's midsection where it was met by the flat of Carl's blade. Carl thrust forward. Lathan tried to lean away from the blow but the tip caught a bit of his left shoulder as he turned.

"Gaah!" Lathan hissed, clutching the scrape with his sword hand as he stepped back with a hop. "You're getting better!" he said, recovering his composure after taking the surprise wound.

"It's because I know I'm going to kill you," Carl said flatly.

"Is that so?" Lathan smiled, raising an eyebrow. "Well, I appreciate you bringing me another horse in your effort." He sunk back into his stance. "I'll need something to ride once I'm done here."

"You're not going anywhere," Carl said, renewing his attack. The sabers flashed and clanged in the darkness with a flurry of swings, parries, and thrusts. Carl swung his blade right to left at Lathan's throat. Lathan brought his blade in to stop the blow, grabbed Carl's sword arm with his left hand, and stepped in swinging the brass hilt of his saber backhandedly across Carl's face. Carl leaned back, feeling the blow catch his chin. Lathan pressed forward bringing his blade back in a broad sweeping swing.

Carl reeled backward from the blow. He reached with his free arm for the knife tucked in the back of his trousers. He caught himself with his back foot then bounded forward, leading with the short blade. Lathan stepped right into it as he swung. He felt the point pop through his wool jacket, shirt, undershirt, pierce his skin, then slide between his ribs into his heart. Carl caught him in his arms. Lathan's swing wrapped harmlessly around Carl's shoulder. His sword fell to the ground.

Lathan clung to Carl, holding him for support. "I believe you've killed me, Cousin Carl," he said into his ear.

"I sure hope so," Carl replied, gently easing him to the ground.

"Ah…" he chuckled lightly, and then with a distant reverence, "All I ever wanted was to matter…matter like you rich boys do so easily."

"You could have, but now you won't ever and it's your damn own fault," Carl said. "The only ones you'll ever matter to now are the crows and worms waiting for you to die."

Lathan coughed up a mouthful of blood as he chuckled, "Well, I guess you got me there, Carl…"

Carl tried to hold on to the hate and anger he felt for the man dying in his arms but he couldn't feel anything. Lathan drifted away peacefully, snuggled in his arms like a child. The moment he had been waiting for suddenly seemed meaningless and empty. Thunder rumbled once more. A raindrop hit the top of his head. He looked up from the dead man's face to the dark sky above the leafless trees that surrounded them. The rain began to fall again.

Epilog

I.
December 17, 1864: Nashville

Elijah came with a wagon in the morning to help collect the dead and wounded that covered Overton Hill. This was where he was told that the 13th USCT fought. The story of their bravery in the face of the enemy's withering fire was already spreading through Nashville. He was proud to hear that some had even made it to the top, but at a terrible cost. Their bodies lay broken and twisted on the slope. Some were stuck in the abatis, suspended in absurd positions of agony as they hung from the sharpened branches like morbid tree ornaments.

"Oh, Jerry..." He let out a sob. He found him lying face down in the mud, halfway up the hill. Jerry was still clutching his rifle. Elijah sat down and cradled the man in his arms. "I'm sorry I wasn't with you, Jerry," he sniffed as he cried.

He looked up at the sound of horses. A group of officers was slowly riding up the slope, their somber faces reflected the grisly scene around them. Their horses carefully stepped around the bodies. It was clear that the bearded man leading them was a general and someone very important by the way the others regarded him.

Elijah suddenly didn't know what to do. He thought maybe he should get up and salute. But he wasn't a soldier anymore and pushing Jerry off him so he could scramble up onto his prosthetic foot in the mud would just be awkward, so he just sat there, holding his friend's head in his lap as this general and his staff approached.

The general stopped and looked down at him, then nodded. Elijah nodded back, wiping away the tears. There was sadness in the man's gray-blue eyes.

"I'm sorry for your friend," he said.

"Thank you, sir," Elijah said, looking up at him through his tears.

The general turned to his staff, "Gentlemen, the question is settled: the negro will fight." The men around him murmured in agreement. The general nodded once more at Elijah before spurring his horse into motion once more.

The pain in the young man's eyes was too much for Major General George Thomas to bear. It was easier to look at the all dead around them than the living young man holding his friend. He let out a sigh as he rode. All the elation he had felt at the moment of victory was dulled by the sight of the cost.

The war had ruined his life. His family in Virginia disowned him for staying loyal to the army that he had sworn an oath to at West Point and fought for in the Seminole Wars and in Mexico. His friends who resigned their commissions and fought for their home states called him a traitor. His colleagues and superiors in the US Army treated him with suspicion, constantly questioning his loyalty even after the press deemed him "The Rock of Chickamauga." He had been passed over for promotion and left behind to watch over the supply hub at Nashville, well before anyone knew the Rebels would make such an audacious attempt to win back the West.

Looking at them now, it was hard to imagine the threat was once real. Thomas and his staff arrived at surrender grounds. Thousands of Rebel soldiers stood in formation. Some shivered as they stood barefoot and dressed in rags hardly suitable for mid-December Tennessee weather. Their dirty faces were hollow from a lack of food.

"Men," he addressed them, "you fought well, bravely, and honorably. You should take pride in that." He took a moment to scan at their faces before continuing. "It's over now. It's time to lay down your rifles and pick up your plows…It's time to go home, boys. For those of you who don't want to be transported to prison camps in the North, I have this offer for you: swear allegiance to the United States of America, promise never to take up arms against her again, and go home." He paused once more, looking at the broken men before him, wondering if his words were reaching them. "We have officers standing by to take your oaths."

To his relief, only a few refused to sign, preferring to be official prisoners of war instead, hoping to be exchanged later so they could fight again. The rest took the oath by the thousands and started their long walk home.

II.

July 5, 1875: Memphis, Tennessee

"Damn you! You cheatin' son of a bitch!" Nathan Bedford Forrest threw his cards down in disgust.

"You wound me to the core, General! I'm the most honest of bluffers!" Gideon Pillow chuckled as he scooped up his winnings from the table. "I can loan you some of your money back if you're in need."

"Now you insult me," Forrest replied gloomily. The men around the table laughed lightly. Forrest squinted as the door opened, spilling sunlight into the dark smokey saloon. Hot summer air rolled in with it. He took a drink of his water as he watched the stranger enter.

The man had a wild mop of blond hair and a long grisly beard. His clothes were ragged and dusty as if he had been on the road for days. He scanned the room with great agitation, walking cautiously among the tables of card-playing men as if he were expecting an attack at any minute. Finely, his wild blue eyes locked onto Forrest's. Forrest leaned back in his chair once he recognized the man and waited with causal amusement.

"Daddy's Boy…" Forrest grinned as Kyle stopped at his table. The men sitting with him turned in their chairs to look at the wild-eyed stranger that had interrupted their game.

"I have business with you," Kyle said, opening his jacket to reveal a pistol, "outside."

"Good heavens!" Pillow said, recoiling in his chair. "I shall fetch the constable at once!"

"It's alright," Forrest put his hand on Pillow's arm, stopping him from getting up. "Mr. Bethune and I are old friends, aren't we, Kyle?" he winked at Kyle with the last bit. "What, may I ask, is the business between us?"

"You killed my friend," Kyle said, his voice trembling with anger and nervousness.

"I killed a lot of people, Kyle. You need to be more specific."

"Francis Beauchamp, your men burned him alive at Fort Pillow."

Forrest closed his eyes and sighed, "Seems I'll never free myself from that day…"

"Son," Pillow leaned forward, "General Forrest has been acquitted time and time again from any responsibility. You can't go on believing everything the Yankee press says. They do the general great injustice."

"Kyle," Forrest said, "I'm not proud of what happened there. It haunts me to this day, but the only man I killed there was one of my own and that was to stop it."

"They were your men, under your command, it was your responsibility," Kyle said, "and today you pay for it."

Forrest let out a laugh and leaned back in his chair. His friends laughed nervously along with him. Their eyes darted between the general and the madman who seemed to have walked out of a cheap frontier novel.

"Ha! I knew you were a killer, just like me, Kyle. I just didn't know you were so damn dramatic. I'll tell you what…I'd be more than happy to oblige you but I have a public engagement this afternoon that I can't miss. If you'd be so kind to allow me to honor my commitment, then I'll be happy to square my business with you, even though, if you'd just wait a damn year or two, I'll be dead anyway. What do you say, old friend?"

Kyle stood blinking at the man he had come to kill. The men around the table sat silently watching him. "Well…I guess," Kyle said, closing his jacket to hide the gun.

"Excellent!" Forrest beamed, "We're going to the old fairgrounds for a barbecue. Won't you come with us? After I say my piece, we can find a quiet place to do our business. You'll be able to slip away afterwards. It's a much better plan than shooting me down in the street, that's for sure." His friends laughed nervously at Forrest's dark humor in the face of this threat.

Kyle walked with them to the train station. "You're not riding with us?" Forrest asked.

"I have a horse. I'll meet you there," Kyle said, looking at the old cavalry leader with new eyes. The transformation was stunning. He could see him clearly now in the full daylight. The man he remembered being so tall, broad-shouldered, and terrifying was now thin, frail, and hunched. His hair had gone completely white, his skin sallow, and his cheeks sunken, yet his deep-set blue eyes still held a devilish twinkle.

"Suit yourself," Forrest said as his friends helped him into the car.

Kyle beat the train to the fairgrounds. He was stunned to see thousands of black people in suits and dresses milling about happily. Red, white, and blue bunting was draped everywhere. A brass band of black musicians played a jaunty rendition of *Kingdom Coming*. A large banner hung over a stage which read, "Independent Pole-Bearers Association."

Kyle was becoming aware that he was one of the few white people there when the train pulled to the platform with a burst of steam. *Good God, they'll tear him apart!* he thought as a crowd gathered on the platform. The band started to play *Dixie* as the car door opened. Forrest and his entourage stepped out to a roar of applause. Forrest smiled and waved at the crowd.

An elderly black man greeted him with a handshake. He was stately and dignified. His fine suit barely hid his strong muscular frame built from a lifetime of labor. The man led Forrest and his party to the stage where they sat in chairs along either side of the podium. The crowd found chairs in the audience as the older black man began to speak.

"Would you like a chair, sir?" a voice interrupted Kyle's thoughts. A young black girl in a pretty dress was motioning him to an empty chair in the audience. Her eyes sparkled with welcome and kindness.

"Umm…sure," Kyle said, feeling the weight of his revolver in his trousers as she led him to his chair. He suddenly felt dirty and unkempt among this crowd of well-dressed revelers. The man at the podium stopped speaking and everyone applauded. Kyle clapped, too, feeling awkward and out of place. The dignitaries were standing now. The pretty young woman that helped Kyle find a seat approached Forrest with a bouquet of flowers. The crowd quieted to hear her speak.

"Mr. Forrest, allow me to present you this bouquet of flowers as a token of reconciliation and an offering of peace in goodwill."

Forrest smiled broadly as he took the flowers, then clutching her shoulders, he drew her to him and kissed her on the cheek which brought great cheers from the crowd.

"Ladies and Gentlemen," he turned to them, "I accept the flowers as a memento of reconciliation between the white and colored races of the Southern states." This brought more cheers. "I accept it more particularly as it comes from a colored lady, for if there's anyone on God's earth who loves the ladies, I believe it is myself." A peal of laughter swept through the crowd.

Kyle sunk into his chair, feeling the weight of his gun as Forrest continued to speak. Suddenly, he realized Forrest was looking directly at him, "I came here with the jeers of some white people," Forrest was saying, "who think that I am doing wrong." Kyle looked around, feeling like all eyes were on him. They weren't. They were enrapt with Forrest, listening intently as he spoke.

"I believe that I can exert some influence, and do much to assist the people in strengthening fraternal relations, and shall do all in my power to bring about peace. It has always been my motto to elevate every man…to depress none." Another round of cheers broke out. Forrest smiled and waited until they died down before continuing.

"I want to elevate you to take positions in law offices, in stores, on farms, and wherever you are capable of going." Loud applause erupted again. Kyle started looking around as Forrest continued. He suddenly felt trapped in the crowd. He knew he'd cause a commotion if he got up and left while Forrest was still speaking.

"I came to meet you as friends, and welcome you to the white people," Forrest continued. "I want you to come nearer to us. When I can serve you, I will do so. We have but one flag, one country. Let us stand together. We may differ in color, but not in sentiment." Once again, wild applause erupted. Kyle dared himself to get up and leave but was frozen to his chair. The heat was oppressive. He wanted to take off his jacket but worried everyone would see his gun.

Forrest finally finished. "I thank you, ladies and gentlemen, for this opportunity you have afforded me to be with you and to assure you that I am with you in heart and in hand." Everyone stood and applauded. Kyle stood, turned, and walked quickly, mumbling apologies as he bumped into people in his haste to get away. He was alone. He had nothing. He had nowhere to go. All he wanted to do was get on his horse and ride west until he could not ride anymore.

Gideon Pillow stood next to Forrest on the stage. They waved to the cheering crowd that had come to hear them speak. He watched the strange vagabond stumble away. He smiled and shook his head, feeling a bit relieved. He leaned over and whispered to Forrest, "I think our friend is leaving."

Forrest squinted as he watched Kyle disappear into the crowd while still smiling and waving. "It's too bad," he said. "He's going to miss out on some good barbecue."

The End

Did you like it? Please give me a review on Amazon, goodreads.

Please join the Engdahl House email list for updates on new releases, discounts, appearances, and more at https://subscribepage.io/EngdahlHouse.

And be sure to read the prequel to this series:

Mexico, My Love

The preview is on the next page.

Preview of *Mexico, My Love:* Chapter One: The Prophecy

The open window didn't help. Claudette threw off her bedsheets in frustration. It was impossible to sleep in the stifling heat. She fanned herself in the darkness, wondering if it was worth lighting a candle to try to read herself back to sleep. Moonlight spilled into her room which was nestled at the very top of her family's countryside home. Perhaps, she thought, if she pulled the chair from her writing desk to the window, she could use the moonlight to read.

She was careful not to bump her head against the steeply vaulted ceiling as she slipped out of bed and softly shuffled across the floor, careful not to cause any creaks that could wake everyone below. She placed her hands on the sill and leaned out into the night air. Below, the moonlight fell on the neatly lined rows of grapevines, giving them an eerie glow. The vineyard rolled out before her and then disappeared over the hills. Somewhere on the other side was Marseille with its cafés, book shops, and life.

She sighed softly. A light breeze rolled in through the window, rustling her simple white shift. It brought a welcomed cooling to her body. It smelled of the sea and the world outside, full of adventure, just outside the harbor. There was life out there, but she was stuck here in this endless maze of grapevines and boredom with only a handful of books that she had already read over and over again. She was hidden away from the rest of the world.

Her family had been hiding for centuries now. They had once been noble, but her line came from a long succession of second and third sons who married into wealthy merchant families instead of seeking titles and peerage. They hid their wealth as they found themselves on the wrong side of politics time and time again. They had backed the Huguenots against Cardinal Richelieu and lost. They had resisted the summons of the Sun King to live in his pampered prison of Versailles, then fell into obscurity in his shadow.

They finally found victory in the revolution and then rode high on the Bonapartist wave. Her grandfather and great uncles had fought in *La Grande Armée*, bringing liberty and republicanism to the rest of Europe. But the Emperor was gone now. He died a prisoner on a lonely island far from France. Those who prospered with him retreated back into the shadows under the return of the monarchy.

So the Moreaus hid, sold their wine, and stashed their money. But most annoyingly, they hid their daughter. "You are too pretty for the eyes of men," her mom warned her. "They will be driven mad with temptation and try to drag you down in their sin." Her mother insisted Claudette be kept away from the eyes of the world until they could marry her into a family that could lift the Moreaus from hiding and into the restoration of nobility under the King.

She sighed again, gazing at the dark hills and imagining the grand life hidden beyond them. Then she heard it. It was thin and bright, too rhythmic to be natural, too melodic. It was dark and lively…it was music!

"Where is that coming from…?" she mumbled. She leaned out further, cocking her head to the side to hear better. It seemed to ride on the sea breeze that swirled around her ears. It was a violin and it couldn't be far! "Who in the world…?" she wondered out loud.

She looked at her bedroom door. Walking across the floor and turning the knob would surely wake the entire house. She looked back into the nightscape outside. There's no way she could sleep now. There was a mystery out there and she was going to get to the bottom of it. She grabbed onto the ivy and swung her body out of the window, clutching the vines with her bare toes.

"Huh…!" she gasped as she slid down the wall, dragging her nails through the vine as she tried to grab onto something to stop her fall. Needles of pain sparkled through her bare feet as they smacked against the ground. She fell flat on her butt, hissing in pain as she shook her hands in agony. Her fingernails felt like they'd been nearly ripped out. She sucked in her breath and listened carefully. Surely all of France had heard her fall. She waited until she was sure that all she could hear were crickets and the lonely violin.

The sound got louder as she crept around the house. The window in the detached kitchen flickered and glowed. She approached carefully. There were stories of wraiths and souls that haunted these hills. They played tricks on the living, enticing them into sharing their damnation. Claudette clutched the sill.

She propped herself onto her toes and peered inside. A dark form was playing a fiddle. It sat at the table next to a candle. Its hair was long with wild brown curls. Claudette found herself mesmerized by the music. *The phantom has captured me!* she thought, trying to will herself to turn away before it was too late, but she was unable to break the spell.

The creature stopped abruptly. "Huh…!" Claudette drew in a breath. She could see a single green eye appear over the top of the instrument. It was looking at her. Icy chills ran down her back. The creature set the fiddle down and waved her in. Claudette wanted to run, but she was trapped in the ghoul's spell.

"You should be in bed, Mademoiselle." The creature spoke French with an accent spiced with Eastern European flavors as Claudette entered the room. She sighed with relief. It was merely a woman, a kitchen servant.

"It is too hot for sleeping," Claudette said, "and I had to know where the music was coming from."

"My apologies, Mademoiselle," the woman said fearfully, "I did not mean to disturb anyone."

"No, not at all," Claudette was quick to assure her. "It was wonderful!" Claudette looked her over with fascination. The woman had olive skin, wild hair, and striking green eyes that reflected the flickering candlelight. "Are you a Gypsy?" she asked.

"I am merely a woman who needs this job, child. My breeding has no bearing on the quality of my work."

Claudette gazed at the woman for a moment, "I think you're beautiful, whatever you are. Please, put yourself at ease."

The woman stared at her for a moment. The fear slipped away and turned into a broad smile that enthralled Claudette with wild mystery. "Thank you, my child. Yes, my people are Romani, but I must be careful. We are not always welcomed in the houses of the French."

Claudette sparkled with happiness. "Well, you are welcome here. I am Claudette," she said offering her hand. "I don't have any friends. It's nice to have someone to talk to."

The woman looked around nervously for a moment, then took her hand, "You're going to get me fired, child. It's not permitted to talk to the masters of the house."

"No, I won't," Claudette protested. "We're friends!"

The woman closed her eyes and sighed with a laugh. She opened and focused them intensely on the girl in front of her. "Okay, my little friend. You can call me Lavinia."

Claudette beamed with excitement. "Is it true that the Gypsies can talk to the spirit world? Can you tell fortunes?"

"That is a myth, child."

"Please, tell me my fortune. Will I ever know love?" Claudette leaned forward in her chair, grasping her hands together in pleading anticipation.

"You are going to get me burned at the stake." Lavinia leaned back in her chair, putting space between her and the girl.

"Oh, pooh! They don't do that anymore!" Claudette scoffed.

"You'd be surprised at man's capacity for violence and cruelty when he fears," she said flatly. Claudette fell silent, blinking her dark eyes at the woman in disappointment. Lavinia blinked back then let out a sigh, "Alright, child, give me your hand."

"I knew it!" Claudette bubbled over with excitement as she thrust her hand forward.

"Careful, my passionate little friend," Lavinia warned as she took the little girl's hand. "There are some things in one's fortune that are best left unknown. Things that only become true because you're expecting them. Be careful not to force the hand of destiny. The spirits are always swirling around our decisions. They're constantly writing and rewriting our destinies." With that, she began to examine Claudette's palm. A wave of concern washed over her face but was quickly replaced by a smile. "Just as I suspected!"

"What?!"

Lavinia looked up from the open palm to the little girl's eyes with a sly grin. "You have a very strong head line, perhaps too strong for your own good!"

"Mamá always says I'm stubborn," Claudette admitted.

"Perhaps you should listen to her."

Claudette rolled her eyes then returned them to Lavinia with renewed excitement. "What else?"

"Let's see…" Lavinia mumbled, looking over the child's palm. "I see a strong life line. You can expect good health and a long life, child."

"I see…" Claudette answered, then with mischief in her eyes asked, "What about love? Will I know great love in my life?"

"Yes, it looks fine," Lavinia said quickly then looked away.

Claudette eyed her for a moment suspiciously. "You're not being honest with me."

Lavinia returned her eyes to the girl, "Chiromancy is not a science, child. It's a game we play to fool the *gadje* out of their money."

"Tell me!" Claudette protested impatiently.

Lavinia stared at her for a moment then sighed. "You have great passion and a capacity to love deeply. Look at how strong this line is as it swoops down from your index finger."

"Huh!" Claudette gasped with excitement. "But then it stops here," she said.

"It does, child, right where it intersects with this vertical line that descends from between your middle and ring finger. That line is fate."

"What does it mean?" Claudette asked with fear creeping into her voice.

"It only means what you make it mean, child. Like I said, chiromancy is a mere game to play on fools."

"Will I have my heart broken?" she asked.

"Child, you must not close your heart, no matter your loss. Let me look again. Ah!" she said. "This line here! It seems your heart line starts again, but later, and it is strong!"

"So there's hope?" Claudette asked feebly.

"So long as you live and you keep your heart young, there is always hope, my sweet little friend."

Claudette looked at her palm in wonderment, looking at the line interrupted by a gap on her palm. "How long must I suffer?"

"It is unclear. Time in the spirit world expands and contracts like the accordion. Remember, you are still in charge of your destiny. The spirit world can only give you hints along the way."

Claudette blinked at her for a moment, her mind running wild with enchantment. "Teach me!" she said at last. "Teach me how to find the spirit world and to read its hints!"

"The spirit world is all around you. You just have to learn how to open your eyes and see it in front of you."

Historical Note

Forrest died two years later from diabetes. His speech at the Independent Pole-Bearers Association was one of his last public appearances. As you probably guessed, I quoted his speech directly in this book. You can find the unabridged version online. It certainly caused a lot of controversy, especially among white supremacists of his day. They called him a traitor to his race for kissing a black girl, and for his speech about reconciliation, unity, and inclusion between the races.

Forrest is certainly the most controversial figure from the American Civil War. He became a millionaire before the war by buying and selling human beings as slaves. A Congressional investigational committee accused him of war crimes for the Massacre at Fort Pillow. He was never brought to trial. He's considered to be the first Grand Wizard of the Ku Klux Klan. He denied any association with the group although it's widely accepted that he was at least a figurehead if not actively its leader

He testified against the Klan before Congress in 1871. He later spoke out about dismantling them, even volunteering to lead a posse against the Klan after they broke into a jail and lynched four blacks. He wrote to the Governor of Tennessee offering "to exterminate the white marauders who disgrace their race by this cowardly murder of Negroes."

So why the change of heart? Many of his admirers say that he was always this way. Some say he found religion toward the end of his life and was trying to make amends. Others say it was for more practical reasons as his post-war reputation harmed his business and political aspirations.

Nathan Bedford Forrest was a real person and I tried to be as true and objective about him as possible using the sources I have which include his own words, biographies written by men who knew him personally, and from modern historians and biographers. There are many historical figures and events in my novels. I take great care to depict them as accurately as modern scholarship will allow.

Of course, the main characters and their stories are fictional, but much of the historical events and real people around them were very much as I described. I should say that I drew the names of my H Company of the 2nd Michigan Cavalry characters from the original roster of 1861. This includes Captain Newman, Sergeant Barnes, and Privates Bates and Scott. Only their names are similar to the real men that served in the unit. Everything else I've written about them is purely fictional. I mean no disrespect to the real men or their descendants.

Francis is also a figure of my imagination. However, there was a real man who fought at Fort Pillow that fits his story. Emanuel Nichols of Company B of the 6th USCHA was a freeman from Michigan who came south to join the regiment. I don't know if he was anything like my Francis, but I'd like to dedicate my Francis Bethune to the bravery of this man. Thank you, sir, for your service and sacrifice.

Young & Brothers Books was a real shop on Front Street in Memphis in the 1860s. You should know by now that if I ever get that specific, it's usually because it's real. I saw it in an 1862 photo and thought it would be a neat detail to include among the saloons and bordellos that were also truly there at the time. The Gayoso Hotel was also real a landmark in Memphis until it burned down in 1899. It was rebuilt in the twentieth century, and I believe it's now used as an apartment building.

Yes, it's true. Alexandre Dumas, the writer of *The Three Musketeers,* was the grandson of a Haitian slave and her French nobleman lover. His father, Thomas-Alexandre Dumas was the highest-ranking officer of sub-Saharan African descent in any European army up to that time. He commanded all of Napoleon's Cavalry during the Egyptian campaign.

If you haven't figured it out yet, Dumas is one of my favorite writers. I've modeled myself after him. Dumas didn't write his works as the novels we know today. He wrote them as serials that appeared in a weekly Parisian newspaper. I try to write chapters like episodes of a serial you might find on a streaming service today. Each book is a season, each chapter is an episode. Hopefully, one of these streaming services will notice and start shooting my series. Stay tuned!

Thompson Station was a humiliating loss for Colonel John Coburn and the three regiments he marched into Earl Van Dorn's well-fortified line while Nathan Bedford Forrest's cavalry hammered away at their left flank and rear.

Cut off from his cavalry and artillery, he eventually had to surrender once his men ran out of ammunition. I may have painted him as somewhat of a jerk. I took my cue from Marshall Thatcher's memoir, *A Hundred Battles in the West*. In it, Thatcher says Coburn "seemed to think the major (Scranton) unnecessarily alarmed, in fact treating that officer and his two battalions of cavalry with contempt." Thatcher lays the blame directly on Coburn for marching his infantry into battle without bringing his artillery forward. Coburn, of course, blamed the cavalry for abandoning him.

Coburn later returned to service after a prisoner exchange. He served nobly under General William Tecumseh Sherman. He and his troops were the first to enter Atlanta and accept the mayor's surrender. He'd later serve as a US congressman and a Supreme Court justice in the Territory of Montana. He died in 1908.

There are two very interesting stories on the Confederate side that didn't make it into my narrative. One is 17-year-old Alice Thompson who picked up the 3rd Arkansas Cavalry Regiment's flag after seeing their colonel and color bearer shot down in her yard. In this Joan of Arc-like moment, she rallied the troops and drove them forward to victory. Even the Yankees were impressed by her valor. Good job, Alice, I salute you.

Roderick, the horse was another surprise hero of the battle. He had taken three bullets while carrying Nathan Bedford Forrest into the fight. Forrest remounted and sent the injured horse back to the corral to rest. But Roderick wasn't done fighting. He broke free from the holding area and jumped three fences to find his master in the heat of the battle. He took a fourth bullet and died at Forrest's feet. Good boy, Roderick, may you forever feast on the green grass of Valhalla.

For the sake of historical accuracy, I should clear up a little of the timeline. I like to write my chapters to be complete stories. Because of this, sometimes their timelines overlap. Chapter Three ends with Francis and Elijah meeting Lieutenant Lionel F. Booth. That would have been after the fall of Vicksburg, which was July 4, 1863. Booth had been a quartermaster sergeant with the 1st Missouri Light Artillery during that siege. He impressed his commanders so much that they promoted him to lieutenant and gave him the task of recruiting for the 1st Alabama Siege Artillery of African Descent which eventually became the 6th USCHA.

The Battle of Thompson Station, depicted in Chapter Four, took place in early March of 1863, some four months before our heroes would have met Booth and joined his regiment. Once again, this overlap was to allow the two chapters to be complete stories in themselves. Chapter Three is about Francis and Elijah in Memphis. Chapter Four is about the 2nd Michigan Cavalry fighting against Nathan Bedford Forrest at Thompson Station.

I should also point out that "Lionel F. Booth" was a *nom de guerre*. His real name was George H. Lanning. Why he used an alias is still a mystery. Booth, which is the name I'll use here, was born in Philadelphia in 1838. He went west at the age of 20 looking for adventure. He found it fighting in Missouri at the outset of the war. He had just recently married a girl named Lizzie Wayt before taking his regiment to Fort Pillow. He left her in Memphis to keep her safe.

Chickamauga was the second bloodiest battle of the Civil War after Gettysburg with a combined casualty count of nearly 35,000 men dead, wounded, captured, or missing. The Confederates actually had higher losses even though it was certainly a tactical victory for them. That said, the battle was still a disaster for both commanders. Both would be relieved of their commands within the months that followed.

General George Thomas did much better, however. He earned the nickname "the Rock of Chickamauga" for his defense on the northern flank that allowed the rest of the army to escape. He was also given command of the Army of the Cumberland which he held onto until the end of the war.

Rosecrans's chief of staff General James Garfield, who I mentioned in the book, would become the 20th President of the United States. He was assassinated in 1881.

I love featuring some of the odd and exotic weapons of the American Civil War, and Lathan's LaMat pistol is certainly one of them. It was a favorite of several Confederate officers. The mid-nineteenth century was a fascinating time for experimenting with weapons before we got to the more standard and iconic weapons of the "wild west" era that followed. The gun was invented in New Orleans by Jean

Alexandre LeMat, a cousin of the famous CSA General P.T.G Beauregard. Beauregard was a financial backer of the weapon and instrumental in winning several contracts with the Confederate military to produce the gun.

The LeMat pistol is a cap and ball, black powder revolver featuring a 9-shot cylinder. What makes it unique is its secondary 20-gauge shotgun barrel. The shooter can opt to use either barrel by switching the firing pin on the hammer to the up position for the revolver, or the down position for the shotgun. They were very effective at close range but not reliably accurate from afar. The novelty and popularity of the gun died out after the war as cartridge-fire pistols like the Colt "Peacemaker" came into the market.

The confrontation between Forrest and Bragg went down pretty much as I described, at least according to Forrest's chief surgeon Dr. J. B. Cowan who was part of his entourage. This includes brushing past the sentries and jabbing his finger into Bragg's face. I took Forrest's dialog directly from Dr. Cowan's account. I edited it slightly to make it more readable. Cowan claims Forrest had a whole litany of complaints which I did not include in this book. Basically, I simplified his rant, but only slightly. The line, "… if you *ever* interfere with me, or cross my path again…it will be at the peril of your life!" is directly from Dr. Cowan's account. I added the swearing. Forrest was known to use profanity quite freely, as did many men of his age, however, most of them were gentlemanly enough not to write it down. I can only imagine this is the case with Dr. Cowan's account which he wrote down sometime later.

Lathan Woods is a fictional character. The part about him holding the sentries at gunpoint is fictional, however, Forrest did brush past them, and apparently, they did nothing to stop the tirade. So I like the idea of Lathan holding them off in his attempt to please his commander.

To clarify one point about Forrest's primary complaint, Bragg had previously taken some of Forrest's men and given them to Wheeler, claiming it was a temporary loan. Forrest begrudgingly agreed. It was after this that he got the order to turn over his entire command and then report to Wheeler for orders. I simplified this into one single event. Either way, Forrest was in a rage. Confronting Bragg and openly threatening his life was certainly a risky and audacious move, but Forrest knew that Bragg was dealing with a whole slew of rebellious officers as well as a declining public opinion. It was a calculated risk and it got him what he wanted. Bragg and President Davis approved of his request to return to Western Tennessee to recruit, apprehend absconders, and build another command.

The near execution of nineteen deserters at Oxford really did happen. I don't know if they had to dig their own graves, but they did have to stand in front of their coffins that were placed next to their freshly dug graves as the firing squad prepared to shoot them. Accounts differ on whether Forrest came himself or sent an officer to halt the execution at the last moment. I don't know if it was from Jeffrey Forrest's influence that he changed his mind on killing the men, but I like to think Forrest had a soft spot for Jeffrey. Forrest had a very special relationship with his little brother. Their dad died four months before he was born. Forrest raised him like a son and sent him to college. Jeffrey's death weighed heavily on him. I like to think of it as one of the steps along Forrest's path that led him to his rage at Fort Pillow.

I should also note that the freckled, buck-tooth boy at the execution was an invention of my imagination. I don't know if the fleeing soldier that Forrest whipped with a stick was one of the men that he spared from the firing squad, but I thought it worked well. The incident in which Forrest whipped the fleeing man really did happen, as did his conversation with Chalmers beforehand. I used Chalmers's own account of both incidents to write those scenes. Once again, I altered what Forrest said to the fleeing soldier just slightly to make it more readable. The actual quote is from Chalmers's recollection years later and sounds a little too wordy to be said in anger. Here's how Chalmers has it: "Now, God damn you, go back and fight! You might as well get killed there as here, for if you ever run away again, you will not get off so easy!"

Colonel Duckworth's bluff at Union City was one of the best-played poker hands of the war. Nearly five hundred men came out of their well-supplied fortification and surrendered to a force that was not much more than half their size with no artillery. General Brayman was on his way to relieve the

Federals. He claimed to have two-thousand men, although a few days earlier he had reported only being able to muster 231. Even with that number, their combined forces could have been a match for the plucky Duckworth and his men. Brayman was within six miles of Union City when he got the news that Hawkins had surrendered. Fearing that Forrest's entire force was there, Brayman ordered his men to retreat back to Cairo instead of trying to rescue Hawkins and his men.

It was certainly embarrassing to Colonel Hawkins. He was exchanged in August later that year and continued his service until the end of the war. He was elected to the US Congress afterward. Many of his men, whom he thought he was saving by surrendering, fared much worse. According to some sources, over two hundred of them died at the notorious Andersonville Prison Camp as well as other places.

The ruse was a glorious win for Colonel Duckworth but may have done Forrest more harm than good. Forrest relied on fear and his reputation quite a bit. The mere mention of his name was enough to take the fight out of many of the Federals. But once the sensational ruse at Union City hit the press, commanders began to question just how tough he was or if he was even outside their walls. This may have led to Paducah's and perhaps Fort Pillow's refusal to surrender.

I should say something about the "black laborers" and their participation and behavior at the siege of Union City. Some sources I've read listed them as slaves, others called them black Confederate soldiers.

There is an ongoing myth about black Confederates. The Confederacy absolutely outlawed the arming of slaves and using them as soldiers until the very last desperate days of the Confederacy, and when they did, those men never saw combat. Both sides used black labor. The Federals called them "contrabands" and often paid them for their work, but not always. Many Confederate officers brought slaves with them to be their personal servants. They sometimes even gave them uniforms. There are several accounts of these servants picking up arms and defending their masters in combat. Human nature is funny that way. People don't always monolithically act the way we think they would or should.

The Confederate army also confiscated slaves from plantations and used them as laborers. These people drove wagon trains, built defensive works, and buried the dead. Certainly, many fled to the Union lines in search of freedom. Many others had been so institutionalized by generations of slavery that they thought their loyalty should be with their masters. I don't know if the men who built the fake cannons at Union City and then taunted the Federal soldiers who fell for their ruse were slaves or freemen. I don't believe they were enlisted soldiers. Certainly, they would not have been issued anything more than the wooden cannons they built at that time. This is why I went with "black laborers." Either way, right or wrong, these guys really pulled a good one on Colonel Hawkins and probably deserved a good laugh at his expense.

The woman dressed as a man at Fort Pillow was Mollie Pittman from Kentucky. She helped raise Confederate troops at the beginning of the war. She commanded a company disguised as Thomas Phillip. She was discovered and discharged in 1862. She then became a lieutenant in Forrest's cavalry under the name "Rawley." Forrest kept her on after her gender was discovered. She became a spy and a smuggler using the name Mary Hays. She purchased small arms and ammunition in St. Louis and smuggled them to Forrest until she was caught by a patrol from Fort Pillow. She attempted to switch sides after she was captured. She warned Major Booth of Forrest's imminent attack and even offered to lead them to Forrest's camps. Booth sent her to Memphis where she was kept in isolation at the Irving Bock Prison. The Federals eventually used her to arrest her source for guns and ammunition in St. Louis. Mollie Pittman disappeared after the war.

The Massacre at Fort Pillow is one of the most painful and controversial events in American military history. Civil War buffs still argue today over what is true and what is myth. The accusation is that Forrest ordered the massacre after the fort was taken and specifically targeted black troops. I drew from the official US Congressional investigation and from many eye-witness accounts of the atrocities that followed, including from some of the personal letters of the Confederate soldiers who were there. These include unarmed men begging for mercy while being shot or clubbed to death. Some were buried alive. One body had been found burnt beyond recognition. He had been staked into the ground inside a tent. The identity of that man is unknown. I made that man Francis who is a fictional character of my invention. There was also a man shot in the foot who survived. I made that Elijah, who's also fictional.

Some argue that the defenders were drunk and refused to surrender which is what led to the high casualty count. They claim that many of the atrocities said to have happened there were mere sensationalism propped up by the Northern press to create public outcry. I tend to believe the eyewitness accounts, especially from the Confederates who believed they were writing privately to love ones and not documenting history for us to examine later. These men had no reason to lie.

Another argument is that Forrest was unaware of the massacre because he was outside of the walls when it started. Some accounts say he tried to stop it and even shot one of his own men. I went with that. I made the man he shot my own fictional character Sergeant Bill Garret. I don't know whether he really did shoot one of his own men or the identity of that man. Much of the massacre is said to have happened after he retired to a farmhouse several miles away from the fort. Unsupervised, it is said his men took their revenge on the black soldiers who had tried to defend the fort.

I believe the truth lies in between the various accounts. I encourage you to read more about Fort Pillow and make your own decision on what really happened and why. *The River Run Red* by Andrew Ward is a great place to start. It was one of my most used sources in writing this book. I also recommend visiting Fort Pillow. It's now a state park. The fort has been rebuilt and has replica cannons placed inside. It's a great window into what it must have been like. I enjoyed my own trip there. It really helped me visualize the events of the battle for this book.

Racism was alive and well in the North, too. The people of Detroit had been very supportive of the war in the beginning but lost their enthusiasm as it dragged on and the draft came. Many became bitter over the black fugitives that entered the city and took jobs. That bitterness boiled over into a race riot on March 6, 1863, a day the Detroit Free Press claimed was "the bloodiest day that ever dawned upon Detroit." At least two people died. Black homes and businesses were burned. Many blacks were beaten in the street. As you may know, Detroit would go on to have more of these bloody days throughout its history. One result of the 1863 riot was the creation of a permanent Detroit Police force.

Coca wine was the rage of the latter half of the nineteenth century. It was quite simply wine mixed with cocaine. People mixed it themselves early on until popular pre-mixed brands began to appear in the 1860s. It was banned in Atlanta in the 1880s, not because of the cocaine, ironically, but because of the alcohol. The solution was to replace the wine with a nonalcoholic syrup. You know this drink today as Coca-Cola. Eventually, they removed the cocaine too and now we're forced to add rum or whiskey if we want to have any fun anymore.

The newspaper headline that Carl read about the Fort Pillow Massacre was from the New York Times, not the Detroit Free Press. The Times headline was much more dramatic and worked better for my story.

The Irving Block Prison was originally an office building. The Confederates converted it into a hospital at the beginning of the war. The Federals then turned it into a prison once they took control of the city. The conditions were so terrible there that President Lincoln himself ordered it closed in 1865. The building was finally torn down in 1937.

The Battle of Brice's Crossroads was probably one of Forrest's most complete victories in which he had an independent command. His band of about 3,500 men utterly humiliated a Federal force more than twice its size. Forrest used his favorite tactic of holding the enemy down in the front while riding around on their flank and rear with his cavalry. I feel what was most effective was the fear and mystique in which the Federals held him.

Samuel D. Sturgis did not command another force for the remainder of the war. He stayed in the army for many years after. His wartime brevet rank of major general reverted back to lieutenant colonel. He was promoted to full colonel and commanded the US 7th Cavalry. George Armstrong Custer was his lieutenant colonel. Sturgis was on a recruiting mission in Saint

Louis when Custer led the regiment to its and his own demise at the Battle of Little Big Horn. Sturgis's son also died at Custer's Last Stand.

The town of Sturgis in South Dakota is named after Samuel D. Sturgis. There's a statue of him on his horse there, but the town is more famous today for its huge Harley Davidson motorcycle rally each year.

The scene in which Elijah and Carl find runaway slaves and white deserters hiding together was common during the war. I thought it was too interesting not to include. We tend to think of historical events through a modern intersectional lens, but the American Civil War was a shared human event that united people as much as it divided them. This is a theme I'm constantly exploring in my writing.

The man falling off the train as it left Memphis prior to the battle of Tupelo really happened. It was just too funny not to include in my story. He was okay but had to walk all the way to La Grange to rejoin his regiment.

Kathryn's anonymous letter to Forrest about the conditions at the Irving Block Prison is my invention, of course, but he was well aware of its reputation. His raid on Memphis was a fantastic and audacious move that played out pretty much as I described, including Bill Forrest clubbing the sentry with his pistol and riding his horse into the Gayoso Hotel lobby. Forrest and his men may have failed to capture any generals or free any prisoners, but they did achieve their main goal. The Federals had to withdraw their troops from Northern Mississippi to protect the city from further attacks.

Although the Rebels failed to capture any generals, they did manage to capture Major General Cadwallader C. Washburn's uniform. Washburn barely had time to flee, let alone dress. He slipped out the backdoor and ran a half-mile to the fort in his undergarments. Forrest returned his uniform a few days later under a flag of truce. Washburn was so taken by this act of magnanimity from an enemy that he found Forrest's favorite tailor in town and had a new Confederate uniform made for him, which he sent to Forrest a few weeks later.

The runaway slave who swam across the Tennessee River and warned the Federals of an eminent crossing was real, however, little is known about him and his life. I filled in the blanks with my own story. The Federals were certainly caught by surprise at the crossing. They assumed Hood would return to Georgia once the Sherman declined to chase him any farther. Hood's invasion of Tennessee is full of *what if's* including the Confederates allowing Scofield's smaller force to slip past them at Spring Hill. Hood blamed corps commander Benjamin Cheatham and his subordinate division commanders John Brown and Patrick Cleburne for this missed opportunity. This blame bothered Cleburne sorely and may have been why he was so eager to demonstrate his bravery at Franklin.

I read several versions of the conversations that took place prior to the Battle of Franklin. I went with what felt right. The handsome general who said, "…let us die like men," is Patrick Cleburne, and he did just that hours later. He was most likely at that meeting, but he uttered those famous words to one of his subordinate brigade commanders later and not to his corps commander. It was just too good to leave out, and who knows, maybe he said it several times that day.

There really was no place for Cleburne in my narrative, but he's so fascinating that I wanted to give him an appearance.

Patrick Cleburne was born in Ireland. He studied medicine but ended up joining the British Army to support his family after his father died. He rose to the rank of corporal in the three years he served before buying his way out and immigrating to America. He was living in Arkansas at the start of the war. His British military experience and personal courage allowed him to rise quickly in the Confederate Army. He was a major general in command of a division at Franklin. It's true that he died on the battlements with his saber in his hand. He had just recently proposed to a woman with whom he was desperately in love. They were going to marry during his next leave. It is said she fainted on the street when she learned of his death from a newspaper boy shouting the headline.

The little German-speaking girl and her father are Matilda and Johann Lotz. They were real people. Matilda had just turned six the day before the battle. Mr. Lotz had immigrated from Germany, started a family, and built the "bullet-ridden" house I mentioned in the story. He was a master carpenter. They moved to California after the battle, wanting to get as far away as they could from the horrors they had witnessed. Matilda grew up to be an accomplished artist and a globe-trotting adventurer. As a little girl, she loved to draw animals in the dirt or on little scraps of paper. The Lotz House still stands today. It is a museum now run by very dear friends of mine. I highly recommend it if you ever find yourself in Franklin.

The Carton Plantation also still stands as does the Carter House where the Lotz family sheltered in the basement during the fight. You can visit these places, as well as Winstead Hill where the Confederate generals conferred before the battle. Franklin is certainly worth a visit in your Civil War travels.

The Battle of Franklin is the bloodiest battle in the American Civil War if you measure it by deaths per hour.

The 13th USCT's actions at the Battle of Nashville are very much as I described them. The injured soldier who was shot and asked his captain what to do was actually in the 12th USCT, but I wanted to include it into the story. It shows just how important it was to these men to give a good showing. This soldier didn't want to look like he was shirking his duty just because he was injured. I don't know if anyone was actually singing the *Battle Hymn of the Republic*, but why not? They were immensely proud and certainly fighting for something they truly believed in: freedom for all.

The 13th suffered 40% casualties during their assault on Overton Hill. Five color-bearers were shot down trying to plant their flag on the Rebel works. Their valor had even impressed the Confederate officers defending the hill. Brigadier General James Holtzclaw praised them in his after battle report saying:

The enemy made a most determined charge on my right. Placing a negro brigade in front they gallantly dashed up the abatis ... and were killed by hundreds ... they continued to come up in masses to the abatis, but they came only to die.

If you were worried about Colonel Edmund Rucker, he made it and lived to be an old man, dying in 1924. The man he fought with was Captain C. Boyer of the 12th Tennessee Cavalry (US). Rucker was hit in the left elbow with a pistol ball as he tried to get back to his line. He was captured and had his arm amputated. He spent that night in a shared room with his adversaries: Major General James H. Wilson and Brigadier General Edward Hatch. Hatch attended to the wounded Rucker through the night and sent him off to the hospital in Nashville with a flask of whiskey the next day.

Colonel George Spalding of the 12th Tennessee (US) found Rucker's saber on the ground and took it home as a trophy. He returned it to him twenty-five years later in an act of goodwill and reconciliation. It is this spirit of gentlemanly honor amongst enemies that enthralls me about the past. It's what I like to write about. I feel in this age of petty online bickering and tribalism, we can learn a lot from those that came before us.

The Battle of Nashville was the last major battle of the American Civil War in the Western Theater. It is also one of the most decisive victories for either side. Hood's army disintegrated as it fled to Tupelo, Mississippi. There, General John B. Hood resigned his command. He'd never command an army again. General Robert E. Lee surrendered his army four months after the Battle of Nashville. Joe Johnston surrendered his 90,000-man army two weeks after that. Soon the rest of the Confederate forces laid down their guns. President Johnson officially declared an end to the insurrection on May 9, 1865.

I want to thank you for reading this third and final book of my American Civil War Trilogy. If you really liked it and want more, don't worry! I have lot more books planned that are connected to this story and will continue the journey of several of the characters, but first: the prequel, *Mexico, My Love* is available now! It tells the tragic love story of Carl's parents. I'm really excited about it.

If you'd like to keep up with me, I'm on all the big social media platforms, and please join the Engdahl House email list for updates on new releases, discounts, appearances, and more at https://subscribepage.io/EngdahlHouse. I also have an Author's page on amazon.com.

Sources

This book is a work of fiction. However, there are many historical accounts in it. I tried to stay as faithful to real history as possible. Below are some of the sources I used in my research. I highly recommend them if you want to learn more about the real history that upon which book is based.

Thatcher, Marshall P. (1884) A Hundred Battles in the West: St Louis to Atlanta, 1861-65, The Second Michigan Cavalry. Detroit, MI: self-published.

Watkins, Sam (1999) Company Aytch or, the Side Show to the Big Show. New York, NY: Plume (Original work published in 1882).

Ward, Andrew (2005) River Run Red: The Fort Pillow Massacre in the American Civil War. New York, NY: Penguin Group.

Hurst, Jack (1994) Nathan Bedford Forrest: A Biography. New York, NY: Vintage.

Hurst, Jack (2012) Born to Battle: Grant and Forrest-- Shiloh, Vicksburg, and Chattanooga. New York, NY: Basic Books.

Bradley, Michael R. (2006) Nathan Bedford Forrest's Escort and Staff. Gretna, Louisiana: Pelican Publishing Company.

Dr. Wyeth, John (1899) The Life of Lieutenant General Forrest. New York, NY and London, UK: Allan Harper and Brothers.

Correspondence of the Chicago Times, FORREST'S RAID; The Capture of Union City, The Repulse at Paducah, The New York Times, April 1, 1864, Page 1.

Ward, Andrew (2009) The Slaves' War: the Civil War in the Words of Former Slaves. New York, NY: Mariner Books

Cimprich, John and Mainfort, Robert C. Jr. (1985) Dr. Fitch's Report on the Fort Pillow Massacre. Tennessee Historical Quarterly 44(1):27-39.

Cimprich, John (2005) Fort Pillow, a Civil War massacre, and Public Memory. Baton Rouge, LA: Louisiana State University Press.

Smith, John David (2002) Black Soldiers in Blue: African American Troops in the Civil War Era. Chapel Hill, NC: University of North Carolina Press.

McGlothlin, John W. (2020) "A Compendium of Information Pertaining to the Composition and Operation of Civil War Mounted Artillery Batteries" Self published.

National Park Service, US Department of Interior, "Manual of Instruction for the Safe Use of

Reproduction Nineteenth Century Artillery in Historic Weapons Demonstrations."

Morton, John Watson (1909) The Artillery of Nathan Bedford Forrest's Cavalry: "The Wizard of the Saddle." Nashville, TN: M. E. Church Publishing House.

LaPointe, Patricia M. (1983) "Military Hospitals in Memphis, 1861-1865." Tennessee Historical Quarterly, Vol. 42, No. 4 pp. 325-342 Nashville, TN: Tennessee Historical Society.

Manville, Craig Julian (1991) "The Limits of Obedience: Brigadier General Thomas J. Wood's Performance During The Battle of Chickamauga" Master of Military Art And Science Military History Thesis, University of Missouri-Columbia.

Frisby, Derek W. (2014) "Campaigns in Mississippi and Tennessee February–December 1864" Center of Military History United States Army Washington, D.C.

Bearss, Edwin C. (1971) Protecting Sherman's Lifeline: The Battles of Brice's Crossroads and Tupelo 1864. Washington D.C., U.S. Department of the Interior.

Parson, Thomas E. (2014) Work for Giants: The Campaign and Battle of Tupelo/Harrisburg, Mississippi, June-July 1864. Kent, OH: The Kent State University Press

Sword, Wiley (1993) The Confederacy's Last Hurrah: Spring Hill, Franklin, and Nashville. Lawrence, KS: University Press of Kansas.

Lardas, Mark (2017) Nashville 1864: from the Tennessee to the Cumberland. Oxford, UK: Osprey Publishing.

Horn, Stanley Fitzgerald (1957) The Decisive Battle of Nashville. Knoxville, TN: University of Tennessee Press.

McDonough, James L. (2013) The western Confederacy's Final Gamble: From Atlanta to Franklin and Nashville. Knoxville, TN: University of Tennessee Press.

Dr. Ranney, Geo E., Surgeon 2nd Michigan Cavalry (1897) War Papers Read Before the Michigan Commandery ... v.2. Military Order of the Loyal Legion of the United States. "Reminiscences of an army surgeon." Detroit, MI: James H. Stone & Company.

Woodcock, Marcus (2001) A Southern Boy in Blue: the Memoir of Marcus Woodcock, 9th Kentucky Infantry. Knoxville, TN: University of Tennessee Press.

Kidd, James Harvey (1908) Personal Recollections of a Cavalryman With Custer's Michigan Cavalry Brigade in the Civil War. Ionia, MI: Sentinel Press.

Volo, Dorothy Denneen and Volo, James M. (1998) Daily Life in Civil War America. Greenwood Press.

Miles, Tiya (1970) The Dawn of Detroit: a Chronicle of Slavery and Freedom in the City of the Straits. The New Press.

Woodford, Arthur M. (2001) This is Detroit, 1701-2001. Detroit, MI: Wayne State University.

The Civil War Podcast

Untold Civil War Podcast

Civil War Breakfast Club Podcast

civilwartalk.com

historicalemporium.com

Works by Cody C. Engdahl

Novels:
The Long Century Series
- Rampage on the River: The Battle for Island No. 10 (Book I)
- The Perils of Perryville (Book II)
- Blood for Blood at Nashville (Book III)
- Mexico, My Love (Book IV)
- The Prussian Prince (Book V)

Nonfiction:
- The American Civil War WAS About Slavery: A Quick Handbook of Quotes to Reference When Debating Those Who Would Argue Otherwise
- How to Write, Publish, and Market Your Novel

Please join the Engdahl House email list for updates on new releases, discounts, appearances, and more at https://subscribepage.io/EngdahlHouse.

Printed in Great Britain
by Amazon